The End of Summer

KJ MICCICHE

cabaret books

Also by KJ Micciche

The Book Proposal
A Storybook Wedding
The Guest Book
One Week Later

To the girls at Dream Dance Fitness, who believed in me
when I didn't believe in myself.

PROLOGUE

I took dance once. Don't let this little nugget of information fool you, though. To clarify, I was like six years old. It was on Saturday mornings. My mom was teaching a painting class at Cape Cod Community College – one of those enrichment-type workshops that mostly appeal to retired folks looking to take up a new skill. My dad worked odd hours back then, steadfast in his resolve to climb the ranks in the Eastport Police Department, so on Saturdays Mom and I were a dynamic duo. We'd grab donuts from Hole In One and eat them as we drove the 25 miles down Route 6 to Hyannis, thankful that we didn't have to contend with the kind of traffic that plagues the Cape's only highway during tourist season. As powdered sugar left white streaks on my black dance tights, we'd chat about the changing leaves, the Brussels Sprout Festival in November, and the stuff I was learning in my big-girl-first-grade-class. Then she'd drop me off in the makeshift dance studio (a converted classroom with a portable sprung floor) so that she could teach the art of mixing watercolors to a roomful of grown-ups in an adjacent hallway.

Our group was called the Twinkle Toes. There were a dozen of us: eleven girls and one boy, all led by a nice, youngish teacher whose name I forget. Maybe I've blocked it out subconsciously. I guess that would make sense, given that the one thing I *do* recall was not exactly my finest moment.

It was close to Halloween, and the Twinkle Toes had been informed that we could wear costumes to class to celebrate the holiday. I proudly donned a homemade unicorn costume which consisted of a bulky, thick pair of furry white footsie pajamas with a hood that my mom lovingly decorated with rainbow ribbons. She affixed a pointy cardboard cone to the top, hand painted and dipped in glitter by yours truly. Unfortunately, my feet didn't fit into my dance shoes on account of the footsie part of the getup, so my teacher let me dance without shoes for the day.

Big mistake.

I was paired up with the boy. At the time, I didn't know his name, because the teacher always referred to him as "Big Guy." He was a *great* dancer. He came dressed up as a cowboy. Flannel shirt, ten gallon hat, Levi's jeans – he even had boots with little spurs on them. We were rehearsing a fairly simple two-step move, but facing each other it was tricky for me to reconcile right from left. The move went *right-left-right-STOMP* to the bass line of Christina Milian's "Dip it Low." It's a great song. To this day, I still love it, despite what happened next.

I was feeling it, I guess. I had my eyes closed, but only for a few seconds, because the STOMP happened just before the start of the chorus – my favorite part of the song. And that was the exact moment that the crushing weight of a cowboy boot forcefully smashed my directionally-challenged, shoe-less toes beneath it.

"Ow!" I cried out and collapsed to the ground, tears instantly pricking at my eyes. The boy crouched down beside me. "Oh, my gosh!" he cried with a panicked expression. "Did I step on you?"

I couldn't answer. I could only sob.

The teacher rushed over. "What happened?" she asked. "Are you okay? Point to where it hurts."

My wailing intensified. The searing pain made me acutely aware of my pulse pounding in my foot. She wanted to see the damage but I guess she realized there was no getting me out of the costume, essentially a full-length zippered onesie, beneath which I was wearing only my underwear. She asked me if I could stand. When I shook my head no, she tried to locate the source of my agony through my PJs, only to be met with feral howling when she came near my toes. "Everyone stay put; I'll be right back," she commanded. Her voice was more serious than our six year-old selves were used to. As she ran down the hall to get my mom, I curled up in the fetal position howling to the soundtrack of Christina Milian, who unironically urged listeners to "pop that thing."

Beside me, the boy pulled in his legs to sit criss-cross-applesauce and, visibly shook in his own right, took my tear-streaked free hand in his own. He ran his thumb back and forth along the edge of mine, in much the way my mother would have done. I was so stunned by the action that I stopped crying, surprised by the comfort I felt from his simple gesture.

"Don't worry. You'll be okay," he hushed me, as tears formed on his lashes.

It was like the calm moment in the eye of a storm.

Next thing I knew, all hell broke loose as my mom and the dance teacher burst through the door with a random man wearing a painting smock. The man lifted me gently off the floor and carried me to the car while my mother jogged alongside us. Mom drove me straight to the emergency room at Cape Cod Hospital. Diagnosis? Three broken piggies: the one that had roast beef, the one that had none, and the one that cried *wee, wee, wee* all the way home. I got a neon pink cast and a hospital-issued little-kid wheelchair, since I was too young for crutches.

And that was the end of my dance career.

Or, in hindsight, I guess you could say it was the beginning.

CHAPTER ONE

GRETCHEN

"So, what exactly happened? Just run me through it so I can jot down some notes."

I sigh. "Well, I suppose it started with the tray of appetizers I dropped in David Krumholtz's lap."

The note-taker – Brenda Dinghy, Employment Specialist, according to the nameplate on the desk – chokes on her cherry Fanta. Coughing into her elbow, she grabs the bottle of fluorescent red soda and I can't help but notice the way it matches my current hair color as she takes a sip. She clears her throat. "I'm sorry, Gretchen. Did you say David Krumholtz? As in the actor?"

I nod. "Yep. He was in private dining."

"You won't believe this. I *met* him once," Brenda whispers. She wipes her brow with the back of her bare wrist, as if the coughing has suddenly catapulted her into a hot flash. "I had a massive crush on him when I was a kid."

"Oh?" The question escapes my lips unintentionally. This is not the reaction I was expecting.

"*Yes*," she seethes. "Did you ever see *The Santa Clause*? With Tim Allen? David Krumholtz played Bernard and it was the hottest reimagining of an elf I had ever seen to that point."

To that point? I struggle not to laugh. "So, how'd you meet him?" I ask, indulging her.

"Well." She straightens up in her chair. "It wasn't until later. I was in college at UCLA, and when I found out *The Santa Clause 2* was coming out, I stood outside the El Capitan Theatre in Hollywood on the day of the premiere. I nearly died when I saw him. Of course, he was more of a man by then and less of an elf."

"Right." I nod, choking back a giggle. "Of course."

"Anyway. I screamed his name, and he was kind enough to come over and say hi."

"That's nice."

"I was wearing a Santa hat, and he signed it for me." She sighs, awash in a new-to-me brand of teenage elfin-heart-throb memories. "So? How did he look? Was he with his wife? I've seen pictures of her online. She's *gorgeous.*"

"No," I say. "He was with some execs from Apple TV. They looked Hollywood-fancy, but I don't know who they were."

She leans in and lowers her voice. "I read they were film-ing at the Diamond Excelsior. There was a whole thing about it in the *Cape Cod Times.* I can't believe you got to see him."

"Yeah. I mean, I guess it would have been cooler if it hadn't ended with me losing my job."

"Yes. Of course." She nods. Her fingernails tap away at the keyboard. "Gretch-en An-drews," she dictates. "Okay, tell me exactly what happened."

"Well, if you're working in private dining, you have to wear heels. And I can't walk in heels. I told the manager, Brady, but he said, 'Rules are rules.' I wasn't supposed to work in that section of the hotel. I'm usually down in the pub, but they put me there because the top server was out sick." I take a breath, exhaling hard, like you do when the doctor puts a stethoscope to your chest. "You can wear normal shoes at the pub. I don't even *have* heels; Brady gave me a loaner pair. Anyway, long story short, David Krumholtz ordered a plate of steamers, and one of the other guys ordered the lobster mac and cheese. I was bringing the tray out from the kitchen and I turned my ankle. Everything spilled all over his lap."

Brenda stifles a laugh. At this point, I'm used to it. Everyone thinks it's just *so* funny. "And, so, now..." Her voice trails off.

"So, I've tried to find work but you know how it is on the Cape. Tragic news travels fast. They're calling me the blazing lobjob. The celebrity scrotum scorcher. The hot clam splasher. The list goes on." I look at my feet, scraping my sensible sneaker against the industrial grey carpet. "Brady belittled me. In front of everyone. I was on the floor covered in sizzling fish juice and instead of helping me up, he just humiliated me." I fight back the urge to cry, remembering how his highness called me *Stumbelina* in front of David Fucking Krumholtz. Brady's father, Chef Braxton Hawthorne, manages the culinary team for the country club and is a grade-A douchebaguette. His minions can only speak to him in subordinate phrases: "Yes, Chef! Heard that, Chef!" as if this was the military and the troop was about to go into full-fledged combat over the best way to flambè the fondue. I've heard horror stories of him verbally assaulting Brady on many occasions, leaving me to imagine that the kumquat didn't fall far from the tree. It's a shame, too, because Brady would otherwise be considered quite the snack, what with his sculpted jawline and latte-colored eyes.

I swallow what feels like a golf ball and run my fingers through my pomegranate-streaked hair. "It's crazy," I say to Brenda. "For a place with an economy that thrives on tourism, you'd think I'd have no trouble finding a job during the busy season."

She nods. "Have you considered looking outside of the service industry?"

I shake my head. "I have school loans to pay off. And a mortgage. Not to mention, I owe my parents five grand. I can't move to a desk job."

Brenda raises an eyebrow.

"No offense," I continue. "The tips are just too good to pass up."

As she taps her fingers on her computer keyboard, whispering "ser-vice in-dus-try on-ly" to herself, I take in my surroundings. The Hyannis Career Center is so drab. Located in a strip mall off Main Street, it's nestled between a vape shop and a now-defunct furniture rental center. The inside matches the outside: neutral cinderblock walls, old metal desks, one other employee stationed by a communal microwave, a single patron using the copy machine (which has metal bars over it like a jail cell and costs 25 cents per page). By the door, the world's noisiest oscillating fan fails to cool down the claustrophobic space. And in the center of it all sits Brenda, the hyper-sexed elf aficionado, tippity-tapping away in her database of dream jobs for a klutzerfuck like myself.

Not exactly an advertisement for a family getaway in paradise.

"How far from Brewster are you willing to travel?" she asks.

"I don't know," I say. "I'd like to stay in the lower Cape, ideally."

"Hm." She scrolls the wheel on her extinct mouse with an excited pointer finger. "I'm not seeing much," Brenda says. "If you had come to me three weeks ago, I would've had a whole lot more to offer."

"I know," I reply. "Peak season's already here." My shoulders slump. I feel the weight of what she's not saying. *Take what you can get, Gretchen.*

"Exactly. The good-paying jobs have all been scooped up." She takes another sip of the Fanta. "Even the not-so-great jobs are mostly gone. You don't want to work at the bowling alley, right?"

"No, thanks," I say, a knee-jerk reaction. Tears begin to build in my eyes. I look up at the drop ceiling, focusing on the water stains, refusing to allow myself to get upset.

Brenda offers me a sympathetic smile. "I'll put your resume into our system," she says, handing me a business card. "And you can check our website for updates whenever you'd like. Sometimes new opportunities come up during the season. J-1s leave, you know. People get canned."

"You're sure there's no way I can file for unemployment?" I ask. I can hear the desperation in my shaky voice. "It's almost June 1st, and I've got a slew of bills due."

"Sorry, honey," she says. To her credit, she genuinely does look apologetic. "When you're fired for cause, there's really not much you can do."

I nod.

"What are you studying?" she asks, perusing my resume.

"Teaching," I say.

"Elementary?"

"Early childhood. I'd like to teach kindergarten."

"What about tutoring?"

I shake my head. "Not in the summer. There's no market for it here."

She nods. "I can see that. Well, at least you know you'll get a job once you finish your Master's degree."

"I hope. I've only got one class left, assuming I can pay for it."

"Listen, Gretchen. You seem like a smart girl. I'm sure you'll find something. You sure you don't want me to add summer camps into your search criteria?"

"I'm sure. The pay is so bad, I could make more babysitting," I say. *If I had any clients who didn't have full-time nannies booked for the season.*

"Okay, suit yourself." She types a bit more, and looks up at me, satisfied, once she's done. "Chin up. It'll all work out. I have a good feeling."

I try not to consider how many poor souls she's said those exact words to.

"Can I ask you one more thing?" Brenda says, smirking now.

"Sure."

"What did he do?"

"Huh?"

"David Krumholtz? When you clammed him?"

I shake my head. "Yelled out some expletives. Jumped up and shook off his pants."

"Did he ask if you were okay?"

"Uh huh. He was as nice as someone could be in that kind of circumstance. I'm sure it hurt. The dish was hot."

Brenda swoons. "I'm not surprised. Class act, that guy."

"I guess," I shrug, pulling my hair back and twisting it into a messy bun with a claw clip. "We didn't really interact once he took his pants off."

Her eyes threaten to launch out of her skull. "He did *what*?"

"It was private dining. There were only a few of us in the room."

"Well played, Gretchen. I've got to say, if you have to lose a job, that's the way to do it. Was he…" She points to her crotch, which I'm guessing means she's asking me about the size of his candy cane and jingle bells, but I've about had it. Thoughts of the bank foreclosing on my condo swirl around in my overcrowded brain. I pause to consider life as a full-time resident of my 15-year-old Ford Fiesta.

It is not a pleasant thought.

"Thanks for your help, Brenda," I say, turning toward the exit.

"Keep in touch. New stuff pops up every day," she calls after me.

I reach my hand up to offer a limp wave goodbye. As I push my way out into the warm, midday air, my phone buzzes. I check; it's an e-mail from UMass reminding me about my past-due student loan payment. Armed with the knowledge that I have $443 in my checking account and a credit card bill of well over $2,000, along with exactly zero receivables pending, I ignore the hunger pangs in my belly and head back home where a box of store-brand Toasty O's and almond milk await me.

Once in my car, the phone buzzes again. This time, it's a text from Jenna.

How goes the job search?

Spectacular, I reply. *I just got a bottle service gig at the Chatham Bars Inn.*

Is that even a thing? she asks.

My thumbs fly across the screen. *Probably not. Nothing new here. Why, you got any leads?*

Three dots. Then a pause. Then, three more dots.

Possibly. Depends.

On?

Three more dots.

Well... how open minded are you?

CHAPTER TWO

GRETCHEN

It is *not* a strip club.

It is a pole dancing studio.

My outfit might make one think otherwise, but I repeat: it is *not* a strip club.

Jenna dug through her closet to find me the fishnet stockings and the barely-there "skirt." I hesitate to even call it that. A washcloth might cover more. The fuchsia push-up bra belongs to me, and the threadbare tank top that I would typically wear as an undershirt has been in my drawer since high school.

The shoes, though, Jenna bought for me. They were the real point of contention when she explained this gig.

"I can't walk in heels," I insisted. "Don't you remember? This is how I lost my last job?"

"These are platforms," she replied. "Yes, there's a heel, but it's not the same thing. It's more like walking on a pair of cement blocks."

"And *that* should somehow be more comfortable?"

"I didn't say it was comfortable," Jenna corrected me. "But I don't think you'll break your neck. Plus, regular platforms are the gateway drug."

"To what?" I asked, incredulous.

"You'll see. For now, just wear them. You'll be fine. Plus, they make your legs look longer. They're cute. You'll get compliments."

"I need cash, not compliments," I reminded her. "Plus, I don't want you spending your money on me."

"Girl, you eat cereal for, like, every meal. These are an investment. Trust me. You're gonna make bank, and when you do, you can pay me back for them."

"I hesitate to ask how much they cost."

"Not much," she assured me. "80 bucks. Not the end of the world. You'll see, Gretch. You'll make ten times that amount on a good day. Now, walk," she commanded. I slid my feet into the shoes and traversed her bedroom. "See? They're not bad."

My center-of-gravity felt off-kilter in the black, patent-leather shoes. In Jenna's full-length mirror, I could see that she was right; they did make my body look longer and leaner, reminding me of the yoga phase I went through in high school. Of course, there were no shoes in yoga, which might explain why I still like it to this day.

I traversed the carpet once, twice, three times for good measure.

"You look hot," Jenna said.

"Thanks?" I laughed.

"It's perfect. They're going to love you."

"And you're sure this is legit?"

"Of course I am. I did it for ten weeks last summer. That job bought me my Jeep."

"And it's definitely not a strip club?" I asked, raising an eyebrow.

"I promise!" she insisted. "Some of the parties like to bring in outside entertainment, but you yourself will never have to worry about stripping, I swear."

My stomach knotted. "Remind me again why you didn't tell me about this place sooner?"

"Um," she grinned, blushing. "You didn't ask?"

I looked at her, deadpan.

"Fine. To be fair, you've always been a little, well –"

I raised my eyebrows and pursed my lips into a smirk. "Be careful with the character assassination, please. I'm in a fragile state."

"Straight-laced?" she offered. "I'm not saying it's a bad thing. You're adorable, with your smarty-pants online Master's degree and your goals to teach little kiddos. But, to be fair, your Instagram is more reminiscent of *Sesame Street* than *Magic Mike*."

"False!" I retorted. "Clearly you've forgotten about the time I worked at Cock Town."

To clarify: Cock Town was a classy joint in downtown Amherst where I learned how to decorate paper penis-shaped bibs for chic patrons to don as they happily drank beer and ate chicken.

"You lasted three days," Jenna said. "Remember? You couldn't handle the menu?"

"Hateful," I laughed. This was sadly accurate, though. On my first Saturday night there, the manager wanted me to push the drink specials, which included the Whisker Biscuit (vodka-cranberry), the Nipple Ring (rum and Coke), and the Spunk Trumpet (seven-and-seven). All of the drinks were served with a Blow Pop sticking out of the top in the spot where a little paper umbrella might have otherwise been. To clarify, I would have been fine *serving* them, but I couldn't bring myself to announce the names of the drinks to tables of total strangers. So, I turned in my apron and high-tailed it out of there, face ablaze from blushing.

"Anyway, that vibe will get you lots of love in a place like this. Everyone loves a good girl with a wild side." Jenna winked at me, knowing full well that all sides of me are as tame as they come.

But hey, a job's a job.

And with that, it was done. No resumé submission. No interview. Just a shady text exchange between Jenna and someone named Arrow. Now, four days later, my first shift – if you can even call it a shift? – starts in exactly 13 minutes, and I'm parked in the Fiesta in an obscure back alley behind the lumberyard off 6A.

Well, no time like the present, I decide, climbing out of my car. I lock the door behind me and walk as gracefully as possible on my 3-inch platforms to the steel, purple-painted door Jenna explained that I should look for. No signage, which I find a touch disturbing, but what do I know about this sort of business?

It's oddly quiet, but as I approach the door, I feel the ground shaking so slightly that I wonder if I'm imagining it. It's as if this warehouse has a heartbeat all its own.

Deep breath, Gretchen.

I open the heavy, metal door and succumb to the shock of sudden sensory overload. Bass thumps harder than my hammering pulse. Rihanna reminds me that I've come here to "work, work, work, work, work, work" through huge, black speakers at a decibel that must be illegal for the sleepy beach town of *Wellingham.* A black banner with hot pink writing hangs on the wall, announcing the name of this fine establishment: *Cosmo-pole-itan.* My eyes take a moment to adjust to the neon purple lighting as the door immediately slams shut behind me. I spy one, two, three... eight silver poles, and – oh – *wow.*

That girl is upside down.

Upon closer examination, I see that her legs are crossed, one over the other at the knee, as if she was just neatly sitting in a chair. Her back is all the way arched, though, and her hair is so long it's just inches from the ground. Her tanned skin is everywhere: bare arms, bare legs, bare stomach and back. Only her essentials are covered – if by covered, you mean spilling out from the sides of an insubstantial sequined bra and panty set, which might actually be a bathing suit, although I can't imagine anyone doing laps in sequins. She's reaching her hands toward the floor, elongating her body, and, yep, by all accounts it appears that she is hanging on to the pole with only her thighs.

Sweet Jesus.

The pole is *spinning.*

The girl – er, *woman* – swings her body back up, hands, then arms, then head, neck and torso, grabs the pole, kicks her legs back like a pendulum, and glides down to the ground.

Which is when I notice her choice of footwear.

The clear heels must be at least eight-inches –

"Hi!" she says, ripping me out of my thoughts with a natural grin.

"Hi?" I reply, a question, because I am unsure of basically everything in this moment. Like, how am I here? What even is this place? I've become a character in what feels like a shroom-induced movie-in-my-mind. Long way from Kansas, Toto. This place is definitely not the future kindergarten class of my dreams. Also, I don't do shrooms. Only multivitamins. And only when I have enough money in the bank to afford such a luxury.

She sashays towards me; my guess is that sashaying is the only way one can maneuver in shoes so tall. Her generous hips sway – boom, boom, boom, boom – to the rhythm of Rihanna and Drake, until she gets to the massive speaker and lowers the volume. Then, she turns back to me. Her platinum blonde hair goes all the way down to her waist.

"I'm Arrow," she says, extending her hand.

It's not a strip club, I remind myself. *There is no stage. Just these poles. These poles are for teaching, not for stripping.* I consciously try to keep my judgment face in check.

"You must be Jenna's friend," she continues.

I try to keep my eyes plastered on a spot in the distance, just above her forehead, in an attempt to not make her feel objectified by her lack of clothing. Not that she looks even remotely apprehensive about her wardrobe choices. Quite the opposite, in fact.

"Gretchen," I say, extending my hand.

Arrow takes it in her own. Her palm is surprisingly dry, and I can't help but notice that her fingernails are painted in zebra stripes. They're not long, though, which – despite only knowing this woman for the past 30 seconds – somehow feels off-brand for her. She holds my fingers hostage and catches my gaze, forcing my eyes down to meet hers. She pauses to wrinkle her nose. "Yeah, Jenna told me. You poor thing." Confusion sets in – is she lamenting my employment status? "I'm sorry, sweetie. I'm sure you can understand why it just won't work for us. Let me think a sec." She closes her eyelids; her fake lashes create a black fan about an inch and a half long on each side, like two creepy jack o'lantern smiles have taken up residence on her cheeks. My hand remains captive; my brain, fully scrambled. *Is this some bizarre greeting ritual?* I steal a glance at our entwined digits and notice the tattoo just under her right breast, a bold, cursive first impression if I've ever seen one.

Boss bitch, it proclaims.

She opens her eyes. "I've got it!" she announces. "You're a temp. Let's call you 'Summer.' You know, since you're seasonal." She purses her lips, dropping my hand like a hot potato.

"I'm sorry?"

"Well, we can't call you 'Gretchen,'" she laughs. "I mean, that's not exactly drip, right? Maybe if we were hosting, like, a quilting circle, your name would be super-cute. But this is pole, babe. We're here to bring out the sexy. 'Gretchen,'" she goes on, using air quotes around my evidently-now-defunct name, "is, well. Just, no." She places one hand on a cocked hip.

Wow.

Discombobulated by the interactions of the past two minutes, I simply nod and accept my fate. I am here to make money. If my moniker – passed down from my beloved grandmother – is a no-go, I can live with that. I smile and nod, affirming my rebirth as *Summer.*

"Slay," Arrow says. "Come. I'll show you where to put your stuff."

I follow her to a bank of lockers in the corner of the room. They look like the ones at the Diamond Excelsior, all wooden laminate fronts and electronic code locks you can set and reset over and over again.

"Nice, right?" Arrow comments. When I look up at her, curiously, she adds, "What? I can tell an impressed face when I see one. I'm *very* intuitive."

I clear my throat. "Sorry. I was just noticing how these are the same lockers as the –"

"Chatham Bars Inn? Wequassett Resort? Diamond Excelsior?" She grins. "I know. I was hooking up with a guy who did spa deliveries for the company that makes them. He was able to score me a bank of these lockers when they were 'damaged' in packaging by a rogue Sharpie marker. The guys at the factory designated them for the garbage. Evidently, no one ever told those fools that a little rubbing alcohol can take Sharpie marker off most non-porous surfaces."

I render myself surprised by this anecdote, partially because I was unaware of that nugget of knowledge about rubbing alcohol, and partially because it sounds rather intelligent, and the speaker of this information is wearing little more than a sparkle panty.

The adage *don't judge a book by its cover* comes to mind. I shake it off, willing myself to be present. "They're nice – um – the lockers. And yeah. I used to work at the Diamond Excelsior."

"Well, good. Then, I don't have to teach you how to program the code. So, you'll lock up your personal belongings when you come in. Cosmo-pole-itan is not responsible for any of your stuff going missing."

"Got it." I nod.

"Put your phone in there, too. None of us have phones during parties. That way, we can't be blamed for sensitive material ending up on the internet."

"Understood." I toss my keys, cell phone, and wristlet into the locker, program my code (9-1-9-9, my birth date) and follow Arrow past a garment rack through a doorway that leads to a cramped office space. It houses an old metal desk with some post-its, pens, an oversized toaster oven, a Maglite flashlight, and a pair of fuzzy handcuffs strewn about – because that makes perfect sense – alongside a shelving unit packed to the brim with oversized shoeboxes. Against the wall rests a broom and dustpan, a tall stack of large, cardboard boxes, and a handful of serving trays. But the centerpiece of the tiny space is a black refrigerator covered in penis magnets and a lone photograph of Arrow (but with brown hair instead of blonde) standing with her arms around a little girl.

"Aw, she's a cutie," I offer, wondering if that's her daughter in the picture.

"Yup," Arrow says. I wait to see if she'll say anything else, but she just lets the unfinished answer hang in the air between us. "This will be your staging area," she continues, clearly not one to discuss anything of a remotely personal nature with a new hire. "Your job is to keep the patrons safe and happy and to monitor the party vibe."

"Uh huh," I nod.

"So, the name of the game is Jell-O shots," she explains, opening up the refrigerator and gesturing to its contents. That's all that's in there – just layers upon layers of Rubbermaid baking boxes filled with red and pink Jell-O in little, plastic shot glasses. It looks like a peculiar advertisement for children's Benadryl.

Oh, wait. There's also one Oikos yogurt.

I chuckle, trying to seem worldly in my Jell-O consumption. "People still drink these?" I ask, in an attempt to look like one of those party girls who regularly consumed alcohol prior to meeting the legal age requirement.

"You have no idea," Arrow replies. "Even people who come in all virtuous like, 'I'm good, I'm not drinking,' can be swayed to partake in a Jell-O shot."

"Pssh. Right?" I interject, hoping she can't see right through me.

She nods. "They're arranged by color based on how the party's going. The red ones mean we need to turn up the heat and get people to loosen up. They're made with Absolut 100. Those have to cook for longer because of the elevated alcohol content."

"Cook?"

"In the fridge. You know what I mean," Arrow says. "Anyway, the dark pink ones are raspberry. They're made with Smirnoff, so instead of being 50% ABV like the red ones, they're only 35. It's like a continuum."

"Right," I say. Again, I'm equally baffled and impressed by her lexicon.

"Then, we've got the strawberry pink shots. They're made with Cruzan coconut rum. Super light, only 21% ABV but they taste good. Once the party hits its peak, we serve up these ones to maintain the vibe."

"The raspberry and strawberry look kind of similar."

"Oh, fuck," she says, standing up straight to look me over. "You're not color blind, right? That's a no-go."

I shake my head. "No, I'm not color blind. I was just noticing that those two are –"

Arrow picks up the Maglite. "In the dark, it's even harder to tell. So there's a few options. One, you use this mack-daddy flashlight here. Two, you open a container and smell them. Three, you taste one. But only one," she warns. "These go like hot cakes, and we can't be wasting our supply. Also, you and I haven't partied together, so I have no clue what your tolerance is. We don't drink on the job unless necessary – like, I might take the welcome shot with a party just to get them warmed up. Anyway, if we get the sense that the group is getting too rowdy – which, to be clear, is when someone starts looking a little green or can't stand up straight anymore – we switch to the lemon drop shots. By that point, they won't care what color they're drinking, and they'll gladly take whatever we give them."

"What are those made with?"

"Nothing. Just lemon juice, gelatin and water, with a lime garnish to make it look fancy. We'll also bring out pretzel bites at that point. We cook those in the toaster oven. The bread absorbs the alcohol, the salt makes them thirsty, which leads to more lemon drops, and the acid in the citrus slows the effects of drinking and rehydrates the body."

I'm stunned into silence. "Hm," I mumble.

"Your job is to be the server, as well as the party barometer. You have to decide what color shot to bring out based on how the party's going."

"Okay," I say.

"You're also responsible for the key box and making all the shots."

"I'm sorry, the what?"

"Oh. The key box. You'll be the party police. The babysitter. Jenna said you're good with kids, so this'll be a good job for you. You know how, at a Chapelle show, you gotta give up your phone at the door?"

"Um, I think I've heard that, yeah."

"Same thing here. When each person comes in, they give you their car keys, like a valet. Just the car. We don't want or need anyone's house keys or extra mailbox key or whatever else they've got. Keys go in the lock box, which works the same as the lockers. You keep the box and when the party's over, you decide if a patron needs an Uber or can drive. We hold keys overnight, and then the next day, we have tow-yard hours in the late afternoon just before the next party. People can come get their cars during that time."

"Wow," I say. "This is a lot more detailed than I expected it would be."

"Listen, Summer. We're here to throw the best party of these people's lives. That shit takes diligent planning. And there are two things that really fuck up a good time. Do you know what they are?"

"Um –"

"Vomit and death."

"Right," I agree.

"So, I won't have those in my house. Every party will be you, me, and three of my girls. We never host more than 30 at a time just based on pole space, but they can bring in whatever they want – catering, additional entertainment, whatever. These are ladies with money to spend: they're getting married, they've come up for the weekend or the week, they're sunburned and horny as hell, and it's on us to show them the time of their lives."

"Okay. Yup."

"You get paid a flat rate of $350 per party. Each party costs them $3,000, which includes alcohol and 3 hours at the studio. They pay half that up front and the balance on the night of the event. We add an automatic gratuity to the bill of 25%. It's listed right there in front of them but usually they still pull me to the side and ask me how much to tip. So I tell them that $100 per girl is customary, and not to forget their shot girl. Usually that gives us an extra $500 added to the bill. Whatever we make in tips, we split evenly. This is a sisterhood, so it doesn't matter if you're dancing or teaching or managing the party temperature, we all need to work together to pull off a perfect night. On a typical day, each of us will make an additional $250 in tips."

Quick math tells me that's $600 for one shift. If I work five days a week, that's three grand.

Holy shit. My mouth turns up into a smile.

"Good?" Arrow asks.

I nod.

"You ready to party?"

The last party I attended was for Sadie's fourth birthday. She's my little cousin. The party was in the backyard of their home in southeastern Connecticut. We played Hot Potato and Pin-The-Tail-On-The-Donkey, and after the cupcakes, the tiny tykes took turns smashing a piñata shaped like Peppa Pig with a yardstick. Everyone was gone by 8:00 p.m., which was way past the bedtime of the children invited, and was not too far off from my own bedtime.

I suspect this evening's festivities will be a bit more interesting.

"Hell, yeah," I respond.

Not in Kansas, indeed.

CHAPTER THREE

BRADY

Obstacles are just opportunities in disguise.

This is the mantra I've been repeating to myself all morning.

"It's about damn time," Big Mike says, chewing on a bite of his breakfast burrito. We're perched on the tailgate of his royal blue Ford F-350. It's a good thing I'm tall, or else I would've needed a ladder to climb up here with those fat tires he's got. Big Mike's a ginger and a sheep in wolf's clothing – the nicest guy you'd ever want to know, but he looks and acts like a thug – which is quite possibly the best mix one could imagine in a human in that it's so obscure. Also, my dude is a tree. But not just any tree: Big Mike's an old, thick-ass oak tree in October: flaming red and orange leaves on a massive trunk. In a stretched out, used-to-be-white Hanes undershirt. With a flat-brim resting on his head, just slightly askew.

Best guy I ever met.

"What's in this? Chorizo?" he asks me.

"Yeah, bro. They call it the Long Pond because the ingredient list just goes on and on." I count off on my fingers. "It's three eggs, cheddar, swiss, avocado, salsa, bacon, ham, chorizo, and hash browns, double wrapped and then pressed on the grill."

"It's dope," Big Mike concurs, taking another hearty bite. "This town needed a good breakfast burrito."

"Agreed." I swallow a gulp of coffee. "Let's hope this little spot makes it past Columbus Day."

He nods. "Well, now that me and this wrap have become acquainted, I'll be back for more. This is worth battling bridge traffic. And thanks for picking up the tab."

"Are you kidding? It's the least I could do. I could never have moved all that shit without your truck."

"You know I got you." Big Mike swallows. "Did your dad say anything before you bounced this morning?"

"Nope."

He slaps me on the shoulder once, twice. "His loss, Bray. He's a dick."

I shrug. "It's whatever. We've been avoiding each other since that day. And to be honest, I should've left years ago. It's just such a shitty market for apartments here."

"Yeah, I feel you. I don't appreciate that you got evicted from your own house, though. Like, that's your son. I don't know. It's not like what you did was so egregious."

Did I mention Big Mike's a high school English teacher? When he kicks his SAT prep vocab into overdrive, I can't help but laugh. Nothing about this man makes any sense at all. I shrug. "Nobody fucks with Chef Brax, I guess."

"Well, I think you'll like your new digs. There's definitely something to be said for autonomy." He sinks his teeth into the handheld and moans something vaguely sexual.

I choke back a snort-laugh. "Did you notice that the hallway reeked of weed?"

Big Mike nods, chewing, holding up a finger until he finishes the bite. "I may have noticed." He licks a speck of hot sauce off his upper lip. "Now you got me thinking it was a contact high that got my ass so hungry." He smiles.

"It was 7:00 a.m. though. Who do you know that smokes at that time?"

"You never know; your neighbors might have still been up partying from the night before."

"I hope not. I'd rather be living next to some landscaper who gets fucked up before his early shift than a bunch of children who plan to keep me up all night."

"You sound like a greybeard, son."

I swallow the last mouthful of my burrito. "Do not."

"Yeah, you do. This thing with your dad has aged you."

I laugh. "I'm just concerned. It seems a little dank. That's all I'm saying."

"Don't knock it. That's some salt of the earth people living up in there. People who fuel the tourist industry: housekeepers, food handlers, gardeners. They work hard to keep our economy going."

"And I'm all for it, you know that. But why do they have to live underground? Bunch of mole people is what it is."

"I like that," Big Mike laughs, wagging a finger at me. "You keep quoting literature. That shit suits you, bro. And it's not underground. Only halfway."

"Anyway, it's just temporary," I say aloud, mostly as a reminder to myself.

"Exactly," he agrees. He crumples up his garbage into a paper bag and hops off the tailgate. "You got trash?"

I shove my burrito wrapper into my empty coffee cup and hand it over. "Thanks."

My dad kicked me out of our family home in a town called Sandwich. Yes, that is the real name of the town. It's an irrelevant piece of trivia now, I suppose, seeing as how I've managed to downgrade to the Cape Cod version of a halfway house more than 20 miles away from there.

I am not an elitist. It's very important that I make that point clear up front. My whole life, people have made assumptions. *Oh, Brady? He's Chef Brax's son. Must be filthy rich.* Wrong. My *father* is rich. My mom took off when I was in high school, and I can't say that I blame her, seeing as how he's such a ball sack. She invited me to come with her, but she was heading to Iowa to chase some dream of becoming a writer, and I was in high school. I had a bustling, teenage social life. I wasn't trying to give that up for a land where corn was the biggest topic of conversation. She enjoyed some nice success, too. Her debut novel came out a few years back, a psychological thriller about a woman who escaped a marriage by poisoning her husband in his very own restaurant. The irony of it all is that she doesn't make much money off of her writing, but her alimony checks are plentiful enough to keep her living her very best life, even if it is in the middle of nowhere.

Anyway, when she left, I didn't consider that I'd be stuck with all of my father's expectations. He wanted me to go to Cape Cod Community College on the culinary track, with the goal that I should get into Johnson and Wales and really learn the craft there. But I have zero interest in cooking. I mean, don't get me wrong, I like a good meal as much as the next guy, but I'm not, like *passionate* about carrots or whatever.

I prefer business. Economics. I think it's fascinating how finances can vary so much from a small town to a big city, and I find it especially interesting in a town where almost 100% of the revenue comes solely from tourism. Against my father's wishes, I went to Boston University to study management – a hellish commute, for sure, but well worth it, as the classes were both thought-provoking and engaging. He and I struck up a deal. I could study whatever I wanted as long as I worked at the country club. And, while that was never great, it was fine when I was younger. But once I graduated, I got an entry-level job as a Market Research Analyst, which drove the old man bat shit crazy. He forced me to continue my Saturday night shifts waiting tables for him at Diamond Excelsior, but the point was entirely moot, because the world came to a screeching halt when the pandemic hit.

I got laid off from my day job – part of the whole *last one in, first one out* thing, and of course all restaurants (including those at country clubs) shuttered their doors, so I proceeded to spend the next year suckling off the government teat like just about everyone else I knew.

Including Chef Brax.

It was really hard on him, being home. He watched a lot of cooking shows and yelled at the TV when he didn't agree with the flour:fat:water ratio in the pie crust, prepped new recipes in the kitchen, and joined the Peloton revolution.

He got through the lonely days just like the rest of us – by distracting himself. I noticed how few people he spoke to. Where I had friends who I could text, have Zoom drinks with, or hang with outdoors, my dad had grocery delivery service that drove him almost to the point of madness, with produce that he himself didn't hand-pick and meat too close to the expiration date for his liking. He was used to being in charge of a huge operation – a man who thrived on the pursed mouth of someone trying his gazpacho and the inevitable compliments that flowed from those lips after swallowing – but during COVID, he had none of that. No praise. No accolades. No minions. No drive.

Which is why, when the club reopened the following year, my father went back with renewed purpose, as if he had to make up for lost time.

"You're coming with me, Brady," he demanded, and seeing as how I had no job and my UI benefits had run dry, I had little choice but to oblige. He said, "You like business? You can manage the waitstaff for me."

So I did. And, not for nothing, I did it well, despite the ever-diminishing quality of workers in the world at that time. J-1s were fine, but they were essentially just kids here on vacation. My year-round waitstaff team was solid. I could count on them to handle the high-end clientele. Nance, my best server, was with me from the beginning of my tenure. She'd been waitressing at the Diamond Excelsior since I was in diapers, she'd often tell me. My other two weekend-must-haves were Trish and Monty: both top-notch waiters. The issue was that they all played poker together on weekends after closing, a tradition which exists to this day. Which is how they all ended up with norovirus when Nance's godson was visiting and caught what she thought was a stomach bug. Twelve hours after a card game I found myself literally scraping the bottom of the barrel to find some random pub girl to work in private dining on the day now dubbed "the incident."

Believe me, I tried to get other servers. But at the beginning of peak season, private dining is a really tough fit, and no one does it quite like Nance. I needed an adult who could be professional around the clients, so the J-1s were definitely out; too many of them are just here looking for a good time and I couldn't be responsible for a celebrity encounter ending up on TikTok. The main dining room was also short-staffed, so I couldn't in good conscience pull from there. I would have served David Krumholtz myself, but I had too much running around to do between the two spaces, and we'd been trained (by my father) that private dining clients are to receive a dedicated server, not a multitasking mid-level manager.

I wasn't responsible for direct oversight of the pub, but these were desperate times and I needed someone immediately. I ran down the flight of stairs separating main dining from the Diamond Mine Tavern. Upon entering, I saw that they were understaffed as well – but they had a bartender plus three, and could stand to lose a body for a few hours.

She was the only native English speaker there. Her hair reminded me of a ripe Honeycrisp apple, red with traces of pink, but it was neatly twisted up into a bun minus the few loose pieces framing her face. She looked about my age, and was hustling a tray of lobster grilled cheese sandwiches over to a party of two in the corner.

As she walked back toward the kitchen, I stopped her. "Excuse me," I said. "I'm not sure we've met, but I'm Brady Hawthorne, Assistant Manager of Personnel –"

"I know you. You're Chef Brax's son." The corners of her mouth turned up.

I looked at her nametag. "Gretchen," I said, holding out my hand. "I'm Brady."

She shook it, and the baby soft skin of her palm lingered on my own. "Can I get you something?"

"I need a favor," I explained. "Do you think you could handle yourself with poise in front of a famous person?"

"Depends," she said. Her pink lips stretched into a smile. "Who is it?" she asked, in an exaggerated whisper.

"David Krumholtz."

She knit her eyebrows together, thinking. "I know that name."

"He's been in lots of stuff. Everything from *Oppenheimer* to *Harold and Kumar go to White Castle*. Most recently, he was in *The Studio* on Apple TV."

"That's it! I watch that show. And I remembered him from *10 Things I Hate About You*." Her eyes got wide. "Wait. He's here? Seriously?"

"I know, I know," I said, not in the mood for games. "Listen, I just need you to be professional."

"Of course," she replied. "Just, damn, you know? That's really cool that he's here."

"Yes. Cool. Great. Wonderful. Come on, then. Follow me."

"Um, okay." She set her tray down on the bar. We climbed the stairs to the lobby, then traversed the grand banquet hall towards the back of the room where the staff quarters are hidden, adjacent the main kitchen. "I'll get you a uniform," I said. "What size?" I gestured at her body, because if there's one thing I know, it's that you should never assume anything when it comes to women and clothing sizes.

Gretchen looked down at her standard-issue oxford pub shirt and black pants. "I don't know. Like, an 8? Medium? Whatever you think would fit?"

"What about your feet?"

"My feet?" she echoed.

"Your feet," I nodded. "You can't wear those shoes. They're fine for the pub, but not for private dining."

"Oh," she said. "I'm a seven and a half."

"Okay. Be right back." I went into the supply closet and pulled a crisp white shirt, black fitted dress pants, and a brand new pair of Nine West pumps, still in the box. The garments were covered in plastic, having just returned from the dry cleaners. I handed the outfit to her and pointed to the staff dressing room. I told her to put her things in a locker and try to change quickly. Then, I sat down and placed my head in my hands, in an attempt to wish away the throbbing.

About five minutes later, Gretchen returned. I gave her a once over. Despite her obvious discomfort, she looked the part. I mean, minus the phosphorescent hair, but really, beggars can't be choosers.

"Great," I said. "Let's go."

"I, um –"

"What?" I checked my watch. David Krumholtz's reservation was for 6:00 p.m., and it was 5:50.

"I'm not great at walking in heels," she confessed earnestly. Her eyes grew wide with the admission. Under different circumstances, I would have found her concern charming.

"I'm sure you'll be fine. This is the uniform. Rules are rules."

She let out a nervous laugh. "You really think David Krumholtz is going to care if I wear my own, significantly more broken-in shoes?"

I shook my head. "No. But Chef will."

"Oh. Okay." She nodded. "Got it."

Gretchen was doing fine. She was composed, got David and his colleagues each a drink, brought out the bread plate with the bean dip and garlic spread, and ground the fresh cracked pepper over it without making a mess. She walked a little slower than I would have liked, but she was being careful, and that was fine.

Until she fell.

I didn't see it happen. I walked in just as I heard the word, "Shit!" and only saw the chaos that ensued after the tray came crashing down. David shot up from the table, holding his pants away from his manhood (smart move, too, because Chef Brax basically lights those steamers on fire before plating them). Gretchen was on the ground, possibly in pain, the tray beside her. Lobster macaroni and cheese dripped from the edge of the table in clumps, hitting the industrial carpet with a splash, like chunks of orangey-pink vomit.

"Oh, my God," I exclaimed, hurrying over to the table. "I am so sorry. She's new – well, not new, just, she's from *downstairs*, and, um –"

"I'm fine," David Krumholtz replied. "It was an accident. I, uh –"

"We have pants in the back! I'll grab you a whole new outfit," I said, realizing that I was about to dress a famous actor like a member of the waitstaff.

"Are you okay?" he asked Gretchen, who was scrambling to get up.

"Yeah," she said, removing her shoes. "I'm so, so sorry. I didn't mean to –"

"I know," he said to her. "Don't worry about it."

Those lips – I could see the bottom one starting to tremble, so I leaned down to Gretchen and said, "Listen, Stumbelina, if you start crying, you'll make this a whole lot worse than it has to be." Then, I left to grab the clothes.

The news made it to the kitchen at lightning speed, and by the time I returned to the private dining room, my father was there. In the havoc that followed, David stripped off his pants, gratefully accepting my offer of pressed khakis and a clean shirt. Gretchen was cleaning up the floor, her feet bare, piling individual steamers onto the tray and swallowing her tears, and my father was clearing the table. "Get a new tablecloth, *now*, Brady," he said to me.

"On it, Chef," I replied. I grabbed new linens, napkins, silverware, dinner plates, and tasting plates. High-tailed it back to the room and Gretchen was gone, along with the fallen tray.

My father and I worked in tandem, wordlessly, to get Krumholtz and company seated and re-situated with fresh drinks and food. Everything was on the house, my father insisted, and I was to stay put in the room and serve them myself. David Krumholtz, class act that he is, didn't make a big stink about it. "Shit happens," he told me. "Really. Every now and again I ask my wife to aggressively throw food at me. Keeps me humble," he laughed.

Some people are just nice like that.

Unfortunately, Chef Brax is not one of those people.

Later that night, my perfectionist father had no trouble eliminating me from both his place of business as well as his house. "That was an *embarrassment* to my kitchen, Brady. How could you call in a rookie for one of the most exclusive guests of the season? You never took my work seriously," he accused me, all but foaming at the mouth. "You try being in the service industry. See how easy it is."

I laughed when he said that – probably not my best reaction.

"Are you kidding me?" I retorted. "I *am* in the service industry! More than you are – you don't serve food; you *cook* it! Do you think it's easy managing the schedules of a bunch of college kids who ride bicycles to work and come and go like the wind? Do you think it's just no big deal handling reservations, seating people, covering two dining rooms with barely any help?"

Instead of a normal response, my father slammed his fist down on the butcher block counter and said, "How dare you speak to me like that? You call yourself a manager? A manager *handles* things, Brady. A chef should never have to leave the kitchen to work the floor. But you think you're so fucking great? Then I'm sure you'll *manage* just fine living somewhere else."

"What does that mean?" I asked.

"I want you gone by this weekend," he enunciated for emphasis. "I'm sick and tired of you belittling everything that matters to me." His eyes overflowed with venom and fire, reminiscent of the fights he used to have with my mother back when she was still around. I knew better than to ask if he was serious. As I walked out of the room, shaking my head, he called after me. "And good luck finding a job as cushy as the one I gave you."

Just like that, I was fired and homeless, all at the hands of my own father. We avoided each other for the remainder of the week. I reached out to my core people directly. Nance was beside herself; she felt responsible, she said, and all but begged me to let her petition my dad to get my job back. Trish and Monty were sorry to hear about my departure as well, but in this business people come and go, and often they run into each other again at some other restaurant. Happens all the time in Cape Cod.

Nance had an in with Luis, a line cook at the pub who had to go to the Dominican Republic for the summer to take care of his ailing mother. This left his apartment vacant. He wasn't planning to sublet it, because it was too much of a hassle to move everything into storage – so Nance was able to get me in there, basically as a couch surfer, for the summer. Luis put all of his personal affects in his bedroom, leaving me a sagging sofa, a bathroom, and a kitchen to call my own until August 31st. All I had to do was cover his rent and utilities.

Of course, nobody mentioned that it was a subterranean situation, as if I was some kind of hibernating gopher.

"Yo," Big Mike says, lumbering over from the garbage can. "We good?"

"All set," I reply.

I climb into the passenger seat and absorb the way the illegal tints make the morning sun look like midnight. "Dark enough in here for you?" I joke.

"Don't talk shit about my whip," he laughs, turning up his system and bobbing his head up and down to the beat of some indie rapper named Larry June. The engine roars as he backs the truck up carefully, creating more air pollution than my Hyundai Elantra could generate in a week. And, while one might expect a truck like this to peel out onto the street, Big Mike cautiously makes a right turn and proceeds to drive the speed limit all the way back to my new digs.

"Sorry I couldn't hang out for longer," he comments with a smirk. "Gina made these plans weeks ago."

"It's all good, bro. I really appreciate your help. Have fun at your spa day."

Mike laughs, a hearty sound that starts deep in his belly. "Someone's jealous."

"Just don't let her try and wax you."

"Nah. We already discussed that the girls could only use me for rubdown practice." He winks. Big Mike's girlfriend is in cosmetology school to become an aesthetician but two of her friends have their final next week in massage therapy. They're "studying" on Big Mike this afternoon. "It worked out perfectly. You strained my poor muscles all morning with hard labor, and now they can knead out all the knots in my back. I earned it."

"You got work tonight?" Unsurprisingly, he's got a decent side hustle as a glorified bodyguard.

"Indeed I do. So, it's extra important that my body be worshipped like the temple it is before I have to go put it at risk in service of others tonight. Should be good money, though. Two-hundred bucks for basically showing up and standing around for like an hour. Can't hate on that."

"You've got the life, man. I'll just be over here scouring the internet for a new job and reorganizing the boxes in my glorified crawl space."

"Could be worse," Big Mike reminds me, pulling into the parking lot in front of my new abode. His flaming hair peeks out from the sides of his kelly-green Celtics hat. He is sunshine, personified.

I bite my tongue, tempted to comment that it could be better, too. But then I remember the thing he said earlier. "Obstacles are just opportunities in disguise, right?"

Big Mike nods, cheesing. "Hard facts, my man." He juts his chin out towards what I imagine is the garbage shed. "I just saw a honey walk right in there. You could wife her up, for all we know."

"Oh, yeah?" I pause, looking for evidence of this sighting. Suddenly, the shed door swings open and a short, bald man emerges carrying a stack of mail. I turn to Mike. "That her?"

"Maybe you're right." He shrugs. "Maybe my tints are a little too dark."

CHAPTER FOUR
GRETCHEN

I am a Cape Cod lifer.

Born and raised in Eastport, I can't imagine permanently living anywhere else. The calm of the tidal flats, the quiet off-season, the quintessential Americana New England summers, replete with clam bakes and bonfires and shark hunting from the shore – all of this was the story of my youth, and I have been blessed with a full and happy existence thus far.

Of course, there are some downsides – like anywhere. Here, the challenges include cyclical traffic, desolate winters, and a shallow dating pool. Everyone knows everyone. There are scant opportunities for higher education on the peninsula that is America's smallest bicep, so most of my childhood friends opted to saddle up and ride off into a more collegiate sunset in nearby Boston, although those who could afford it went even further. Some ventured south after 18 years of nor-easter-laden Januarys, and some even decided to leave the country altogether on gap-year backpacking adventures through Europe, Latin America, and the Caribbean. Alternatively, some of my classmates found a cranial escape in recreational drug use and mass consumption of spirits. Destined for a future bouncing from holding cells in local police precincts to the Barnstable County Correctional Facility, these poor souls let the yawntastic redundance of the off-season stifle their potential for greatness.

There were confused dreamers, too – teenagers whose senioritis and mediocre grades conflicted with any hopes their parents may have had for them of a life beyond the Cape. Jenna was one of those kids. Her compass lacked a true north – one day she wanted to be a veterinarian, the next she wanted to go into competitive pickleball, then she decided she was best suited for nursing. She was a prime candidate for 4Cs, better known as Cape Cod Community College to out-of-towners. She has since spent her time piecemealing a part-time Associate's degree together with online classes towards a Bachelor's, landing her a placement in the ER at Cape Cod Hospital. Young adults like Jenna took a little longer to find their way, but eventually figured it out. Jenna didn't stay on the Cape because of her great love for it; she stayed because there was really nowhere else for her to go.

Then there were the kids like me. Few and far between, we were goal-oriented and thirsty for learning but also loved growing up here and couldn't imagine settling anywhere else. I begrudgingly moved to Amherst to pursue a degree in elementary education at UMass, fully intending to bring that knowledge back home with me and offer it up to the very school system that raised me. And that's exactly what I did. I got my initial teaching certification, then moved back in with my parents after graduating college a semester early. I enrolled in a Master's program online at Framingham State University and started working at the Diamond Mine (the pub at the Diamond Excelsior), while beginning the interview process for a full time teaching position in the early months of 2020.

Cue the screeching halt otherwise known as COVID.

The job market for teachers suddenly evaporated. The pub shut down and instead of spending my time pursuing meaningful career opportunities, I gratefully banked unemployment checks from the government while continuing my remote graduate classes. My relatives lived in Boston, and as the mass exodus from big cities began later that spring, we welcomed a houseful of extended family members to stay with us for the foreseeable future. This included my aunt, uncle, three teenage cousins, and one very poorly behaved chihuahua named Foofie, who took pleasure in terrorizing my new pandemic rescue kitten, Zoloft. I'd adopted him as an antidote to the sadness I would have otherwise battled on account of not being able to pursue my calling of working with young people. I found it exceedingly difficult to study amidst the constant ruckus at home, so I decided it was time to find my own slice of local real estate.

Now I live in a cute little condominium. I bought it just before the prices skyrocketed. Like, literally, *weeks* before. I'd been able to save up a modest nest egg thanks to my waitressing gig at Roberto's, an upscale Italian restaurant in Amherst. It was there that I learned just how lucrative the service industry could be. That plus the bit of money I was able to bank from the Diamond Mine and a few months of unemployment grew my savings account to a whopping $12,000.

My one-bedroom walk-out apartment cost me $110,000. I put down my entire savings account and my parents loaned me the remaining $10k so I wouldn't have to pay PMI.

The thing about Cape Cod is the rent is batshit crazy in the summer. So if you're a local and you plan to stick around, you need to own your own place.

Not everyone is as lucky as I am. I live on resort property, so the landscaping is beautiful and there's a golf course right behind my building. There's an indoor/outdoor swimming pool complex directly across the street that's bustling with kids and families all summer. I'm not allowed in there because I'm not a country club member, but it's still nice to have it so close. There's a horse farm down the hill, so when I go for walks, I get to gaze upon these lovely creatures just roaming in a wide, green field.

Sure, not everything is perfect. The building can sometimes be a little damp. To navigate one's way to my humble abode, one would open the main door to the communal residence and walk down a flight of steps to a hallway laden with dehumidifiers that smells vaguely like incense from my neighbor down the hall (the one who leaves every pair of her shoes on her exterior doormat, as if that's intended to be common space). Inside, my home is a very standard 570 square feet of living space. Tiny kitchen, normal-sized bathroom, single 10x10 bedroom, living room-dining room combo, and a sliding glass door that leads to a small cement patio where I can sit outside and have a drink or read a book. I have a beautiful picture window that overlooks the 5th tee and a spectacular hydrangea that blooms fragrant violet and blue flowers in the summer. Unfortunately, the floral scent can't mask the odoriferousness of the black Labrador retriever three doors down whose clockwork defecations in the muddy grass between the building and the golf course are reminiscent of a sack full of assholes. By mid-July, the horseflies come, and I can't sit outside anymore because in the late-afternoon sun, all I inhale is the warmed aroma of canine fecal matter.

Still, it's paradise.

I suppose I should mention that recently, there have been some issues. Our HOAs are about to skyrocket because evidently, the building (and all of its companion buildings in my "village," aptly named *Tidewater*) has massive leakage issues due to improper insulation from back when they were built in 1985. Whenever it rains, I have to lay out a thick stack of towels at the base of my slider because there is active precipitation *inside* the house. Accordingly, stains bearing evidence of black mold are forming on my ceiling, looking like the transmogrifying ink blots one might flip through during an intense cognitive therapy session. I have decided not to consider what breathing in this toxicity might be doing to my lungs, especially knowing that the condo board is on it – they're all homeowners, too, and a structural concern is no laughing matter.

But they don't live on my floor.

Many of the owners use their condos as investment properties and lease them weekly to vacationing families. The condos on my floor, however, are mostly owned by Diamond Excelsior's management, and are then rented to the year-round club employees, because it's incredibly difficult to find affordable housing in Cape Cod. So, not only are the employees earning minimum wage and hoping to bring in tips to supplement their paltry paychecks, they also get the added bonus of giving most of that money back to management once a month in the form of a rent check.

For me, this is a starter home. And to be fair, it could be a lot worse. The J-1s, who are seasonal, live in barracks reminiscent of sleepaway camp cabins tucked into the woods in a clearing that management didn't even bother to pave. They get to ride company-issued rental bicycles down a bumpy gravel path each morning to get to their assignments. Some work at the beach club, others at one of the seven swimming pools, still others on the golf course. J-1s come to America *looking* for an adventure. I suppose it would be fun to leave Norway, where the average temperature in July is 50 degrees, to have a summer abroad in the balmy-by-comparison northeast corridor of the United States. The gravel biking situation might seem like a small price to pay in that scenario. Alas, the tundra is not my natural habitat. Also, I am not a child. I am a *grown-ass woman*, according to my new employer, Arrow.

So you can understand my frustration at being woken up so early on a Saturday morning with unwelcome neighbor-noise, especially after getting home so late last night.

Arrow's staff-member-sisterhood arrived about an hour after I did. Three girls dressed in loose pajama pants and oversized T-shirts giggled through the door, immediately smiling my way. Arrow introduced them to me as Saffron, Cherry, and Indigo. (I later learned their government names are Maria, Cheryl, and Kim, but forced my brain to immediately forget this intel as I would otherwise inevitably fumble and refer to one using her parent-issued nomenclature.) The first thing I discovered was that these girls are super body-positive. After exchanging brief pleasantries, they headed straight for the locker bank. No one even flinched when they began to strip off their outer layers, as if this is something one just does at work, like a chef peeling an onion.

Except for me.

My jaw involuntarily hit the floor when Cherry dropped her Gymshark joggers to reveal a pair of high-waisted, leather hot shorts that exposed 90% of her posterior and appeared to be lodged in between her cheeks like a permanent wedgie. Indigo's torso was wrapped in unseasonal Christmas lights with a battery pack tucked into her bra, and Saffron – a diminutive firecracker at 4'11" – wore a leopard-print, one piece situation with a V so deep, it went all the way down to her belly button and left very little of her top shelf to the imagination. They made Arrow's outfit look demure by comparison.

"Not nice to stare," Saffron admonished me, half bent over, strapping on a shoe that gave her the additional inches to bring her up to my height of 5'6". She hit a switch on the underside of the shoe and the platform lit up.

I cleared my throat. "I'm sorry. I'm just not used to –"

"She's kidding," Cherry interjected. "Don't even listen to her."

Saffron stood up straight. "I'm fucking with you." She smiled, smoothing her hands down the sides of her body, adjusting the fabric of the outfit she had on to make sure it was properly in place. "Hand me that tape?" she went on, pointing at a Ziploc bag in the open locker. I grabbed it and passed it to her. "Gotta keep the hammers in the tool box, you know what I'm saying?" She proceeded to remove strip after strip of double sided tape to affix the leopard fabric to her skin.

Indigo flipped on her lights. "You guys don't think these'll burn me, do you?"

"Nah," Saffron said. "I've done Christmas photos with those. They get a little warm, but nothing crazy. Just be careful not to slam into the pole. If you break one, you could get all scratched up."

Indigo nodded. "Maybe I'll tape them in place, too."

"Can't hurt," Cherry added.

"So, Summer," Saffron wondered aloud, "You gonna dance with us?"

"Not wearing that," Cherry laughed, gesturing toward my outfit with a nod.

I looked down at the not-quite-couture situation I was sporting. Admittedly, the tank top looked, well... ratchet, but I sort of thought that tracked with the kind of party we were throwing. I didn't realize there were legit costumes we could be wearing. Also, Jenna did not mention anything about me having to –

"She's only here to babysit," Arrow interjected, laughing. "Besides, I doubt she could dance."

"Damn, Arrow. That's cold," Cherry said.

"No, she's probably right," I interjected. "I don't think I could do all that upside-down business you were doing when I got here."

"My moves are advanced," Arrow replied, rubbing a fingerful of Icy Hot on the back of her shoulder, atop a tattoo of a glass heart shattered by – you guessed it – an arrow. "We don't teach that at parties. We just like to show off."

"It impresses the clients," Indigo added, pressing a piece of tape to her ribcage.

"You could learn," Cherry said. "But you'd have to upgrade your look. Although, I'm obsessed with your hair color. Where did you get that done?"

I touched my ruby locks. "4Cs. I was a cosmetology final."

"Super cute."

"Anyway, we all started from scratch. We could teach you how to pole." Saffron offered.

"I took dance as a kid," I offered.

Arrow rolled her eyes. "Totally different."

"You should try it. We work out on Mondays and Tuesdays, when there are less likely going to be parties," Cherry said. "We do all our own choreo. It's great exercise."

"Plus, it's fun," Indigo added. "You might like it."

"I could never wear what you guys are wearing, though," I admitted. "I thought *this* was scandalous." I gesture at my current getup.

"You're a grown ass woman," Arrow said with a smirk. "No shame in flaunting it."

A few minutes later, the hot-mess-express came roaring into the station just shy of the party's designated 8:00 p.m. start time. 27 girls barreled out of a huge white party bus, already lit from whatever pre-game cocktails they'd enjoyed. Arrow rolled her eyes. "Ugh. I hate early birds."

Arrow pushed up her boobs in her bra before swinging open the door. "Hey, ladies!" she waved, welcoming them in with her fakest smile. "Who's ready to get fucked up?"

"Woo!" the one dressed in a short, tight, white lace getup who I could only assume was some lucky man's bride-to-be screamed out, punching a fist high in the air.

Arrow brought the girls into the studio, Cherry cranked up the music, Saffron climbed one of the poles and began spinning up by the ceiling, and Indigo launched into a headstand from the floor which resulted with her wrapping her legs around a different pole. Arrow showed the partygoers where they could put their personal belongings. I was grateful to not have to worry about collecting car keys because that would have been akin to herding feral cats; there was no semblance of order whatsoever among these women. Instead, I tried to gauge the vibe of the room, but felt so overwhelmed that I was tempted to just start handing out bottles of water. (As it turns out, Arrow may have chosen the wrong girl for the job, seeing as how my idea of a party vibe involves a mug of hot cocoa and a nice crossword puzzle.)

"You okay?" Cherry asked me.

I nodded, grabbing her by the hand and pulling her in close so I could whisper-yell. "What color shots would you start with?"

"I'd go middle of the road. This group seems okay so far." She pulled back to look at me. "Relax, bae. This is nothing."

I took a breath and grabbed the raspberry Smirnoff Jell-o shots. I counted ten trays of 32 shots each, two of which were the "lemon drops" (aka glorified Gatorade). I put on my best attempt at a cool-party-girl face, which may have come out doppelgangering as a constipation face, and held the plastic platter out in front of my stomach, heading for the ladies who were already dancing in a weird junior-high-school-type circle.

"Hey, girlfriends!" I screeched at the group, bopping my way on my clunky shoes into the middle of their proverbial "Ring Around the Rosy" formation. Carrying a cafeteria tray of shots through the strobe-lit-darkness, I was desperately trying to make sure none of them fell while DMX barked at me through the speakers, God rest his soul.

"OhmyGod, shots!" someone hollered, and I was bombarded by the greedy crowd, as if I was an untended bag of chips at a seagull-laden beach. Swarmed. Pummeled. Stunned, I stood there, amidst the slurping of mouths on plastic, which would probably have sounded like a dick-sucking contest were it not for DMX not-so-gently assaulting my ears with his repeated use of expletives. Tiny cups flew back onto my tray and excited obscenities came at me from all sides as the ladies resumed their sad attempts at sticking out their mostly flat hindquarters in the name of dance.

Thankfully, Arrow put an end to the mass hysteria by momentarily lowering the music and explaining that the group should split up, no more than four per pole, so they could be led through a series of moves by her team. There would be four basic maneuvers taught, she explained. "We'll begin with a dip turn, followed by a fireman spin, a back knee hook, and a fan kick. We'll also practice some floor work and then we'll put together a short piece of choreo using both the pole and a chair. But first, we need to stretch. Everybody spread out."

She commanded the room, and I was in awe. It was oddly reminiscent of watching an elementary school teacher direct a classroom of sweaty, post-recess children. Saffron, Cherry and Indigo headed to stations throughout the dance floor. Each of them was responsible for covering two poles, so Arrow modeled a move, and they did it with her before coaching their respective partygoers on how to execute it. The whole thing was conducted with precision: Arrow made it clear when I was to bring around more shots to keep the mood level, she gave the girls time to practice, and the place hummed with the nervous laughter of satisfied customers. They practiced "walking sexy" for each other, spun, slipped, and slid around the poles, learned how to crawl across the floor and how to fake a split off the pole. Generally speaking, the girls were terrible at it, but they were having fun, which was obviously all that mattered.

When the trays of shots were halfway gone, my colleagues performed a little number they'd be teaching to the room. An amalgamation of all the moves they'd taught in isolation with some simple transitions both on the pole and on the ground, somehow they made this 90-second situation look extremely hot. The ladies cheered, excited to learn a "whole pole dance," and continued gratefully accepting my shots as they practiced and ultimately performed for each other in small groups.

Then, just as the last group was finishing up, a heavy knock landed on the steel entry door. Arrow looked around at the party as if she was uneasy and walked over to answer it – in pole heels and her underwear – while 27 pairs of concerned eyes followed her, mumbling to each other, as if they were about to be caught doing something wrong.

Alas, in walked a stone-cold fox of a man – all angles and lines and muscles under his tight t-shirt, dressed in a pair of waders and carrying a tackle box, evidently unfazed by Arrow's lack of proper clothing. "Excuse me," his voice boomed. "I'm with the Cape Cod Shellfish Association." He paused for dramatic effect. "We heard there were some clams here that needed shucking."

"Yeah, there are!" Arrow exclaimed. "Right, ladies?" She proceeded to grab him by the bulging forearm and pull him into the space. The tackle box dropped along with the beat, this time belonging to "Closer" by Nine Inch Nails. All of a sudden, the man's hips began to gyrate and I realized that this was not, in fact, a poor, wayward fisherman. He was followed in by a giant bodyguard-type-gentleman, dressed in a black t-shirt, black jeans, and a black hat, undoubtedly in attendance to protect the talent.

Which was a good thing, too, because *holy estrogen.* You would think these women had never seen a man before. Arrow cried out for the bride and sat her in a chair and before I knew what was happening, the man's waders were gone and his bulge was on full display, covered only by a triangle of shiny, camo fabric. He ground his hips into an overwhelmingly eager soon-to-be-espoused partygoer under a sudden thunderstorm of dollar bills. Meanwhile, I attempted to protect my strip-club-virgin eyes from the dry humping that ensued. The entertainer dipped the chair back and held the bride in place with one arm while situating his admittedly-plentiful junk directly over her face.

She was wildly mesmerized.

Variations of this continued on for approximately 30 more minutes. I delivered two more trays of the lighter shots during this time and marveled at this man's dance moves. The stripper got up on chairs, interacted with almost every person in the room, and nearly impregnated the bride while Indigo and Cherry morphed into pole-swinging backup dancers. He was beautiful – a perfect combination of strong muscles and lean meat and good man smells, and then, as quickly as he appeared, he was gone, leaving me to wonder if it was all just a fever dream.

Somehow, tacos arrived exactly then. (Of all the things!) A catering van from Papi Chulo's in Harwich delivered trays upon trays of premium Mexican cuisine, and, evidently, 27 suppressed orgasms became infinitely hangry. Corn tortillas went a-flying as inflated dopamine levels demanded to be satiated with ground beef, cheese and endless guacamole. Papi Chulo's also brought a bucket of margaritas. Thank God; these ladies were so thirsty, they bordered on dehydrated. I would have recommended they put some electrolytes in their margaritas, but it was not my place to offer suggestions.

After inhaling their Latin snack (the food, not the stripper), the party came to a very natural close. Arrow reminded everyone to grab their personal belongings and we all waved at the bus as it exited the parking lot, as if it were a summer camp cheese wagon driving a group of children off to their first sleepaway adventure – instead of a liquor-stocked trollop-tour headed to an after-party drag show in nearby P-Town. Saffron put on some Camila Cabello and we wiped down the poles with rubbing alcohol, disinfected the surfaces, cleaned the bathroom and swept the floor. When it was time to go, Arrow handed each of us a fat envelope. I counted the bills in my Fiesta.

$620.

In one night.

It would have taken me a week to make that much in tips at the pub.

Once I got home, I had a tough time coming down from the adrenaline rush. So many of my cherries were popped last night: I'd never watched a striptease, never seen anyone pole dance, never been a shot girl. So I did what anyone would do: I devoured a box of taco leftovers like a savage trash raccoon in front of my TV, inhaling the latter part of an SNL repeat as an accompaniment. I followed the hefty meal with a single lime-flavored High Noon and two melatonin gummies, hoping I would get some good, well-deserved shuteye. And I did, with Zoloft curled up at my feet. In fact, I was so overwhelmed with sudden exhaustion that I allowed myself to fall asleep in my fishnets and tank top, hair up in a messy bun, face unwashed, looking like a commercial for a hangover remedy.

The next thing I know, there's sunlight beaming in through my slider. And banging. I roll over in bed, groaning. I check the time on my phone: 8:45.

Seriously?

It's coming from Luis' apartment – which is odd, because Luis is in the DR for the summer. Could be the management company, checking on the status of our constant leaks. But it didn't rain last night – so why would they be banging like this?

I try to suffocate the noise with my pillow, but to no avail. A whirring sound starts.

Ugh. What the hell?

I peel myself up. *This shall not stand.* Is it too much to ask for a little common courtesy? I grab my bathrobe and put it on over my ludicrous getup. Glancing in the mirror, I cringe. But I don't care what the Tidewater Management Company thinks of me. And Mr. Smoot, our building handyman, has seen me look way worse.

I pad over to Luis's in stocking feet, willing the grating sound to stop. I'm not hungover, but I sure am tired, and this is a most unwelcome alarm.

I knock on the door.

No answer. *Of course. Old Smoot probably can't hear me.*

I try the knob. It turns. I lean my head in and scan the area, trying to locate the source of the noise.

"Hello?" I call out, stepping into the apartment.

Like a fucking jack-in-the-box, a man pops up off the floor, revealing himself over the tiny island separating the kitchen from the rest of the living space. He's holding – *ohmygod is that a gun?*

I startle, and my hand lands on my chest reflexively. "Shit!" I seethe.

"Um, can I help you?" he asks in a tone that balances aggravation with politeness, a surprising combination for an obvious felon wielding a mortal weapon.

I clutch a fistful of my bathrobe against my heart, catching my breath in a fashion that is, to be fair, a *smidge* dramatic for this hour of the day. It's not a gun. It's a drill. Or, like, a screw gun. Some kind of power tool. I exhale.

"What are you doing?" the annoyed dude asks.

It takes a second to realize that I'm familiar with the exact cadence and tone of that voice. I remember it like a heart palpitation, or like one of those unwelcome songs that gets stuck in your head. As the recognition floods my body like the panties of last night's bride when the stripper raw-dogged her romper, I become acutely aware of how I must look in this moment.

I try to respond, but there's a morning frog stuck in my larynx. "I –" I croak. I clear my throat, the hearty cough of an 80 year-old pack-a-day smoker. "I *live* here." I point in the general direction of my apartment. "Well, *there*."

He – Brady – *the* Brady Hawthorne who made a complete fool of me at my previous place of employ – scrunches up his nose, his expression shifting as his brain tries to place me. He looks different, dressed in mesh shorts and a t-shirt, a far cry from the funeral-director getup he had on when he had my sorry ass fired. I elect not to notice the fact that his biceps are large enough to strain the sleeves of his T-shirt.

He looks normal. As in, *not* a complete stuffy country club asshole.

Good, even. With that drill in his hand, flexing his forearm.

Ew. Stop that, I tell my brain. "What are *you* doing here?" I ask.

"I'm subletting," he explains, eyeballing me. The confusion that dances across his face lasts only a moment. In the end, I know it's my hair that gives me away. Nobody pulls off the Ronald McDonald color quite like I do. "Shit," he mumbles, which is how I know he's figured out who I am. Still, he puffs himself up like he's got a leg to stand on, trying to regroup. "Why are you inside my rental?"

"I thought you were the management company," I squirm sheepishly.

"Even if I was, do you make it a habit of barging into other people's condos?"

"Luis is away," I point out.

"So, does *that* make it okay?"

"Oh my God!" I exclaim. "You're the one making all this noise first thing in the morning!"

"Well, I'm sorry, but I'm building myself a bed. And it's, like, 9 o'clock."

"It's 8:50, actually, and it's *Saturday*. Were you raised in some sort of *barn*?"

This makes him laugh, a brusque puff of air cut off by his own incredulous expression. "Pray tell, what is the *correct* time for one to partake in such activities?"

Smug bastard. "How about never?" I retort, fully aware that this is the reasoning of a toddler.

Brady huffs. "Listen, I really am sorry to have bothered you. It's obvious that you're coming off some sort of *night*." He gestures at my bathrobe and fishnets. "I'll give it an hour, so you can nurse your hangover, or whatever it is you need to be doing right now."

My blood boils. "I'm *not* hung over," I fume.

"Tell that to your outfit," he mutters with a smirk.

"Ugh!" I grunt. "It's the weekend!" I proclaim. "And this is *communal* living. Don't you know that you're supposed to respect your neighbors?"

He tilts his head at me, his eyes bearing a curiosity that closely resembles a puppy dog, but way hotter, and in mesh shorts that may or may not give me a mild understanding of the size of his chowder cannon. "Gretchen, right? I'm sorry – are you supposed to 'respect' your neighbors by availing yourself of their entryways without even so much as a knock? Is that the kind of building etiquette that I've defied by merely trying to assemble a simple piece of furniture?"

I want to stab him with a pair of needle-nose pliers.

He crosses his arms with indignation, still holding the power tool, forcing all sorts of muscles to tighten. It's a standoff. I can't come up with a clever retort fast enough, so I put my hands on my hips and sneer at him. He continues to mansplain his existence to me. "I'm sure you understand. I need to get this bed built so I have somewhere to sleep tonight. Such is the quandary we find ourselves in. Hence, the hour I'm willing to give you. That is called compromise."

I am mute, incapable of a response.

"Cat got your tongue?" he asks.

I shake my head. "You're a dick, Brady." I turn and head back out into the hallway.

His laugh follows me. "Aren't neighbors supposed to bring you cookies or something?" he yells toward the still-open front door.

I slam mine behind me.

"Have the *best* day!" I hear him call out from his side of the wall. "Thank you for stopping by!"

"Fuck," I whisper, opening the pantry and grabbing the shareable-size bag of M&Ms I keep in there for emergencies. I pour out a handful of rainbow deliciousness, and pop the candy bits all into my mouth at once, letting the chocolate melt into my tongue.

What kind of cosmic karmageddon is this? I wonder. *Of all the people in the world, why is Brady Hawthorne living next door to me?*

Also, why does he have to look like that?

CHAPTER FIVE

BRADY

*T*hat's about right, I decide.

Cape Cod's small, but it's not *this* small. So of course the universe should plant me right next door to the girl who got me fired from my job.

Of all people.

Oh, I can just picture it. Perhaps she can bring home updates from my dear old dad about how business is going. It's obvious she would get nothing if not sheer delight out of watching me squirm.

I'm actually a little surprised that she behaved so, um, *spicy*. There was definitely an edge to her that I wouldn't have expected based on our previous interaction. On the contrary, Gretchen seemed pretty cool that first day when I met her. She saw that I was in a tough situation and was willing to do the job – she even *tried*. And yes, she fell, and that was awful, but even at that, she didn't cause a big scene about it after. She cleaned up the mess. True, she *almost* broke down in tears, but I caught her before that could happen – effectively *saving* her job, thank you very much. She left – embarrassed, I'm sure. Covered in food. Also, possibly hurt – a twisted ankle or perhaps an injured leg. She was a good enough waitress, so I'm sure she's just back down at the pub where I found her.

Not in those tights or the tiny robe that barely covered her ass, but whatever.

It *is* a cute ass.

Ugh. Enough, man, I tell myself. First of all, she works for your father, so that ass is off limits. Secondly, she's your neighbor, so get in the habit of locking your door lest she barge in here on the reg like some bad recurring episode of Everybody Loves Raymond. Plus, she should be at the club almost every day in season, so she won't be hanging around here lurking in the hallway or anything.

Anyway, the hope is soon enough I'll find a decent 9-5 in my field of interest and won't have to worry about the wackadoo pub schedule of the server next door. That's all. In fact, once I'm done building this bed, I've got a hot date with the internet to find myself a new gig. Because money doesn't grow on trees, you know. And I've got about enough saved up to cover the two months of rent and utilities I have to pay Luis, but beyond that, I'm not exactly rolling in it.

It's true. Despite what you'd think, country club wages – even those of an Assistant Manager at a whopping $22 an hour – only get you so far, especially when you have to pay rent to your own father to live in the bedroom you've been inhabiting since birth. I've also been footing the bill for my car loan, insurance, cell phone, and groceries ever since I left to go to college. I was able to bank a few hundred bucks a month once the pandemic ended; then, I spent a chunk of it on a camping trip to St. John for an eco-tourism class I decided to take through the National Park Service, another chunk on new tires and brakes for my Elantra, and another chunk on a girl, who, at this point, is better left nameless. (Fine. Her name is Miranda. We went to BU together. Let's leave it at that.)

It's a locally well-known fact that scoring a job on the Cape in the height of the season is not going to be the easiest thing. A lot of business transactions happen via word of mouth; when a job is available, it's usually gone before it even makes its way to the internet. I'm not averse to driving out of the immediate area, say, to Plymouth, or maybe even a little further, but I don't think my car could survive the daily commute to Boston long-term, especially given the fact that I just moved 30 minutes further away from the mainland, smack into the elbow-crease of Cape Cod.

It will be fine, though, I decide over a breakfast of microwaved quick oats. I rearrange boxes for the next 40 minutes, determined to keep my promise and be a better neighbor than my counterpart on the other side of the living room wall. At 10:00 a.m., I go back to assembling the bed, and by 10:45, that task is officially crossed off my to-do list. The mattress I ordered – alas, my dear father wouldn't allow me to bring my own bed with me since "he paid for it" – has a delivery window of between 12:00 and 3:00 p.m., so now there's nothing left to do but wait.

I park myself at Luis' dining table and search the main job sites I know of: indeed.com, LinkedIn, and CapeWorks, a division of the Massachusetts Department of Labor. I find a few postings, but nothing that jumps out at me. I check my e-mail, where my mother has forwarded me information about a slam poetry collective that's starting in Hyannis, as if I am a candidate for anything remotely artistic. In some ways, she's as bad as my father, projecting her hopes and dreams onto me as if I am the giant movie screen at the Wellingham Drive-In, just some blank slate in need of someone *else's* vision to transform me into something worth watching.

When I was in kindergarten, my mother had the brilliant idea to enroll me in the Saturday Academy at 4Cs. It was an "enrichment program for the Cape's best and brightest kids," which feels like an antiquated thing to even say nowadays. "Best and brightest" implies that others could be classified as "worst and dimmest," but what was really funny was the fact that it was a self-selected, fee-based program, so there were no gatekeepers. My mother alone was the deciding party determining my luminosity, and she enrolled yours truly in all the things: Creative Writing (of course), Oceanography, a program called "Junior Emerils" – as in, Lagasse – to appease my dad, no doubt – Painting, and Modern Dance.

One might wonder what my well-intentioned (if misguided) mother was up to with her choices. Well, in my later years, I asked her. She informed me that she was trying to "unlock my potential as an artist and an informed citizen of our world."

At six years old.

Here's how that played out:

On the first day of "Junior Emerils," I cut my finger with a plastic knife and cried so hard that I needed to be sent home. "You see?" my mother declared to my father. "Brady isn't cut out for cooking!" (No pun intended, I'm sure.) "We can't send him back to *that* class. We mustn't *endanger* our son."

Just like that, five classes became four.

Creative Writing was, to her dismay, a bit of a disaster. See, I hadn't begun *reading* yet, at least not independently, and so writing was a bit of a stretch. As I progressed in school, I was a late bloomer with the whole reading thing. It was bad enough that they made me repeat kindergarten. I was placed in resource room for additional help with reading and spelling from first through fourth grade. I'd bet good money that I'm dyslexic, but my father was absolutely not about to accept a child with any sort of disability, learning or otherwise, so we just swept my B/D confusion permanently under the rug. As I got older, the reading thing sorted itself out but I was still an awful speller. Thankfully, computers and cell phones became my predominant sources of communication, and spell check helped me not look like an asshole most of the time. But back when I was six, I had a real time of it in the 4Cs Saturday Academy Creative Writing class. The teacher, Miss Flora, didn't have the heart to speak to my mother about my lack of ability to read, so instead she let me dictate my (undoubtedly awful) attempts at stories and poetry to her, and she'd write them down for me. The final project was a group exercise where all of our work was collected and synthesized into a "literary journal," which included a poem I "wrote" about puppies. It went like this:

Dogs are good.
I like small ones.
Cute, cute, cute.

Woof, woof.

Puppies.

My mother proceeded to carry that publication around with her for the next six months, proclaiming me a "published author" to anyone who would listen.

After Creative Writing, I had Oceanography, which wasn't so bad. I thought it was cool to study marine life, and they let us go outside to the marsh to look at things like hermit crabs, which I now know have little to do with the actual *ocean*, but alas, I was a mere tyke at the time. Also, we got to wear swim trunks for outside play, and I rendered it fun to sit on the ground in the muddy marsh, because I could pee out there with my trunks on and nobody would know. Just my little secret with the earth.

Best and brightest, folks.

Painting was next, and I was good at that. If by good, you mean someone with a talent for splashing and splattering and making a real big mess. "He's like Jackson Pollack!" Mom would exclaim. I thought she meant Percy Jackson, from the cool movies my cousins let me watch, and I was like, "Yeah! I'm a Greek God!" which I thought meant I could carry a sword and kill monsters and other cool stuff like that. But when I asked the teacher of that class when I would get my sword, she just laughed politely and gently wiped the paint out of my eyebrow with a Kleenex.

Last but not least was Modern Dance. I was surprised to find that I was the only boy in the class. Just me and ten little girls. In a move that I now recognize was a genuine attempt at being inclusive, the teacher (Miss Wanda) created an entire routine around me. We danced to the remix of

Christina Milian's *Dip It Low* and I was front and center with a solo during the part where Fabolous raps. I had so much fun in that class – I could pick up the footwork with ease, and Miss Wanda showered me with praise, constantly saying that I was a natural. "Watch out for this one," she told my parents at the recital. "Your boy can *dance*."

At the recital, I think my father expected me to be hidden away in the back corner of the stage or something, but one of my earliest memories is killing it out there, really bringing my A-game to the performance, and the look on his face that could best be described as *aghast*. I overheard my parents fighting later that night in their bedroom with the door closed. The following morning, my father informed me that Saturday Academy would no longer be a thing I participated in.

That man has been dismissing me ever since I was six years old.

He started a war, though, and his sorry ass was fighting a losing battle. I *liked* dancing. So, as soon as I was old enough to do it without him knowing, I went for it. In high school, I joined a b-boy crew and learned how to breakdance, which gave me insane upper body strength thanks to all the tricks. Some of the breakers were also on the boys' step team at my school, so in my junior year I joined that too, at their urging. It was extremely competitive. We practiced every day, and there wasn't a damn thing my father could do about it since I'd just gotten my driver's license and could come and go as I pleased. Our team that year was recognized regionally in the State Qualifier for the National Step League, and camera crews came to cover it. We didn't win, but we were on the local news at 10:00 p.m., and I made sure it was on every television in the house. Seeing my father's disappointment at my popping, locking, and stepping was all the win I needed.

My mom has always believed that I have art in my blood. She didn't want to admit that my stint as a b-boy and a stepper in high school were fueled by a passion for revenge against my dad way more than passion for the art of dance, though. Not that her fervent convictions that *my son is an artist* translate into anything of use with regard to my current job hunting situation, though. If only her unfailing cheerleading for my hidden talents (yes, we're using that term loosely) could translate into a meaningful income, I'd have significantly lower blood pressure right now. She means well, though, and Lord knows she loves me, so I feel compelled to respond to her e-mail, however misguided or ridiculous her ideas of my potential future in slam poetry might be. I write her back – a quick, "Thanks, Ma, I'll def look into that! Love you too, - B," to appease her, before turning my attention back to the real job search.

I scroll through sponsored ads, widen the mileage radius, and momentarily consider the idea of getting a CDL license because according to Zip Recruiter, I could make up to $100,000 a year with benefits as a truck driver. (I cross the idea off my list when I read a thread on Reddit about fashioning a commode out of a bucket and a cushioned toilet seat and keeping it in the cab of your truck so you can pull over on the side of the road when you need to take a shit without having to worry about your ass cheeks getting cold. Um, no thanks.)

It won't be slam poetry, and it won't be trucking. But I'll find something.

I have to.

I mean, what other choice is there?

CHAPTER SIX

GRETCHEN

A few weeks into June, I feel like I've won the lottery.

I settle into a new routine: On Mondays and Tuesdays, I work out with Saffron, Cherry, Indigo and Arrow for most of the morning and then we go to the beach in the afternoon. (Not Arrow. She claims to not like the beach, but one time I tried to switch it up and do the community pool instead so Arrow could join us and Cherry told me not to bother. When I asked her why, she shrugged and said that Arrow's too busy to hang out.) The rest of the week, I have shifts at Cosmo-pole-itan. I run tow-lot pickups, followed by party hosting, and I make more Jell-O shots in those few weeks than I ever thought I'd see in my lifetime. I am good at this job. I even learn to walk in the platform shoes Jenna got me.

I pay her back for them, because in three weeks I've somehow managed to bank a little over $7,000 cash. I've earned more than that; I spent some of it on bills and two hefty trips to the mall – specifically to Victoria's Secret – to buy more "work clothes." (The single skirt and fishnets wasn't going to cut it for a daily uniform, I quickly learned.) Also, my body feels different. I'm eating better – having *groceries* in your house will do that – and the daily workouts appear to be toning up muscles that I haven't used in ages.

Also, it turns out that pole dancing is fun. I'm not very good at it, but I've learned a few spins and how to use various grip aids, depending on the weather and the moisture content of my body. It's crazy how much science is involved. There are days where I need to douse my palms in rubbing alcohol just to keep them from sliding down the pole, and then others where I can get by with just a touch of a liquid we stock called Dry Hands. The pole has to be warmed to a specific temperature, and if it's too hot or too cold, it can become slippery. Different parts of the body can be used for grip too, Cherry taught me. "The pits," she said. "Armpits, knee pits, elbow pits. Anywhere the body bends naturally can create a good, strong hold."

Pole dancing is not without its downsides, though. For one thing, holy hell, the bruising. My thighs and shins look a bit like those of a rambunctious first grader, all black-and-blue marks that I cover up with makeup before every party we host. Also, it can leave you really sore. We do crunches on the pole, shoulder and arm workouts on the pole, even pole lunges and pole squats, and I have a standing date with a bottle of Aleve first thing each morning.

There's also the issue that my parents still think I'm working at The Diamond Excelsior. I wanted to tell them about being fired, but not until I secured another job. Now, anytime my mom and I chat, I have to narrowly avoid the subject of work altogether. This leaves me with very little to talk about, seeing as how I have no boyfriend. (Unless you count Zoloft, since we share a bed. Unfortunately, there's not much to discuss on that front, other than his new love of stealing shrimp tails out of my garbage can – a gross hobby, sure, but so adorable that I can't stand to stop him. Also, let's not lose sight of the bigger picture, which is the fact that I can afford things like shrimp now. Mic drop.)

There is no doubt in my mind that Mom and Dad would kill me if they knew what I was doing to keep myself afloat financially. You think I'm kidding, but you don't know them. Allow me to paint you a picture.

My father's name is Andrew Andrews. He goes by Drew, but that doesn't make what my grandparents did by calling him that any less horrific. I love my Nana and G-Pops, don't get me wrong, but when you have a name like Andrew Andrews, you don't exactly begin your life with the ancestral real estate of a glambassador of excellence. No Trendy McFabulous are you, no sir. Instead, you come bursting onto the scene with the equivalent of social jaundice, and you can't even speak yet. You peer down the road that lies ahead and you can almost smell the teasing, the mockery, the disdain for your mere existence. So you learn how to fight. By second grade, you've been to the head nun's office at your Catholic school more times than you've been to the dentist in your entire life. And even *she* feels bad for you! By the time you get to high school, you've changed your name to AJ – short for "Andrew Just-wish-I-had-any-other-first-name," because your middle name is not John or Jack or Jim, it's King. *King.* Fucking King! As in Dr. Martin Luther? No, indeed. It's your grandmother's maiden name. Which gives you the initials AKA.

Also Known As.

As you get older, you spend far too much time trying to figure out how to score the most badass job in the world so nobody will make fun of you. At least, that's what my dad did. He's the Chief of the Eastport Police Department. The high honor of Chief was bestowed upon him when I was in the fourth grade, and he's never looked back. Every year, we sing "Hail to the Chief" instead of "Happy Birthday" when he blows out his candles, and he wouldn't have it any other way.

I don't blame him one bit.

My dad grew up in Brooklyn, New York – Bay Ridge, to be exact. The son of second generation Irish-Scottish immigrants, he went to parochial school all the way through twelfth grade and then, because his grades were nothing to write home about and he couldn't figure out what else to do with himself, he decided to enlist in the military after a recruiter came to the all-boys school for a presentation. He joined the Army right out of high school and not too long after boot camp, he was deployed to serve in the Gulf War in the fall of 1990. Lieutenant something-or-other Andrew Andrews then got himself hurt overseas – a non-battle injury resulting from a training accident that left him with three herniated discs. The hernia was so bad that my dad had to endure spinal surgery at the ripe old age of 21. On the upside, the honorable discharge set him up for pretty much any federal job he wanted, not to mention a heavily-supplemented ride to any public college he saw fit, a perk which he took to the bank when he enrolled in the John Jay College of Criminal Justice in Manhattan.

By contrast, my mother Annie (that's right, you sleuth – she's Annie Andrews, as if the name situation needed more salt poured into its gaping wound) grew up in the tiny hamlet of Provincetown, in the curled-up baby fist at the end of Cape Cod's arm in the sea. Eldest daughter of the Town Manager and his stay-at-home wife, Annie (then Myers) was a headstrong young lady who wanted nothing more than to see the world. She grew up in the art capital of Cape Cod, and from a very young age was drawn to the P-Town cultural scene. She excelled in the visual arts and, with her parents' blessing, went to Sarah Lawrence College in Westchester, New York courtesy of the generous tuition support delivered by three different scholarships. Annie found her calling in sculpture, particularly ceramics. She made beautiful pottery – large earthenware pieces, slow roasted in the kiln with low-fire glazes that caught the attention of galleries in the West Village and Soho. During her final semester, she was taking an art therapy class, and there was a series on Art Rehabilitation for the Imprisoned, hosted at John Jay.

She was seated next to my dad, and as the story goes, he asked her out for a burger after the session.

Within weeks, they were head over heels in love with each other.

Graduation loomed over both of their heads that spring, and Annie Myers planned to move back home to the Cape and work under her father's purview on projects for the Provincetown Cultural Council, but alas, Andrew Andrews couldn't stand the thought of losing her to distance. It was bad enough making his way from the west side of Manhattan up to Westchester via mass transit; there was no way he could tolerate a five hour schlep up to the Cape on a regular basis. So, in an act of desperation, on what was to be her last night in New York, Andrew Andrews proposed to Annie Myers. "Make me the happiest man in the world, Annie. Marry me, and I'll follow you anywhere."

She said yes. And he kept his promise.

Two weeks later, once the fanfare of their respective graduations had died down, Andrew Andrews moved in with the Myers family in Provincetown. Annie's parents – my Gigi and Papa – wouldn't allow the lovebirds to live under the same roof, but as luck would have it, they had a guest cottage on their property that they were happy to allow him to stay in, in exchange for help with the grounds. My dad was eager to assist with landscaping, cleaning the gutters, washing the windows, basically anything that would keep him in good stead with my Papa. He began applying for jobs and just after Labor Day, he took the written exam for an entry-level position as a police officer in nearby Eastport. He was selected for a live interview, and then a second round interview with the chief.

When Andrew Andrews got the job, the Myers family celebrated with a traditional New England clam bake, the last of the season as it was almost October of that year. Andrew and Annie began the search for houses in Eastport. "It's important to live where you serve," Andrew said. "Nobody will care more about keeping this town safe than the people who live here." With the help of the (then) Chief, the pair found an adorable, if somewhat dilapidated, beach cottage west of route 6, just three blocks from Last Encounter Beach off Sarasota Road. Annie was entranced by the scent of the bayberry and salt air, and Andrew saw the full potential the cottage could offer with a bit of effort and elbow grease. He would refinish the wide-planked pine floors, lay a new roof, get new kitchen appliances, replace the rotted drywall, fix the outdoor shower, and repaint the living room and bedrooms. Thus was born his project for the next three months.

Annie Myers became Annie Andrews in a small church ceremony on December 23rd at St. Peter the Apostle Church in P-Town. The reception was held down the street at the Provincetown Inn, and Andrew Andrews' parents came all the way from Brooklyn to watch their eldest son take his bride. The old photographs in my parents' attic depict what I would imagine was a rager in the late 1990s. Guests donned plastic sunglasses and glow necklaces in a festive conga line, and my aunts and uncles sipped unseasonal frozen cocktails with paper umbrellas in them. The happy couple took a picture kissing under the inn's mistletoe which still sits on my mother's dresser in a teakwood frame to this very day. By all accounts, the affair was small, sweet, and genuine, much like my parents.

In lieu of a honeymoon, they moved into their Eastport home on Christmas Eve, as my mom wanted nothing more than to wake up that Christmas morning in her new home with her husband by her side. Dad bought a tree off a lot on Route 6 the same day he moved all their boxes from P-Town to Eastport, and it filled the cozy house with the scent of pine. They each placed one, single wrapped gift under the undecorated tree and opened it the next morning by the fireplace. My dad gave my mom a piece of pottery he made for her at a ceramics workshop offered by the Truro Center for the Arts – an ashtray-type thing to hold her jewelry. He stamped her name in it with block letters, and it too is a permanent fixture on my mother's dresser, right next to the mistletoe photograph.

My mother's gift to my father was an even bigger surprise: it was a framed photograph of her holding a positive pregnancy test.

I'm sure you thought that they were virgins until marriage, right? Well, first of all, ew. I still don't like thinking of them as human creatures capable of reproduction and such. But also, no. They were young and in love, and as gross as it is, it's also really kind of sweet. Their wedding was far from a shotgun situation; my mom didn't even realize she was pregnant until just a week before the nuptials. She wrongly assumed she missed her period due to the stress of the wedding, bless her heart.

Unlike their sweeping romance, pregnancy was not all roses and sunshine for my mother. She managed to escape morning sickness, so she incorrectly assumed that would equate to an easy coast through the remaining trimesters as her little belly grew to be the size of a lobster pot. She suffered from endless exhaustion paradoxically met by an inability to sleep. Insomnia plagued my mother for the last eight weeks of my gestation, and in the rare moments when she was able to nod off, night terrors awaited her. The doctor ordered bedrest, and one could only laugh at the irony. Still, when her water finally broke, my poor mother was so physically drained that she couldn't push, and after laboring for 22 hours, I was born via C-section.

Once I was delivered, the drugs they gave my mom induced a sleep so deep, legend has it, she was out for almost two whole days. Well, those two days scared the very life out of my father, who spent his time beside her, periodically checking her pulse, learning from the kind nurses how to change my diaper and bottle feed me. Mom would rouse when hospital personnel came to check her vitals and change the dressing on her lower abdomen. The lactation consultant asked her if she wanted to try nursing, and she did, but when I didn't take to it the first time, my father suggested she continue sleeping. She held me briefly, always nodding off as the rhythm of our heartbeats merged into one. *Thump, thump, thump.* We were together, the three of us. A family. And she could finally relax enough to drift away into a long-awaited rest.

On the third day, my mother woke up, achy and sore, with rock-solid, swollen breasts. It was then that we were able to begin nursing, which helped my father calm down a bit. He treated my mom like a casualty of war, and to this day, he'll tell you the experience scarred him. Andrew Andrews is good in a crisis unless the crisis involves his family. And because they loved each other as much as they did, my mother agreed that they would stop at one child.

With boundless gratitude for their blessings, my parents and I left the hospital an unbreakable unit. It's been that way ever since.

In elementary school, I was the pigtailed little policeman's daughter. In middle school, I was the orthodonture-clad Chief's kid. Nobody messed with me, not that there was much to mess with. I was friendly, artsy like my mom, serious like my dad. Honor roll student. I joined my local 4-H club and learned about our town's affinity for brussels sprouts, among other local agriculture. I was in my high school's productions of *Grease*, *Bye, Bye Birdie*, and *Mamma Mia*. I played softball. Babysat. During my senior year, I got a volunteer gig at the Boys & Girls Club down in Hyannis, and it was there that I realized how much I loved working with children. I wrote about it in my college essays. And then, much to my father's chagrin, off I went to UMass to pursue my teaching degree.

This is not to say that my dad didn't want me to be college-educated. He knew the only way to do that was to leave, but he was sad to see me go. Sentimental. Four years without me after 18 as the Trusty Trio made him wonder at how quickly time could pass. When I returned home, he was overjoyed. "The Cape needs good teachers," he said, ever an advocate for my future. Even when the pandemic hit, he was okay with me waitressing, as long as I was safe and healthy. He helped me move into my apartment, background checked the guys I dated, and always looked out for my well-being.

To say he would be less-than-pleased with the idea of his baby girl working at a place where her ass cheeks were barely covered by a children's sized pleated skirt would be the understatement of the century.

So keeping it hidden is, obviously, a critical component of this whole scheme.

We used to have Sunday dinner together. Dating back to when I was really little, it was kind of a sacred tradition in my house. Mom would make us a beautiful meal – like, holiday-worthy – and the three of us would gather at the table around 4:00 p.m. and feast. If it was summertime, we'd eat outside on the back deck. Dad would grill up kebabs or skirt steak or chicken cutlets and Mom would make every manner of salad-based side-dish you could imagine: potato salad, pasta salad, quinoa salad, a robust Greek salad or strawberry summer salad. When I got old enough to cook, I'd bake brownies as a dessert. Always the same Duncan Hines box-mix brownies, but my Dad would take a bite and tell me they were the best he ever tasted. Wintertime Sunday dinners always included some carb-heavy, casserole dish: lasagna, beef stroganoff or chicken au-gratin, that sort of thing – and yes, still with the salad and always, the brownies.

I had to back out of Sunday dinners a long time ago, on account of my job at the pub. My parents understood that weekend evenings are really important for tips. The best servers get those shifts, and because I work really hard in everything, I even worked hard to be a great pub waitress. Once they realized Sunday nights would no longer work for my crazy schedule, my parents switched our weekly gathering to Sunday mornings. So, instead of dinner people, we became brunch people.

Thankfully, I can keep the brunch schedule going with the new job. I don't have to get to get to Cosmo-pole-itan until later in the afternoon for the tow-lot pickups, so the mornings are still free. Even if I'm exhausted from being out late, I can still make it up to my parents' house for a 10:00 a.m. brunch date, brownies in tow (because that is the expectation, regardless of whether or not they go with my mom's quiche).

But it's obvious I'm tired. Mom's like a bloodhound when it comes to my health. They both are, really.

Allow me to present Exhibit A: last week's brunch.

The menu included a spinach and artichoke frittata, ham croissants, a fruit platter, and locally sourced cranberry juice. And my brownies, which I made super last minute and which were definitely a little undercooked, on account of me pulling them out of the oven early (so I wouldn't be late). I was wearing running shorts and a t-shirt. Flip flops. Sunglasses on my head to keep my messy hair out of my face. I opened the door, holding the tray of brownies with my potholder-clad hands, and I kid you not, I was greeted with, "Hi, baby. What happened to your leg?"

Mom took the brownies from me and set them on the counter. I dropped my potholders next to them and wrinkled my brow. "What are you talking about?" I asked.

"Your left leg. The inside thigh – it's covered in bruises," she said.

Fuck. It didn't even dawn on me to wear body makeup over my pole bruises. "Um, I don't know," I said. "I didn't even realize that was there."

Dad walked in and gave me a hug. "Hiya, buttercup."

"Look at her leg, Drew."

"It's nothing," I insisted.

"It's *not* nothing. Look," she replied.

"What happened?" Dad said.

"I'm not sure, Dad. It's just a black and blue mark."

"Let me see." He held me back from him and studied my legs. I turned my left foot out to second-position-in-ballet to reveal some wicked nasty bruises that honestly, I should have known were there but wasn't looking for in my mad dash to get to brunch on time.

He narrowed his eyes. "Who did this to you?" he growled.

"No, Daddy. I swear, nobody did this."

"You know what this looks like? Annie, do *you* know what this looks like?"

"I swear I'm fine."

"What does it look like, honey?" Mom asked.

"Assault," my father announced.

My mother gasped.

Dad couldn't stop there. Ever the chief, he continued to push. "So, then, you tell us how you got these bruises, before I –"

It's hard to think on your feet when you're exhausted. Which, I guess explained my answer. "Oh, *I* know. It must have been the horseback riding."

"Horseback riding?" my dad raised an eyebrow.

"Yes. For Jenna's birthday. A group of girls went horseback riding."

"Isn't Jenna born in April?" Mom wondered aloud.

"Wow – good memory, Ma. Um, yeah; it was a belated celebration. Very hard to coordinate schedules."

"I don't remember you saying anything about going horseback riding," Mom replied.

"No? I could have sworn I told you."

She shook her head. I immediately felt bad for making her so confused.

"And when was this little equine adventure?" my dad asked.

"Um," I considered the color of the bruises. Bright purple. Means they were probably about three to four days old. The daughter of a cop knows details about things like this. My palms began to sweat. "Wednesday," I said.

"Didn't you have work?" Dad retorted.

"Yup, but I went in late," I lied. "We did the ride first thing in the morning."

"Trail ride?" he asked. *This is becoming an inquisition,* I thought. *Best to shut it down as quickly as possible.*

"Uh huh," I replied, knowing the only way he'd let up was if I give him something to hang on to. "The horse's name was Boomerang. The trail was in Sandwich. Afterwards we went to Café Chew for brunch. It was a really nice time. She loved it."

"So, how did you get the bruises?" Dad asked, but his shoulders were no longer up by his ears, so I could tell he was relaxing a little.

"Must have been from mounting," I went on. "My horse was super tall."

Dad nodded, a touch of skepticism still firmly lodged in his expression.

Mom said, "Well, next time, be careful. It looks awful."

"I'm sorry. I didn't mean to scare you," I replied. We went about our meal then, but I made a mental note to just wear pants next time.

To be clear, I felt terrible lying to my parents. I typically don't lie well, for one thing. Also, I know my Mom and Dad just worry about me because they're good parents, and I would never want to take advantage of that. But, some things you can't share with your overprotective father.

You know, unless you want him to lock you up in a holding cell for the foreseeable future.

Still, despite my parental deception, I'm in a bit of a sweet spot, and I really can't complain. I've never had a job that transformed my body *and* my bank account in a matter of weeks.

The only thing that sucks is having what's-his-face living next door.

For someone who's supposed to be the Assistant Manager at the Diamond Excelsior private dining shit parade, this dude is *always* around. He put an admittedly cute small table out on the back patio with two chairs, and he eats breakfast out there every morning, always in a different color pair of those damn *shorts.* I think he goes out for runs and then comes home and has his little bowl of cereal and cup of coffee while perusing God knows what on his phone. Probably toe pics on Onlyfans or some other equally heinous offense, I've decided.

I can see him out the sliding glass door in my bedroom, and typically, this is the image I wake up to in the morning. My curtains are floor-length, white sheers, which (thanks to Zoloft) have taken quite the beating courtesy of his sharp-AF kitty fingernails. I don't think Brady can see in, but I can see out, and in the early morning sunlight, with the remnants of sweat from whatever workout he's putting his body through, well... suffice to say there are worse things I could wake up to. I just can't reconcile his hotness with the fact that he got me canned from my last gig. Although, joke's on him, as I've made an entire summer's worth of tips at the Diamond Excelsior in just a few weeks at Cosmo-pole-itan.

I saw Brady one time last week with his laptop outside around nine in the morning, having some sort of Zoom call. He looked – I don't know – pensive, maybe? Nervous? Whatever. It annoyed me that he felt like it was okay to take his online business meetings in our shared outdoor space. *He's no better than the dog from the C apartment down the way,* I thought. *No regard for others.* He wasn't being particularly loud, and Lord knows he didn't pollute the air with stench like the Labrador does, but it was auditory stench, with his chatter, or maybe visual stench – just his presence in the space made it impossible for me to get ready for my morning workout with the girls. I kept being distracted by his jawline, his scruff, his stupid calf muscles in those shorts. *Like, please. We get it. You're hot. You don't have to constantly flaunt it.*

I began to feel like he crawled into my head and took root. As if he was the human equivalent of lice. Or maggots. Or some equally offensive pest that requires professional extinguishing.

I started to catch myself looking for Brady. First, out my sliders. Then, like, if I went to throw out the garbage or get my mail. Or walking through the hallway to my apartment. Or even at the grocery store. I learned that he drove a blue Hyundai Elantra with exactly two stickers on the back bumper: one granted him beach access to all the Brewster beaches, and the other was a Diamond Excelsior VIP parking pass. On the occasions when I was out driving, I'd keep an eye out for his car. Subconsciously, of course. That exact shade of blue. The side-by-side stickers. That white and red Cape and Islands license plate that started with the letters CIJ. Not that I had memorized it intentionally. It just happened. Sometimes, I'd park beside him the lot, and when I'd climb out of my Fiesta, I'd casually glance inside his car. He kept it neat in there. Neater than my car, that's for sure. He had a "new car" scented little cardboard tree hanging from the gear shift, a pack of Trident gum and a travel-sized hand sanitizer in the cup holder, and a burgundy hoodie sweatshirt in the backseat.

Not that I noticed.

On more than one occasion, I thought I saw him out somewhere – not his car, but *him* – and then got up close and discovered it wasn't actually him at all. The first time it happened was at the beach with the girls from the club. There was a guy jogging in the distance whose muscular torso triggered me to squint my eyes. He had a navy and teal brimmed baseball cap on – no shirt, mind you – and I popped up from my towel to "take a walk," I announced. I headed in the direction of the runner, like a magnet was pulling me towards his Hawaiian-Tropic-commercial-tan body, but when I got a little closer, I realized it wasn't Brady after all. This guy didn't have the same nose – that was the first giveaway. Brady's nose is the tiniest bit upturned, and this guy's nose was longer and pointier. Then, I saw that the hair color was off – random jogger dude had blonder hair than Brady. I walked away feeling something. Definitely *not* disappointment, in case you're wondering. It was probably relief. There was a little bit of a lump in my throat, but that's common with the feeling of relief. I'm sure of it.

Another time, I was down at the mall in Hyannis looking for more work clothes – that is to say, half-shirts from H&M

that showed off my entire belly and bikini bottoms from PacSun. (This is a common outfit, and paired with platform heels it's incredibly sexy.) But, anyway. I was walking past Dick's Sporting Goods and could have sworn I saw Brady perusing the sneakers, but when I went in, he was nowhere to be found. Again, not that I was looking. I just *happened to notice*, that's all.

This ridiculous new habit has been filed away under "annoying side effects of living next door to your ex-boss." Don't cry for me, Argentina. I can still go about my daily life and be about 96% okay. (Sure, the remaining 4% is on *constant Brady alert* but I can't help the fact that I haven't had sex since my last boyfriend, Keith, back in – well, let's just say it's been awhile.) Anyway, since then, my body has slowly morphed into a wanton, salacious frightmare on account of my internal frothing of the ovaries. I'm serious. They have a collective mind of their own and always behave like the apocalypse is coming. I can almost feel them shooting out my eggs every month like darts out of a Nerf gun, loosely aiming for anything that looks like potential baby daddy material. It's bad-news-bears, because my flirting game is about as tight as a wizard's sleeve.

The good news? Today I have a shift at Cosmo-pole-itan. Thus, to exactly no one's dismay, I have no time to consider the rambled musings of my hyperactive (if ignored) libido.

I get myself ready (new tiny T-shirt and glossy, mermaid panty under a loose fitting, cotton romper to hide the getup), apply a shit ton of makeup, first on my pole bruises and then on my face, grab my platforms and throw them in a Stop & Shop reusable bag and slide on my Birkenstock sandals. I drive up to Wellingham with the windows down and the music up loud, truck-stop sunglasses on and my hair whipping around in the wind tunnel that is my front seat.

When I arrive at Cosmo, I open the front door and head straight for the locker bank. The door to the office is closed, but behind it, I hear what appears to be the end of a difficult conversation.

"I'm sorry, honey," the voice says. It's Arrow, but you wouldn't know from the tone. This voice is sweet like Nestle Toll House cookies, rich with the unique combination of sorrow and comfort that can only come from a mom. "I wish I was there with you, baby girl. But, listen to me," she continues, firmer now. "You're my strong little kitten. Anytime you get scared or nervous, I want you to hold onto the tiger stuffie I sent you, and remember that you are fierce. Just give it a big squeeze, and know that I believe in you." There's a pause, and I realize that I am 100% eavesdropping at the door now. I can't help it – I'm hearing a side of her that I never could have dreamed existed. "Of course, my angel. You did the exact right thing. That's why I gave you that kind of phone, so you could always call me if you needed me." A deep breath. "No, little lady. You should never be sorry for that. You're a good girl, Kit. You're *my* good girl." Another pause. "I love you more, baby. Now, let me talk to Daddy, okay? Yes, sweetheart. I'll talk to you soon." She makes a kissing noise three times and then, silence.

About 30 long, quiet seconds pass, and I'm tempted to knock on the door just to let Arrow know that I'm there. I don't want to seem like a creeper and end up pissing her off. This job pays way too much for me to risk losing it over something as innocent as overhearing a conversation. I consider sneaking back out and coming in again in five minutes, much louder this time. Just as I'm about to turn and walk out, she says, "Listen fuckface, if I find out that you left her home alone again, I'll get on the next flight out there and slit your motherfucking throat, you hear me?" *Shit.* Now I really want to disappear. "No, I don't want to hear it. She's a *baby*, for Christ's sake. I don't give a fuck if it was ten *seconds* – you never leave a child alone like that. You scared the shit out of her!" A sigh. "Don't you dare raise your voice at me even a hair, you hear me, Ricky? I swear to God, if you upset that child any more today..." Her voice trails off. "Just don't, got it? I'm financing your entire life out there and I can come get Kit and pull the plug on your cash flow at the drop of a hat, understood? Now, put on your fake smile Daddy voice and say something nice to me before hanging up like a gentleman. I don't give a shit what you think of me. You have a daughter who's watching your every move. You owe it to her to at least pretend to not be a total piece of fucking garbage."

Another few seconds passes, accompanied by a long string of "mm hms," and then I hear her slam the phone down on the old metal desk.

I'm terrified that Arrow will discover me outside, so I calmly knock three times before opening the office door and popping my head inside. "Hey!" I say, in my most cheerful voice. "I just got here, but I heard you on the phone and didn't want to bother you. Just saying hi!"

I avoid making eye contact with her as she spins away from me, towards the wall, and grabs a paper towel from the roll on top of the fridge. It's clear I've startled her. "Oh, hey," she says, trying to be cool. She blows her nose, a heavy honk, into the paper towel. "Fucking allergies," she says, then grabs her phone off the desk and looks at it while blotting the edges of her eyes. "You're early."

"Just a few minutes. Sorry," I reply.

"No. It's fine. I gotta go, anyway." Arrow grabs another paper towel, and swipes her keys off the desk. "You're fine with tow lot, right?"

"Uh huh."

"K. I'll be back later."

Like a flash of lightning, she's gone.

Well. That was certainly something.

I'm trying to reconcile the fact that I just saw Arrow tearing up when I hear the front door open again. It's a partygoer from last night – and so begins the next hour of tow lot. I remain fully dressed to greet hungover girls and hand out their car keys. After the last Lexus has left the lot, I strip down for a workout with Saffron, who shows up early because she promised to help me work on my pole climbing. When she arrives, I debate whether or not to mention what I heard on Arrow's phone call. But, admittedly, I don't know Saffron that well, and I don't like to gossip about people, so I leave it alone. Plus, she swirls in like a tornado, ready to spin all night – and she's singularly focused on getting my pole climb up to snuff. She's convinced me that it's all in the shoes. "The stickier your pole shoes are," she says, "the better you'll be able to get up. It's got way less to do with upper body strength than it does with your footwear."

I make a face. "Sticky? That sounds gross. Who wants their shoes to be sticky?"

"Not sticky like covered in bubble gum. I mean the fabric. The best shoes are the patent leather ones. They're made out of a vinyl-plastic combo that just naturally adheres to the pole when you put pressure behind it. Trust me. You've got to try them."

So, begrudgingly, I go into the little back office with the Jell-O shot stocked fridge and I slide my finger down the stack of shoeboxes until I find a pair my size. They're open-toed boots with a seven inch heel, but the three inch platforms make the heels only four inches insofar as my arches are concerned. I text Jenna a picture. *So, *this* is happening,* I write. She texts back a mind blown emoji. I try the shoes on, and am unsurprised to find that I can't walk in them – at least not naturally – but am delightfully bemused to learn that I can swing from the pole without much trouble. When landing, I'm careful to make sure both feet are firmly connected to the floor and I'm standing fully upright before I let go of the pole, as if it is a walker intended for a 90 year-old instead of the strip club essential that it actually is. After all, nothing's worse than a shot girl on crutches.

I need more practice in the shoes, but not so much practice dancing as practice just *walking.* "You should try wearing them tonight," Saffron offers. "You can always change out of them if they become too much."

I shrug. "Maybe."

"This one's going to be an easy party. Arrow told me there are only 15 girls coming. It would be a really good night to test them out."

That sells me. I've never worked a party that small yet. Surely, if I move a little bit slower than usual, it won't kill the vibe with so few ladies in attendance.

So, I keep my usual platforms on standby in favor of the toeless boots once the party begins at 8:00. It's a cute little group. They're throwing a masquerade-ball-themed shindig, so each of them has on a fancy eye mask. One's laden with neon blue and purple feathers (reminiscent of a peacock), another's covered in glitter. The bride is wearing a mask covered in white lace, which reminds me of something I saw on one of my mom's old Madonna cassette tapes from back in the day. She's got little fingerless gloves to match, but she'll learn soon enough that you can't use gloves on the pole. They give each of us a mask to wear also. Mine is neon green faux snakeskin – which doesn't exactly match my mermaid-inspired outfit, but really, who cares? The only issue I have with it is that it slides a bit more than I'd like, so there are moments where it gets in the way of my actual line of sight. Which feels a little scary, given that I'm trying very consciously not to resemble the walking dead when I strut around in the dimly lit space with my trays of Jell-O.

The party progresses as usual, with rounds of shots interspersed by a dance lesson in small groups. The girls perform the choreo they've learned between the poles and the chairs, and I continue to work on my balance as I deliver the trays of shots and pretzel bites. While they're dancing, I work a bit on pacing back and forth, just to keep my calf muscles moving. A part of me is concerned they might cramp up from this constant tippy-toe action.

Right on cue, when the dancing part of the night is over, we get a firm knock on the door. I'm accustomed to this now; I know the stripper has arrived with his bodyguard in tow. I wonder what kind of ridiculous treat the group has in store on this hot, summer night. Arrow sashays over to the door, dramatically pretending to wonder aloud, "Who could that be?" and when she swings the door open, she's greeted by the bodyguard. He's a huge man – broad shoulders, with biceps that threaten to tear through his black t-shirt. "Dude, go," he whispers hard at the guy alongside him. The bodyguard opens a flask, hands it to the man beside him – who, from here looks like he's wearing some kind of mask (in keeping with the theme, I suppose). The masked bandit takes an enormous swig from the flask and hands it back to the bodyguard. Then, bodyguard guy places an oversized hand on the upper back of the masked bandit, pushing him through the door.

Which is when I notice that he is wearing not only a mask, but a complete Zorro getup. Cape, vest, the whole nine. He looks... well, it's kind of hard to say how he looks given the snake mask waging war with my fake eyelashes. But his vibe is decidedly different than our previous strippers. He seems uncomfortable, as if maybe something's got his little Zorro whip all twisted up.

I adjust my mask and see the stripper glance back at the bodyguard, who shoots a real stern look at him like, "Don't fuck this up, man."

Then, the stripper turns to face Arrow and gulps once before saying, "I am Zorro, um, the outlaw?" He says this in a real shitstorm attempt at a Spanish accent, and two things run through my mind. The first is that I am immediately reminded of Puss N' Boots, probably because Antonio Banderas is the voice of the fiery orange cartoon cat and is also the man behind the mask in the actual Zorro movie. The second is – and I assume this is because it's become a recurring theme in my life – that the stripper looks a whole lot like Brady Hawthorne.

But that *can't* be.

I mean, right?

"Oh! Welcome, Zorro," Arrow purrs.

He spins his cape around to face the group of ladies. "I, um. I'm here to... um..." Zorro looks back at the bodyguard with what appears to be real panic.

"Nobody cares!" one of the ladies screams. "Just take off your pants, Zorro!"

They all begin to cheer and whoop and Cherry turns the music on. Through the speakers, Luis Fonsi and Daddy Yankee beg the ladies to "let me trespass your danger zones," (solamente en español), and the stripper is fed to the den of hungry lionesses like a sad, lone wildebeest. The bass thumps and Saffron affixes herself to a pole and begins to swing around it, tossing her hair and moving her hips like the pole itself is a long-lost lover. Arrow pushes Zorro into the crowd of ladies and flips open a folding chair. The gagglefuck of penis-starved, masked maidens push their friend, the bride, into the chair, where I hand her a ruby red shot, which she gratefully accepts. Zorro helps himself to three of the shots on my tray and crushes them with his fist, the Jell-O dripping into his mouth. He swallows, tosses the plastic cups back onto my tray, stops to look at me as if he's confused, and then mumbles, "Thanks." He shakes his head quickly, as if trying to situate himself, takes a big, deep breath and approaches the chair slowly. His walk, tentative at first, morphs into a slow strut (amen for alcohol), and I cannot help but notice that through his Zorro mask, he gives me a sideways glance. Like, even though he's walking towards the bride, his gaze is trained on me.

It's Brady, my scrambled brain decides. *But, no. It can't be. That makes no sense at all. He's working. It's a Friday night! He's definitely at the Diamond Excelsior. This is just your mind playing tricks on you.* My eyelashes choose this exact moment to affix themselves to the edge of the eye-hole on my right side. I turn and carefully walk away into the tiny office, where I set down my shot tray and pull the eyelashes apart from the mask with the utmost caution. I blink several times, making sure I'm free of the glue trap that is the inner edge of this dumb snake face.

While in the office, I grab a fresh tray of shots and fluff up my hair. I emerge into the darkness of the studio to see Zorro – now *sans vest*, but still with his cape on – doing something with his hips. *Sweet Lord, those abs,* I think. They're like perfect little boxes, all lined up neatly, leading down to a gorgeous V-shape that dips below the waistband of his black pants. Zorro's lower half undulates like the waves at Nauset Beach, slamming into the shore, thrusting from the dark blue ocean onto the sand. Pounding into the personal space of the bride, whose obvious enjoyment is making me feel perhaps the tiniest bit snakeface-green... with envy.

Fucking control yourself, Gretchen. It's not *Brady.*

And even if it was *Brady (which it's definitely* not*), he's your asshole neighbor, not your friend, and especially not your boyfriend. So let him fuck the air in front of this random, betrothed bachelorette. No (snake) skin off your back.*

I breathe in the warring scent of plumeria body spray from the ladies and Malibu from the Jell-O, mesmerized by the angles and lines on Zorro's hard-as-a-rock body. Until – my *God* – he rips off his pants.

Wow.

The pouch of the barely-there man-thong that remains is *filled* with stripper sausage. Like, *whoa.*

The women screech and howl. "Fuck, yeah!" one yells, shoving dollars into his underwear. He pauses and takes a deep breath – before diving smoothly onto the floor and dry-humping the ground, putting his entire hindquarters on display for the adoring bridal bandwagon. He slithers up from the ground and – literally just centimeters away from the bride's body – slides his torso along her silhouette, until he places his hands on her face, cupping her cheeks with his palms, leaving the poor bride to stare into the face of Zorro and wonder if she's making a gigantic mistake by marrying anyone other than his fine ass. He runs his hands down her jaw and into her hair, smiling as he gives a gentle tug on her blonde curls before bending backwards into the ground, motioning with his finger for her to follow him, which she does, naturally. Now, with dollars raining down around them like confetti, she is basically having dry-outercourse with him on the filthy floor. Yes, her clothes are still on, and yes, her friends are all there, hollering like a feral pack of pants-burrito-craving horndogs. "Ay, papi!" the whitest girl in the crowd yells, and I laugh at the ludicrousness of it all.

At some point, Zorro makes his way over to the area where the poles are. Saffron, Cherry and Indigo are swinging away, climbing, spinning, spreading their legs in fankicks and a move called "Hello, Boys," in which they pole-sit atop one fist while they lean back and split their legs open as wide as possible. The partygoers attack the remaining poles as Zorro takes turns grinding on each girl, making sure nobody leaves without having had the chance to slide their manicured fingers along his rippled stomach or paw at his ass cheeks like a tribe of horny circus clowns. It's funny – well, sort of, until he begins to saunter up to yours truly.

I tend to stay out of the way during this part of the night. I mean, I'm just the shot girl. No need to interact with me. Tonight, I look like a cross between a reptile and a fish-woman, so yeah, we're not exactly working with A-game material. Plus, poor Zorro is undoubtedly awash with every germ known to man, so it's not like I'm trying to bathe all up in his pornflakes.

But he's coming this way. And he's licking his lower lip with the tip of his tongue.

Oof.

I can't seem to look away, despite the mask sliding down my nose, trying to blind me with my own fake eyelashes. I push it back up with my forefinger as he places his hand on my waist, pulling me closer to his winding hips. Char-ly Black's "Gyal You A Party Animal" blares through the speakers, the dancehall delight making it impossible not to sway my body from side to side. Then, when my knee is solidly between his legs and we are rocking together, he releases my waist and places his hands on the back of my head, lightly pulling at my hair in what is possibly the most sexual touch I've ever experienced before. Zorro silently runs his fingertips down my arms, starting at my bare shoulders and sliding all the way down to my hands, where he twists his digits around mine as we move in time with the music. He's not exactly grinding *into* me, but if I were to push my pelvis forward even just an inch or two, I can all but guarantee that I'd accidentally bump into his massive package. In some strange way, it's almost hotter that we're not pressed fully up against each other.

Wordlessly, he raises my hand in his and drops it up over his head, suspended in mid-air. Then, he does that famous move from *Dirty Dancing* where he slides his one hand down the inside of my arm, which tickles me as he nears my armpit. I tug my hand back instinctively, laughing, and my finger gets caught on the elastic of his face mask. I pull so hard that before I realize it, the cheap elastic has snapped, and the black mask of Zorro snaps off, floating for a split second like a puff of black smoke before falling to the floor.

It's Brady Hawthorne.

I stop dancing. *It can't be.*

He winces, touching the side of his eye line where the mask snapped. A red welt is forming. He rubs it and looks up at me, crossly, before his face swiftly changes. His gaze sweeps over my barely there T-shirt and mermaid panty, then down my fishnet-clad legs to my sky-high platforms. He looks back up again and settles on my blood-red hair.

It registers.

He knows it's me.

Zorro – er, Brady – takes three steps backwards before turning hastily and high tailing it out of there, leaving in his wake the groans and miserable sighs of Team Trashelorette. His bodyguard follows him out the door, with Arrow hot on their tails, shaking her head. Meanwhile, I force myself out of my deer-in-the-headlights moment and wobble back to the office to grab more shots, which I set down on the table and the girls gratefully devour. Right on time, the caterers enter the space, a pair of men from Añejo in Hyannis who are swiftly setting up a fajita station, as I excuse myself from the building and teeter outside into the parking lot.

"You don't just fucking leave!" Arrow yells. "That's not how it works!"

"Yo," the big bodyguard guy says, pulling off his hat to reveal a head of bright orange hair. "Don't come at my man like that." He takes a lumbering step towards Arrow. It's not threatening exactly, but I would be scared if it were me. "He's *new.*"

Arrow shoots a sharp look at me, while Brady fumbles into a pair of sweatpants, leaving an oil streak along the passenger side of the blue Hyundai Elantra that is unmistakably his. "What, Summer?" she asks, annoyed. "What do you want?"

"Summer?" Brady asks.

"What do you *want?*" Arrow asks again, more firmly this time.

I shake my head and adjust my snake mask so it doesn't stick to my eyes. "Um, nothing."

"Get back in there," she seethes at me.

I go.

But not before hearing Brady say to his bodyguard, "Bro, I could have sworn she was my neighbor."

CHAPTER SEVEN

BRADY

Big Mike talks the boss chick down and collects my money. It's a *lot*. I can't count it at that exact moment because I'm shook – a combination of adrenaline and nerves and *fuck* I am like 99% sure that the redhead in the fishnets was definitely Gretchen. How the hell am I ever going to look her in the face again?

But, *no*. It wasn't her. That was some girl named Summer. With the same color hair, and the same exact fishnet-clad apple-bottom booty.

Big Mike drives me home in my car. I'm so grateful that we carpooled over to that wretched place.

"You okay?" he asks.

"I don't know, dude. That was… something."

"You did a good job, though. Those girls were *about* you."

"I felt like an idiot. Also, like a cheap piece of meat. And thongs are so uncomfortable. I don't know how women do it."

"There's a thought you should never share in mixed company." Big Mike guffaws.

I breathe deeply, trying to relax. "So, is that what it's like every time?" I ask.

He shrugs. "I mean, yeah. Basically. That was a smaller party than usual, though."

"It felt like an out-of-body experience."

"I'm sure. I mean, for real? It was a little weird for me, too. I'm trying to reconcile the fact that I've seen your bare ass now. And not, like, locker room ass. Stripper thong-ass. It's a whole new level of friendship for us."

"Please, don't remind me."

"Seriously, though? You did good, Brady. I've seen way worse. You got moves."

"I used to dance when I was young."

"Not like *that*, I'm sure."

"No," I concede, smiling. "Not like that."

"It's just a shame you flipped at the end. That probably lost you some street cred."

"It's fine. I'm not trying to make this, like, a regular thing."

"You say that now. Wait till you count what's in that envelope."

I shake my head. "It was just a one-time thing, to help with my bills this month."

"You mean to tell me that you can't spare another hour of your life for $800?"

"Is that how much you think it is?"

"Ballpark, yeah."

I pick up the envelope from my center console. It's very fat. "All in singles?" I laugh. "That'll look classy when I go to the grocery store."

"That's why you just take it straight to the bank and deposit it."

"Great. So the ladies at TD can all make fun of me."

"They don't care. Money's money," Big Mike assures me.

"And how much do you get?"

"Oh, I'm flat rate - $200. Steve pays me direct."

"I think I'd be happy doing what you do. That's decent money. And you get to keep all your clothes on."

"Sorry, my man. You're too scrawny to protect the talent."

"Scrawny?" I echo, feigning offense. "How dare you?"

Big Mike laughs, patting his belly. "I've got easily a hundred pounds on your little Slim Jim ass."

"Rude," I announce – but he's right, and we both know it. "I'm solid muscle," I reply. "And I'm almost as tall as you."

"That's true, but you weigh like a buck ninety-five soaking wet. I'd kill you if I sat on you."

"Well, then, how about don't sit on me?" I grin. He shakes his head, and we remain silent as the still summer air blows in through the cracked front windows. The words "sit on me" call to mind a moment, frozen in time – me, facing the shot girl who *I swear to God* is a doppleganger for Gretchen Andrews, the feeling of my fingers wrapped around hers, the fever from her body merging with the heat from mine to create a blazing chemical reaction that still stirs my lower half, even thinking about it now.

"You good?" Big Mike asks.

"Yeah, I'm okay," I say, shaking the memory out of my head. "I still can't believe that I ran out into a parking lot in a fucking thong."

"Not your finest moment."

"What exactly *should* I have done?"

"Well, typically, the night ends with you excusing yourself into the back office. I bring you your clothes and you get dressed, and then I get our money from Arrow and we slip out the back door. The ladies always have food delivered right after the stripper leaves – it's like if they're not going to get laid, they need to satiate themselves *somehow* – so they're usually too caught up with tacos or sandwiches or whatever to even really notice the talent heading out."

"Stop calling me the talent," I say. "That sounds weird."

Big Mike pulls us into the Villages at Diamond Excelsior and drives down the road toward the Tidewater. I spot his truck in the parking lot, sticking out like the behemoth it is, and he parks my car next to it.

"Thanks for driving, man," I say. "I appreciate it."

"Well, you were certainly in no kind of state to do it yourself."

He hands me the envelope of cash, and I shove it in my drawstring bag. "Talk to you tomorrow?"

"You got it."

"Get home safe, bro."

We leave my car and I head inside. At Gretchen's door, I pause to listen. It's quiet. *Maybe she's sleeping,* I think. A normal person would be asleep on a Friday night at – *what time is it, even?* I check my phone. *Midnight.*

But I'm wired. I go into my apartment and count my cash. It's $883. That's a fucking *lot* of money for one night. Definitely enough to cover the next month of groceries, hands down. And so what if it cost me my dignity? I don't have to do it again if I don't want to. This was only supposed to be a trial run, anyway. At least that's what Steve, the guy who owns the company, told me on Zoom last week.

"Good audition video," he'd said. "You dance often?"

"Not really," I replied. I'd watched the movie *Magic Mike* and learned the steps to the *It's Raining Men* number Channing Tatum does with the umbrella. Luis had a golf umbrella like that in his dining room, so I used that – though it wasn't black like the ones in Magic Mike. Instead, it was white with *Diamond Excelsior Golf Club* written on it in royal blue block print. But I digress. I stood my bedframe and mattress up against the wall and pushed back all of the other furniture in the living room to make space, then set my cell phone up against the television to record myself doing the dance. The moves were pretty easy to learn – just lots of hip stuff. The guys in the movie crawled around on the floor a lot, I noticed. The women liked that – yes, I *know* they're actresses, but I don't know. It felt convincing, as if real women might enjoy it, so I snaked around on Luis' Pergo floors for my audition, too. Also, I didn't have the right outfit – a trench coat and a rain hat – so I improvised with a zip up hoodie and a baseball cap. For the part where Channing jumps off the stage and starts grinding on the ladies in the audience, I just improvised using poor Luis' kitchen chair. I cut the filming after that, since I didn't have a pair of tearaway pants or anything like that.

"You ever strip before?" Steve had asked.

"No, but I'm a quick study," I assured him.

"And how do you know Mike?"

"Oh, me and Big Mike have been friends since grammar school. We grew up together."

"He's good people," Steve said.

"The best," I agreed.

"And you're cool with keeping this… discreet?" Steve asked.

"Um, yes. Absolutely. I definitely wouldn't want anyone to find out about it."

"Okay. Then we'll try it out. I've got a small gig next Friday. Mike will be there. It's all cash. You just need the clothes. They're doing a masquerade themed thing – so I was thinking you could wear a Zorro costume. It's one of our easy go-to costumes anyway. The pants snap down the sides. Make sure you practice with them at home so you know how hard to pull in order to get them off quickly. There's also the mask, the hat, and the cape. And a vest. Also with snaps. Oh, and we use a whip instead of a fencing sword. You know – for safety."

"Right. Um. What about… well, for *under* the pants?"

"Oh, yeah. So, you're going to need a dance belt. It's like the male dancer's equivalent to a jock strap. It's got some padding and support, gives you some lift, and fits nice and snug around your junk so nothing falls out when you're dancing. You need to wear it under your G-string. The G-string for the Zorro costume is black with some bedazzling on it."

"Where do I get that?"

"We'll issue it to you. It's the only part of the costume we don't want back."

"So, hold up." I lowered my voice. "I have to wear a thong… *over* a thong?"

"Trust me, you'll be glad you did. It makes everything look bigger, keeps an extra layer between you and the partygoers, and tucks it all up in there."

"And I can buy these things from you?"

"Yep," Steve says. "It's $50 for the dance belt and $30 for the G-string."

Fuck, I thought. *That's a pretty big investment for some tiny pieces of cloth I'll never want to wear again.*

"Trust me, if you perform half as good as you did in your audition video, you'll make ten times that amount back next Friday."

I nodded. "You take Venmo?" I asked.

"Uh huh. I'm at Steve the Skeeve."

I grimaced. Not wanting to be offensive, I didn't respond.

"Old college nickname," he added.

"Great," I said. "I'll send it over once we get off this call."

"Good. I'll get your gear to Big Mike."

"Okay. Is there any, like, paperwork you need me to fill out?"

"Nope. We're entirely off-the-books. Next Friday will be your trial. If you like it, and the girls like you, great. We'll add you to the lineup. If not, we part ways, no hard feelings. Fair?"

"Sounds good," I replied.

"Stripping's not for everyone," he told me.

"I'm sure you're right," I laughed. "But if it pays the bills..." my voice trailed off.

"Exactly," the Skeeve agreed.

With that, we ended the Zoom call. I sent over the cash from my (dwindling) bank account and called Big Mike.

"You in?" he asked.

"I'm in," I said.

"It's easy money, dude. You'll be fine."

"You never told me the guy's name was Steve the Skeeve. What the hell is that all about?"

"Oh, you know. Just jokes."

"He said you'll get me my clothes in advance."

"Yeah, that's fine. I'll save you the trip of having to go meet up with him. What's the character? Fireman? Pizza delivery guy?"

"Oh my God, gross. Is that actually a thing?"

Big Mike laughed. "You'd be surprised."

"Well," I replied, my voice down to a whisper, "I'm Zorro."

"Bahahahaha!" Mike sputtered.

"Shut up, dick!"

He took a second to calm down. "Yo, my cheeks hurt now. Fucking Zorro. That's classic, Brady. I can't wait."

"Thanks, man. I hate you, too."

"You'll be fine. I'll get your outfit for you. I'll grab it this weekend."

I spent the next several days regretting the decision to try such a ridiculous get-rich-quick scheme. It was just really fucking hard to find a decent job when the season was already underway. In the resort world, my split from my dad had turned into fodder for the gossip mill, so none of the big chefs in the area wanted to work with me. The stories were so exaggerated, ranging from me screaming in his face in public dining to me pulling a butcher knife on him in the kitchen, like some kind of psychotic monster.

I got a Zoom interview for a Market Research Analyst position with a firm based in New York City, but it wasn't for another two weeks (since the recruiter was on vacation) and would also require a second round interview live in midtown

Manhattan, if I got that far in the process. That job had solid earning potential, but the hiring process would probably take the entire summer. See, that was the thing. The long-term employment opportunities were never a quick fix, and since I hadn't really been prepared financially to get kicked out of my living situation at the hands of my fucknut father, I found myself struggling – and out of cash – a lot sooner than I expected to be. Sure, I could use my credit cards, but if there's one thing I know from my background in economics, it's not to abuse credit. *Don't spend what you don't have*, my freshman year econ professor warned. I always took that advice to heart.

Which is why, when Big Mike said he had an idea for a way to get me paid quickly and in cash, I listened. Sure, it sounded suspect. But I wouldn't have to sleep with anyone. The job was simply to dance for 30 minutes to an hour and make the women feel attractive.

$800 for 60 minutes or less? *Fine,* I decide now, after a (thorough) shower, a toasted English muffin with butter, and a glass of water from the tap. *Maybe it was worth it.*

It's just as I'm turning off the faucet from washing my plate in the sink that I hear keys jingling out in the hallway. Before I can stop myself, I grab the dishtowel and dry my hands, then swing my door open and pop my head out.

Gretchen startles, dropping her tote bag by accident. "Shit!" she seethes. "You fucking scared me!"

I study her. Same color hair. She's wearing a pair of sweatpants and an oversized UMass t-shirt. She could be coming from anywhere. Until – *shit, there it is* – I notice the mermaid scales on the underwear that spilled out of her bag onto the ground. She bends down to pick up her things, hastily sweeping the panties back into the bag. Then, she stands up and looks at me. I'm awkwardly facing her, each standing at our apartment doors. Wordless.

Until –

"You!" we both scream and point in unison.

"I *knew* it was you!" I exclaim.

"How is *this* what you're doing on a Friday night?" she retorts.

"Shh," I admonish her. "Keep your voice down."

"You're the one sneaking up on people in the middle of the night, popping out of your condo like a fucking Whack-a Mole!"

Just then, the door down the hall opens and our massive neighbor, the one with the dog that shits everywhere, steps out into the hallway. "Yo," he says, in a voice so deep it sounds cavernous, like the great and powerful Oz. "Can the two of you please have a little respect? Some of us are trying to sleep."

Gretchen's eyes bug out, as if there's something she wants to say. I glare at her, trying to silently warn her that perhaps now is not the time for her to air whatever grievances she might have about this particular giant (who stands at least 6'5") when I am the only one around to protect her from being murdered here in the hallway. "Yeah, man. Got you. Sorry," I say, and he shuts his door with a grunt.

I walk toward Gretchen. It's about a dozen steps. "I *knew* it was you," I repeat, more quietly this time.

"What are you doing working as a *stripper*?" she replies, louder than I'd like. I'm not interested in engaging with the gargantuan down the hall again.

"Shh," I whisper. "We should have this conversation inside."

"Inside where?" she asks, as if I've just suggested we hop in a rocket ship and fly to the moon together.

"Your house? My house? I don't care," I say.

"Not *my* house," she declares.

"Fine – my house. Just not here," I murmur.

She sighs. It's not exactly a sound of acquiescence. More like – I'm not sure – relief, maybe? She gives me a pretty hard side eye, like she's contemplating whether I might be a murderer.

"You were fine barging into my house weeks ago," I remind her.

"I *thought* you were Luis."

"Okay, well, I'm going to go in there," I whisper, pointing into my condo. "If you decide you'd like to discuss this like mature adults, you know where to find me. But I am not going to stay out here and get clubbed to death by *that* neanderthal." I jut my chin out towards the C apartment.

Gretchen sighs dramatically. "Fine. Let me put this down. Hang on." She fumbles to put the key in the lock, turns it, drops her bag and follows me back to my condo, keys in hand. She steps inside, closing the door behind her quietly. "Well?" she says, shifting uncomfortably from one foot to the other. "Go ahead."

I narrow my gaze at her. "Summer, huh?"

"I'm sorry, *Zorro*," she replies, smirking.

"Why the name change?" I wonder aloud. "Is it just so people don't know that it's you?"

"I wish," she says. "Apparently my name is not acceptable."

"According to who?"

"Arrow. She's my boss. The one who was screaming at you in the parking lot?"

"Ahh. I see."

"But is that the *real* elephant in the room, though?"

"What? You working at a strip club?"

"It's *not* a strip club. And even if it was, *mine* was not the junkbucket on full display tonight," she says.

"No? You just walk around in your underthings on the street, then?"

"Not on the street. Only in the studio," she responds. "But at least my dumptruck was fully covered. That's more than I can say for you, my friend. You and the ol' dick in the box really caught me by surprise."

At this, I can't help but laugh. "Um, you and me both. I feel like you were suffering an identity crisis. Is she Ariel? Is she a gecko? You were like a walking riddle tonight – what's green, shiny, and wobbles when it walks?"

"Excuse me!" Gretchen retorts. "I was trying out new shoes! You of all people should know how hard it is for me to walk in heels. And the snake mask was courtesy of the *bride*, thank you very much."

"It seems like every time I see you, you're about to fall down."

"Not right now," she points out.

"No, I guess that's true."

She folds her arms across her chest and sizes me up. "What?"

"It's just, the last time I was standing here, you were kind of a dick. And this time is proving to be more of the same."

"No, I wasn't. You were the one who stormed in here, telling me when and where I could use my power tools. *I* was actually quite delightful."

"This is a sad turn of events. First, he goes off to become a stripper. Then, he develops early onset dementia."

"I think I know why you're so salty," I reply.

"I'm *not* salty."

"You like me."

"Gross."

"Fine. You *want* to like me. You thought I was the hottest Zorro you ever saw."

"Correction: you are the *only* Zorro I've ever seen."

"And now that we work in the same industry, you want to be friends with me."

"I would never be friends with you, Brady. You're the reason I'm in this industry in the first place!" She gives me a tart look.

"How's that, exactly?"

Gretchen huffs. "Please. Let's not rehash it." She puts up a hand and takes a step towards the door.

"Wait! Don't go," I say.

"Why not?" she snaps, flipping that fiery hair over her shoulder and looking at me with a sneer.

"I just think we've got more to discuss, that's all. And I genuinely don't understand why you say you would never be friends with me."

Gretchen groans with resignation, turning back to face me. "Well, if you're going to trap me here, I suppose I'm welcome to check the refrigerator for snacks." She walks the few steps into the miniscule kitchen and swings the fridge door open wide. "Yikes," she says. "Slim pickings, huh?" She holds up a half-eaten jar of pickles.

"Don't eat those," I say. "They're not mine."

"Whose are they?" Gretchen laughs.

"Those belong to Luis. He didn't clean out his condiments before leaving."

"So, your fridge is basically empty and you can't even claim the condiments as your own?"

"I have oatmeal if you want some. Or microwave popcorn."

"Popcorn, please."

I grab a package of movie-theater popcorn from the pantry and toss it in the microwave. As it pops, Gretchen hoists herself up to sit on my kitchen counter, next to the sink.

"Make yourself at home," I comment.

"Thanks," she says, not picking up on my sarcasm. Or, possibly, just ignoring it. "So," she begins.

"So," I reply. *Pop, pop, pop.* The scent of butter begins to permeate the airspace.

"Far cry from private dining, huh?"

"Yeah, I'd say so."

"I guess Daddy gave you a flexible schedule so you could go parade your tubesteak around for the almost-married contingent of the Outer Cape?"

I laugh, pleasantly surprised with her humorous observation. "No, princess. Or should I call you Chicken of the Sea?" She snickers at the quip. "I haven't worked at the Diamond Excelsior since our last time there together, actually."

"Wait – what?"

"You heard me."

"Why not? Did you quit?"

"Far from it. My fabulous father fired me."

"Really?"

"Indeed," I say. The corn pops like fireworks, not a far off metaphor from the sparks I felt flying around Gretchen before she snapped off my eye-mask earlier.

Somehow she's even cuter now, perched on my kitchen counter like she lives here or something.

"Why? Was it because of me?"

"Nah." I figure she doesn't need to know that she was the proverbial straw that broke the camel's back. "I had it coming."

"Really? But you always seemed so... uptight. Professional. Like a neurotic penguin in your fancy suit."

"Neurotic? That's real high praise," I say. "And it was a uniform. If anyone should understand about a uniform, it should be you, Fishnets McGee." Smirking, I take the popcorn out of the microwave and carefully pull apart the edges of the bag. Then, I hand it to Gretchen. "Careful. It's hot."

She accepts it and places it in her lap. "I'm serious," she goes on. "Believe it or not, I actually didn't hate you – until you fired me."

"Wait." I let her words sink in. "*Fired* you?"

"Yeah," she says, sheepishly. "After the David Krumholtz thing."

"I never fired you. I came back out with new table linens and you were gone."

"You called me Stumbelina and told me to stop crying."

"I know. But I didn't *fire* you. I thought you still worked there."

"No. Your dad told me you wanted me to leave. Once I cleaned up the mess, I went back into the kitchen and Chef Brax told me I should go."

"So, *he* fired you." I consider this new piece of information. "Seriously? He had no right to do that. It was *my* job to manage the wait staff."

"He specifically said that *you* wanted me gone – immediately. He told me that if I put up a fight or made a scene, he'd call the police. And I couldn't risk him doing that, because my dad's the police chief in Eastport, and word travels fast on Cape Cod."

"What a fucking asshole. First of all, he would never intentionally bring the cops to the restaurant – that's just ridiculous. Secondly, I never said any of that!" I insist, feeling my blood boil. "I swear, Gretchen. I felt bad about what happened to you. Anyway, that night I came home – back then, I *lived* with my dad – and he fired me, too, and kicked me out of the house."

"Which is how you ended up subletting from Luis."

"Exactly."

"Wow. Brady, your dad's a real taint."

I laugh. It's such an accurate depiction. "You're right. Point is, it wasn't me. I would never have let you go for tripping, even if you did spill the steamers on a celebrity. You were doing me a favor, working outside of your station at the pub."

"I just assumed you were mad. Your dad was furious, and even when he wasn't in crisis mode, he was always intimidating. So I kind of assumed that you could get angry like that, too. Or, rather, that you *would* get angry. Sorry," she rambles. "I'm just surprised. I really thought you fired me. He said it with such rage. I thought you were both just assholes. No offense."

"Oh, believe me, none taken," I say. "I'm sorry you thought that. I guess that explains why you had such an ax to grind with me when I moved in here."

"Can you blame me?"

"No. I suppose not," I concede, grabbing a handful of popcorn and putting a few pieces in my mouth. "Anyway, I'm sorry."

"It's fine. Glad we cleared the air, though."

"Yeah," I say. "Me too."

She sets the half-empty popcorn bag down on the counter and hops down. "Well, this has been enlightening. But I've got to go. I'm beat."

I nod, feeling my throat constrict.

She walks to the door. "It feels weird."

"Which part?"

"The not hating you thing," she says. "It's going to take some getting used to."

"Well, you know what they say."

"What's that?" she asks, with her hand on the doorknob.

"Practice makes perfect," I grin.

She smiles. "Tell that to your dance moves," she says, raising her eyebrows. She shoves her hand into the pocket of her sweatpants and pulls out a crumpled dollar bill. Tossing it on the floor with the same motion one might use for a mic drop, she smirks at me and says, "Night, Zorro." Then, she slips away, leaving me bemused, awash in the scent of popcorn, listening to the echo of her apartment door opening and closing behind her in the hallway.

CHAPTER EIGHT

GRETCHEN

I wake up the next morning flustered from my active hippocampus, which kept me dreaming about Brady all through the night. Dreaming, remembering. I'm not sure.

I'm probably just ovulating, I decide.

Because I can't help myself, I call Jenna and I gush about running into Brady in his new role as Zorro. She lets me go on like the good friend she is, ultimately reminding me that the universe works in funny ways.

After our impromptu therapy session, I make the conscious decision to put my brief dance with Brady out of my mind. Yes, it was *insanely hot* and yes, it's true that no man has *ever* danced with me like that before, but it was probably his last time ever doing it, and that's fine. I can't afford to be distracted while I'm working, anyway. I didn't like the way Arrow spoke to me, scolding me like a child for – for doing what, exactly? For stepping outside? As if that was some egregious offense? Well, lesson learned. If I want to keep this job, at least for now, I can't allow myself to get rattled.

Lucky for me, today is Saturday, so I have a chance to redeem myself.

Summer Saturdays on Cape Cod are the worst. It's something us locals refer to as "turnover day," meaning all of the tourists in weekly rentals will be leaving and all of the following week's tourists will be arriving. If you live here, you know never to make important plans to go somewhere off-Cape unless you're in the mood to sit in hours of bridge traffic on Route 6. I always use Saturday mornings for laundry, taking a walk on the Rail Trail (if I feel the need to be extra healthy, since it's also the day that has the least bicycle traffic), and more recently, I've been working on my moves at the studio. It's the one time of the week where I can be there alone, so I feel less inhibited since no one is watching me.

Cherry taught me to record myself when I'm dancing, which is a common practice among the girls. I like it because it gives me the chance to see what I look like up there and to perfect my movements so the shapes I create with my body look the way I want them to. Saffron recently instructed me on how to invert, and that's been a lot of fun. It's not too far off from gymnastics, really. This morning, I choose to practice something called a "chopper inversion." I set the pole to spin, and after stretching first, I begin with a few simple moves from the ground. The pencil, where you lift yourself up, body straight and still, in perfect vertical alignment with the spinning pole, is great for conditioning but also for getting used to the motion. The first time I ever did a move on spin pole, I became immediately nauseous, so I always remember to start with something simple to get accustomed to the movement.

To do a chopper, you first have to know how to invert on a static pole. Essentially, you stand alongside the pole, with your inside hand holding the pole up high and your outside arm reaching across your body to hold the pole as well. Then, you do a pole crunch, but with legs straight out and in a V shape. Basically, you just swing your legs up over your head. Once you get good at that, just pull up a little higher and you'll be upside down in a true inversion. On spin pole, this move looks awesome because your legs create the appearance of a helicopter.

I'm at the studio, working on the move with the stereo pumping out the newest Charlie Puth track, when the door opens, letting in a stream of bright sunlight.

"Oh, hey girl," Arrow says.

I flip myself back down and land as gracefully as I can. "Hi, Arrow. What's up? Early for you, no?"

She drops her purse on the table near the front that we use for catering. "Actually, I'm glad you're here. Did you get a text from Cherry?"

I shake my head. "I don't think so. I haven't checked my phone recently, though. Why?"

"She's in the hospital. Appendicitis."

"Oh, shit. That sucks. Sorry to hear it," I say. "Is she okay?"

"Yeah. She'll be fine I'm sure. Thought it was food poisoning, but when the pain just kept getting worse and worse, her boyfriend took her to the ER."

"Thank goodness. Isn't it, like, really bad if your appendix bursts?"

Arrow shrugs. "I guess. I'm no doctor." She checks something on her phone, then swipes the screen and looks at me. "Listen. Tonight's party is a big one, and I need all hands on deck. We've got 30 girls coming down from Boston. The bride is some locally famous author chick, so it's a little more of a high profile crowd."

"You want me to make extra shots?" I ask.

"No – that's not the issue. I need to make sure all the poles are staffed."

I say nothing, because I'm not quite sure what she's getting at.

"I need you to *dance* tonight, Summer."

What? I can't be hearing her correctly. My jaw drops. "Me?"

She nods. "Please. Let's not get all dramatic about it. You know the choreo. It's simple. And then, for the in-between times, like when the guys are here, just dance on a pole. We can put the shots out on the table."

"What about the keys?"

"Party bus," Arrow explains. "No worries tonight."

My heart thumps with Charlie Puth's bassline. "You sure, Arrow? I don't know if I'm ready."

She looks at me sternly. "You'll be fine, Summer. You can do this. You know the old saying *Dance like no one's watching*?"

"Yeah?"

"Just do that."

"Maybe we can ask Jenna to come back?"

"No offense, I know she's your friend, but Jenna's about as sexy as a teddy bear in a tutu. Also, she can't dance for shit."

"Really?" This surprises me, given the fact that she's the one who introduced me to this place.

"No cap. And, not for nothing, Cosmo is exit only. Once you're gone, you can't come back."

"Oh." *I didn't know that.* "Seriously?"

"Deadass."

"Why not?" I wonder aloud.

"It's just my policy." She shrugs, tracing a sparkly purple fingernail along her ear to keep her hair from hanging in her face.

"Oh. Um. Okay," I say. I can't imagine Jenna doing anything to piss Arrow off (other than not wanting to pole dance for the rest of her natural life) but Arrow's a bit of a strange bird, in my opinion, so I opt to just leave it alone. Instead, I gather my things, turn off the music, and head out. "Well, I was just about to get going. I've got some errands to run, but I'll be back for tow lot later," I tell Arrow.

"'Kay. And hey, don't forget. No fishnets if you're dancing. Wear the lower heels so you don't have to worry about falling. And, since you're new at this, I would recommend a bra and booty shorts – that way, all your business will stay tucked in. Get the ones that are ruched down the crack – you know, with the pads? That'll give your ass more curve. I need you to give me as much skin as you possibly can. None of this tank top bullshit. Nothing kills a vibe quicker than a pole dancer who's dressed like it's wintertime." She waves at my current ensemble, a boyfriend tank from Old Navy and a pair of Soffe shorts – which would only keep one warm in winter if one lived *on the actual Equator*.

"Got it," I reply, and escape to my car. I dial Cherry, who picks up on the third ring.

"Hello?"

"Hey. It's Summer. You okay?"

"Ugh," she moans. "It's been a rough night."

"Arrow told me. I'm so sorry," I offer. "Anything you need? Anything I can do?"

"Nah. Thanks, though. I have to stay in the hospital for one more day, but then I'm stuck home for two to three weeks until I get clearance from my doctor to come back to work."

"What happened?"

"So I got home last night after the party, right? And I ate some leftover pizza. It had been sitting out for a while, so when my stomach started to hurt, I figured, ah, fuck. It was probably bad cheese. You're not supposed to eat pizza if it's been left out, right?"

"How long was it out for?" I ask.

"Mmm. I'm not sure. Maybe like a day or so?"

A day or so?

"I just assumed it's so chock full of preservatives that it would be fine. But then my stomach started to turn. I'll spare you the gory details. Let's just say, there was lots of cramping, and all on one side, and it just kept getting worse and worse. So finally, I called Bobby and he came over. When it wasn't getting any better, even after I got sick, he convinced me to let him bring me to the emergency room."

"Good thing," I say. "Your boyfriend's got good instincts."

"Yeah, I guess. They got it out before it burst, but the whole thing still sucks," she adds. "Anyway, now I'll never eat pizza again."

"You feel better now, though?"

"Tons," she says. "Although I have stitches now, and I'll have a scar, which sucks."

"I'm glad you're okay, Cher."

"Thanks. Sorry I'll be missing work for a bit. I know Arrow's freaking out about it."

"Um, not going to lie, I'm right there with her."

"Nah. You guys will be fine."

"Everyone else, maybe. Not me." I swallow. "Arrow has me dancing tonight."

"That's cool," Cherry says. "You'll do great."

"I'm terrified," I admit.

"Don't be. Remember – the girls are all going to be wasted, for one thing. And none of them have ever poled before. So you'll look like a rock star even if you're only doing basic moves. Trust me."

I take a breath, putting her on speaker and backing the Fiesta out of its parking spot. "I guess."

"Seriously. You're a great dancer – especially for someone who just learned. I wouldn't feed you a line of bullshit. And, Arrow really likes you. She told me so herself."

"Really?" *This, I find hard to believe.*

"Scout's honor," Cherry insists. "Oh! You know what used to help me get over the jitters?"

"What's that?" I ask.

"Edibles. I've got some in my locker. Feel free to help yourself. The code is 6-9-6-9."

Classy, I think.

I'm the daughter of the chief of police. I grew up on those tired old "this is your brain on drugs" commercials – and not from the television; my father used to just play them for me randomly on his phone as a supplement to whatever life lesson he was trying to offer. Legal or not, I will *not* be indulging in random edibles from Cherry's locker. "Thanks," I say, hoping to sound polite and not judgey.

"Yup. Don't even give it a second thought." She pauses. "I've got to go. One of the nurses just came in for something."

"Feel better," I say.

I go for a drive to Last Encounter Beach in Eastport in an effort to create space from Arrow and just breathe. I need to calm down.

The beach helps. It always does. Me and the briny salt air have our own special deal: when things get rough, or if I'm stressed out about something, I put my toes in the sand and look out at the tidal flats and remember that the world is way bigger than just my miniscule problems.

By the time I get back to the studio for tow lot, I've gone home to change into a more "appropriate" outfit (and no, Brady's car was not there, not that I checked or anything) and I've put on sweats and a t-shirt because I'm not trying to go out in public wearing only a bra. Arrow's gone when I get back, leaving me to run tow lot pickups on my own, which is fine, since being busy is helping me get the butterflies in my stomach to calm the hell down. I take a break between tow lot and preparing for the night to run up to Cumberland Farms for gas station PB&J, which sounds disgusting but is the best two-dollar meal-on-the-go this town has to offer. When I return, Saffron's there, and I lament my life to her.

"I'm just worried I'll look ridiculous," I explain.

"Listen Chica, you're gorgeous. You could just stand there and it would be fine. But –" she lowers her voice, "Do you have any idea what kind of entertainment this crew is bringing in tonight?"

I shake my head.

"Oh my God, I'm *so* excited. The bride is a huge Red Sox fan, so the Skeeve is sending over a whole baseball team of strippers!"

"What? Won't it get, like, *crowded* in here? And what exactly is a *Skeeve*?"

"Oh." Saffron giggles. "Steve the Skeeve. He's like Cape Cod's resident pimp."

I bust out laughing. "There are no pimps on Cape Cod! This is the world's most Norman Rockwell place to live. I love how you're making it sound like Vegas."

"Well, he's definitely not a guy you'd find in a Rockwell painting, that's for sure."

"What exactly does he do?" I wonder aloud.

"He's the procurer. Arrow pays him a flat rate per guy per night. It's part of the bill for the ladies who come here. And his job is to find a dancer who will match what the girls want: so, like, tonight, the bride-to-be wants a baseball team, and it's up to the Skeeve to deliver that."

"That sounds… about right for someone who goes by the name *Skeeve*," I surmise. "Do you think it's legal?"

Saffron shrugs. "No clue."

Well. This is a bit much for me to process at the present moment. I do think that Brady might want to look into this if he's working for some suspect operation.

Perhaps I should give him a heads up.

Yes, I decide. And not because it gives me a reason to knock on his door. I'll do it because it's the right thing to do. The *neighborly* thing.

After all, I am nothing if not a gracious neighbor.

But not right now. Right now, I need to stretch. *Nothing worse than pulling a muscle on the pole*, I think.

I shake my head. *Wow. When did my headspace make such a huge departure from thoughts of nursery rhymes and basic language arts?*

Who even am I right now?

CHAPTER NINE

BRADY

I could not sleep last night.

I mean, don't get me wrong. I was definitely tired, but I kept tossing and turning, thinking about those damn fishnets.

I had a filthy dream about Gretchen. We were in my kitchen, only it was pitch black, except for a lamp in the corner that glowed fuchsia. She was up on the counter, but instead of sweatpants, she was wearing her mermaid-inspired bottoms with her loose t-shirt, and she begged me to rip off her clothes. I couldn't picture her naked body, but I could feel its curves and her baby soft skin as if it was really happening. Dream Gretchen wrapped her legs around me and buried her face into my neck, leaning up to lick and bite my earlobe. She closed the gap between our bodies by grabbing my ass cheeks and thrusting me into her, and just as kernels of popcorn rained down around us, I woke up to discover that I was, quite actively, stroking myself.

I checked the clock on my phone. 3:00 in the morning.

There was no way I would be able to fall back to sleep with a boner the size of Idaho under my covers, so I grabbed a hand towel out of my laundry basket and milked the popsicle in an attempt to clear my head (no pun intended). *My God,*

I thought. *This hasn't happened to me since high school.* I was fairly sure I'd be able to nod off after that, but my mind kept replaying the more innocent parts of our time together: the conversation in the kitchen, how embarrassed she looked recounting the mishap that got her fired, the way she gently blew on the first bite of popcorn so she wouldn't burn her mouth.

I wondered how I might find a way to see her again that seemed natural, not forced or contrived. Then, I wondered if any of the bizarre events that twisted our worlds together were lodged in Gretchen's mind, keeping her awake.

Chemistry's a weird thing.

Lying there, I remembered my last serious girlfriend, Miranda. We met the summer before my senior year of college. I was covering a shift for Big Mike (after he had one too many the night before) parking cars at the Sidewinder, a hot spot in Wellingham known for its shorefront party vibe. Miranda rolled up in a Jeep with no doors, wearing a triangle bikini top, unbuttoned denim shorts, and a pair of Ray Bans. She was with three of her girlfriends, a rowdy group with the radio blasting the Zac Brown Band into the otherwise fairly quiet airspace. It was just shy of noon, and I could feel my already sunburned shoulders taking a beating. She left me to valet her car, giving me a flirty once-over before hopping out, barefoot. The Sidewinder is conducive to the dress code Miranda and her friends donned that day: it's all fish tacos and live music and people laying out in the sand or playing beach volleyball.

But anyone with half a brain knows it's a mistake to walk around barefoot in the gravel parking lot of a bar.

So, not three minutes after she and her girl-crew exited the vehicle, I returned to my station to find her doubled over, bloody and crying. Surprisingly, her friends were nowhere to be found.

"Shit! You okay?" I asked.

She looked up at me from under her tear-streaked sunglasses. "I stepped on a piece of broken glass," she hiccupped.

"Hang on – I think there's a first aid kit in the booth." I ran to the key booth and found the kit tucked away in the corner. I pulled out a small stack of alcohol pads, the biggest Band-Aids I could find, and a roll of gauze.

Back at her side, I crouched down beside her, uncapped my Poland Spring bottle and carefully poured water over the wound. "Where did your friends go?" I asked.

"They went inside to find help," she sighed. "But they had mimosas at brunch, so it's no surprise that they're taking so long."

"Jeez," I said, examining her foot. "Well, the good news is I don't think you'll need stitches." I ripped off a piece of gauze and pressed it against the cut. Then, I tore open an alcohol swab and said, "This is probably going to sting. You can squeeze my arm if you need to." I cradled her foot in my hand and swiped at the cut, lighting up her sensitive nerve endings. I blew on it, like one might blow on a child's scraped knee, and she dug her fingers into my bicep, sucking in her breath. I fanned the cut with my hand, inspecting it to make sure it was clean. I placed the Band-Aid over it and wrapped the pad of her foot up in gauze. "This is going to mess up your beach day, you know."

"Yeah," she replied. "I know."

I introduced myself. "By the way, I'm Brady," I said.

"Miranda," she replied. "Thank you for helping me."

I nodded. "You here on vacation?" I took my folding chair out of the booth with one hand and helped her up with the other. She sat down in the chair and squinted up at me from behind her sunglasses.

"My family has a house in Truro."

"Nice," I said.

"What about you?"

"I live here year round. But not out this way. I'm actually just here covering for a friend of mine today. I'm from Sandwich."

"Cool. Are you in college?"

"Mm hmm," I nodded. "I go to BU. You?"

"Wait. BU as in Boston University?" she asked.

"Yeah."

"For real? Me too," she smiled.

"Really? Small world. What are you studying?"

"Political science. I'm thinking about becoming a lawyer."

"I'm an econ major," I replied.

The conversation continued for the rest of the afternoon, interrupted by my running off to park and retrieve cars, to grab her a turkey avocado wrap and several glasses of water, and by her drunk friends coming out "to check on her" about 20 minutes into our conversation. Miranda assured them she was fine but probably shouldn't go barefoot into the sand, and they were more than happy to ditch her in pursuit of a group of jacked up guys carrying a volleyball.

At the time, I thought we had chemistry. I mean, the whole damsel-in-distress meet-cute was kind of sweet, and she laughed at my jokes and gave me her number when her friends decided it was time to go. We saw each other several more times that summer and by the fall we were officially a couple. In retrospect, our time together was predictable. The beginning was fun; we went on dates where I spent more than I could afford in an attempt to impress her. The middle was less exciting and more mundane. Miranda complained that I studied too much, that I forgot our six-month anniversary (I didn't realize that was even a milestone), and that I wasn't paying as much attention to her as I had during our summer on the Cape. By the spring of that academic year, as the calendar was barreling toward Graduation Day, we'd begun having those "what will become of our relationship after college ends?" talks. To be honest, I wasn't expecting us to last, given her dreams of going to law school in New York and my plans to find work in Boston.

But that wasn't why we broke up.

In an effort to make me jealous, Miranda took up the habit of flirting with other guys. For example, we'd be at a frat party and she'd go off and dance with someone else. When I questioned the behavior, she'd claim he was "a friend from back home" or "some guy she used to hook up with." Not exactly the kind of warm-and-fuzzy behavior that made me think she'd be good in a long-distance situation.

So I began to create a little space between us. Then, about a week before graduation, she didn't return my calls or texts for over 24 hours. I figured this was another attempt to make me jealous or upset. Until I stumbled upon the *Boston Globe* on a routine coffee run to Dunkin'.

That was how I discovered the torrid side-relationship Miranda was having with a partner at the law firm where she was interning. It was right there on the front page: *Attorney's Affair with Student Ends in Arson*, it read. Miranda was accused of trying to "Lewinsky" her way to the top, and when a series of lewd photographs was discovered by the furious fourth wife of Stacks "tha hustla" Phillips – as in Phillips and Burns, injury attorneys, 1-800-GWAP-SHOP, Miranda's sorority house was mysteriously set on fire, and she disappeared virtually overnight. Rumor had it she left in the custody of Massachusetts' witness protection program, but I eventually heard through the grapevine that her wealthy parents decided to give her the "Fresh Prince of Bel Aire" treatment; namely, they sent her across the country to live with her (equally rich) family out in California. Her phone number was cut off, and I didn't care to pursue it any further after that.

So, yeah. My relationship record is about as stable as my current employment situation.

With Gretchen, though, I feel like there's a world of possibility out there. She seems adorably innocent for someone working at a pole studio, which makes her even sexier, and if I could just find a way to see her again, I decided while tossing and turning in the wee hours of the morning, *I'd* – hm. I'm not really sure what I'd do. I'd like to think that I would grow a pair and ask her out, but I've been remarkably single for several years, and I don't feel like my swag game is particularly on point at the moment. In fact, I'd be willing to bet that any street cred I might have had at the Diamond Excelsior went out the window once she saw me run into a parking lot wearing nothing but a Zorro thong.

Which is why, when I get the call from Steve the Skeeve, I decide it's fate.

"Hello?" I answer.

"Yeah. Brady. It's Steve. Just checking in. How'd you make out last night?"

"Um. Pretty good, I think. I wasn't sure how to end the night, so I might have messed that part up a little bit, but overall I think it went well."

"Mike said you did good for a rookie."

"Great. Well, thanks again for the opportunity. I appreciate it."

"You busy tonight?" he asks.

"Uh –" I pause to consider the question. "Not really. What's up?"

"I got a bigger gig. Bride wants ten guys."

"Ten? That's a lot."

"You ever dance in a group before?"

Recollections of my kindergarten Saturday Academy Modern Dance recital – and the revenge dance career that ensued in high school – flood my brain. "When I was younger, yeah."

"You think you could learn some basic moves kind of quick? I had ten guys, but one got picked up by the cops last night for public indecency and his folks haven't posted bail yet. Apparently, they're pretty pissed."

Can't imagine why. "Yeah, I'm pretty sure I can. It's like riding a bicycle – but using only your hips." I laugh at my own joke. "Wait. I have a question."

"Shoot."

"Would this be at the same place?"

"Yup. Cosmo is my big spot. Outside of that, we do private parties, but there aren't any real clubs out here on the Cape, you know?"

"Right." *Hmm. Another chance to see Gretchen, without it being weird. I mean, obviously it's weird, the thought of stripping in front of her again. But because she's all decked out and uncomfortable, somehow it makes it less weird that I'm only covering my cod-piece with a snapper-wrapper.* "What's the getup? Zorro again?"

"Nope. You'd need to be a baseball player. Lots of bat-action. Two choreographed routines. You think you could make it down to Harwich to practice with the guys? 1pm?"

Two hours? "Yeah, I can be there."

"Great, kid. I'll even throw in the thong this time since you're doing me a solid."

"No problem." The butterflies that have suddenly appeared in my stomach threaten to wreak havoc on my gastro tract. "Where's the practice, exactly?"

"Harwich Cultural Center," he says. "Friend of mine has a dance studio there." He gives me a phone number, which I write down. It belongs to Max, one of the people I'll be dancing alongside. "He's been with me the longest. I'll let him know to expect you."

"Okay," I say. We hang up, and I exhale, looking at myself in the mirror.

"Well," I say to my reflection. "Batter up." I shake my head, laughing at the absurdity of it all. I wash my dance belt by hand in the kitchen sink and toss it in the dryer before heading into the shower to start getting ready.

I'm not from this part of the Cape, so I type in Harwich Center in the GPS and I end up giving myself just enough time to arrive at the Harwich Community Center at 12:55 p.m. I briskly walk inside. The place is nice, and it looks like fairly new construction, right across the street from a high school. But it definitely gives off a geriatric vibe. There are three elderly women behind a circular front desk, and I try to get my bearings and find some sort of center map to figure out where in this building the dance studio Steve told me about is located. A quartet of old men are playing racquetball through a glass wall straight ahead, all hiding behind rec specs, and a woman in a wheelchair with a ball of yarn and a pair of knitting needles in her lap is being rolled down the hallway by a middle-aged aide. There's a Harwich Community Center bulletin board that boasts upcoming events, such as a field trip to the Sandwich Glass Museum and a "movie night" featuring the movie *Cocoon*, which must be well before my time because I've never even heard of it.

Befuddled by the lack of clarity as to where the dance studio might be, I approach the desk. One of the women, with a badge that says "AGNES, here to help" comes up to me. Slowly.

"Can I help you, young man?" she asks.

"Can you tell me where the dance studio is?"

"What's that, now?" She leans in closer.

"I'm looking for the dance studio. I'm here to meet some guys."

"Dance studio?" she asks.

"Yes, ma'am. If you could just tell me where it is, that would be great."

Confused, she looks up at the ceiling. "For dancing?" she asks me.

I nod. "I'm here to meet a group of guys," I add.

She looks at me and offers what I'm sure, back in the day, might have been the Agnes version of a devilish grin. "I haven't seen anyone here for dancing," she says. "But I would be happy to cut a rug with you, if you're looking for a dance partner."

I shake my head and look at the clock on the wall. It's 1:00. "I'm sorry, I'd love to do that another time, ma'am. But right now, I'm late for a dance rehearsal with a group of guys. Now, please. Is there a dance studio here or not?"

"I'm afraid there's not," she replies, sadly. "Betty?" she calls out to a different white-haired lady at the desk.

A diminutive thing with a four pronged cane who I can only imagine is Betty turns around.

"Betty?" Agnes repeats. "This young man is here looking for dance classes?"

"No, that's not it," I interject, not wanting to be rude.

"Huh?" Betty asks, adjusting her hearing aid.

"I'm sorry," I say, trying not to get flustered. "I'm supposed to be meeting a group of guys here to learn a dance number for a bachelorette party tonight."

"Oh," Agnes says. "Ooh-la-la," she nods at me.

Betty startles, as if perhaps she's turned up her ears too loud. "He's a stripper?" she yells across the desk.

"I don't know," Agnes replies, looking me over. "He could be."

"Please, ladies. I'm just looking for a dance studio. If there's not one here, I must be in the wrong place."

"You might check the Harwich Cultural Center. It's over on Sisson Road. You know where that is?" Betty asks, loudly.

"Isn't *this* the Harwich Cultural Center?" I ask.

"Oh no," Agnes replies. "This is the Harwich *Community* Center. We welcome everyone, but it's really mostly a senior activity center."

Fuck. That explains it. "Oh," I say. "I'm sorry for the confusion. Hope you both have a lovely day," I add, and turn to leave.

"Come and see us again sometime!" Agnes hollers after me.

I pull up the number for Max in my phone. I dial it.

"Hello?" a man answers.

"Yeah, hi. My name's Brady. I got your number from Steve?"

"What's up, man? We're all down at the HCC. You coming?"

"I'm on my way. Just got a little lost. Sorry. Where exactly is it at?"

Max offers me directions; turns out I'm just a few minutes away. When I arrive, he meets me at the door. "What up, bro? I'm Max." He holds out his hand and gives me a pound. "Nice to meet you."

Max has to be about 6'5". He's huge, not to mention ripped. Hard to imagine him as a dancer. Now, a baseball player, *that* I could see.

I follow him down a long hallway. "This some kind of school?" I ask.

"Used to be," he says. "Now it's an artist's collective. Groups rent out the old classrooms to set up shop for all sorts of things – fiber arts, pottery, you name it. We just borrow space from the Zumba group that meets here. I'm friends with the girl that runs the classes."

"Cool," I say, as we turn the corner.

When we get to the dance room, Max introduces me to the other guys. You would think I was entering a Greek God competition or something. It's impossible not to notice how good they look.

Max explains that there are two numbers we need to rehearse. The first is a mash up of classic walk up songs, *Enter Sandman* by Metallica, *Seven Nation Army* by the White Stripes, *Welcome to the Jungle* by Guns N' Roses, and a few others. For that number, we'll be using the bats. There's a bag with a dozen or so wooden bats in it, and Max explains we're using wood because it's heavier, so our muscles will flex harder when we hold the bats up. For that dance, we'll end up shirtless but still wearing our pants.

The second number, which abandons the bats – is a hip hop compilation including Notorious BIG, DJ Khaled, and Drake. This is the one where we strip all the way down. "It's a slow burn," Max explains. "We'll make more money if we keep the ladies at bay a bit longer. So the two dances combined will take us about ten minutes. By then, they won't be able to keep their hands to themselves," he grins.

"Or their money in their purses," another guy named Tommy adds.

We begin with some basic stretching, and I'm surprised at how much it feels like a dance class. Most of us will stay in formation as backup dancers, so the work for the first song is pretty minimal. It's a lot of hip thrusting and hands sliding down our chests. The bats are (of course) synonymous for our pork swords, so there's a good amount of holding them upright and grinding our hips while slowly stroking the wood. Then there's a part where we freestyle – each of us finds a lady in the crowd and has to give her our baseball cap while we body roll up against her.

My position in the lineup is in the back row, all the way to the right. This is good because no matter what, I'll be able to watch the guys in front of me on the off chance that I forget the moves. They've all done similar versions of this dance before – they've pretended to be a hockey team (same thing but with hockey sticks), construction workers (with levels), even farmers (with hoes). There's a lot of repetition, which makes learning the dance pretty easy. About halfway through, we abandon the bats for folding chairs, and there's a good amount of flexing and posing – each of us, one at a time – followed by a synchronized dolphin dive to the ground that marks the beginning of the end of dance number one. Once we emerge from the ground, the shirts and belts have come off, and after that it's a whole lot of gyrating and sharp, precise thrusting until the end of the number.

The second dance comes up almost like a flash mob sort of thing, because we're expected to mingle and dance with the girls on the floor for a solid five minutes first. "That'll prime them," Max says. "That way, when they're all hot and bothered, sweaty and ripe, that's when we'll break out into the second number. This one is a little more tricky because of the water."

Water? I wonder.

"It's during the DJ Khaled song, 'All I Do is Win.' The confetti will go off and then we'll do the water cooler dump. So, Brady – you and Dex are going to pop the confetti canisters from the back corners and I'll be in the middle, holding up the trophy, when Billy and Jay come up behind me with the cooler full of water. It's the best part of the dance. We can't spill actual water in here – or use *real* confetti – so we'll improvise those parts."

Max shows us the various formations we'll need to get into and we practice the part where we rip off the pants – which is kind of funny, given how all of us are currently in regular underwear underneath. It looks smooth, though, and after several takes we get it right.

By the time we finish up, it's almost 4:00, and I'm surprised at how fast the afternoon flew by. "Nice work, everyone," Max says. I follow him to his car and he gives me my baseball-inspired thong, a navy blue and white undergarment that's got *Big Ballers* written in script across the center. I laugh and shake my head.

Big Mike meets up with me again to drive up to Cosmo. We take his truck this time. I'm surprised at how nervous I am, and he's surprised that I'm doing this again, especially two nights in a row. "Didn't think you caught the bug, after how you dashed off last night like Cinderella," he jokes.

Instead of telling him the truth about Gretchen and the fact that I just want to see her again, I shrug and say, "You were right. It's great money."

"I told you, dude. You won't have to worry about bills for a hot minute after this."

When we arrive, we wait out in the parking lot as instructed. The steel door keeps the thumping bass at bay, and at exactly 9:30, all ten of us line up at the door behind Max. Big Mike is at the back of the line, as he'll remain by the door once we go inside, and I'm right in front of him, last stripper in the lineup.

Arrow opens the door. "Oh, hello," she says in her over exaggerated, dramatic voice. "How can we help you?"

"We were just on our way to a game and our bus broke down," Max announces. "Any chance we could use this space for practice?" he asks.

"Hell, yeah!" Arrow shouts. "Right, ladies?"

Screaming ensues as we file in and get into our formation in the area of the studio designated to be our makeshift stage. As we do this, Big Mike shuts the door hard behind him, and I scan the room looking for Gretchen. I see the three pole girls headed towards their – *wait a second.*

The girl in the middle – it's – *no, it can't be.*

I thought Gretchen was just a shot girl?

The music starts, and I need to focus, but she's up there spinning and the ladies of the party are howling and I can't quite think straight. *What was the opening move?* I look in front of me. *Oh, right. Bat resting on your shoulder.* Gretchen climbs the pole. *Fuck, Brady. Pay attention.*

Somehow, I manage to get myself in the zone and get through the first part of dance #1. When it's time to grab a girl and put my hat on her, I want to go after Gretchen but she's – *holy shit, she's upside down* – not available at the current moment. So I sidle up to the lady closest to me, and everything is going fine until I actually look at her face. It's a very specific combination of amused and horrified.

"Brady?!" she exclaims.

No. Fucking. Way.

It's Miranda.

Other ladies turn around with raised eyebrows, but they're easily calmed by the elixir of soon-to-be-wet stripper dancing all around them. Up on the pole, Gretchen stops gyrating for long enough to make eye contact with me, and now she looks shook as well. Not, like, *Hey, fancy meeting you here* happy to see me; more like *oh my God is that actually you* panicked. But I can't worry about that right now because my ex-girlfriend is directly in front of me, threatening to destroy what little self-respect I have left. Miranda looks like she's seen a ghost, and I can't exactly evacuate the dance floor mid-routine, so I put my hat on her head and just plead with my eyes for her to keep her mouth shut.

That plan does *not* work.

"What are you *doing* here?" she asks, much louder than I'd prefer, her voice overflowing with curiosity.

I pull her close to me and grind my hips up on her. I really, really don't want to but I desperately need her to be cool. "Shh," I say into her ear. "Let's not make a scene."

She pulls her face back from me, bewildered. I do a spin and drop down to all fours, hump the floor a few times, then hop back up to my feet and snake my way back up her body. "Besides, you're one to talk," I go on, back next to her ear now. I'm holding her by the hip with one hand – the other hand is up over my head when I say, "Shouldn't you be in California?"

"I moved back east last year," she replies. "I'm staying at the Truro house for the summer." I thrust my junk at her in time with the music, as if this isn't the world's most awkward situation. I pretend not to notice Gretchen watching me from her bird's eye view on the pole. "What about *you*?" she asks. "How did you become a –"

"Nope," I say, placing my forefinger on her lips to cut her off, letting out a surprised chuckle at the irony of our chance encounter. "Gotta go," I add. It's true; it's time for the second half of the first dance. I'm back in my spot in the formation of guys, thankfully able to remember all the moves and keep time with Billy, who is directly in front of me. We each grab a folding chair and set it up with a quick flick of the wrist. Then, we put one foot up on the seat of the chair and thrust away into the darkened space around us. Flip the chair and straddle it. Half the guys (not me, thank God) lean backwards, do a complete backbend and kick up and over into a standing position. I am not a gymnast, so my move is to stand up, slide the chair between my legs, pick it up in a flip twist, set it back down and sit in it normally, reclining my shirtless, slathered up body and sliding my hand down my chest to my stomach before grabbing myself and thrusting a whole bunch more. The ladies are quite happy with this, it seems, judging from the screaming. I keep my eyes trained on Gretchen, who seems reciprocally laser-focused on me. I'm not sure what it is about this environment but I'm pretty sure that if we ran into one other in the grocery store we wouldn't stare each other down like we are right now.

Or maybe I'm wrong.

By the time the first dance ends, we're back out in the crowd, expected to dance with the hot and bothered ladies who are sucking down Jell-O shots as if it's their last meal on Earth. This is the moment where I want to go over to Gretchen and dance with her, but she's still doing combinations on the pole with the other girls. I try not to stare but it's killing me – just when I thought she couldn't get more beautiful, there she is, legs for days and a body that could make a priest blush, and she's gazing down at me like watching me watching her is doing unthinkable things to her.

So that's going well, until Miranda reappears in front of me. This time, she's more determined. I spin out, trying to avoid full frontal contact with her, but she grabs me by the hips and pulls me to face her. "Brady, how did you get into this?" she asks, moving in time with the beat like *it's cool, we're cool, let's just make small talk like old friends* – as if her sexual indiscretions of the past didn't have repercussions aside from the arson. Once upon a time, this girl actually *hurt* me, and the last thing I need is for her to fuck up my chances with a woman I actually like who *isn't* rumored to be in the custody of the state. So I dive down onto the ground and begin crawling away towards literally anybody else – but when I stand back up, she's right there in front of me again. "I had no idea you were such a good dancer," she says.

Nope, I think, *this is not going to be like some Love is Blind reunion show, where I'm the ignorant asshole who didn't know you were trying to sleep your way into a job at a law firm, only now you see me with my shirt off and you think twice about what you missed out on. No thank you,* I decide, as I catch the waist of a different lady to my left and lift her up so she looks like she's dry-boning me in the air.

"Woo!" the girl shouts.

"Courtney!" Miranda hollers up from *right next to me.* She taps the girl on the arm. "This is Brady! You know, my ex? From college?"

The woman – *Courtney* – loses her smile as her mouth forms the shape of an O. I place her back down on the ground, glaring at Miranda. "I'm here to do a *job,*" I say.

She leans in close to my ear. "I just want to talk to you," she replies.

"No need," I reply, spinning away from her and lifting my leg up to grind on a different nearby party patron.

From the corner of my eye, I see an obviously frustrated Miranda pull an airplane-sized bottle of Tito's out of her bra. She cracks it open and sucks down the contents, shaking her head and grimacing at the taste. Miranda never had much of a tolerance for alcohol. I body roll into the blonde in front of me, and she squeals with delight.

If I had to venture a guess, I would say about 30 seconds pass. Of course, when certain things happen, they appear as though they're occurring in slow motion, so it *feels* more like entire minutes – but before I can register the next series of events, Miranda has pushed my temporary dance partner aside. "I need to talk to him," she says. Her words are dizzier than before. The blonde shrugs and two steps over behind Billy, who's eyeballing me with an expression that silently asks if I'm okay.

"I never said I'm sorry," Miranda says, leaning in to make sure I can hear her.

"It was a long time ago," I reply. I place my hands on her hips to create distance, but she smacks them away and takes a step in closer to me. Uncomfortably, I continue. "Water under the bridge."

"I felt bad. It wasn't what you thought. Come outside, Brady. Come and talk to me."

"I'm working," I say. It's code for *leave me alone*, although the fact that I'm currently not wearing a shirt maybe sends mixed signals.

"So, you can work on me," she replies, and before I can stop her, she's got her lips on mine and she is forcing her tongue into my mouth like a serpent.

I put my hands on Miranda's shoulders and remove her from my face. Next thing I know, Billy's beside me. "Yo – you can't do that, bro," he whispers in my ear. "You could get fired. Don't kiss anyone."

I nod, unable to say anything because the music jacks back up and the first few beats indicate that it's time for our flash mob hip hop dance to begin. We step out – one, two, three, four – slide to the left, put up one bicep, two, then kiss each one, grab the front of our pants on our upper thighs and pop, pop, pop, rip them off. The ladies squeal with delight, and Miranda's eyes grow so wide I think they might just fall out onto the floor. In matching thongs, we shake our asses, lean back, hip thrust our junk into the eager crowd of ladies and then me and Dex head to the back of the makeshift stage to grab our confetti cannons while Billy and Jay grab the Gatorade cooler. It's only a little bit full, just enough to create the illusion of water splashing everywhere. Once we hear the beat drop – boom, boom, boom, boom – and DJ Khaled shouts his own name, Dex and me pull back the cannons and then – *pow!* – confetti rains down everywhere and Max stands in the middle of the stage with his arms up to the sky, relishing the water being spilled all over him. It's a fucking spectacle, to say the least. But the dollars rain down too, and I know that the rehearsing was worth it. The ground is littered with tens and twenties, none of the amateur hour situation from yesterday with all the singles.

It is *so* much money.

Gretchen and the girls finally come down from the poles and each of them grabs a tray of shots to distribute. Now that the show is coming to its finale, the goal is to get the ladies as lit as possible without making anyone sick. I watch her as she smiles while doling a tray of shots out to the girls nearest my side of the stage, which is perfect because the song ends, and I'm finally able to get close enough to talk to her.

"Got an extra?" I ask, nodding at the shots.

She hands one to me, but I can tell something's off.

Of course. I can smell the Chanel permeating off her skin before I even see Miranda standing beside me.

"I'll take a shot," she slurs, sliding her arm around me.

Gretchen's brows knit together. "Um, here," she says, handing off another shot to Miranda. "How do you two know each other?" she asks.

Miranda looks at me with an intoxicated blank stare. Her body leans into me. "Brady and I used to be in *love*," she swoons.

I try to stand her upright and offer my two cents, but Gretchen shoots me a death scowl and says, "How nice for you." Without another word, she turns and glides off.

CHAPTER TEN

GRETCHEN

I guess that explains it, I think.

That explains the way he was making out with her on the dance floor in front of me.

Here I thought we had some – I don't know, chemistry or something! But I was obviously wrong because not only did he show up here on the worst night ever for me, where I'm out here humiliating myself pretending to be some kind of dancer, but he brought along some groupie *chick who obviously is totally familiar with every* sexy as fuck *dance move the guy can throw down.*

The guys are all down on the dance floor so I storm away from Brady and his long-lost lover in the only direction that's wide open – the stage area. I walk as quickly as I can given my choice of footwear, holding the few remaining shots I have on the tray out in front of me. The shot tray, coupled with the darkness, seems to create a blind spot for me because the next thing I know I'm flat on my ass in a puddle of water in the middle of the stage.

Dumbfounded, I sit there for what feels like an eternity despite realistically being only a moment or two. I feel the tears sting my eyes and Arrow yell, "Seriously?" My ass and my left elbow hurt, and pink Jell-O in tiny plastic cups is strewn about amidst the wet dead presidents on the stage floor. But, before I can even collect myself to stand up, I'm being lifted up and swiftly carried off like a groom carries his bride over the threshold of their new home.

I know it's Brady without even looking at him.

First of all, I can feel it in his grip – he's firm but not rough.

Secondly, I can smell it. It's the same smell from last night when he danced with me – a particular combination of Irish Spring soap, Old Spice deodorant, and coconut oil.

A tear slides down my cheek, and he leans his face down to mine and whispers, "I got you." The smooth sound of his voice puts me over the edge.

More tears fall, and all I can think is that I can't stand to lose a second job on account of not being able to walk in high heels.

Brady carries me into the back office and sits me down on the desk. I move my hand to wipe my eyes but he stops me. "Wait," he says. "Let me do it. You'll smudge." He grabs a paper towel from the roll on the desk and dabs under my eyes gently, saving me from destroying my face but also from inadvertently pulling off my fake eyelashes. It's very sweet, and if it weren't for the fact that *the love of his life or whatever* was just steps away, I might have found myself insanely attracted to him in this moment.

"Are you okay?" he asks. "Did you break anything?"

"I think I'm fine," I say.

"What hurts?"

"Other than my pride?"

"Yes. Physically."

Arrow bursts in the room. "Summer! What the actual fuck?" She shoots Brady a fierce look. "You," she says. "Why are you in here?"

"She fell," he says. "I wanted to make sure she was okay."

"Okay, there, knight in shining nutsack armor," she says, the words dripping with sarcasm. "Get out there and air-fuck my customers, please. You don't need to be back here."

"Jesus," Brady says.

"It's okay, Brady. I'm all right."

"Listen, Arrow," he begins. "With all due respect, I was trying to help one of your employees. You know, if she got really injured, something tells me you don't exactly carry a workers' comp policy. You could have one hell of a lawsuit on your hands."

She smirks at him. "Are you threatening me? In *my* house? Wearing a fucking thong?" She throws her head back in a laugh that sounds demonic. "That's priceless. Seriously, dude. Get out there and do your damn job."

"Brady," I say, but my eyes say significantly more. "Go. I'm fine, I promise."

He sighs, turns and leaves.

I inhale, preparing for Arrow to unleash her fury on me.

But she doesn't. Instead, she just says, "Get yourself together and come back out as soon as you can, okay?"

I nod.

"You can walk, right?"

"Yeah. I think I just bruised my ass, to be honest."

"You can take off the shoes, if you want. Pole barefoot for the rest of the night."

"Okay. Thanks."

I'm surprised at the shift in her tone with me as compared to Brady, almost as if she has some personal ax to grind with him. "He's not supposed to be out there hooking up with them," she comments. "He should know better."

"Oh, that," I say, remembering.

"I could get him fired if you want me to."

"No, no," I say. "It's fine. I, just. He's my neighbor. He used to be my boss. We have kind of a - um - complicated thing going on."

"Are you two…" she trails off.

"No, nothing like that," I clarify.

"Okay. Just checking. Because you know we look out for each other here. Chicks over dicks."

I laugh. "I never heard that one before."

Arrow nods. "I've told you before, Summer. Pole is a sisterhood. We always take care of one other. I could annihilate him for you, if you ever needed me to."

"Got it."

I don't know why - I mean, Arrow's one scary woman - but somehow, it makes me feel a little better. Maybe it's just the idea of feeling like I'm a part of something, or like someone would stand up for me if came down to it.

If we're being honest, for as much as my gut tells me not to like or trust any of it, there's something about this place that makes me feel like I belong.

I don't know what comes over me, but I feel like the moment might never come again. There's a crack in the armor. Arrow feels remarkably *mortal*, if temporarily. A person capable of genuine feelings. My mind swirls with curiosity over her story, over what made her become the way she is, and the only evidence I have is stuck to the refrigerator. Boldly, I turn to Arrow and ask, "Is that your daughter? In that picture?"

She looks at me with an expression on her face that I can't quite read. It's... wistful, maybe? But masked by her always-tough exterior. "No," she says, shaking her head. "That's my niece."

"Oh. Well, she's beautiful," I say. I've overstepped, I know it.

"Thank you," Arrow replies. She exhales, and there's so much more behind those two words, but she's done sharing. Her chest heaves. "C'mon. Get yourself together. We've got a job to do."

I nod. Arrow gets back to the party, and after a few deep breaths, I take off my shoes and inspect my ankles. I'm okay, thank goodness. I rub my butt cheek – I'm sure there will be a bruise tomorrow – and consider what awaits me on the other side of the office door. The guys should be leaving soon, so whatever's going on between Brady and that girl won't continue (at least not in my sight), but I'll be stuck with her for the rest of the night. Food will be here soon, so that will bring the party down naturally.

I'm trying to relax but my heart won't stop pounding. I peek out the door, looking around for Brady.

He's dancing with the bride-to-be and – yup, there she is – the one who was "so in love" with Brady. To his credit, Brady is totally facing the bride. The other girl has her mouth up against his ear and is grinding on his bare ass like a rabbit in heat. He's not pushing her away, but he's not paying her any attention, either. Still, I feel like I want to stab my pole heel through her eye.

I've never really been the jealous type, but I've been on the other side of it, once, and it was very unbecoming.

Just after graduating college, I came back home to Eastport to live with my parents. I got my job working at the Mine in the Diamond Excelsior and was getting ready to start online graduate school in the fall. During my free time, I volunteered for the town in whatever ways I could. This act of citizenship was ingrained in me from childhood; when your dad's the chief of police, you just grow accustomed to showing up at town events, manning a table, helping with a float for Windmill Weekend or running a craft activity for kiddos at the annual Brussels Sprout Festival.

It was during one such event, the Orleans Police Block Party, that I met Keith.

Orleans is a town closer to the mainland by a few miles. It's way more populated and has things we lack, like a big grocery store and a TJ Maxx. They also have the block party at the end of August every year put on by the police department, and we are obliged to help out in solidarity.

I was manning the hot dog station; that is to say, I was handing out hot dogs to hungry dads and their children and accepting their food tickets, cleaning up the ketchup and mustard station, and restocking the napkins. The grill guy, an Orleans officer named Anthony, was coming off his wiener-cooking shift to go man the dunk tank, and to relieve him was none other than my dad's newest hire, Keith Fullerton. I knew *of* Keith – the Cape is small, so everyone knows everyone to some degree – he grew up in Chatham and went to Monomoy High School (I went to Nauset, the other high school out this way), played football, and after graduation, enrolled at 4Cs for an associate's degree in Criminal Justice. He was a lifer here, just like me, but we ran in very different circles, and he was two years my senior.

"Reporting for duty," he announced. He pulled on an apron that said, "Proud to Serve" with a picture of an array of barbecue utensils. He stood about 5'10", was thick-necked and muscular, and had several tattoos on his forearms. But he was a master on the grill, insofar as one can master cooking a Ball Park hot dog to perfection. Keith took the job seriously, and only stopped to make small talk with me when the lines died down. He offered me a hot dog, and I accepted it. Then, he asked, "So, are you a ketchup girl or a mustard girl?"

"Relish, actually. And sauerkraut," I replied.

"Really?" He raised his eyebrows and gave me an approving nod.

Yes, folks, that was it. That was his version of flirting.

We got to chatting, and at the end of our shift together, he said, "You ever been to Depot Dogs?"

I shook my head. "Heard of it, though."

"Want to try it? I'll take you after we're done here."

"You're not sick of hot dogs at this point in your day?"

"Nope. I know it may not look like it," he laughed, patting his belly, "but I can eat."

"I can, too," I joked, patting mine in response.

"Yeah? So prove it."

"You're on," I replied. "Just let me check in with my dad." This was standard operating procedure in our house. I could not go out with anyone without my father's approval. I didn't mind it; it was just the way things were.

I shot my father a text: *Cool if I go to Depot Dogs with Keith?*

Fullerton? he replied.

Yeah. He asked me.

Is it a date?

Not sure. Don't think so. I think it's just hot dogs, Dad.

Then it's fine with me, Gretchie. Thx for asking.

"Got the green light," I told Keith.

He drove us down to the food truck spot at the intersection of Depot Road and Route 28, parked at Buca's, and we walked up to the guy at the stand. "Get this girl an English Dog and a Red Rock Dog," Keith said. "And I'll take the same."

I scanned the menu to figure out what he'd just ordered for me.

"They're great – don't question it, just trust me."

The English Dog was slathered in beer cheddar cheese sauce and bacon, and the Red Rock Dog was a compilation of chili, onions, kraut and mustard. The truth was, I didn't really love hot dogs. I would eat one once in a while, like at a picnic or a baseball game, but outside of that, I wouldn't *choose* them as a destination for my taste buds.

So, having two of them, neither one prepared the way I actually preferred, was maybe not the best decision.

It was, however, a fabulous metaphor for how our relationship would go: Keith telling me what I *should* like, what I *should* do, how I *should* behave. I hadn't had lots of boyfriends as a younger person. I had Ethan in high school – he was fine, but we had known each other since we were in diapers and it was just young, puppy love until we both went off to college. Then I dated Noah when I was 19, and I really liked him but he really liked sleeping around, so that didn't end well. I followed him up with Trent – a guitarist in a local bar band in Amherst who saw fit to write a song about me called "Let Me In Your Tail Pipe" and then Alphonse, an exchange student who begged me to "Viens à Nice avec moi" when his student visa ended.

And yes, I know what you're thinking – *didn't you ask you father if you could date these guys?* The answer is, *sort of.* Ethan: yes, Noah: no, Trent: no, Alphonse: no. But since moving back home post-college, I had gone out on a single date with Ed, a guy from the fire department (yes, with permission from Dad; sadly, exactly zero sparks ignited – ironic, given his work with flames), which brought us up to this moment with Keith, the hot dog king.

Date or not, I figured that it was the respectable thing to do to ask my father's permission, especially considering the fact that Keith worked for him.

The thing is, if you want to stay on Cape Cod for the long haul, you need to find someone who you're compatible with who wants to stay here, too. And I was having no luck in the dating department. So, yes, despite the gastrointestinal distress our first unintentional date put me through, I decided to buck up and let him have my phone number when he asked for it. Then, in a celebration of optimism (however misguided), I said yes when he asked me out the following weekend to a Red Sox game in Boston.

Keith was a die-hard Red Sox fan. I guess this is why I'm reminded of him now.

Well, that and the jealousy thing.

We went to the Sox game and he thought I was hitting on the mascot. Yes, that fluffy, green guy. I asked Keith to take my picture with him, and he obliged, but spent the rest of the night asking how me and Wally the Green Monster planned to spend our honeymoon and wondering aloud if our babies would be green. You would think I made out with his Muppet-face the way Keith went on about it.

A few weeks later, we were at the mall in Hyannis when I bumped into Olivia, a friend of mine from high school. She was with her husband, Joe, who had their brand-new baby strapped to his chest in a Bjorn. We chatted outside of Target for all of three minutes, tops, and when we walked away Keith said, "He's lucky I didn't kick his ass."

"Huh? Why?" I wondered.

"You didn't notice the way he was looking at you?"

"He was *wearing* his child! He barely said two words to us," I replied.

"He was eye-banging you."

"Please, Keith. That's ridiculous."

It became a trend. Anywhere we went, he'd contrive an indiscretion from his hyper-active imagination. It became so annoying that I was willing to break up with him over it, only I really didn't know how, given the fact that he worked with my father and had the unofficial Chief Andrews Seal of Approval.

COVID saved the day the following spring, when all of a sudden we were forced into solitude. I told Keith I didn't think we should compromise our respective families by intermingling, and eventually we fizzled out enough that I was able to break it off. Then, I got Zoloft (the fur baby, not the drug) as an antidote, under the pretense that I would remain single forever.

To be clear, I do not miss Keith, but sometimes I miss the *idea* of him, the security of knowing that someone is yours. This early stage flirting business has never been my strong suit. So I blame myself for developing whatever little crush this was on Brady – no, I blame *him*, for invading first my home life and then my work life with his clothes off and muscular body on display. I am not a jealous person by nature, I remind myself, and Brady was absolutely never mine, despite any cuteness we might have shared in his apartment last night. If he's out there making out with random strangers, that's his prerogative. Nothing I need to concern myself with. Envy is an ugly trait, and any guy who's going to bring that out in me is definitely not someone I need to waste my time on.

With this in mind, I inhale one more time, buck up, and head back to the party.

CHAPTER ELEVEN

BRADY

I swear to God, if Miranda doesn't get off my ass, I am literally going to scream.

I see Gretchen emerge from the office and head straight for an available pole. She does a basic spin, followed by some move where she kicks her legs in the air in a rainbow, and then begins to dance alongside the pole, feet planted firmly on the ground. She's noticeably shorter now – *ah*, I realize, *no shoes*. I smile at her, but between the darkness and the noise, I don't think she sees me.

Meanwhile, I choose to dance with the bride, who I figure is the safest bet in the whole place. Arrow shoots daggers at me from across the room, as if I myself tripped her employee and caused the scene on the stage, but we exchange no words. Miranda tries to turn me around so that I can pay attention to her, but all I am watching is the glow-in-the-dark clock on the wall, counting down the minutes until this particularly hellish nightmare can come to a close.

Finally, after hoisting the bride up into an aerial hoop with Max and pretending to worship her à la Cleopatra, our dance crew's last song comes on, and with less than three minutes until my inevitable departure, I attempt to make my way back to Gretchen.

I'm steps away from her when Miranda pops up in front of me like a bad game of Peek-a-Boo. "Hey, lover," she slurs. Despite being cut off from Jell-O shots, I've seen her take at least two more airplane bottles of alcohol out of the bras of her friends.

"Nope," I say. "I'm just the entertainment."

"Tell it to the girl-boner I've been nursing all night."

Gross. I shake my head and try to circumvent her.

"Brady, will you *please* just come outside and talk to me?" she pleads. "Two minutes. That's all I'm asking."

"My God," I say. "Miranda, what part of *no* don't you understand? We have nothing to talk about. All conversations came to an abrupt halt when you cheated on me and disappeared. That was your doing, not mine," I remind her.

"Jesus, Brady, I don't want to do this here!" she says, exasperated but also definitely wasted. "It's not what you thought it was."

"So, you weren't trying to sleep your way to the top?"

"No!" she cries. "I mean, yes, I wanted the job, but it all got blown out of proportion," she says.

"See? And you got even more than you bargained for! You got yourself a whole new life on the west coast! But please don't come back here and try to pick up where we left off."

"Brady," she begins, placing her hands on my wrists.

I pull away. "No," I say, firmly. "It's fine, like I said. I don't care. Please, just let it go, sober up, and uh, you know. Have a good life."

Her expression morphs, and now she's smiling. "It's fine, Brady. Besides, I'm engaged."

What? I wonder. She holds up her left hand, and sure enough, there's a diamond. "Then why are you out here trying to hook up with me?"

Miranda shrugs, then tips sideways a little. I reach out to keep her from falling over. "Like I said, I just wanted to explain myself to you. I thought maybe if I reminded you how good we were together, you'd at least hear me out," she says.

How good *we were? Is this girl kidding?* It doesn't matter, because the song ends, and it's time for us to go. "Not tonight, Miranda. I've got to run. Good luck to you," I say. I turn towards the door, wishing I'd had the chance to talk to Gretchen, but when I turn back to see where she is, she's busily helping the guys from Three Fools set up a buffet of what appears to be ballpark snacks on the catering table.

This time, I adhere to the standard protocol of not darting out into the parking lot in my skivvies. I follow the guys to the back, where Big Mike delivers us each a pair of shorts and a t-shirt, and we head out as a pack into the parking lot. Arrow doesn't follow us out right away. It takes her an extra 15 minutes to emerge into the lot, but when she does, she hands Mike a large yellow envelope and thanks us for our time. "Almost ten grand," she says. "You guys should be proud; I think that's a record."

Mike and Max work together to split the money ten ways on the back of Mike's tailgate, while the rest of us just hang around, checking our phones and generally staying quiet so as not to cause a disturbance in the neighborhood this late at night. *The soundproofing on the converted warehouse is really incredible,* I think. From out in the parking lot, you really can't hear a thing, whereas inside the building, one's eardrums are assaulted with a constant, heavy thump of bass.

When all is said and done, we each walk away $955 in cash, and by the time Big Mike gets me back to my apartment, I only have one thing left on my mind.

I make myself a bowl of ramen soup and wait to hear the jingle of late-night keys in the lock. When I finally hear Gretchen coming down the hall, I carefully open my door and cough three times so I won't startle her.

She looks at me, pushing her own door open, lugging the same tote bag from last night. "Hey," she says.

"What's up?" I ask quietly, so as not to disrupt the precious slumber of the zoo creature down the hall.

"Nothing," she replies.

"I'd really like to talk to you, if you're not too tired," I offer. The words sound borderline pathetic, but they're genuine, and I think she can sense that.

She eyeballs me, pursing her lips in thought. Then, Gretchen tilts her head to the side and says, "Got any snacks?"

"Nothing great," I respond honestly, "But I make the world's best ramen soup, and I would be honored if you'd let me whip up a package for you."

She nods, sets the bag inside her door, and follows me back to my place. I shut the door behind her, grab a package of ramen out of the pantry, and measure out two cups of water into my saucepan, which is still on the stove.

"Nothing gives off a summer vibe quite like a late night bowl of noodle soup, am I right?" I joke.

"Brady," she says, her voice softer than it was last night. "Why am I here?"

"For the fine culinary experience?" I joke.

"I mean it. Why'd you wait up?"

"I, uh. I wanted to talk to you. About that woman."

"You mean, the love of your life?"

"Oh my God, nothing could be further from reality. Also, I had some questions for you – namely, since when are you a pole dancer? I thought your job was glorified shot girl."

"Cherry called in sick," she explains. "What about you?"

"Huh?" I ask.

"Well, you're one to talk – I thought last night was a one-time thing for you? What – you had a taste of the limelight and now you're addicted?"

I laugh. "Not the limelight, nope."

"The money?"

I shrug, hoping my honesty won't make me seem soft or desperate or worse, entirely financially unstable. But Gretchen just nods in silent understanding. "Okay, so we've got several items on the late-night chat agenda, then," I say. "I'd like to start with Miranda, if it's all the same to you."

"Sure thing," she says. "Shoot."

"I dated her back in college."

"Lucky you."

"Then she slept with someone else behind my back."

"Oh," Gretchen says, her expression changing from Himalayan-salty to cloudy with a chance of ramen noodles.

"And as if that wasn't enough, the *wife* of the person she cheated on me with decided to set fire to the sorority house where she was living."

"Holy shit! Seriously?"

"Mm hmm," I nod. "Which resulted in Miranda moving across the country, only to show up at my place of employ all these years later."

"You mean, *my* place of employ?"

"Correct."

"Wow. That is not what I thought."

"What did you think, exactly?"

"Old girlfriend, sure. Reminded of all the good times she had with you, on account of getting a glimpse of you in your little baseball outfit."

"You make it sound like I'm a little league champion."

"You know what I mean."

"Well, as explained, you had it all wrong. And I kind of knew that you were harboring some misguided notions, which was why I wanted to clear the air."

"You don't owe me anything, though," she points out.

"I know. But I wanted you to know."

"Okay. So now I know." She smiles, and I feel a little better.

"I just don't want you hating me again."

"Brady, it would be really hard to hate you now that I've seen your bare ass cheeks."

I feel the heat rise up into my face. "Thank you for reminding me."

"Okay. My turn for a question."

"Please." I motion to her with my wooden spoon. Then, I stir her soup. *Almost ready.*

"Are you planning on stripping every night?"

"Truth?" I ask. "I think I've found my heart's passion, the art of the full-body shave." I laugh. "No. I honestly didn't plan to do more than just one night – yesterday should have been my first and last time visiting you at work."

"So, what brought you back?"

"Opportunity knocked. I mean, you really can't hate on a place that's doling out cash like that. Also, I've got bills to pay, and much to my surprise, money does not grow on trees."

"I still can't believe your father kicked you out of your house."

"Yeah, he's a delight," I agree, pouring her soup into a bowl. I grab a spoon and a fork from the utensil drawer and carry the meal over to Luis' dining room table. "Here. Have a seat." She does. Gretchen wraps a long braid of noodles around her fork and blows carefully before taking a bite.

"This actually hits the spot," she says once she swallows. "Thank you."

"House special," I reply. "Anyway, to your point, it was all just stupid family drama. I didn't want to work for Diamond Excelsior long term, anyway. Being an assistant manager at a country club restaurant is not exactly my dream job."

"No, I can see that," she deadpans. "Swinging around your sperm worm for the masses, though. Life goals, am I right?" She takes a sip of the broth from her spoon.

I grin. "Last night was actually a new low for me. That was the first time I'd ever done that."

"Same. It's one thing to hand out shots, but it's quite another to swing around on a pole all night long. I may have given myself vertigo at one point. I'm not exactly what you'd call a natural."

"Think you'll do it again?" I ask.

She considers the question. "Depends."

"On?"

"How bad you think I was." Her expression challenges me.

"You were great," I reply, meaning it.

"Stop it." She takes another bite of noodles, smirking.

"You were," I insist. "You were beautiful."

"Were?"

"Are."

An awkward silence descends upon the space between us. She's smiling into her soup, and a hearty slurp punctuates the otherwise possibly sensual moment.

"What about you?" she asks. "You think you'll keep stripping?"

"Depends," I say, echoing her answer.

"On what?"

"My grocery situation in a few weeks?"

"That's fair."

"I'm sure this can't be what you dreamed you'd be doing, though, right? Or maybe I'm wrong," I surmise. "Did you study fashion design in college? Because your getup these past few times I've seen you has really been some red-carpet business."

"Ha," she says. "Cute, Brady. No, actually my degree is in Elementary Education."

"Stop lying. You've got a teaching degree? What were you doing working as a waitress?"

"I'm still in grad school. I've got one more class and my field work left, and then I'll be done."

"So, help me understand something. Is this what teachers do to make ends meet? Good lord. All my childhood fantasies about Miss Johnson are coming true right before my very eyes."

"Who's Miss Johnson?"

"She was my sixth grade teacher. I had the biggest crush on her. I used to keep my sixth grade class photo on my nightstand."

Gretchen coughs, almost spitting out a mouthful of soup. "Gross." But there's a light in her eyes when she says it, and it intoxicates me a little bit. I feel a shift in my shorts. "And, no, as I *said*, I'm not a teacher yet. Just a waitress. Well, I used to be. Now I'm just – a glorified shot girl, I guess."

"In mermaid panties."

"Not tonight, thank you very much! Besides, who are you to judge, Zorro?"

"No judgement here. On both nights, you looked... convincing," I say.

"Careful," she warns me. "If you insult me, I might just have to spill this hot bowl of soup all over your junk. It's kind of my specialty, you know. Falling down? Spilling things?"

"That's fair warning, thank you. Let's just say, last night you had the Ariel look down. I mean, all the way down to the hair." I restrain myself from touching it again. "I never saw a mermaid in fishnets, but you definitely pulled it off. And then tonight, well." I pause, intent on *not* delivering a commentary about her sex appeal. "Let's just say that any man who gets to be with you is incredibly lucky."

Her lips purse together. "Thank you," she says, looking down at her soup bowl. "That's very sweet. If we're doling out compliments, I suppose I can share that I think you're a great dancer."

"Thanks. I'll add it to my resumé. All the marketing firms will be so impressed."

"Is that what you studied? Marketing?"

"Economics," I clarify. "I think money is interesting."

"Interesting? That's an odd way to describe it."

"Think about it," I say. "How whole economies thrive based on particular industries. Like here on the Cape. We're a tourist economy. That's why I can't find a job. Supply and demand, you know? The jobs are in high demand but the J-1s come in from all over the world to fill those jobs. So, high demand is met by an even higher supply."

"I'm glad you didn't lead with this lecture in your baseball uniform. The ladies might not have been quite so worked up."

I laugh. "Sorry to bore you."

"I'm teasing you, Brady. I understand completely. I tried so hard to find a job that was more along the straight and narrow, but everything was gone by the time you – um, your *dad* – fired me. I mean, well, not *everything*. But I wasn't going to match my Diamond Excelsior tips over at the bowling alley."

"Exactly."

"You may just be the smartest male stripper I've ever met." Gretchen smiles at me.

"You know a lot of male strippers?" I ask.

She shakes her head, but she's got that smug look on her face again. The sight of those lips smirking like that takes me back to our dance last night in the darkness of the pole studio. But I'm an awkward mess – just a jumble of adrenaline, exhaustion, and cheap ramen. The few drinks I had at the studio wore off a long time ago and I've got no social lubrication to replace them with. Nervous that the conversation might hit a lull, I suddenly remember I wanted to ask Gretchen something else. "Hey, I was wondering – how come that girl – Arrow?"

"My boss?"

"Yeah, her. What did she think was unacceptable about your name?"

"I guess it wasn't on-brand for her studio. All the girls have fake names. She calls them Cherry and Saffron and Indigo. Instead of their real names, which are Cheryl, Maria, and Kim."

"What's Arrow's real name?"

"Funny. I have no idea. I always just assumed it was Arrow."

"Well, I like the name Gretchen."

"Thanks," she replies. "I've never had a problem with it. It's my grandmother's name."

"It's pretty."

She smiles, setting her fork and spoon down into the bowl and pushing the chair away from the table. "So, you working tomorrow?"

"No. I don't think so, anyway. I only snagged tonight's gig earlier this afternoon."

She nods. "I have tow lot in the afternoon."

"What's that?"

"It's where I hang out so the girls who were too drunk to drive can come pick up their cars."

"I thought they came in on a party bus."

"Three of them met the bus there. So I've got those ones to wait for."

"Is there another party tomorrow night?"

"Yeah," she confirms. "Not as crazy as tonight. Sunday night parties tend to be a little more tame."

"Would you like some company?"

"At the party?"

"No," I laugh. "At the car pickup thing. I could hang out with you if you didn't want to just sit there alone."

Gretchen smiles at me with her eyes. "It's your life, Brady. I can think of like a million things I would rather do on a Sunday in the summer than wait for three hungover girls to come get their cars."

"You really know how to sell it."

"I'm happy to have you there. But no pressure if you change your mind," she clarifies. "Now, at the risk of never seeing you in a thong again, I'm going to head home." She stretches her arms up over her head, revealing a sliver of her stomach. "I'm exhausted, and my ass hurts. I need to take some Aleve."

Inside, I feel a pang of panic. *I don't want her to leave,* I realize. "Did you *want* to see me in a thong again?" I ask, then immediately regret it. *What the fuck? This is your A-game?*

"I'll be honest. The thong didn't do it for me. I mean, you've got a nice –" here, she waves at my posterior, "but I'm not really into guys wearing thongs."

My mouth develops a mind of its own by making things worse as I blurt out, "So, what *are* you into? Boxers? Briefs? Commando?"

She looks up at me. I can't help but notice how short she is without those stupid heels on. "I'm into dancing," she says, giving me a look that suggests she could be into a whole lot more than *just* dancing. "Like I said, you're an excellent dancer, Brady."

I feel my cheeks get round as my mouth curves up. "Maybe we'll dance together again sometime," I say.

"I'd like that – but not for money."

"No, not for money."

"I'd rather you be dressed."

I laugh. "Me, too."

"Just one last question, and then I should really go."

Please don't go. "Shoot."

"How come you took off the other day? After I broke your mask? Was that, like, the moment you realized it was me?"

I let go of the breath I didn't realize I was holding. "If we're being honest, yeah. The mask was pretty hard to see through. I thought the shot girl *looked* like you, but it was totally out of context. I recognized the fishnets from the day you came here to yell at me. And the hair color – because, well, I mean that's kind of your signature thing."

She nods, thinking. "So, why did you leave so suddenly?"

I shrug. "I was embarrassed. I wasn't sure it was you, because you still had a mask on. But I thought it might be. And you could see me. Like, *all* of me." I take a deep breath. She stands there, waiting for me to continue. "Also, I thought you hated me."

"That's fair, I suppose," she admits.

"So I was scared that if it was you, and you saw my face, you'd freak out."

"So you freaked out before I could?"

I chuckle. "Basically."

I don't say the rest of what's spinning around inside my head. I don't tell her that I can't remember the last time I felt the kind of instant chemistry I found with her hands in mine, the way our bodies could have fit together like a glove, if we'd let them. How vulnerable I was, wearing basically nothing, shaved from the neck down, slathered in coconut oil, my pride and my anatomy on full display. And how every time I looked at her and she looked back, even through the stupid snake mask, it felt as if we connected on a visceral level. At least, that was how I experienced it. I don't tell her that the memory of it all kept me up the entire night and almost resulted in the embarrassment of sticky sheets. Instead, I stay silent. Staring at her. Searching her face for clues about any impressions our encounter left on *her*.

I take a step towards her, slowly, tentatively. My gaze travels down to her mouth, and I notice the way her top teeth chew on the flesh of her juicy lower lip.

"Gretchen," I whisper.

But she takes a step backward.

"I, um. I should probably go," she mumbles.

I freeze. "Okay," I reply begrudgingly. I can't read the moment. I feel flooded – like I could just float away, and she looks at me like maybe she feels something similar – but, she's leaving. Aching for her to stay, I spit out more words.

Anything to keep her here another minute. "I'll come to the car thing with you tomorrow," I say. "What time?"

"Oh. Um. I usually get there around three. Tomorrow, I have brunch in the morning with my parents and then I'll probably head straight there."

"Okay. I'll meet you."

"Sure," she nods.

"I scream inside my head. *Sweet Jesus! You are the worst with women! Do something hot, for fuck's sake!* "Uh, Gretch?"

"Hm?"

I grab a pen out of the junk drawer in the kitchen, click it, and take her by the hand. I'm not sure what comes over me as I hold her, palm side up, and press the pen into her skin. "IOU 1 dance," I write. She watches me, amused. I feel the warmth of her hand in mine. I lift her palm to my face and press my lips against it.

When I let her go, she looks at her hand. She blows out a breath – this is more than just an exhale. I've left an impression on her. I can tell. Then, she smiles – one of those expressions that transcends just her mouth and sets her whole face aglow. Without words, she burns her image into my brain, letting herself out of my apartment but locking herself in my thoughts. "See you tomorrow," she whispers.

"Bye," I reply, biting back a grin.

Fuck, I think. *I've got it bad.*

CHAPTER TWELVE

GRETCHEN

Okay, okay. You're fine. Just breathe.

Holy shit.

Was Brady Hawthorne really looking at you like he wanted to take you?

Fuuuuck.

I study the palm of my hand. That's, like, probably the *cutest* thing any guy has ever done – writing on my hand like we're in the fifth grade. And what the hell? He's *smart* too? All that talk of economics... from a *stripper*? Although, it was just twice, really. I mean, this is not his *intended* line of work.... Still, the boy can *move*. He was sexy as Zorro, but the group dance with the baseball getup was about all that I could handle.

You asshole! Why did you leave? It was pretty fucking obvious he wanted you to stick around, at least for a little while. What were you thinking?

I inhale, hold my breath, and wait for my heartbeat to slow down. I'm tingly all over. I'm supposed to hate Brady Hawthorne. But, first I found out that he *didn't* actually fire me, and in fact, he *also* got fired (which – sidebar – 100% *had* to be my fault), and then, just when I wanted to write him off as a complete douchebag for hooking up with some random chick in front of me, I find out *she threw herself at him* and *she also cheated on him* way back when. Okay, and so then, I'm like *it's fine, whatever, we can co-exist as neighbors who occasionally work together,* but he goes and feeds me ramen, tells me I'm beautiful, and declares his intentions on my palm.

And, let's not forget the princess carry.

Okay. Okay! I like him. Whatever. It's fine. I can be cool about it.

I'm about to head into the bathroom to wash my face when I hear a knock. It's a light tap, really, but my heart stops, because I know it can only be one person.

I go to the door, my entire stomach lodged in my throat. I open it, trying to keep myself from trembling.

"What's up?" I say, thinking maybe I left something behind at his place. I scramble to consider what I had on me over there. "Did I, uh, forget something?"

"No," he says, quietly. "I did."

Then, he places his forefinger and his middle finger just under my chin and gently tilts my face up towards his. "May I?" he asks.

I'm paralyzed. Things like this don't happen to girls like me. I can't even speak. I just nod, ever so slightly.

His kiss takes my breath away. He closes his eyes and leans, slowly, into me. When I feel his lips on mine, they're soft, moist, full and delicious. His hand slides around to the hairline at the back of my neck, and as he pulls me in closer to him, his long, thick fingers weave their way into my messy waves. He massages the back of my head with the calloused pads of his fingertips. His tongue parts my mouth and he tastes me, tentative at first, then hungrily. As if I'm a decadent dessert, he revels in the meeting of our taste buds with a soft, appreciative moan. I'm instantly overcome with a combination of exhaustion and elation, in much the same way as a triathlon competitor must feel when approaching a long-awaited finish line. Finally, he seals the moment with a soft bite of my lower lip and a single brush of his nose against mine.

Brady exhales, untangles his hand from my hair, and runs his fingers down my cheek. "I'm sorry. I just –" he begins.

"Don't be," I say. "Sorry, I mean. That was –"

"Mmm," he breathes. "Yeah, it was." He lightly puts his lips to my forehead and lingers there for a second. "Goodnight, Gretchen," he whispers.

"'Night, Brady," I reply.

I wait until he's all the way inside to close my door.

CHAPTER THIRTEEN

BRADY

I sleep surprisingly well that night.

In fact, I wake up with a new lease on life. I'm a badass! I grew a pair! I went for what I wanted and it was spectacular!

Today, I get to meet her at the studio for the tow yard thing and to spend some time together in the daylight with clothes on, like normal people.

I feel *great*. I head out for a run, go to the bank to make a huge deposit in my checking account, and hit the fitness trail at the park, where I bang out push-ups, crunches and chin-ups. I have no idea if I'll keep dancing or not, but keeping my body in shape is important to me either way, if for no other reason than to acquire the endorphins I'm chasing.

I go home, shower, change, eat. Later in the morning, I get another call from Steve checking in. He says he heard good things, and while he doesn't have anything immediate for me gig-wise, if I want him to, he'll gladly keep me on the roster for upcoming stuff. Given the fact that I was able to accumulate over $1,800 in two days, I tell him I'd be happy to have him consider me for future work.

I run to the grocery store; no more of this popcorn and ramen bullshit if I might be having company in the near future. I get real food, stuff I can cook, produce, meat, and seafood from the perimeter of the store that doesn't come in cans or freezer bags. Items with expiration dates. I spend over a hundred dollars, something I haven't had the luxury of doing since I lived here. Also, I buy a jar of pickles, just so I can say that I have my own now.

At 2:30, I leave to head up to Cosmo. It's a gorgeous day out; I feel bad that Gretchen has to spend it holed up in a dark warehouse. Maybe tomorrow, she'd like to hit the beach with me. *I'll ask her*, I decide.

There are four cars in the parking lot when I arrive. One of them, I've come to know, is Gretchen's ridiculous little Ford Fiesta. There's also a Lexus, a BMW, and an Acura in the lot. Those cars are all gleaming white, reminiscent of new veneers in the mouths of wealthy summer people, lined up all neatly on the gravel like that.

I park my car next to Gretchen's and head to the door. When I open it, music spills out, wrapping around me like a blanket. It's a slow song that I don't recognize, something very reminiscent of Nine Inch Nails' *Closer* but sung by a female voice. "How do you want me?" the breathy voice asks. The music and the darkness work in tandem to make me feel like I'm entering some kind of sex den. Which is right on trend for me in my mesh shorts, flip flops, and Hog Island Beer Company t-shirt.

When my eyes adjust to the light (or lack thereof), I spot Gretchen swinging from a pole, attached by long, black silks. The silks come down in a pair, and she has wrapped them around her waist in some kind of knot so that, with one foot against the pole, she can use languid, deliberate movements to hoist herself into a fully reclined position. Straight as an arrow, perpendicular to the pole, she lifts one leg up and grabs it with her free arm, and she slowly spins in a beautiful circle, silks careening off her back like something out of a dream.

My. God.

"Oh, hey!" she calls.

I walk towards her as she maneuvers her way out of the silks, landing as gracefully as a bird coming down from the sky, all wings and feathers and floating.

"Don't stop on my account," I say. "That looked really cool."

"Yeah, they're fun," she replies. "Pole silks – but they'll burn your skin something fierce if you're not careful." Gretchen shows me the inside of her forearm, where she has what looks an awful lot like a rug burn.

"Ouch," I say. "That just happened today?"

"Uh huh. I'm still learning," she smiles, sheepishly.

Gretchen grabs a bottle of water that's in the floor over by the wall of mirrors. The light shines neon purple all around us. "Want some?" she asks, holding the bottle out to me.

"I'm good, thanks," I say. "What time did you get here?"

"About 30 minutes ago," she replies.

"How was your brunch?" I ask.

"It was great, thanks. How was your morning?"

"Busy, but good. Got some errands done." I try to sound nonchalant, as if I didn't spend all morning thinking about this moment right now.

"So, are you working the party tonight?"

"Nope. But Steve – he's the guy who organizes everything – he said he'd keep me on the roster for the future."

"That's nice. I honestly can't imagine keeping up the pace of doing this beyond the summer. It's a lot."

"Well, sure, I mean especially if you're dancing all night long. I only have to humiliate myself for under an hour. You guys have to do this all night, right?"

"Not exactly. The way it works is the group of girls arrives and first we let them dance and hang out, just warm up, give them some shots to get them to relax, you know? Then we do a pole dancing lesson. That's actually really easy because we show them a move and they practice it over and over for each other."

"That doesn't get boring?"

"Well, sure, for us it does, but not for the girls. Most of them have never been on a pole before, so they feel like deviants even going near one. It takes a lot of time just for them to learn how to walk around a pole. Some of them have what Arrow calls 'elephant feet,' like, their step is just so hard that nothing looks sexy. So, we try to teach them how to walk, for starters."

"Show me," I say.

She laughs. "You want me to show *you* how to walk around the pole?"

"I do."

"You've got no shame, huh?"

"Please. You've seen me in a baseball thong. Pretty sure nothing's off limits with us."

This makes her snicker, and the sound does something to my chest cavity.

"So, come on." I grin. "Let's see if I've got elephant feet."

"Okay," she replies, shaking her head. "First things first. Come stand here." She leads me over to a different pole and directs me to stand in front of her. The pole is to my left. She taps on my left shoulder. "This is your inside arm."

"Inside arm," I repeat, raising my left hand.

"Good. And this," she taps my right shoulder, "is your outside arm."

"Got it."

"So, scooch over a sec." I shuffle to the side. "When you walk, you want to hold the pole up high using your inside arm. Follow the natural flow of your body, which means that as you walk forward, you'll automatically be moving counter-clockwise, like this." Gretchen takes a few steps around the pole. "Now, watch me."

Gladly, I think.

"I've got good posture, right? Head high, shoulders back, and be sure you make eye contact with the audience."

I try to imitate her posture, which makes her giggle.

"Now, for the feet. With toes pointed, you'll start with your inside foot and take a step. Then, you drag your outside foot behind you until it comes up in front, and again, toes pointed, slowly step into a walk. Your hips need to sway dramatically and your free hand should do sexy stuff, like trace up your side or run through your hair – not that you have long hair, but you know what I mean," she continues. "So, it would look like this."

Gretchen pulls a remote control out of her sports bra and points it at the stereo, turning the music up a few notches. It's *Body Party* by Ciara (another great throwback). The slow, sexy R&B rhythm reverberates through the space, charging the moment with electricity and heat. She waits for the beat to drop and then walks exactly as she described, with her hips alternating out into each step, her toes dragging, her head swaying so her hair cascades down her back, and her free hand snaking its way up her torso, over her right breast, and into her tousled locks.

"God damn," I cannot help but say.

This gets her chuckling again. She hops away from the pole and says, "Okay, big talker, Your turn now."

"I can't do that. First of all, I'm a guy. Secondly, that was *hot.* I'm, like, lukewarm at best."

"Just try it," she encourages me. "Remember, you asked me for this."

I begin to walk, letting my performance exude the humor of the moment. Gretchen's laughter is an elixir to my soul, so I play it up even more dramatically, and she hollers and catcalls at me in response. "Woo! Yeah, hottie!" she yells.

Finally, I stop walking and attempt to catch my breath from laughing so hard. "Who knew just *walking* could be so challenging?"

"See? So, you can imagine how the girls who come here take forever practicing it," she explains. "Plus, they're in groups, like three or four of them sharing one pole, so they all have to take turns, which sucks up a lot of time."

"Gotcha. So, then what happens?"

"Well, then we teach them the most basic spin, which is called a dip turn. Ever heard of it?"

"Can't say that I have."

"Okay, so watch me first." She approaches the pole again, in the same spot as before. "Inside arm high, outside arm reaches across to grab the pole. Take one step with your inside foot, and then lift your outside leg and let it trace a nice big circle around the pole. Next, lift the inside foot and step it back through the space between your body and the pole. It's simple and pretty, and you can make it very dramatic with the leg extension." She does the spin once, twice. "Nice, right?" she asks, when she's done.

"Very nice," I agree.

"You think you can do it?"

"No. But I'll give it a whirl."

Gretchen steps back, and I approach the pole. I follow the steps she showed me and inadvertently end up tripping over my own foot. I try again. Still no good. "Well, it's confirmed. I think I have elephant feet."

"Definitely not. It's not easy," she explains. "Lots of people assume it's simple, but so much of it is core strength and honestly, like, basic gymnastics."

"Okay, but it makes me feel like a clown, so I think we should stop now, before I make myself look any worse."

"I think you look cute, for what it's worth," she says. I'm pretty sure she's blushing but it's too dark to be 100% certain.

"If elephants are your thing, then sure. I'm killing it."

"Fine. Let's be fair about this. It can't be much easier dancing the way you do. So, go ahead. You teach me a move now."

At this, I can't help but snort. "Really? You want *me* to teach *you*?"

"Well, not the *stripping* part, obviously. But one of the dance moves, sure. Why not? You don't think I can hack it?"

"Oh, I'm sure you could," I say. "You've got plenty of upper body strength. Which move do you want to learn?"

"Teach me that thing that looks like you're doing the worm."

"The worm? You mean a dolphin dive?"

"Yeah! The one on the ground. I think that one's my favorite."

"Ha," I reply. "You and every woman in America."

She stretches out her arms like she's preparing to lift something heavy. "So, how does it go?"

I can't believe we're doing this, I think. *This is not at all what I expected.* "Can you do a push-up?" I ask.

"I think so. Haven't tried in a long time."

"Okay, so get down on the floor and try to do, like, five push-ups."

"The guy ones or the girl ones?"

"The guy ones."

Gretchen drops down to all fours and then springs out into a plank position. She lowers her body carefully and then pushes up with her arms. Twice, three times, four. By the fifth one, she's wobbling. "That's hard."

"You get used to it after a while. Takes practice. But, you see how all the strength really comes from your shoulders, your back and your arms?"

"Yeah," she nods.

"Okay, now we're going to do a yoga pose. This is called a cobra stretch." I get down next to her and lay on the ground, flat on my belly, then push my upper half up in an arch, facing my chin up to the ceiling.

"I know that move," she says. She lies beside me and mirrors my position.

"So, this is our ending pose for a dolphin dive. Essentially, you jump up first, just a little hop, and then sort of swan dive onto the ground. You want to land in push up position, but your front half lands first and your legs and feet follow. By the time your legs hit the ground, you're pushing up your upper half in a cobra stretch. It gives the illusion of your whole body having made a big curve," I explain. "You want to try it?"

"Sure," she grins. She shuffles back and forth in time with the music and then does a jump but lands hard, almost like the dry-earth equivalent of a belly-flop.

"Shit! Are you okay?" I ask.

She cackles. "That was so bad!"

I crouch beside her. "Did you hurt yourself?"

"No, I'm fine," she laughs. "I just can't believe how not graceful that was."

"That's why it's a guy's move. I think we should just stick to what we're good at. No more dolphin dives for you."

"Deal. And no more dip turns for you," she retorts, grinning.

I stand up and hold out a hand to pull her up off the floor, just as the music shifts to another old school song, *Pony,* by Ginuwine. According to the Skeeve, it's a strip club anthem.

The music overtakes me – it's *such* a sexy song, and in the darkness, all alone, there's an unmistakable opportunity that I don't want to laugh off awkwardly. Instead, I grab a folding chair from against the wall and flip it open. Then, I look at Gretchen and begin to slow-walk over to her, giving her smoldering bedroom eyes. Her amused smile vanishes, replaced by something very different – still a smile, but also, an understanding. There's a vibe here – dark plus music plus solitude. No eyes to watch us. No embarrassing spectators throwing money at me. Just us, and the involuntary way my hips move to the bass line as I strut towards her. No question about it: I owe her one dance, and I'm here to see that she collects it. She purses her lips together as I take her by the hand and lead her to the open chair, gently pushing her body down so she sits in it.

With the beat, I trace two fingers across her shoulder blades as I walk around the back of the chair. As I emerge on the other side, I place her hand on my stomach and push it towards my chest, revealing the bare skin of my abs. Her eyes light up, and I take one step back and pull my T-shirt up over my head, tossing it to the side. Next, I dolphin dive right on top of her, holding the sides of the chair for the pushup motion instead of placing my hands on the ground, my nose close enough to her chest and neck that I can smell the faintest bit of sweat from her workout mixed with the soap from her shower. I push back off the chair and I'm on the floor, down on one knee, sliding my hip through my arms onto the ground then pushing back up and doing another dolphin dive as she watches with what appears to be building anticipation. I crawl across the floor in front of her and arch backwards so I'm lying with my back to the ground. My pelvis juts out in a series of smooth hip thrusts from the floor, arms raised over my head, facing her as if I'm lying in a bed while she sits at the foot of it.

Next, I pop up and casually walk towards Gretchen until I am completely straddling her in the folding chair. I grab the back of the chair with one hand so that I can work my hips on top of her and then – one, two, three times, I wind them in a circle – my inevitable erection throbbing noticeably through my mesh shorts. I snake my arms around her neck and lean forward into her as if I'm going to kiss her collarbone – but it's just a dance, and I am *relishing* in how good it feels to tease her, so I keep my lips to myself and instead I just breathe on her skin, still grinding into her lap for a few counts more. Next, I retreat, standing back up and pulling her to her feet. I lift her hands until her arms are over her head, and I slide my palms down both sides of her body until I get to her thighs. One quick bend at the knees and – *boom* – she's up in the air with her legs wrapped around my waist. I bend down with her in my arms, lean down to touch the floor with one hand so the she's almost parallel to the ground, and then –

"Um, helloooo," I hear, the annoying screech of a rich woman who can't be bothered to *just wait a second while I finish seducing this woman, please.*

I come back to standing and carefully set Gretchen down. The moment is gone – as fragile as a bubble, popped in the wind.

"I'm here for my car," the woman says, wearing sunglasses even though it's as dark as night in this space. "That's my Lexus outside." She flips her hair and points to the door.

Gretchen is speechless, likely on account of my wild overtures, so I am left to interact with the loaded Lexus lady. "Yup, be right with you," I say.

I turn towards the wall to adjust myself so as not to be accused by the Lexus-leaser of any lewd (if unintentional) propositioning. "Where are the keys?" I whisper down at Gretchen, still seated in the chair beside me.

She gulps. "Office. Desk."

"I love that I just made you incapable of forming multi-word sentences," I say in her ear.

With a grin, I head to the office, grab the Lexus key off the desk, and bring it to the Interrupter. "Here you go."

"Hey," she says. "You're one of the guys from last night."

"Guilty as charged."

"Brady, right? OMG. My friend, Miranda, told us *all* about you."

I have no idea what she could have said, but I also don't care, seeing as how I was just about to show Gretchen the full ability of my mouth when the SUV queen appeared. "Great," I say.

"So, I guess we'll be seeing you soon," she says.

Huh? Nope. Don't care. "Sure thing," I reply.

"Ohmigod, wait! There's Chloe!" This one waves a hand up in the sky. "Chloe!" she yells. "In here! I'm with Miranda's dancing fuckboy!"

"Excuse me?" I ask.

"No offense," the Interrupter winks at me.

Chloe walks in, looking tore up in oversized flannel pajama pants, a sports bra, and the world's largest sunglasses doing nothing to mask her obvious hangover. "How are you so chipper?" she asks the Interrupter.

"I'm sorry, which car is yours?" I ask.

"I'm the Acura," she says. I leave to get her keys.

"Look, Chloe! It's Miranda's boy," the Interrupter claps.

I shake my head.

"Don't worry, she'll be here soon," the Interrupter says. "I just texted her. She's in an Uber."

"Terrific," I say. "Well, you two are all set, so feel free to head on out. We need to close up here anyway."

"M'kay," the Interrupter replies. "*So* excited we got to see you, though." She reaches out and traces a finger down my forearm.

I pull back and shoot a finger gun at her, like, *hey now, that'll be a hard pass.* "Yup. Same," I reply, the sarcasm dripping off my words like sweat in a sauna.

Chloe and the Interrupter leave and I look at Gretchen, who is busily putting away the folding chair. "Hey," I begin. "I'm not trying to end our time here, but I would really rather not run into Miranda if I can avoid it."

"Ohmigod," she jokes, flipping her hair. "I can't imagine why not."

"Exactly," I reply. "But what are you doing after work tonight?"

"Probably sleeping, Brady. I'm not sure if you know this, but I typically get home pretty late."

"Yes, I'm aware. Well, what about tomorrow? Do you have work tomorrow, also?"

"No. Tomorrow and Tuesday are our two days off."

"Want to go to the beach with me?"

"Depends." She cocks an eyebrow. "Is this a date?"

"I would like it to be, yes."

"Okay. Then, yes. I would like that too."

"I mean, just for clarification, I don't dance like that for just anybody."

"Really?" she laughs. "Because I'm pretty sure that's *exactly* what you do."

"Touché," I reply. I shoot her a wink before leaving. "Tomorrow, then."

"Can't wait," she says.

"Same here," I reply.

I'm pretty sure she means it.

Lord knows I do.

CHAPTER FOURTEEN

GRETCHEN

When I return home after my shift that night, I see a folded note taped to my door. *Here's my number*, it reads, *so we can communicate more efficiently during daylight hours. -B.*

The rest of my day – meaning the space between Brady's impromptu dance lesson at the studio and the end of the night when I find his note – quickly unraveled into a disaster. Still, seeing his scrawl on a piece of paper with my name on it teleports me back to our afternoon together, and the past eight, messy hours at Cosmo somehow evaporate. All that remains are memories of his smile, his touch, his breath on my neck – and suddenly, I'm giddy all over again.

That *dance*.

After Brady high-tailed it out of there, Miranda came to tow lot to pick up her car, and (other than asking if he was there), we didn't say much to each other. I closed up shop once she left and grabbed a few things at the supermarket for a quick dinner, headed back home, ate, and got ready for my night shift.

When I got back to the studio later on, I was surprised to find a very different kind of note inside my locker. It was a Post-It note. From Arrow.

Had to go to Tucson, it read. *Not sure how long I'll be gone. Since Cherry's out, I need you to be in charge of bookings and any office business. All the info is on my laptop. Password is kitten414. Call Cherry if you need anything. You guys can operate without me for a few days until I return. xx, Arrow*

Tucson?

Really?

And she was leaving *me* in charge? Via directions on a Post-It?

Huh.

I called Arrow in an attempt to get actual intel, but it went straight to voicemail. I hung up before leaving a message, hoping someone else would know what this was all about.

When the girls arrived, I showed them the little yellow square of paper. I tried not to panic at the thought of being down to three girls running an entire party.

"Does anyone know why Arrow would go to Tucson?" I asked.

"I think she has family there," Saffron said.

"If anyone would know, it's Cherry," Indigo added. "She's known her the longest."

I debated calling Cherry, since I wasn't sure when she was getting out of the hospital. I shot her a text instead asking her to call me when she had a free second. No sense in worrying her, since she really couldn't do anything to help us in her present state.

"Okay, well, in the meantime, we need to figure out how we're going to get through today." I pulled out the laptop, pressed the power button to turn it on, and waited for the welcome screen to load. Indigo and Saffron sat down by the locker bank seemingly unfazed and before long, be-came engrossed in something on one of their phones. When prompted, I entered the password as instructed. A bunch of windows opened up, and there was a pop-up that read, "Google Chrome did not shut down properly. Restore all pages?" I automatically hit "yes" because that was my brain's knee-jerk reaction, but I was not prepared for the e-mail that appeared on the screen.

And, because I'm human and the subject line was in caps... I couldn't help but read it.

To: cosmopoleitan12@mail.com
From: clientrelations@desertbreeze.com
RE: URGENT

Dear Ms. Cooke,

I hope this e-mail finds you well.

I am writing to follow up on a phone call I placed to you a few minutes ago regarding your sister. Unfortunately, your voice mail box was full so I was unable to leave a message but it is urgent that you get in touch with me. Please note, Jennifer is not hurt or in any danger; her rehabilitation is proceeding well this time around. However, we just received a call from the Tucson Police Department, who informed us that her boyfriend was arrested this morning at home and is being held at the Pima County Detention Center until someone posts bail. Jennifer's daughter was taken by the authorities and risks being placed in an emergency shelter by the Pima County Department of Child Services if they cannot locate a family member to come get her. You are the only person listed as her next of kin, and I'm concerned that since your voice mail is full, you may not have received any messages from them, which is why I'm writing to you.

Please call me as soon as possible so that I can make Jennifer aware of this situation and assure her that you are taking care of it.

Thank you,

Stella Franklin, Client Relations Manager
Desert Breeze Rehabilitation Center

"Um, guys?" I said to Saffron and Indigo.

The girls looked up from Saffron's phone, where a famous pole influencer was demonstrating an advanced move called the Broken Doll on TikTok. "What's up?" Saffron asked.

"Look at this," I said, passing them the laptop. I waited quietly while they read.

"Who's Jennifer?" Indigo asked.

"Arrow's sister, I'm guessing?" I replied. "I know she has a niece. That's the girl in the picture on the fridge."

"Jeez," Saffron said. "That explains her vanishing act."

"She didn't say anything to you guys? Haven't you been working together for a long time?"

"Yeah, but she never gets personal. At least not with us," Saffron added.

Indigo shrugged. "She's only tight with Cherry."

"She never even hangs out with us," Saffron reminded me. "Arrow's not about mixing business with pleasure."

"But she always says 'pole is a sisterhood,'" I argued. "I just assumed she was closed off with me but was friends with you guys."

"Nope." Saffron shook her head. "And I always thought the girl on the fridge was her daughter. That was why I figured she never did the beach days. I assumed she was doing grown-up parenting things."

"No one ever thought to ask her?"

"She's not exactly approachable, Summer." Indigo laughed.

I nodded. "That's true."

"Anyway, I'm guessing she'll be gone for at least a few days," Saffron said. "Judging from that e-mail, it could be even longer than that."

I sighed. "I guess we better get to work, then."

There were a bunch of Excel spreadsheets on the home screen. One was marked with today's date, so I opened it.

"Check it out," I said, and the girls huddled around me. "Looks like 17 people are coming tonight. Not bad; I think we can handle that on our own. The entertainment is a cowboy. Okay, so it's a country theme, I'm guessing. That's fine. There's cowboy boots in here somewhere, right?" I scanned the wall of shoeboxes.

"Yeah," Saffron said. "A few pairs in different sizes. They're up top." She pointed to an upper shelf way above the fridge.

"Cool. I would so much rather wear cowboy boots than regular pole heels," I added.

"Just keep in mind you won't be able to climb in them," Indigo pointed out.

"That's fine. I'll stay mostly on the floor. I can take keys, run the shots and handle the front door, and I can teach the choreo in boots. Should be no sweat."

"What should we do?" Saffron asked.

"If you can cover the music," I said, "that would be great. And Indie, if you can be the hype person when they first get here, to get the party started, that would help too."

"No sweat," she agreed.

"We can all do the money stuff together at the end of the night. But I'll collect the cowboy's cash and put it in the envelope for him when it's time for him to go." I paused to think. "Is there anything I'm missing?"

They shook their heads. "I guess we're lucky it's Sunday," Saffron offered.

"Seriously," Indigo echoed.

The evening was smooth and uneventful, minus a little mishap with Between The Lines (a crazy popular food truck that drove all the way out from Sandwich to cater this event). They got lost on the way to the studio and couldn't find the barely-marked warehouse space, so I ended up jogging down to Route 6, where I waited at the turn for the truck, flagging them down like a lady of the night on the street corner, a human advertisement for The Village People in my little cowgirl vest, booty chaps and ten gallon hat.

Once they arrived and set up the food, the girls gorged themselves on something called the Sloppy Chopstick, which is a sloppy joe made with brisket, grilled pineapple and Asian coleslaw. It's a huge sandwich that smells incredible but ended up all over the ladies as well as the floor. They should have ordered bachelorette bibs to accompany their fine dining choice. In fact, so much barbecue sauce and slaw wound up anywhere but on plates or in mouths that the girls and I stayed late to mop, which is something we usually don't do – but we wanted to make sure we covered all our bases since we had no idea when Arrow would return from her sudden sojourn to Tucson.

I considered trying to call Arrow again after we were done cleaning, but when I checked my phone, I saw that I missed a call from Cherry during the party. I decided not to return her call so late at night since she was probably settling in at home after being discharged from the hospital. Instead, I set a reminder in my phone to try her the next day.

By the time I got home, I was exhausted, but as I walked down the hallway towards my apartment door, I couldn't help but feel butterflies in my stomach. I half expected Brady to pop out from behind his door as I passed by. He didn't, though, which was probably for the best since I didn't want to go to the beach the following morning looking like a zombie.

But the little note taped to my door with his phone number on it was a pretty sweet surprise.

Now, I fumble with the keys, unlock the door and head inside, where I strip off my work clothes and pull on a pair of comfy sweats and a fresh tank top. I head to the bathroom to wash my face and brush my teeth. I plug my phone in and set it on my nightstand on top of the note, testing every ounce of restraint I've got. I close my eyes, but all I can see is Brady's face.

Nope. I'm not that strong.

I punch in the numbers and save Brady's info in my phone. Then, I let my thumbs fly across the flat panel keyboard on the screen.

Hey there. Thanks for your number. Figured you should have mine, too. Hope I'm not waking you.

I hit send, then realize I omitted an important piece of information. *It's Gretchen, btw. Not sure if you tape your number to lots of doors on the reg, but figured I should probably clarify just in case.*

I see three dots appear. My heart begins to race, despite my body's exhaustion.

I heard you come in. Glad you're home safe. Looking forward to our date tomorrow.

I smile. My stomach twists up like a pretzel. I'm not sure how to respond, so my thumbs just hover over the screen.

The dots come up again, and then this message pops up: *And, no. You're the only person whose door I'm leaving my number on.*

Good, I type. Then, I stop before hitting send. I'm tempted to say something flirty but I don't want to come off as thirsty. I delete the word, replace it with *Well, that's nice. I hope you had a nice rest of your day.* That feels more tame, but it's late, and I'm tired, and my conversational skills are maybe not the best at this exact moment.

I'm sorry for leaving earlier, he writes. *I would've liked to hang out longer and finish our dance.*

My lips pucker together. This could very easily become a late night *U up?* text exchange, but I consciously summon up all of my will power. If Brady has dated Miranda, who strikes me as a wild child, maybe that's what he's used to. But I'm not that girl. I mean, sure, my *body* would like me to be that girl, but... he lives right next door, at least for now. The part of my brain that has any common sense at all knows that I'd like to be in a committed relationship with Brady before I hop in the sack with him. Or, at the very least, I should at least go on a date with him first.

Me too. But it's okay. My day sort of unraveled after that anyway, so the timing was probably not the best, I type.

Everything okay? he responds.

Yeah. Arrow went on a sort of impromptu vacation and left me in charge. It was fine, just unexpected.

Gotcha. Well, hopefully tomorrow will be a better day.

I'm counting on it, I reply.

Three more dots appear, then stop, then start again. *10am good?*

Perfect. Looking forward to it, I write back.

Quick question. Are you in bed already?

My heart skips a beat. *I am. Why do you ask?*

The stop and go of the dots on the screen begins again. *I was going to offer you some ice cream. It always makes me feel better when I have a shitty day. I've got cookies and cream and rocky road. Happy to share, if you want in. But if you're too tired, I totally understand. No pressure at all.*

Who am I kidding? It's adorable and sweet, and I'm grinning like a fool. *Ice cream sounds amazing, actually.* I pause, overthinking, as usual. *But, just making sure, this isn't code for something else? Like, when you say cookies and cream you don't actually mean condoms and lube?* I type, then think better of it. I'm about to delete that last part when Zoloft jumps on the bed hungry for snuggles, and the phone fumbles out of my hand onto the mattress. As I pick it back up, I accidentally hit send. I mean, of *course* I do.

Classic Gretchen.

I can hear his laughter through the condo wall.

Nope. Actual ice cream. Be right there.

I climb out of bed, catch a glimpse of myself in the mirror - no makeup, huge sweatpants, a tank top without a bra - I feel like a walking advertisement for freshman year of college. I consider putting on something else but there's a knock. *Here goes nothing,* I tell myself. I pull open the door and my pulse thumps in my ears when I see him standing there, a pint of ice cream in either hand, a grin that brightens as I invite him in.

Brady gives me a peck on the cheek. "You look beautiful," he says.

My insides throb. I feel like a teenager with a crush. My mind flashes back to Eddie Marken, my first boyfriend. I'm transported to the boy-girl dance where we shared our first kiss. It was sloppy and rushed, and he broke my young heart just weeks after when he ended our relationship because school was out for the summer and he was leaving for sleep-away camp. I was "geographically inconvenient," my mother explained when I cried about it later that night. But in the fall, when we returned to school and I started dating Aidan Ralph, I still carried a torch for Eddie, and my heart would race every time I passed him in the hallway.

That racing – the uncontrollable pounding in my chest – it rushes over me like a tidal wave now, here in my apartment well after midnight as Brady stands before me double-fisting frozen treats in an attempt to brighten my day.

"Hi," I say.

"So? Which one?" He holds up the rocky road, then the cookies and cream. "Pick your poison."

"Scoop of each?" I ask.

"Ooh, a girl after my own heart. I'll have the same."

I grab two bowls from the cabinet, and two spoons from the drawer. I set them on the counter and fill each with a generous serving. I gesture at the table. "Wanna sit?" I ask, turning around. Brady looks up, as if he's just woken up from a daze.

"Sure." He pulls out a chair at my modest dining table. "So?" he asks, as I place the bowl in front of him and sit down across from him. "Best and worst part of the day?"

I smile, taking a spoonful of ice cream and savoring it before answering. "You first."

"That's tough. I'd say the worst part was leaving you at your tow lot thing earlier than I'd hoped to." I try to ignore how his voice makes my skin tingle. "And the best part is right now."

"Really?" I ask. "This?"

"Yeah." Brady shrugs. "I like having you next door."

I nod. "I have to agree with that. No offense to Luis, of course."

"Of course," Brady echoes. "Now. Your turn."

"'Kay. I'll start with the worst part. It wasn't exactly *bad*, just weird."

"I'm ready. Take it from the top." Brady licks some rocky road off his spoon, and I'm so focused on his tongue that I forget what I'm supposed to say for a sec. "Um. Earth to Gretchen?"

"Sorry. Right." I feel the blood rush to my cheeks. "After tow lot was over, I ran around and did some stuff, and when I got back to Cosmo, Arrow was gone. She went to Tucson and left me in charge."

"Tucson?" His nose scrunches up in confusion.

"Yup."

"As in, Arizona?"

"You guessed it."

"Well, that's far."

"I know."

"When's she coming back?"

"Few days, I think. I'm not really sure."

"Okay. So, that's bad why, exactly?"

"Not bad, necessarily. Just, there were only three of us to run a whole party. It was busy. And weird. I feel like she disappeared out of nowhere."

"Been there," he quips.

I raise an eyebrow.

"Miranda? Remember? In college?"

"Oh. Right."

"Anyway, in my experience, when someone disappears out of nowhere, it usually isn't for a fun, happy reason."

"I know. Which is why it was weird. Also, I don't like the responsibility of holding down a room full of potentially drunk grown people while they pretend to have skills on the pole. Feels like an insurance nightmare waiting to happen. If they were kids and just came for normal dance classes, I could be okay with that, but these women are an absolute liability."

Brady laughs. "Aw. I could see you chasing a bunch of little ones in tutus."

"Not through a pole studio."

"No, definitely not. What about the other ladies, though? Why wouldn't Arrow put one of them in charge?"

"Cherry knows her the best, but she's sick. Appendicitis."

"Yikes."

"Yeah, and we've been sort of playing phone tag. Anyway, I'm sure I'll find out more tomorrow."

"Everything will be fine," Brady assures me. "And if you feel like you need backup, just call me. I'll come help out."

I sigh. "Thank you. I really appreciate that."

"No worries at all. Okay, so what was the best part of your day?"

"Well…" My voice trails off.

"Right now?" Brady guesses, his mouth upturned, suppressing a smile.

I shake my head. "If I'm being totally honest, that dance from earlier was –" I wave my hand to fan my face. "Caliente," I say.

He grins, and I feel my face flush. "Yeah. It was."

"Can I ask you a weird question?"

"Sure." He does that tongue thing with his spoon again and it takes all the restraint I've got to not lean across the table and invite him to do that inside my mouth.

"How did you learn to move like that?"

"What do you mean?"

"It's more than just dancing. It's like a whole other level."

He smirks. "Think so?"

"It's like a combination of dance moves, of course – sharp lines and angles and all that, but it feels like there are also fluid moments, as if you're melting into your dance partner."

"You think I do that with everyone?"

"I mean, don't you?" I remember the kaleidoscope of emotions I felt in my stomach when I watched him dance with Miranda.

"I think there's a distinction, actually."

"Do tell."

"Well, when I'm dancing for an audience, it's this combination of vulnerable and empowered."

I raise an eyebrow, listening.

"One thing that's interesting about this line of work is the way the women behave," he continues. "It's like they're ravenous. Ready for a good time. They know it's not really sex, so they don't have to perform or worry about my needs or any of the other things that might cause someone to get in their head too much during an intimate experience. They get to just enjoy the feeling of being wanted. Admired, you know?"

"But it's all fake."

"Of course it is. But my job is to make it feel like it's not. So, if I look at you like this –" he lowers his eyes, looking up at me from under his hooded lids, and glides the tip of his tongue over his lower lip, "you might feel some kind of way."

I shift in my seat. "Yeah, okay. I see what you mean."

"So, I'm in charge, then. It's low-stakes for her. She just gets to sit back and enjoy feeling desired. And when she lets me take her by the hand, I can move her, lift her, sit her down in a chair, whatever. I won't touch her in a compromising way – I'll get close enough to make her excited but not cross the line. It's an intense amount of control."

"So, where's the vulnerability you mentioned?"

"Well, I have to convince her that I want to do filthy things to her. In front of an audience. *While* I take my clothes off. I'm human, though. Having all those eyes on you can make you feel sort of like a museum exhibit. Lots of room for people to judge you."

"I'm pretty sure you're not getting any complaints."

"Still doesn't stop me from feeling nervous."

"Seriously?"

"Well, maybe a little less now. But that first night? I was terrified."

"Really?"

"Yes. The whole time. But especially dancing with you."

"Me? Why?"

"Because there was chemistry. Heat. I *felt* something. Like underneath all the showy stuff, there was something real."

"Mmm."

"Does that make sense?"

"Yes." I swallow, sucking the marshmallow swirl out of my teeth. "But you," I say, pointing my spoon at Brady, "have nothing to be nervous about."

"Do you ever feel that way?" he asks.

"About dancing?"

"Yeah."

"God, yes. It's terrifying. I mean, you saw me fall."

"Even still. You're really good."

"Compared to a zoo animal, maybe."

"Don't do that."

I wrinkle my nose. "What?"

"Don't be self-deprecating. Just say thank you and accept the compliment."

Goosebumps appear on my arms. "Thank you," I say.

"I wouldn't say it if I didn't mean it."

I nod, feeling my neck get red.

"What about you? Do you like having an audience?"

I shrug. "Not really. I prefer being alone in the studio. It's freeing, because if I make a mistake, no one's watching."

"Do you feel sexy?"

"Sometimes," I admit.

"Dancing is liberating. It can bring all different emotions to the surface."

"I guess that's true of most art forms."

"It is. My mom's an artist, and she says she only feels like her true self when she's creating something."

"Really? My mom's an artist too." I smile. "What's her medium?"

"She's a writer. How about yours?"

"Pottery."

"Nice," he replies.

"She's really talented. And yeah, like yours, she's happiest when she's making something."

"You don't feel that way about dancing?"

"I think I feel that way around kids. I'm very passionate about working with children."

"Yeah?"

"Uh huh. I love that feeling of when you teach something new to a little one, and they get it – the way their eyes light up. It's like magic."

"I can see it. You, teaching children."

"What makes you say that?"

"You're sweet. Patient. Even the way you were when you were trying to coach me through those pole moves. I don't know." He scrapes at the bottom of his ice cream bowl. "I just feel like you'd be a good teacher. You're confident in that kind of role."

"I guess."

"I think confidence is really sexy."

"Do you, now?"

Brady puckers his lips. The corner of his mouth has the tiniest trace of chocolate on it. I don't know where the sudden burst of courage comes from, but I reach across the table and use my thumb to wipe it off. His jaw goes slack. He's surprised, but doesn't move to push my hand away.

"Sorry," I whisper. "You had a little something there."

"All good," he says, looking down into his empty ice cream bowl.

Then, silence. My lungs compress, waiting for him to say something more.

Finally, he raises his eyes to meet mine. "So, you enjoyed it?"

"What?"

"Our dance earlier today?"

"Did you?" I counter.

He catches my gaze and locks into it. "I'd like to finish it."

"Here? Now?"

"I mean, this is where we are."

I gulp. "We need music."

He holds up his phone. "Got us covered." He pokes around on Spotify. "I'll stick with your theme of early 2000s club music."

The intro to the song reminds me of a xylophone, or chimes, or some plucked string instrument that I can't exactly place but in this moment, it's like a shot in my gut. Muscle memory. I immediately recall the melody. My mom commented that it "wasn't appropriate for a kids' dance class anyway" as she raced me to the hospital with three broken toes.

I stand there, trying to place the tune. The lyrics begin, and I remember. It's *Dip It Low* by Christina Milian.

Brady pushes his chair back from the table, stands, and holds his hand out to me. "May I?" he asks.

I tilt my head, considering him. Then, I take his fingers in my palm, noticing how long and thick they are, like they're better suited for building a house instead of being an assistant manager at a country club restaurant. He pulls me up to standing and angles my body so that I'm facing him. With one hand on my waist, he gives me a look I can't quite place – a cross between brooding and mysterious, until he breaks it with a mischievous bite on his lower lip. Brady rolls his hips into me slowly while gently pushing my head toward my exposed shoulder, presenting my bare neck to his waiting mouth. He doesn't kiss me, though. He breathes me in, glides his face up to my earlobe and breathlessly whispers, "Where were we?"

The beat drops, and his movements become a current of ins and outs, sharp and smooth, curves, shapes, and lines. Brady drops to the floor in some flip that he makes look absolutely effortless before he pops right back up in the reverse of the exact same move. In his T-shirt and sweatpants, he has full range of motion. My crowded little living room can barely take the length of his 6'2" body writhing around me on the floor. As Christina's voice builds toward the chorus, Brady sidles up in front of me and places his knee between mine. Hands on my hips, he rocks me back and forth in time with the beat. The sweatpants leave little to my fertile imagination as his arousal becomes evident beneath the cotton. This isn't the club, though. This is my house, and my body betrays my better sense of judgment.

My hips match Brady's movements, as if to say, *You think you're worked up? I'll show you worked up.* I body roll once, twice, pushing myself into him. It feels... otherworldly. My hands begin to wander, first around his neck, then down his back, my nails frustrated with the fabric that separates them from his skin.

Until it doesn't.

Brady licks his lips and nods at me once before slithering down my body. With my legs still shoulder-width apart, I feel his hands wrap under my thighs and in one quick motion, he's got me in the air, in the position of straddling a chair, and he pulls my pelvis straight into him, making sure that I can feel every inch of what I'm doing to him. We sway together with the music, and because Brady is securely cradling my ass and thighs with his open palms, I've got my hands free to tug at the hem of his shirt. I lift it as much as I can, revealing his abs, which are glorious.

"Jesus," I inadvertently whisper aloud.

He sets me back down on the ground and crosses his arms at the base hem of his T-shirt, then drags it over his head to give me a glimpse of what I'm dying to see. I bite down so hard on my lower lip I'm afraid I might bleed. The shirt drops to the floor.

Brady does three pelvic thrusts before wrapping an arm around my waist and pulling me in close again. He puts his lips to my ear and grazes the lobe with his tongue. My eyes roll into the back of my head. "More?" he asks.

"Mm hmm," I reply, a guttural sound that comes from somewhere in the back of my throat. Before I can say anything else, he spins me in a 180 and I'm backing myself up into him, able to feel him from a whole new angle. His hands pull me in by the waist, gripping my thin tank top, balling it up into his fists at my sides. He slides it up my belly, then pauses just below my breasts. "This okay?" he breathes into me. I turn to face him and, with a bravery that comes from somewhere metaphysical, I pull the shirt off over my own head. The central air hits my nipples; they instantly morph into solid pink berries. The hunger that burns in Brady's eyes is mirrored in my own gluttonous desire.

He stops moving, despite encouragement from the directive-based lyrics of the song. He just stares, his gaze transfixed on my breasts. "God damn," he mutters.

Just then, my phone rings.

I pick it up off the kitchen table with the intent of silencing it, not even considering the fact that it's after one in the morning and the only reason anyone calls at this time is for tragic news or for a booty call – and the only booty call possibility in my life right now is standing right in front of me.

I check the screen. "Shit," I say.

"What's wrong?"

"It's Cherry."

CHAPTER FIFTEEN

BRADY

I urge Gretchen to take the phone call.

Not that I *want* her to, mind you. It's just – I know it'll crawl inside of her head, and she strikes me as the type of woman who won't be able to relax knowing there's something hanging over her.

And I want her to be totally relaxed when we do what it seems like we were just about to start doing.

"Hello?" she says, mouthing *I'm sorry* to me, a pained look on her face.

I shake my head to indicate she's got nothing to be sorry for. I pick her tank top up off the floor and hand it to her. "Uh huh. Well, yeah, that's why I called," she says, sliding the shirt over her head with the phone still in her hand.

I excuse myself to use her bathroom. *This is probably for the best*, I decide. I'm so wound up, there's no way I could have lasted for her anyway. I splash cold water on my face as my erection subsides, noticing the fluffy white bathrobe she wore that first time she barged into Luis' apartment hanging on the hook behind the door. The room smells like peaches from the hand soap, and she's got a lineup of hair and skin products on a shelf above the toilet. There's a box sign on the wall that reads *True beauty can't be found in the mirror*. It's sweet. *She's* sweet, with her aspirations to teach children and the way she clearly cares about other people. Such a far cry from some of the girls I've dated in the past.

This one is different, I realize.

Suddenly, as much as I want to devour her, I also want to help her through this issue and show her that I'm not just some asshole whose sole objective is to get her into bed.

Besides, maybe if we hold off a little longer, it will mean more when we finally go there.

I exit the bathroom. She's still on the phone with Cherry, and I don't want to sit here listening in on their conversation. I grab the ice cream bowls off the table, place them in the sink, and leave a note on the magnetic whiteboard on her fridge.

Thank you for a fun nightcap, I write. *I'll see you tomorrow at 10 for our beach date. Sweet dreams.* I draw a heart, even though that seems... well, not exactly macho.

I don't care.

I like her.

She pouts as I point to the door, shaking her head in a silent request for me to stay. She's perched on the arm of the sofa, so I walk over, plant my lips lightly on her forehead, and whisper, "I'll see you tomorrow."

CHAPTER SIXTEEN

GRETCHEN

I hate watching Brady leave, and to be honest, I'm sick and tired of people interrupting our time together. But when I hear what Cherry has to say, it's all heavy enough that I probably wouldn't be in a real sexy mood afterwards anyway.

We exchange pleasantries, and after learning that she's no longer in the hospital but is now at home on bedrest, I discover that Arrow never told her about this trip to Arizona.

"Really? She didn't mention it?" I ask.

"Nah, but this happens from time to time," Cherry replies. There's a slight change in her octave, though, reminiscent of a child who's been caught sneaking candy after bedtime.

And so we begin a passive-aggressive verbal tug of war. She shares nothing further; I hesitate to deliver the details of Arrow's private, family-related e-mail. For one thing, I don't want to gossip, but also, I don't want Cherry to tell Arrow that I was snooping around in her personal business. Instead, I play dumb.

"What's in Tucson? The girls thought you might know."

"Her sister lives there."

"I didn't know Arrow has a sister."

"Yeah – a twin, actually."

"Wow. Really?" *So it's the* sister *on the fridge.*

"She keeps it all pretty quiet, because she and her sister have kind of a strained relationship."

I wait for more, but Cherry stops there. So, I fish. "You guys are pretty close, right?" I ask.

"Best friends since elementary school."

"That's sweet; I didn't realize that."

"Yup," she says, but that's it. I wait through another awkward moment of silence, piecing together that Cherry either knows what's going on with Arrow and doesn't want to tell me, or might actually *not* know... and what if Arrow needs help? My conscience pulls at me.

"If I share something with you, will you promise to keep it a secret?" I ask, my resolve eroding like the bluffs at Cahoon Hollow Beach.

There's a pause. "I guess. I mean, it depends on how serious it is."

I appreciate her honesty. "You really don't know what's going on with Arrow at all right now? Like, you swear you don't know why she left for Arizona out of the blue?"

She sighs. "Like I said, she's got family there. But this time, specifically? No, I don't know." Another pause. "Is her sister okay? Is something bad going on?" There's concern in her voice. It's genuine. *Just tell her the truth. It's the right thing to do. Also, who's to say that the other girls won't say something to Cherry?*

"I saw something I shouldn't have seen," I admit.

"What?"

"An e-mail."

"From?"

"Someone at a place called Desert Breeze."

"Oh." She sounds sad but not surprised.

"I didn't mean to see it," I continue, explaining about how when a computer shuts down too fast or the wrong way or whatever, when it restarts, it saves your pages.

"Don't worry," she assures me. "You don't strike me as the diabolical type. What did the e-mail say?"

I tell her the gist of it.

"Fuck," Cherry says under her breath.

"It's bad, right?"

"Yeah," she concedes. "Listen, Summer. I believe you have a good heart, so I'm going to lay some truth on you and I need to know that you'll hold it in the strictest of confidence."

"I will. I promise."

She sighs. "We're from Plymouth, originally. Growing up, the three of us were like the Three Musketeers: me, Joyce, and Jenny."

"Joyce and Jenny?" I repeat.

"That's Arrow's real name. Jenny's her sister."

"Shut up. Arrow's real name is *Joyce*?"

Cherry laughs. "Yeah. It's always been a point of contention for her. That's why she never lets anyone keep their name when they come to work at Cosmo. 'No one's going to pay top dollar to take pole lessons from some grandma named Joyce,' she used to say."

"That's too funny," I reply.

"Can't hate; she's definitely right," Cherry says. "Plus, I think she prefers anonymity. Dancing can make you feel exposed. By changing your name, it's like you put on a fake persona and don't have to feel so close to it emotionally."

"I get that."

"Anyway, Joyce and I went to 4Cs together after high school. We were totally coasting, but Jenny was the put together one. She was super smart. She went to Tufts, and she was studying to be a dentist. Everyone was always on Joyce. 'Why can't you be more like your sister?' they'd ask. It drove her crazy, but she figured, *whatever*. Jenny got the book smarts but Joyce got the street smarts."

"Uh huh," I say.

"So fast forward two years. Me and Joyce got our Associate's degrees from 4Cs. Her parents came to the graduation, but Jenny didn't come down from Tufts. She had some big biology final or something. After graduation, Joyce and her folks went out to dinner in Hyannis, and then her parents drove home to Plymouth. They had to get home early because the next day they were leaving early in the morning for a vacation – just her parents, not Joyce. But they never made it."

"What do you mean?" I ask.

"Her parents were killed in a car accident on the way to the airport."

"Oh my God."

"I know. It was the worst thing you could ever imagine. I was with Joyce when she got the call. They were driving at like four in the morning for an early flight. They were supposed to go to the Bahamas – what's that big resort there? Atlantis? I think that's the name. They were supposed to celebrate their 25th wedding anniversary there. So they were heading up Route 3, and it was basically empty, but then a car came flying at them out of nowhere. It was going the wrong way down the highway at top speed, like something out of a horror movie. Like the driver had a death wish."

"Holy shit," I say.

"I know. He was totally high. They said he died on impact."

"Jesus."

"Yeah, and Arrow's mom was in the passenger seat. The car flipped over and the first responders couldn't get her out in time."

"What about her dad?"

"He went through the windshield. Wasn't wearing a seatbelt."

I exhale, thinking about my own parents and what something like that would do to me. There would be no coming back from it. I'd be devastated. "That's unthinkable."

"That's why she runs tow lot."

I connect the dots as she says the words. It's not just a good business practice. Tow lot is a life or death situation to Arrow. All of a sudden, it means everything that I'm responsible for it. "I don't know what to say."

"I know. It's a lot."

"What does this have to do with Arizona, though?"

"Well. I'm sure you can imagine that Joyce had some survivor's guilt, but there was also a part of her that was so grateful she got to see them one last time. Meanwhile, Jenny fell apart, only we didn't know it at first because she was heavily medicated at the funeral, and as soon as it was over, she went back to Boston. She still had two years left of dental school, and she'd made a life for herself with her college friends and whatnot. Joyce was heartbroken. She felt like Jenny was the only family she had left, and she was choosing not to deal with any of the aftermath of it. Joyce had to handle everything. Big things, like funeral arrangements, but also the small things that nobody thinks about, like cutting off her parents' cell phone service and managing their home in Plymouth. Cleaning out their closets. Donating their clothes to Goodwill. All that stuff."

"By herself?" I ask.

"Well, she had me. But Jenny wanted nothing to do with any of it."

"That's so sad."

"I know. It really hardened Joyce. She got her first tattoo then – the one with the shattered heart pierced by an arrow. We were worried about Jenny but Joyce was also really mad at her. At the time, we didn't realize that Jenny was going through her own guilt about not having come to the graduation, not being able to have that one last dinner with them as a family. She was beating herself up about it pretty bad."

"I get that. I'm sure I'd feel the same if it were me."

"Me too," Cherry agrees. "It got worse, though. She got into prescription drugs. I don't even know the names of all the shit she was taking. She was getting it from the dental office where she was interning. But when her internship ended, she needed a new supplier. That's when she met Ricky." She clears her throat. "He was bad news. She met him on the internet. But not, like, on Hinge or Tinder or some *normal* place. *Craigslist.* Can you believe that? And then, she went all the way out to Arizona to meet him during winter break."

"Craigslist? Is that even a thing anymore?"

"Maybe for apartment rentals, but it was *never* a thing for dating! I don't know why she thought she should look there. Sadly, like I said, Jenny never really had much in the way of street smarts. That was more Joyce's department."

"That makes no sense, then. Why would Arrow – uh, Joyce – let her go?"

"Jenny lied. Said the trip had something to do with school. She never told any of us she had met someone. And she came back – well, not home, but to school – and continued behaving normally. So, you can imagine Joyce's surprise when out of nowhere, a few months later she dropped out and told us she was moving to Arizona permanently. She only had a few credits left, so it was crazy, right? Like, why would you do that? Nobody understood what the hell she was thinking. Turned out she was pregnant."

"Oh. Shit."

"Yup. I guess she decided she wanted to start a life with him out there. I think she was scared to come home, to live here without her parents. But Ricky was a disaster, and me and Joyce felt some sort of way about the two of them together. We tried to get Jenny to come back home. Joyce majored in business at 4Cs and wanted to start her own company on the Cape. She told Jenny if we all worked together, we could open up a dental practice. Joyce could manage the business end of things, I could do all the marketing and social media, and Jenny could be the dentist, if she'd finish up her degree and get her license. But Jenny was hell-bent on staying put, and we couldn't understand it. Jenny didn't tell us that she was pregnant until the third trimester. She didn't want anyone to try and talk her out of keeping the baby."

"Wow," I say. "That's a whole lot of family drama."

"I'm not done," Cherry says. "So, Jenny goes out there. And she and Ricky were living together, right? Well, one day, like literally *a week* before the baby was born, the cops issued a warrant for Ricky's arrest and he skipped town on her."

"Seriously? Arrest for what?"

"Identity theft. Apparently, he stole dozens of social security numbers during the pandemic to collect unemployment benefits. He opened up PO Boxes in several different locations and had the checks sent to them. And then, when the cops came after him, he took off. They caught him at the border of Nogales, Mexico, and he was sentenced to two years in prison. So Jenny had the baby all by herself out there, and of course she called Joyce for help, because – well, who else was she going to call? Joyce was royally pissed at her for being so stupid, but still, she begged her to come home. Like, now you're going to stay in Arizona for some *criminal*? And put the baby in potential danger once he gets out of jail?"

"Shit."

"Jenny was a total wreck. She suffered from post-partum depression on top of still having residual feelings about what had happened with their parents, and she desperately wanted to stay where she was. She had a little girl, Katherine. We call her Kit. Joyce went out there to be with them and to help raise Kit for the first few months. She fell in love with the baby – like, real deal love at first sight. I always thought Kit was the biggest blessing in disguise that ever happened to the two of them. She gives them both something to live for, you know? Like, something positive to negate the sadness of what happened to their parents. Anyway, by the time Kit was four or five months old, Jenny's post-partum faded, which was good, but she still didn't want to come back here."

"Was she still taking meds?"

"Yeah. She did a brief stint in rehab at that same place, Desert Breeze. That's how I know the name. But it seemed like that helped her. At least, it did at the time. She got herself some job in retail. Not exactly living the dream, but at least she was able to take care of her daughter." Cherry clucks her tongue. "Comparatively speaking, of course."

"Right."

"Joyce was still upset, though. Jenny would call asking for money from time to time so we worried that things weren't all roses and sunshine, you know? Ricky was in jail, and he had to pay a hefty fine that wiped out any financial assistance he might have provided them, so he was useless. Joyce kept trying to convince Jenny to come home. She promised we would all pitch in and take care of Kit. But I think Jenny was embarrassed."

"I get that."

"Joyce even considered moving to Arizona. But she had a life here: friends, her parents' house to take care of, not to mention the memories of her entire childhood that she wasn't ready to walk away from yet."

"Wait – Arrow still lives in Plymouth?"

"Yeah. She couch surfs at my place in Hyannis sometimes, but her actual house is in Plymouth. It's the house she grew up in. My parents live across the street."

"That's a hike."

"Yep. Truth be told, I think she's been holding on to the house instead of selling it in the hopes that Jenny will come back home with Kit," Cherry explains. "Anyway, right after Kit's first birthday, Ricky got out early for good behavior and moved back in with Jenny. That was when Joyce decided to buckle down and open Cosmo. She knew she could be making real money if she set it up the right way. Now, she Venmos Jenny and Kit money every week. She just couldn't stand the thought of them living in squalor with an asshole like Ricky because Jenny's too proud to do the right thing and come back here."

"How old is Kit?" I wonder.

"She just turned four."

"So, Cosmo has been around for three years?"

"No," Cherry says. "Joyce opened it last year. We had to study pole first, which is how we met Saffron and Indigo. Joyce also had to figure out all the necessary parts of running her own business. We had to scout out a location, paint, get the poles, find clients, all that stuff." She pauses, as if she's remembering. "It's been really good for Joyce, though. It's given her something to focus on, especially since it benefits Kit and Jenny."

I let everything she's told me sink in. "Man," I exhale. "It's crazy, if you think about it."

"What is?"

"How little you can know about someone who you see every day."

"Yeah. Joyce keeps everything real close to the vest," she says. "I mean, I get it. This is the only family she's got. She's protective. I would be, too."

"So, how long do you think she'll be gone for?"

"No clue. Doesn't sound good, though. I'm sure she'll be out at least a few days."

"And you're not coming back for..."

"My post-op care plan says two to four weeks. But I can probably come back in about a week and a half. I just can't dance for a while, because of the incision."

"Got it," I reply. I take a breath. "Okay. So, what can we do to help?"

"You're doing it. Just keep the business running smoothly. I'll be back in action next week. I can run shots if you can cover the pole for me."

"That's fine. And I'm here if you think of anything else."

"Try not to worry. Joyce chose you for a reason. I mean, you're smart, you've got a good work ethic, you're always on time, you're willing to do basically whatever she tells you to, and your job includes running things that matter a lot to her without anyone around."

"I don't get any of those vibes from her, to be completely honest. But I'll take your word for it."

"How do you mean?"

"She's not particularly nice to me."

"Joyce isn't nice to anyone. She figures that if she gets attached, she'll only get hurt. You're a temp, Summer – it makes sense that she would put her faith in someone who's going to leave no matter what. That way, she doesn't have to get all invested in caring about you personally. Like I said, you're a hard worker, so I think she expects that you're not going to disappoint her, but if you do, she won't have to worry about losing a friend over it, seeing as how you have an expiration date."

"Wow," I say. "That's... that's a pretty sad outlook."

"Yeah. Well, she's had a pretty sad life."

I let this thought marinate. *It all kind of makes sense now,* I decide. *Hurt people hurt people, right?*

"I'll keep you posted if I find out anything else," Cherry says.

"Thanks, Cherry. Same here."

"Catch you later," she says, and ends the call.

CHAPTER SEVENTEEN

BRADY

After last night, I'm ready to take this whole thing with Gretchen to the next level. So the following morning, I get myself together, pack up my Yeti cooler, roll up a pair of beach towels and knock on Gretchen's door promptly at 10:00. It's sunny and 80, perfect beach weather, and I'm convinced it's going to be a great day.

When she opens the door, she's sparkling. Her hair is up in a high ponytail and she's got on a loose tank top over a black string bikini, a pair of cutoff jean shorts and flip flops. She tells me I look nice. I kiss her on the cheek, noticing how the scent of sunscreen mixes with her shampoo. "You smell incredible," I reply.

I offer to drive, because I stashed the beach chairs in my trunk this morning and because it's the gentlemanly thing to do. This is a date, and I want to treat it that way. We get to First Light Beach in minutes; it's a stone's throw from the Diamond Excelsior resort. First Light is on the bay side and the tide is out so we trudge out to a sandbar in the middle of the crystal clear Brewster Flats. I hope that I give off five-star boyfriend material vibes instead of male stripper vibes. I really want her to take me seriously.

We unfold the beach chairs and settle in. I offer her a bottle of water, which she gratefully accepts.

"So, how did everything go last night after I left?"

"Good, I guess," she says. "It was weird, though. I learned a lot about Arrow and her personal life."

"Bad stuff?"

"Just complicated. I feel bad for her. She's had a lot of rough things happen in her younger years that have made her pretty guarded."

"I hear that."

Gretchen wrinkles her forehead. "Was your childhood…" Her voice trails off, the trace of a question resting in the inflection at the end.

"Bad? No. I mean, not really, anyway. I've been pretty fortunate overall. But, you know, my dad's always been an asshole. When I was younger and my mom left, she told me to go easy on him, and I couldn't understand why she would say that when all he ever did was act like a piece of shit towards her. So, on one of my visits to see her, I asked her how she could forgive him like that. And she told me that he had a terrible childhood – his father was abusive to everyone in the household, and he had to grow up much, much faster than most kids do."

"That's sad," she says.

"It is sad. It doesn't excuse the way he treats people now, but at least it provides an explanation."

"So you're not mad at him for kicking you out?"

"No. I don't appreciate it, that's for sure, but I think it's just part of who he is. He's happiest alone, I think. Also, I try to channel those feelings into something positive. I keep a running list in my head of all the things I'll never do when I become a parent, just based on the things that have been done to me that I didn't think were right."

"I like that. I think it's a smart way to cope with a difficult relationship," she says. "Still, I'm sorry. That sucks."

"It's really okay," I assure her.

"Are you close with your mom?"

"I am. She's in Iowa. We talk several times a week on the phone and I visit her a few times a year."

"That's sweet. Does she ever come here?"

I shake my head. "Not to the Cape. Sometimes she'll visit someplace that's not too far away, though. She's done author events and things like that," I explain. "She's actually got a writing conference in Connecticut in a few weeks. I might see her then," I say. "But I'm sure she'll come visit more once I settle down somewhere."

"And where are you hoping to settle, exactly?"

"I'm not sure. I need to start by finding a job. The stripping is incredible money, but you know. It's not a life plan – at least not for me."

"No, I hear you. This is definitely a temporary thing for me as well," she says. "How's your job search going?"

"Slow. But not bad. I'm always looking. And I've got a few open applications, so that's good. Also, I have a Zoom interview this Friday."

"That's good – what's the position?" she asks.

"It's an Market Research Analyst job at a marketing firm." I leave out the part about it being located in New York. *Cross that bridge if we come to it*, I figure. *No need to worry about it now.*

"Cool," she says.

"What about you?" I ask. "Are you looking for a teaching job for the fall?"

"Yes, but only as a sub. I told you I still have a few grad credits left, right?"

"Uh huh," I nod.

"So I need to make sure that my schedule's pretty free for all of that. The good news is I only have one semester left. And I've done a projection for how much money I'll have by the end of summer at the rate I'm going at Cosmo. It's good. Like, I might not even need to work for a little while."

"Mmm. You're speaking my language. I love economic projections."

Gretchen laughs. "Noted. If I ever want to get you all hot and bothered, I'll start using words like 'net proceeds' and 'commodities exchange.'" She claps her hands and doubles over. "I have no idea what a commodities exchange is, actually."

"I would explain it to you, but you'd fall asleep," I reply. "Really, though, I'm sure you'll have no trouble getting a job as a teacher when you're ready to apply. I feel like the market for teachers is pretty open on the Cape."

She nods. "It's not bad right now. It just makes more sense to finish up the credentials so I can start fresh at a school next September. If I can sub in the meantime, I'll be able to make a name for myself in the field, and who knows? Maybe I'll get hired at the school where I sub."

"Sounds like a solid plan," I tell her. "And you definitely want to stay on the Cape?" I wonder aloud.

"I do. My whole family is here. I love it here," she says. "What about you?"

"I could go either way, to be honest. I love Cape Cod. I think it's a really special place. But I think it would depend on a lot of different factors."

"Like?"

"Like the money, for one thing. My housing situation, for another. Luis will be back at the end of August. Stuff like that."

"That makes sense," she agrees. A mosquito lands on her shin and she gives it a smack. "Do you have any other family on the Cape? Any siblings?"

"Nope. Just me."

"Really? Me too. I wouldn't have pegged you for an only child."

"Funny. I was about to say the same thing. You seem like you could be the oldest in a tribe of many." I smile, envisioning Gretchen chasing a brood of little ones around.

"I think my parents would've had more kids," she says. "They had a tough time with me when I was a baby. My mom went through a lot."

"Are you guys close?"

"Me and my mom? Yeah, definitely. My folks live in East-port. I still see them every Sunday."

"Right. For brunch," I recall. "Do they know about your current job?"

She shakes her head. "No way. My dad would lose his shit."

"Protective?"

"Extremely. He's a police chief. He'd kill me."

I nod. "Yeah, I haven't told my mom about it either."

"It's temporary," she shrugs. "And it would only worry them."

"Exactly," I agree. "So what do they *think* you do for work right now?"

"They don't know about what happened. They still think I work at the pub. I was going to tell them once I got a new job, but that never materialized the way I'd hoped it would have. So I haven't said anything, really."

"Ah, I see."

"What about you? What do your parents think you're doing?"

I adjust my feet in the sand. "My mom knows I'm looking for work. There's nothing she can do to help me from so far away anyway. And I haven't spoken to my dad since he kicked me out."

"That's a shame for him," Gretchen says. "He's really missing out."

"On knowing I'm a stripper?" I laugh.

"On being your dad," she explains.

We continue like this for hours. We talk about our closest friends (I mention that Big Mike can probably help Gretchen find a job as a teacher), our favorite restaurants, our college experiences, and so much more. We feast on the (fairly elaborate, if I do say so myself) lunch I've packed for us. There are several sandwich options to choose from, since I wasn't sure what she would like. We polish off a bag of Cape Cod sea salt and cracked pepper potato chips together, and each drink a vodka seltzer. I love that with every passing moment, I'm learning more and more about her: about her friend,

Jenna, that she's a turkey-and-cheese kind of girl, that she's never seen any of the Star Wars movies but has seen every Pixar movie (she's a huge Pete Docter fan), that she loves chocolate and is scared of heights. I file away each new bit of information like a puzzle piece.

By the time the day comes to an end, I feel like I've known her for a lifetime.

There are no parties tonight, and I would love to hang out with Gretchen until the wee hours of the morning, but I made plans to help Mike pick up a piece of furniture that Gina found on Facebook marketplace that is apparently gigantic. Given the fact that he's done me several solids over the past few weeks, I can't cancel on him, despite how badly I want to. So I bring her home, kiss her goodbye, and tear myself away.

I can't remember the last time I was this happy.

CHAPTER EIGHTEEN
GRETCHEN

L ife is so good sometimes.

Brady and I fall into a routine quickly, almost as if we're both making up for the time we've lost being single for so long. I feel like I've hit the dating jackpot – he's warm, sweet, kind, smart, and absolutely delectable to look at, like the human version of an aphrodisiac. We go to the grocery store together, we eat dinner together, and we've gone on more dates in the past two weeks than I've been on in the past two years. He keeps a stash of Gifford's ice cream in the freezer for our post-work chats, and he dances at Cosmo two more times – once as a firefighter and once as a pilot. Both times, he keeps his eyes trained on me when he takes off his clothes.

July 4th falls on a Tuesday, so there are no parties booked, which leaves us available for what Brady says is going to be a memorable evening.

He's cryptic about our plans, so I'm really excited. Just the fact that he puts thought into stuff is incredible. Even Jenna, who is skeptical of almost every guy, tells me he's a keeper.

Brady tells me to dress nice and that he'll pick me up at 5:00 p.m. I opt for a white sundress with yellow trim and a pair of white wedge sandals. The whole outfit accentuates my tan. I purchase new underwear for the evening: a white lace thong and a matching strapless bra, just in case we end up in one of our respective beds.

Which, to be clear, hasn't happened yet.

His fault, not mine. I would rip his clothes off in a heartbeat, but he says he wants it to be special – which, obviously, just makes me want to rip his clothes off even more.

At 5 on the dot, he knocks on my door. He's wearing a pair of pressed khakis and a white collared shirt, rolled up at the cuffs to reveal his bulging forearms. He tells me I look beautiful, asks if I'm ready, and takes my hand as we walk out to his car.

We catch up on the long drive to Provincetown. I'm surprised that's where he's taking me, but I've come to learn that nothing about this man should surprise me. On the way there, we chat about work stuff – he's nervous because he hasn't heard back yet from the employer who he had the Zoom interview with a few weeks ago. He thought the meeting went well, but nothing's happened since, and he even made it a point to send them a thank you e-mail. I share that I'm starting to think about classes for the fall and that I have a meeting with my advisor next week to receive my placement for student teaching. We talk about sub jobs, and I explain that I can only sub for half the semester because the other half I'll be reporting to a school every day. But I have started looking, even though it makes me nervous. I never used to be nervous thinking about my long term goals, but now I feel like I just want to live in the twisted little bubble of Cosmo forever. We've fallen into a different groove without Arrow around. Cherry's back at work now and it's become a really friendly environment. For the first time, pole *feels* like a sisterhood. Nothing lasts forever, I remind myself. But I'm enjoying this summer immensely.

It's also so nice to be able to talk to Brady about work stuff, because Lord knows I can't share any of that with my parents. It's a wonder they haven't figured me out yet. I'm in the best shape of my life, I only wear leggings to their house for brunch (since the debacle with the pole bruises, I don't need any further commentary) and I don't talk about the Diamond Excelsior at all, when I used to complain about it constantly. I've mentioned that I'm dating someone, so I think that's making my mom really happy. Maybe they're chalking any changes in my appearance or my general attitude up to that. They ask when they'll "be able to meet this young man," and I promise them I will bring him to brunch sometime soon.

The drive to P-Town is easy – a straight shot up Route 6, no traffic, which is also a little surprising. My guess is that because it's a Tuesday, this July 4th will be a bit less crazy than if it were on a weekend.

But it's P-Town. In the summer. Which basically means it's one gigantic party.

He takes me to a restaurant called The Pearl Necklace. Yes, I know. Maybe not the best name for a food establishment, but surprisingly, it's a very high-class place. I've never been there because it's so expensive. When we walk inside, I'm surprised to find that the place is completely empty, except for a single waiter dressed in what looks like a tuxedo, minus the jacket. Brady shakes his hand.

"Gretchen, this is Gabe," Brady says.

"Enchanté," Gabe says, taking my hand and planting a light kiss on the top of it.

"Gabe and I have known each other for years. High end dining has its perks."

"Are you the manager here?" I ask.

"I do a little bit of everything," he replies.

I raise my eyebrows. "Where is everyone?" I wonder aloud, as Gabe motions for us to follow him into the dining room. The room is empty, except for one lone table against the window, offering a stunning view of Race Point Beach.

"We're closed on Mondays and Tuesdays," Gabe explains. "But Brady's hooked me up before, so I was happy to return the favor. Anyway, please sit. I've prepared a menu for you, curated by your date here. Your hors d'oeuvres will be out momentarily. Enjoy the view."

Brady pulls out a chair for me, and I sit down. My eyes take in everything – the insane view of the endless sand with the blue waves breaking in the distance beyond it, the lavender hue of the sky just above the water, the ambiance of the room itself, with its cathedral ceiling and pristine wainscoting. Not to mention Brady himself. He's sparkling. It's almost like he's giddy with the excitement of having brought me here. I can only imagine what the meal is going to taste like.

To exactly no one's surprise, it's a feast for the sensees. Hors d'oeuvres are a combination of charcuterie, apple-baked brie with a honey-balsamic reduction, and lobster crostini with rosemary butter. It's paired with Bollinger champagne, which goes down very smoothly. We toast to summer. I'm so overwhelmed that if the night ends right here, it'll still be the best date I've ever had by a long shot.

But it turns out we've barely scratched the surface. Salads arrive: watermelon and feta cheese over microgreens with bacon-infused house made croutons, topped with lime vinaigrette. Next, the main course is delivered: New York strip with roasted lemon-thyme carrots and scalloped potatoes. Each part of the meal is more decadent and spectacular than the next, and we have time to enjoy without rushing, leaving plenty of space for conversation, laughter, and gazing at each other in the setting sun, wondering how we got so lucky.

And then, it happens. Brady asks me to be his girlfriend. I lean in and kiss him, and we toast once more. We're so cute it even embarrasses *me*.

After dessert (a white chocolate mousse that is literally to die for), Brady excuses himself from the table. I assume he's going to the restroom, but again, I'm incorrect. Instead, he sneaks out to his car and gets a blanket and a Bluetooth speaker, which he's brought so that we can sit outside on the sand and watch the fireworks.

He sets us up about 20 feet back from the ever-changing bend of the shoreline where the ocean waves crash down on the beach. There's a bonfire quite a way down on one side, and several smaller scattered parties in the other direction. The noise of happy people carries on the breeze with the salt from the sea. I'm not sure if I'm buzzing off the food, the champagne, the general vibe of this perfect night or all of the above, but I feel amazing. It's only 8:30, so we've still got about 30 minutes until fireworks will begin, and on this private stretch of sand, I decide now is as good a time as any to finally finish what we started weeks ago.

Brady secures the blanket with a few rocks and oversized clam shells. He takes off his shoes and socks and sets them on the edge of the blanket as well. "Wait – don't sit down," I say.

"Why not?"

"Can you play some music on your phone?"

He smiles. "Of course. That's why I brought the speaker."

I look up and down the beach once more, just to be sure we're really alone. My eyes finally settle on Brady. "Put on the song we were dancing to in my apartment."

"*Dip It Low*?" he asks.

"Yeah." My voice sounds far away, as if it belongs to someone else. My gaze feels misty. I'm trapped inside a cloud. Everything inside of me is soft and warm.

"I'll have to dance with you if I play that song," he says. He's flirting with me.

I like it.

"Good," I say, my lips upturned slightly into a hint of a smile.

He smirks, then slides his hand into his pocket to take out his phone. He searches for the Christina Milian song and tosses the phone on the blanket when the music starts. Stepping towards me, he says, "You sure you want to start this here?"

Instead of answering, I kick off my sandals, place my hands on his hips and pull him into me.

He groans quietly.

Maybe I'm drunk. I don't think I am, but this behavior is not exactly on-brand for me. I consider the fact that I might end up losing this dress in the minutes to come, and realize that I don't care. It's P-Town, one of the sexiest places on earth. Nobody will even bat an eye if my ass cheeks are on full display.

Brady spins me around, then, with the exact right amount of force, pushes on my upper back so that I bend over and touch the floor. He pushes himself into me from behind, and – *wow* – I can already feel his rigid erection. I keep my palms in the sand while he slides his hips forward and back a few times, imagining how it might feel without all this clothing in the way. Slowly, I flip my head back up so my hair cascades down my back and I raise my upper half back up to a standing position. His lips find my neck, his breathing fills my ear, and his groin continues to press against me as we rock together. I twist my fingers around his and encourage him to explore my upper half, all the while continuing to match his hip action with my backside. When his hands reach my breasts, I exhale, arching my spine to lean further into his touch. I scan the beach again quickly. Still empty.

"I want to look at you," Brady implores me. "Turn around."

I do.

His hands slide my straps down over my shoulders, and he tugs the elastic top of my sundress down to reveal my bra. He plants a kiss on my collarbone, then another, and another, working his way down my body until he arrives at the upper edge of my bra cups. His hands squeeze my breasts from the bottom up, giving him the opportunity to catch a glimpse of what's under the fabric in the space that appears. "Tell me if you want me to stop," he whispers, and slides his fingers beneath the lace, working the undergarment down around my ribcage, revealing my top half to the humid night air. His lips surround one nipple while his fingers tweak the other, and before I can even process how wet this makes me, Brady's tongue sends waves of pleasure between my legs by alternately sucking and licking the hardened peaks of my flesh.

By the time we reach the bridge of the song, I need to feel him. I glide his face back up towards mine so he's standing upright, and I snake my hand between us, wrapping my fingers in a semicircle around his straining bulge. I stroke up and down, appreciating his length and imagining him filling me. He kisses me, hums of pleasure choking in the back of his throat. I can't help myself. With my top half still exposed, I tug at his belt. Brady opens his eyes and sweeps the area. "You sure?" he whispers.

"I want to see it," I reply.

He helps me then, unbuttoning his pants and lowering his zipper so I have full access. He's wearing boxers, a stark contrast to his usual getup of a stripper thong, and this revelation strikes me as extremely sexy because it's so *real*. There's no alter-ego here, no showy persona. Just a beautiful man who's hard as a rock because of me. The realization nearly sends me over the edge as his tongue resumes its residency inside my mouth.

I reach back down and tighten my grip around him. Skin against skin, I feel his heat and the anticipation pulsing through his shaft. The song ends, and a new one begins but I can't even register it because his hand slides up under my dress and traces up my thigh. When his fingertips reach the edge of my panties, my hips grind forward, letting him know that *yes, this is good,* and *no, please don't stop.* He pulls his neck back for a second, long enough for me to hear him say, "I need you to lie down," and then I do. We do, together. He lowers me onto the blanket and begins to work my panties off under my ass with one hand while cupping my face with the other. "Can you keep watch?" he asks feverishly.

"Uh huh," I manage to mumble.

And then I lose him beneath the skirt of my sundress.

I can't keep my eyes open; Brady's tongue cracks me open like an oyster and I clutch the blanket and involuntarily push myself into his eager mouth. He licks me, tasting my sweetness and reminding me of his tongue on the spoon the first night we had ice cream together. My mind briefly registers that fact that I'm indecently exposed in the middle of a beach, being feasted upon in the most arousing situation my brain could ever conjure up. I surprise myself once again when, instead of being embarrassed or shutting down at the thought, I spread my legs wider, welcoming Brady's fingers to explore me. He finds my g-spot right away and focuses his attention there while working his mouth against my starved sex.

I don't take long to come. Bucking my hips, Brady strokes his finger back and forth to build me towards release, alternating his mouth between sucking gently and licking me with the tip of his tongue. His free hand reaches up to my chest and pinches my right nipple. I paw at my left breast and match his movements, while my other hand holds his head in place through my skirt. When I finally let go, a swell of ecstasy breaks in choppy spasms. I feel a surge between my legs as my brain floods with dopamine, endorphins, and oxytocin. When I'm done, all that's left are lingering kisses on my inner thighs and the gentle breeze off the Atlantic Ocean.

I exhale deeply, shrouded in satisfaction and relief.

Brady works his way back up beside me. "Good?" he asks.

I kiss his earlobe. "Amazing," I reply. I close my eyes and smile.

"Good," he says. I can hear the smirk in his voice. He's pleased with himself.

Now it's my turn.

"Take these off," I say, tugging at his pants.

He laughs. "Seriously?"

I nod. "It's a big blanket. We can wrap up in it. Take them off," I repeat.

I inhale the briny breeze off the water and summon up a second wind as Brady follows directions and removes his pants.

"Shirt too," I say. He dutifully works the buttons open and slides the dress shirt off his arms. I gaze upon him in his t-shirt and boxers. "You are the most intoxicating sight I have ever laid eyes on, do you know that?" I ask.

"Like this?" he asks. "In an undershirt and boxer shorts?"

"Absolutely. Can I just tell you? You're insatiably hot when you're doing your stripper thing, but natural Brady is fucking fire."

He scrunches up his nose as if he's going to question me, so I cut him off. "Take the compliment, babe. Just say thank you." I grin, using his words against him.

"Thank you," he says. I think he might be blushing, which strikes me as funny given the fact that he just spent the last several songs working my body into a frenzy.

"Now lie down."

He does, and I sit up beside him. "Are you always this bossy?"

"Never," I retort.

"Bummer," he says, pulling me down over him. "I kind of like it."

"Noted," I say, pushing up his T-shirt and kissing his chest. "Cover me with the blanket please?"

"You cold?" he asks.

I kiss down his stomach. My tongue is a paintbrush, swirling color down the canvas of his torso. "No. I just don't need all of P-Town to watch what I'm about to do to you."

"Jesus," Brady says, but he can't speak after that, because the words get stuck in his throat.

I feel the blanket land on my back and his hand rests on the top of my head as I work his length in and out of my willing mouth. He's longer and thicker than anyone I've ever been with, and he smells like a masculine blend of Tide laundry detergent and Irish Spring soap. Inhaling him is exhilarating up close like this, and I savor it, not caring about who might see. I am protected by this blanket cocoon, swaddled by the darkness of nightfall around me. I use my hands to stroke him while I tease his head with my tongue, then take in his full magnitude until he hits my tonsils. In and out, back and forth I devour him until I feel him constrict into his body. I slow down then, give him one final kiss, and emerge from the blanket like a butterfly.

Without a word, I straddle him and pull my dress up over my head, depositing it on the sand next to us. Brady still has on his T-shirt and I'm in a bra, so even if someone was to approach us, we're not exactly indecent – at least not from afar. I'm about to slide him inside my body when he asks, "Do you have a condom?"

I shake my head. "I'm on birth control. Do I need a condom?" I ask in return.

"No, I'm clean."

"Same," I say. Then, I angle his manhood at my entrance and push him inside. He fills me, stretching me open in the most pleasurable way. He moans as he enters me, and my eyes roll into the back of my head. We begin to move together, waves cresting, crashing, and retreating on the shore, our fingers interlocked by the sides of his head, hips bucking up and down. It's untamed and animalistic, wild and raw – pure lust mixed with an emotional connection so deep it defies measure. I pound my body into his, building his orgasm with intention, not even focusing on the enjoyment my own body is receiving from the unfiltered, natural experience. I can feel my own climax developing, which surprises me. I'm not the type to come twice in a night – but then again, I'm also not the type to ride someone in public.

Only, maybe with Brady, I am.

I move faster, and his hands unclasp mine so he can help me along with his fingers as we move towards an inevitable grand finale. The thought strikes me that Brady *wants* to make me come again, so I don't hold back. I let him bring me to the brink and just as I gasp and shudder, his face contorts.

With a grunt, I feel him explode inside me – once, twice, three times, followed by a long series of smaller aftershocks.

I collapse on top of him and we lay like that for a minute, fully spent atop his beach blanket.

"God damn," he whispers into my hair. His heart pounds through his T-shirt.

I lift my face off his chest to look at him. We lock eyes and both start to laugh. "That was really good," I say.

"Yeah," he agrees.

"I can't believe nobody caught us."

"Me too. I didn't plan this, you know," he says. "I mean, I *hoped* for it, but not outside. I thought maybe later, like, at home…"

"I know. I didn't plan it either."

"But, my God. That was –"

"Yeah," I interject. "I know." Brady takes off his shirt and uses it to clean us both up. I put my panties and my dress back on, and he pulls back on his pants but keeps his T-shirt in a pile for the time being. We lie there, his arm around me and my head on his chest. *Because of You* by Ne-Yo starts up on the Bluetooth speaker. *This is like the greatest hits of 2007, I think.*

"Can I ask you something totally random?" he says.

"Of course."

"What's your affinity with the Christina Milian song?"

"I don't really know," I reply. "I just like it. You want to know something funny?"

"Sure."

"I broke three toes to that song once. I should hate it."

Brady stills. "Wait. How?"

"In a dance class, back when I was a little girl."

"Did someone –" he starts.

"I got stomped."

"Oh, my God." His eyes grow wide. "That was me."

"What?"

"I was the cowboy."

"Shut up."

"Miss Wanda was the teacher."

"That's right! I could never remember her name."

"I could never remember yours. Just that you were a unicorn."

"I didn't know yours either. They always just called you 'Big Boy' or something like that."

"Big Guy," he corrects me. "Because I was tall."

"Holy shit. So we go all the way back to –"

"Six years old," he says.

"That explains so much."

"About what?"

"About our connection. I guess it's deeper than even we realized."

"That fucking song," he says.

"What about it?"

"I *knew* there was something. It always made my pulse speed up a little."

"Maybe it made you nervous," I suggest.

"No," he says, shaking his head. "It's not that." He pauses for a moment, and I see a lightning bug flash nearby. "I think my heart remembered you," he says. "My brain might not have, but my heart did."

A lump forms in my throat and I swallow it, just as the first fireworks go off against the black backdrop of the clear July night.

It's about the only thing that can make this moment any more perfect than it already is.

CHAPTER NINETEEN

BRADY

Just like that, we are *serious.*

I can't get enough of Gretchen, and the feeling appears to be mutual. Actually, I *know* it is, because exactly one week later we're having dinner at her parents' house.

We've come up with a story that is 75% true. We work together at the Diamond Excelsior, and I live next door for the summer. That's it. Nice and simple. She doesn't feel comfortable explaining our real occupations and I don't blame her; it's embarrassing, and especially considering these are her *parents*, I really don't want them to lose all respect for me straight out of the gate.

She explains that her family is very tight knit. She and her mother share almost everything, and her father is your typical, overprotective dad. He happens to be the Eastport Chief of Police, too. Not that I'm intimidated by that, but... well, you know. It might be a little less nerve wracking to meet her dad if he was, say, an investment banker or an accountant – someone with whom I might have a little in common with. I could make myself seem like a guy who's on the up and up, worthy of his daughter, as opposed to a couch surfing glorified waiter, which sadly is a huge step up from my current reality of sausage-slinging stripper.

The fact that we're having dinner on a Tuesday makes sense given our respective "professions," since Tuesday was always a slow night at the restaurant and the pub. I pick Gretchen up (read: I walk 30 feet and knock on her door) at 4:00 p.m., and she lets me in with a smile. She's wearing an apron.

"Smells delicious. And you look adorable," I say, giving her a kiss.

"Thank you! Brownies. They're always my contribution when we have a family meal." She points to the bouquet of flowers I'm carrying. "Aw. Are those for me?"

I shake my head. "Sorry, babe. These are actually for your mom."

"Oh my goodness, Brady! She's going to love you. That's so sweet."

"I didn't know what to get your dad, so I was thinking maybe we could swing by the liquor store on the way up and you can tell me what he likes to drink?"

"Dad's fine with beer. We can grab a six pack of Cape Cod Blonde and he'll be very happy. I never bring him anything. Except the brownies, of course."

We head to the car, stop at the store, acquire provisions. By the time we get to her parents' house, I find that I'm working extremely hard to keep the butterflies in check.

"I promise you, Brady. They're going to love you," she whispers as we walk up the crushed seashell driveway to the cottage. It's robin's egg blue with a lineup of hydrangeas in the front surrounding a modest porch. The window boxes are overflowing with petunias in every color imaginable.

This home is clearly occupied by an artist. My mother would adore it.

Gretchen's mom swings the door open wide. "Sweetheart!" she exclaims. "Don't you look beautiful!" Then, to me, "Hello! You must be Brady. I'm Annie. It's so nice to meet you." She leans in and with both arms, brings us in for a warm, if awkward, three-way hug.

"Hi, Mom," Gretchen says. Annie Andrews smells like lavender. When the hug ends, I can't help but notice that she and Gretchen look like peas in a pod. The only major difference is Annie is brunette and Gretchen's hair has faded to pink. But they both share the same freckles, the same rounded cheeks and the same button nose. Gretchen hands over her square pan of brownies. "You cut your hair. It looks great."

"I did!" She fluffs up her bob and offers a wide smile.

"Here, Mrs. Andrews. These are for you," I say, handing over the bouquet.

"Well, aren't these lovely? Thank you, Brady! Such a gorgeous mix of happy colors. I love them. Please, call me Annie," she goes on. "We're not super formal here. Come inside! I can't wait to hear all the details about how you two got together."

We follow her through the door, and as expected, the inside of their home is just as pretty as the outside. There are paintings of nautical landscapes on the walls, several family photos, and no shortage of pictures of Gretchen as a little girl. The skylights let the late-day sun into the living room, and the kitchen spills out onto an expansive back deck, where a man stands holding a pair of barbeque tongs, facing a wide grill with his back to us.

"They're here!" Annie sings, and Mr. Andrews turns around. He's a tiny bit taller than I am, has salt and pepper hair, and is wearing an apron that reads *Trophy Husband.* I see Gretchen in him too, the way his smile lights up his face when he looks at his daughter, and in the warm brown of his eyes.

"There she is," Mr. Andrews says. "How's my girl?" He wraps her up like a giant burrito in his mammoth arms.

She gives him a kiss on his shaved cheek. "Dad, this is Brady." Gretchen gestures at me.

"Good to meet you, son," he says. He shakes my hand firmly, and I offer him the six-pack. "Ah, thank you. Let's get these in the cooler. Annie, would you mind?"

"I got it, Dad." Gretchen takes the beer from her father and heads to the other end of the deck.

"Please, make yourself at home," Mr. Andrews says. "You like to grill?"

I nod, leaning against the railing. "Haven't done it in a while, though."

"What do you prefer: charcoal or gas?"

"Gas is more convenient, but nothing beats the taste of a burger cooked over the coals," I say. It's funny because I don't grill. My dad would never let me anywhere near his outdoor kitchen. But it sounds like the right answer, and all I care about is impressing this man.

"Atta boy," Mr. Andrews replies. "I'm with you. Gas is just much cleaner. How do you like your steak?"

"Medium's fine."

Gretchen hands each of us a beer. "Here you go, guys. I'm going to go help Mom with the salad." She winks at me and then turns to Mr. Andrews. "You be nice to him," she warns.

He laughs. "When am I ever anything but nice?" he replies.

"That one boy she brought home – Max? Matt? I forget his name," Annie calls from the kitchen.

"It was Mack," Gretchen reminds them. "And you scared him so bad, he almost peed himself."

"How'd you do that?" I wonder aloud.

"I handcuffed him to that bench over there." With his tongs, he points to a carved wooden bench alongside what appears to be a vegetable garden.

"Daddy said he needed to be put on time out after he said he didn't like the Patriots."

I laugh. "Really?"

"It was the *way* he said it. Said he thought Tom Brady was a punk who couldn't catch. Meanwhile, the little shit was – what – 15 years old? He could barely catch a cold, much less a football. So I put him out for a few minutes."

"It was the most mortifying date I ever had," Gretchen says.

"Who names their kid, Mack, anyway?" Mr. Andrews asks.

"It was short for MacArthur! His first name was Herbert."

"Well, that explains it. And I'm not one to talk about people's names. But that guy had it coming to him. And, see? You're welcome. As a result of my discipline, you never heard from old Herbie Mac ever again."

"Please don't discuss football with Brady," Gretchen says.

"You got strong feelings on the subject?" Mr. Andrews asks me.

I hold my hands up in surrender. "No, sir. I'm a baseball guy."

"Red Sox?"

"Yep."

"Good. Don't worry, Gretchie. He can stay."

"Thank goodness," she laughs, and opens the screen slider to let herself back into the house.

My phone goes off in my pocket. I pull it out intending to silence it when I notice the call is coming from a 212 area code. *I think it's the job I've been waiting to hear back from.*

"You can take that if you need to," Mr. Andrews says.

I shouldn't take it, I tell myself. I check the time. It's 4:47. *Just before 5:00 p.m. on a Tuesday. Could be bad, but could also be good. Fuck, fuck, fuck. I'm awful under pressure like this.* "Excuse me just one sec," I say. *If it's good news, I might look a little more like a prospect for their daughter.*

I take a few steps to the side, by the edge of the deck. "Hello?"

"Yes, hi. Is this Brady Hawthorne?" a man's voice replies.

"This is he."

"Brady, hi. This is John Stellaris, from Gildersleeve Marketing Group. We met a few weeks ago?"

"Of course. Nice to hear from you, John."

"I discussed it with the partners and we'd like to invite you down to New York for a second interview."

"That's great. Thank you. When would you like to schedule that for?"

"Well, unfortunately one of the members of our team is out on vacation through the end of the month. Lucky bastard's on a yacht trip in the Mediterranean. He's back on Monday the 30th. Think you can do a little later that week? Maybe that Friday, the 4th?"

"Sure. I can clear my calendar."

"Great. Thanks, man. Sorry for the delay. Summer's a tough time to get everyone in a room together."

I try to offer a hearty chuckle, but it comes off sounding a bit like Santa Claus saying *ho, ho, ho.* In my peripheral vision, I see Gretchen's dad look up at me. I clear my throat and say, "No worries. I understand."

"So, you'll come to our midtown office on Madison Avenue. Say 9:00 a.m.?"

"Perfect," I reply. "Anything I should bring?"

"Nothing I can think of right now. I'll reach out if I think of something, though."

"Sounds good. Thank you, John."

"Yup. I'll see you then."

"Looking forward to it."

He hangs up without saying goodbye.

"Everything okay?" Mr. Andrews asks.

"Yeah. I'm sorry," I say, sliding my phone back into my pocket. "That was actually a call about an interview."

"Oh, yeah?" he asks. "Where at?"

"It's a firm in New York. Gildersleeve Marketing Group, it's called."

"What kind of job?"

"It's a Market Research Analyst position."

"Sorry, son. No idea what that means."

"Basically, it's just studying and compiling data to help companies understand trends in sales."

"So, remote then?"

Good question. "I'm really not sure, actually."

"Better find out. I know my Gretchie won't be moving to New York City. She'd break her old man's heart."

"I'm sure it's virtual. I mean, it's basically sitting in front of a screen all day. Who cares if that happens in New York or on Cape Cod? The work is still the same."

"Hey, Brady? Do you like crushed red pepper in your pasta salad or should I put it on the side?" Gretchen asks, popping her head out of the slider.

"In the salad's fine, thanks."

"Gretchie, did you know about this big fancy New York job your friend here's got on tap?"

"Huh?" she asks.

Your friend? Don't love the way that sounds. "You know, the firm I had the Zoom call with a few weeks ago?"

"Yes, that's right," she replies. "I didn't realize they were in New York. Or that they contacted you again."

Not the right time to go into this, I think. But I don't want to end up handcuffed to a bench, so I just try to downplay it. "They just called – just now. Said they'd like a second interview."

"Oh my gosh, Brady! That's so exciting!" She steps onto the deck and throws her arms around me, then pulls away and plants a big kiss on my lips. Right in front of her father.

"New York is five hours away," Mr. Andrews adds.

She pulls back. "Is that where the job will be?"

"The headquarters is in the city. I'm not 100% sure if the job itself is virtual or not."

"Seems like a question one might ask on a first interview, but what do I know? I'm just a cop," Mr. Andrews adds.

"Daddy," Gretchen says. The inflection in her voice pleads with him to ease up on me. "When's the interview?" she asks.

"Few weeks. We can talk about it later," I add.

Sensing my discomfort, she attempts to change the subject. "That reminds me. I have my meeting with my advisor tomorrow."

"When will you get your student teaching placement, honey?" Mr. Andrews asks.

"Hopefully at the meeting. I can't wait to find out. I hope it's close by."

"You put in choices, right?" her dad asks.

"Yeah. They asked me for my top three. So I chose Eastport Elementary, Stony Brook Elementary in Brewster, and Orleans Elementary."

"In that order?" I wonder.

"Yeah," she smiles. "I would give my left arm to work at the school I grew up at."

"Live where you serve, that's what I always said," Mr. Andrews chimes in, flipping the steak tips over on the grill. "Did you grow up on Cape, Brady?"

"I did. I'm from Sandwich."

"Ah. Nice community."

"Agreed. It was a nice place to grow up."

"Your folks still live there?"

"My dad does, yes."

"He's the chef, Gretchie tells me. I guess that's where you got your grilling skills from, then?"

I nod.

"You know, we've never actually eaten there. The Diamond Excelsior. That's fancy business."

"I guess. Sort of overpriced, in my opinion."

He laughs. "All those resorts are, though. They cater to the tourists."

Yes... now this I can talk about. "Agreed. Summer people are the single driver of all pricing in the Cape and Islands economy. Just look at the housing market."

"Were your parents also raised here?" he asks.

"No, sir. Technically, I'm a washashore. My parents moved to Sandwich when I was a baby."

"Where from?"

"Boston. My grandfather was a chef at the Four Seasons there, which is where my dad did his apprenticeship. As I understand it, my father didn't want to live in his shadow, so when he got the opportunity to work at the Diamond Excelsior, he packed up my mom and I and the three of us left."

Mr. Andrews nods. "And where's your mom now?"

"Dad*dy*," Gretchen seethes.

"What? She's not – I'm sorry, she hasn't passed, has she?" he asks me, earnestly.

"No." I shake my head. "My mom lives in Iowa now. She's a writer. Moved out there about ten years ago," I explain.

"Oh." He nods. There's a lot he's not saying in the silence, though.

"Gretchen tells me that you and Mrs. Andrews have quite the whirlwind love story," I offer, trying to maintain a positive vibe.

This makes him smile. "That we did. Still do. Every day with Annie is an adventure."

"Aww," she hollers from the kitchen.

"I'm sorry for the inquisition, Brady. You just need to understand, me and Annie, we just want what's best for our little girl. Gretchie's all we got, and she deserves someone who's going to make all her dreams come true."

"I agree," I say. "She's a very special woman."

"You know, Dad," Gretchen says. "They say girls look for a man who reminds them of their father."

"She's not wrong," Annie calls out.

"Well, son," he says. "If you're anything like me, you'll do whatever it takes to make her happy. Because she deserves it." Mr. Anderson drapes a protective arm around his daughter.

I smile, but I can very clearly read between the lines. That's a threat, a guarantee, and a challenge all rolled into one.

Gretchen rolls her eyes. *I'm sorry*, she mouths at me silently.

I inhale, contemplating how to respond. "Mr. Andrews, with all due respect, I've learned a lot about relationships from watching my parents go through their divorce. So I can't stand here and give you my word that everything between Gretchen and I will be perfect. I can only promise that I'll show up, even when it's hard, or inconvenient, or uncomfortable. In my experience, relationships succeed or fail based on whether or not both parties make the choice to actively put the other person first, every day, no matter what." I rub my hand along the back of my neck. "For as long as Gretchen will have me, I give you my word, I'll show up for her."

He stands there, frozen. A lump forms in my throat as I try to read his expression. But then, a slow smile plays on his lips. He reaches out and shakes my hand. "Good in my book, kid," he says, patting me on the back with his free hand. "Good in my book."

CHAPTER TWENTY

GRETCHEN

Jane Bishop is my advisor at Framingham State University. She was also my teacher for a Science of Reading class I took last year, which was the single experience that solidified my belief that my calling in life is to become a teacher. She's a certified dyslexia therapist and her lectures are famously informative, largely because she explores brain neuroplasticity and how best to create a strong academic foundation for children by using techniques that build both skills as well as confidence. She's busy, though, because she trains entire school districts on how to work with learning disabled children in addition to being a faculty member at Framingham. So, when she hosts her advisory meetings online, they're usually during a lunch break in her schedule, or they're squeezed in during an independent exercise she's running with a larger group of teachers. Advisory meetings are 30 minutes tops. She's brilliant, so I'm thrilled to be working with her, but still. 30 minutes at a clip is all that any of us get.

30 minutes to plan my entire upcoming semester.

"How's everything, Gretchen?" she asks. "It's so good to see you. How's your summer been?"

"Good. Fine, thanks. You?"

"You know, same old. Doesn't feel like summer, to be honest. I'm running a project with the city of Burlington. We're collecting data on an aggregate of 877 students there. It's a beast, but it's trailblazing work. We're developing a whitepaper to deliver to the state education department in Vermont with clear data on the benefits and value to a science-based reading approach to language acquisition for kindergarteners – so I've been synthesizing data for the past six weeks. Super fascinating stuff."

This is why I chose her as my advisor. Jane Bishop is working to change the landscape of public education and early literacy in several states, which – as a potential future kindergarten teacher – truly amazes me.

"Wow," I say. "That's very cool."

"At some point, we're going to use Massachusetts as a model. Maybe by the time you're a teacher, I can enroll your class in one of my future studies."

These words are like music to my soul: the idea of being a teacher worthy of participating in a Jane Bishop study.

"I'd love that," I respond.

"Okay. So." She swipes something on her phone and sets it down on the desk in front of her. "This semester you need to take a Digital Pedagogy class and get your observations done. Then in the spring you'll do student teaching and be all set."

I nod. "I can't believe that's all I have left. So exciting."

"I made some calls to make sure you'd have your observations and your student teaching placement in the same school, and because I have a former student who's an administrator at Eastport, I was able to get you in there."

My heart races. "Seriously?" I exclaim, trying not to sound like a kid. I take a breath, catching myself. "Thank you. That's wonderful. I went to that school as a child." *Wonderful* is an understatement. It's a dream come true. "My dad's going to flip."

"Why's that?"

"He's just super committed to the notion of giving back to the community."

"I love that." She claps her hands. "Ah. So happy it worked out, then."

"Really, thank you."

"My pleasure, Gretchen. All that's left is for you to complete the basic pre-req stuff. I'll let them know at Eastport that you're good to go for a September start for your observations. They'll issue you a drug test at the end of summer. They'll also send you directions on how to get fingerprinted. This allows the state to run a thorough background check. Results will go back to the school, and you should be able to get started right after Labor Day."

"Perfect, "I say.

"Now, observations will be Monday through Thursday," Jane explains. "Digital Pedagogy is Wednesday night from 7-9 and also Friday from 10 to noon. So, it's a pretty full schedule."

"Wait," I say. "Quick question. I was planning to start looking for sub jobs for the fall. I thought observations were only 2-3 times a week."

"No, it's four days. And, I mean, you could go for sub jobs but honestly I wouldn't recommend it, for a number of reasons. First of all, you want the continuity for observing.

Sub positions are completely reactive, and could last longer than a one-off day here or there."

"I just thought it would be a good resumé builder," I say.

"I think you're better off looking into an after-school position. Something where you can make a difference. What are your hobbies, Gretchen?"

I ponder this. "Um. Dancing, I guess." Yes, I realize that the *style* of dancing I participate in would not exactly qualify under "transferable skills," but it's not a lie, and it's the only thing I can think of at the moment.

"You have any formal training for it?" she asks.

"I guess," I say, stretching the truth. "Nothing that I'd put on a resumé, though."

"That's okay," Jane says. "If you're enthusiastic and can create a simple curriculum for a dance club, you'd be able to prove that you can be a resource both in and out of the classroom. So I would sooner advise that you go that route. You'll have more of an impact that way, and honestly, you'll make more money too, because it's consistent work."

"Okay," I nod. I jot down *dance club* on my notepad.

"I'd check out the websites of schools in the area. Many of them have postings up for the fall already. Even if it's not specific to dance, you could help with homework, lead arts and crafts, play games, things like that. I'm sure you'd have no trouble finding an after-school gig."

"Got it," I reply. "Thank you." *After school,* I scribble.

"Obviously, you should look at Eastport first, just for convenience and ease. But if they don't have anything, you can expand to Wellingham, Truro, Orleans, wherever else is close by. Just don't build yourself too much of a commute because an after-school program is going to need you pretty close to the time that school ends. I know this sounds like it should be pretty straightforward, but you have no idea how many students I've worked with who don't realize some of the basic mechanics of time management." She laughs.

"No, I get it," I assure her. "I appreciate the idea. It sounds like more fun than subbing anyway."

"Yes, and even more importantly, you'll make a name for yourself in a local school, which will lead to a higher likelihood of that school considering you for employment once you're certified."

"Exactly."

Jane taps her pen against her lower lip. "I'm trying to think. Is there anything else we need to discuss?"

"I don't think so. Eastport will contact me?"

"Yes, via e-mail, late August, with directions for drug testing and fingerprinting."

"I think that's all, then."

"Okay. Then make sure you keep me posted on the job search for an after-school position. I'll keep an ear to the ground as well and let you know if I hear of anything."

"Thanks," I say.

Jane sighs. "I love this part of advisory. It's so rewarding to watch students when they're right at the brink like this. Like, you're so close to your goal that you can taste it."

"It's definitely exhilarating. I can't wait for September."

"Me too. Anyway, you know where to find me if you need anything in the meantime. Hope you enjoy the rest of your summer, Gretchen."

"Thank you! You too."

She grins, nods, and with the click of a mouse, she disappears.

I spend the next hour diving down an internet rabbit hole, searching for after-school positions and making lists of sites to return to. My resumé is updated from when I went to the Hyannis Career Center, but now I want to consciously include more child-friendly stuff as well as references. I babysat for a set of twins two summers ago, and the mom, Mrs. Girardi, always said I could list her as a reference if I needed to. So, I dig through my phone and find her number. My brain continues to spiral in this way until I realize I'm late for prepping the Jell-O shots for the party tonight, so I need to get myself together and head up to Cosmo.

I call Brady on the way up Route 6 just to say hi. He's on his way down to the Cape Cod Mall to buy a new pair of shoes for his upcoming interview. I like that we're both preparing for the future. It's nice, feeling like we're about to take a big step forward into a much more adult life together.

I consider the fact that Brady could be my forever-person, and it makes me feel warm inside. I slip into a daydream for the rest of the ride to Cosmo. I picture him proposing to me on a beach somewhere. I imagine my father walking me down the aisle at a sweet backyard wedding at my grandparents' house in Provincetown where the romantic camellia vines have been growing wild for years. I picture the end of the aisle, Dad lifting my veil and looking at me with happy tears in his eyes. "I trust you, son," he says to Brady. "I know you'll take care of my little girl."

When I get to Cosmo, my daydream is put on the back burner upon the realization that I'm out of Jell-O. I've got plenty of alcohol, but sadly, one cannot make Jell-O shots without the Jell-O. I climb back into my Fiesta and begin the sojourn back down 6 to the Stop and Shop in Orleans. It's as I'm approaching the Orleans Rotary that a man on a bicycle pops out onto the road at Log Cabin Farm. I swerve to the left to avoid hitting him, and then I overcorrect back to the right, which is how I end up slamming into the curb with my front tire.

Which pops. Of course.

I hear a noise, but I assume it's the sound of the collision with the curb. I'm able to keep driving, so I don't realize the tire is rapidly deflating until about 30 seconds later, when my pulse (which is already pounding from the scare of the biker) shoots through the roof as my car begins to wobble. *The rotary's too big,* I realize, and decide instead to pull off into the grassy area on my left directly opposite Wild Care, the wildlife rehabilitation center. I get out of the car and walk around the front to the passenger side. *Yup. That tire's shot.*

I have a donut, but it's very old and lives underneath the carpet in the hatchback of my car. Also, if we're being real, I don't know how to change a tire. I don't even know if the donut is any good. What I *do* know is that if I call my father, his first question will be *Where were you going at 3:00 p.m. all the way out this way?* According to him, I should be at work from 3-11 at the Diamond Excelsior on a Wednesday, not stuck at the Orleans Rotary wearing a pair of leopard print booty shorts and matching bra underneath a pair of loose overalls. Not that he has my "work schedule" stuck to the fridge. Never in my family.

Nope. Can't call Dad. And yes, I do have AAA but it's my dad's policy, so I'm not sure if that would somehow end up being reported to him. My dad's the *chief of police*, you understand. The man is basically a cross between Sherlock Holmes and the Terminator.

That leaves Brady.

I punch my phone screen with my forefinger, locating him in my recent contacts. It rings twice before he picks up.

"Well, hello again. What's up?" he asks.

"Hi," I say. "I'm sorry to bug you, but I'm stuck at the Orleans rotary."

"Stuck? What do you mean?"

"I hit the curb and my tire went flat."

"Oh, shit. Are you okay?"

"Yeah, I'm fine. Just don't know how to change a tire, exactly."

"Okay. No worries. I can change a tire. I'm on my way home from the mall, so I'll just come straight to you. Figure no more than 30 minutes? Can you stay where you're at safely?"

"Yeah, I'm on the grass right off the rotary. If you head around it once, you'll see me."

"Okay. Stay in the car. I'll get there as fast as I can."

True to his word, Brady comes to my rescue in 28 minutes, not that I'm counting. Only problem is, the metal piece that holds the tire iron and jack in on top of the donut is rusted shut. Brady can't get it to come loose.

"Do you have a donut I can borrow?"

"Yes, but it might not fit your car. The lug pattern has to match." Brady scratches his head, thinking. "Maybe you should just take my car. I'll stay here and figure out how to handle this."

"I don't want to leave you stranded," I say.

"Nah, no worries. I'll be fine. I have AAA, so I'll just get the car towed to Cape and Islands Tire. It's right up the road, maybe two miles tops."

"But what if they don't have a tire?"

"Then they'll get one. Might take a day or two, but the guys who run the place are good. And the prices are fair."

"But you'll be stranded," I point out.

"Gretch," he says, reaching out for my hand. "I can get an Uber. It's no big deal."

I sigh.

"Anyway, no sense in arguing. You need to be at work, don't you? It's almost 5:30."

"5:30? Holy shit," I say. "I gotta get the Jell-O. I need to make the shots!"

"Okay, so go. I've got this." Brady gives me a kiss on my forehead and hands me his keys.

"You're a lifesaver," I say. "I owe you one."

"Happy to help," he says, and the fact that I know he genuinely means this makes me want to curl up in the backseat of my busted Fiesta and do all sorts of unthinkable things to him to express my gratitude.

Unfortunately, I really need to go.

I kiss him goodbye and head to Stop and Shop in Brady's car. A basketful of Jell-O boxes later, I'm back on the road to Cosmo, and I honk the horn when I pass Brady. He's on the phone, and gives me a wave from the driver's seat of my flaming orange ride.

By the time I get back to the studio, I begin mixing and pouring the trays of shots as quickly as I can. At 6:30, they're all in the fridge and I'm cleaning up the boxes just as Saffron and Indigo arrive with a Domino's pizza in tow.

"Hey, girl!" Indigo hollers. "Cherry's right behind us. She had to stop for some yogurt or something because she didn't think her body could handle pizza after the appendicitis issue," she explains.

"So, feel free to join us," Saffron adds. "We can't finish a whole pie before a party."

"I'll bloat," Indigo laughs.

I grab a slice and sit with them. Cherry walks in moments later.

"Hey!" I say. "You look great. How's the patient?"

"I think I'm finally ready to dance again," she says. "No climbing, just to be safe, but I think I can do the basics and teach the choreo and all that."

"Thank God," I say. "I'll be more than happy to go back to my role of partysitter."

"Dress to pole anyway, though," Cherry says. "Just in case I need backup or start to feel less than wonderful, okay?"

"No worries," I reply. "So, your stitches are all healed, then?"

Cherry pulls down the left side of her sweatpants to show us her scar. "They're mostly dissolved, yeah."

"That looks badass, Cher," Saffron says.

Indigo giggles. "When people ask, you should tell them you got in a knife fight."

"I hate the way it looks. Eventually, I'll probably get a tattoo to cover it."

"It's not bad," I say. "I'm sure the scarring will fade."

"All I can say is thank God for the high rise trend," she says, pulling her pants back up. "I can still wear bikinis and booty shorts."

"Amen," Saffron offers, chewing on the crust of her pizza slice.

The girls finish eating and then change into their eveningwear, which is as much of a process as ever. I obsessively check on the shots in the fridge, but, like the saying goes, *A watched pot never boils.* I can't get my shots to cook faster. By 7:50, I realize this is actually going to be an issue. I pull Cherry off a pole, where she's warming up.

"Cher. We've got a problem."

"What's up?"

"The shots aren't ready."

"When did you prep them?"

I sigh. "About 90 minutes ago."

"Well, that explains it."

"What should I do?"

Cherry shrugs. "I'm not sure. This has never happened before."

"I would've had them done on time, but my car got a flat and I had to wait for Brady and switch cars and it took up a bunch of time," I wail.

"Okay, relax. Listen, the girls paid for a good time, so we'll just give them one. We good on alcohol?"

"Yeah, we've got cases in the back."

"Then just run the party using regular shots. Nobody will complain."

"We're going to burn through bottles way faster that way."

"Yeah," she agrees. "But it's one party. What other choice do we have?"

I nod. "Okay," I say. "I'll get the shot cups and start filling trays up." *I don't have a good feeling about this.* I look down the other end of the room, where Saffron and Indigo are practicing a move called the Bird of Paradise. "Cherry?"

"Yeah?"

I look at her solemnly. "Have you heard from Arrow?"

She nods, turns her back to the girls and lowers her voice. "She had to take Kit to a hotel. They're staying there together until Jenny gets out of rehab."

"When will that be?" I ask.

"July 21st."

I calculate this in my head. "So, like, just over a week."

Cherry nods.

"Then what? Will she come back?"

"She's trying to get Jenny to agree to move back here, from what I understand. But Jenny's in rough shape. Ricky's back in jail. It's a mess over there."

"Okay," I sigh. "How's Kit?"

Cherry smiles. "Thankfully, she's like a beam of light in a really dark situation. She's doing well, all things considered. She gets to visit with Jenny a few times a week, and she and Arrow are like two peas in a pod. Kit calls her Auntie Joy, which is maybe the cutest thing ever. She put her in a half-day summer camp at the YMCA so she gets to swim and go to the playground and stuff, which is a whole lot better than being stuck in some random hotel room all day."

"That's good," I say. "Please send her my best."

"I will," Cherry says. "Now, go get those shots ready. They're going to be here any minute."

The party consists of 23 guests, all from New Jersey. They roll up in limousines (thank God, no tow lot tomorrow), come decked out in micro-dresses with sky-high heels and hair extensions and extra-plump lips. Many have flashing penis necklaces on, and the bride is wearing a pink plastic crown made up of tiny upright penises. Several of them come into the space double fisting bottles of hard liquor: Patron, Absolut, Jim Beam, Smirnoff. One girl has a bottle of Boone's, which would strike me as funny if I wasn't undergoing a current alcohol crisis. They're not supposed to bring in outside booze, but maybe if we make an exception just this once, we won't burn through our own supply. I mean, they're going to do shots either way. Might as well let them drink what they want. I look at Cherry, silently asking her the question of whether or not we should allow this, and when she shrugs, I get the sense that she's thinking the same thing I am.

So, shots become more of a situation where most of the girls have affixed themselves to the bottle of their choosing, as if these were water bottles during a workout. I put the pretzel bites on early, because the group gets turned up pretty quick. They're grinding all over each other, all over the poles – one of them gets sloshed so quickly that she actually starts licking a pole. *Nasty.*

By the time the strippers come, the group is largely out of control. The three guys are dressed as wealthy businessmen in a *Fifty Shades* type of tribute, and before long the girls begin using silks and handcuffs and all sorts of other

BDSM-light toys that seem a bit over the top for the way we usually run things. But, hey, who am I to say what's okay and what's not? Cherry's back now, so I look to her for guidance. Only, she appears to be just as much of a deer in the headlights as I am. Even the guys look a little surprised, but they're busy being pawed at by the parched partygoers, one of whom clearly has a testicle fetish and keeps grundle-grabbing our guys. I can only shake my head and pray this all ends soon.

I pay out the boys in the back office as the food arrives: they've ordered edible phalluses in every variety you can imagine, in keeping with their penis vibe, I suppose. There's sausage and peppers, foot long Sabrett hot dogs, pigs in blankets, you name it. It's actually quite repulsive, the stench of all that processed meat and condiments, but, um, the heart wants what it wants, I guess? And if it wants dick-shaped dinner doused in sauerkraut? Ugh. I don't even know.

It doesn't take long for madness to ensue. There's a girl by the end of the buffet who loses her footing. Another girl catches her. As soon as the first girl stands upright again, she vomits.

Right into the tray of Polish kielbasa.

I am reminded of the first time I met Arrow. "There are two things that fuck up a good time," she said.

Vomit and death.

Saffron, Indigo, and I eyeball each other when it registers that this has escalated in to one of those, "If you're going to puke, then *I'm* going to puke" situations, and before I can figure out what to do, a second girl throws up. The vomit gets into the first girl's hair. Cherry's eyes bug out of her head.

I shift into crisis mode. *Get them outside*, I tell myself. I hesitantly wrap my arm around the first girl and begin to usher her toward the door. She stops to throw up once more on the way out. Another partygoer follows me with the second sick girl, thank God. I leave her out there with the two friends to get sick all over the gravel lot in front of Cosmo-pole-itan.

Back inside, the remaining girls have been ushered away from the food. Indigo tries to get them back on the pole, and some of the more inebriated ones follow her, while Saffron offers each of the ones who are complaining of still being hungry a dry hot dog bun. I guess she figures bread will keep this from continuing. Meanwhile, I grab a black garbage bag and begin to throw the contents of the buffet area into it, trying desperately not to inhale the scent of regurgitation that lingers heavy in the air. Cherry grabs the mop bucket and fills it with water and disinfectant, and she begins to mop the area.

I prop the door open to remove the filled garbage bag and check on the girls outside. *I'll have to hose down the lot*, I realize. *It reeks out here.* The first puker, whose name I learn is Amber, seems to have gotten most of it out. The second puker, Jessica, is only getting started, and I narrowly avoid getting a fresh round of splatter on my shoes as she gets going again. The caretaker, Fiona, is studying to be a nurse, I learn. She asks me if we have any water or electrolytes.

A lady walking a dog by flashlight notices us, but thankfully, doesn't stop – just gives us all a disgusted, judgmental look. *I get it lady. I'm grossed out, too.* I go back inside to get some water bottles.

Which is when I see Cherry holding her side.

"What happened?" I ask.

"I think I pulled something," she says. "It hurts."

She lowers her hot shorts and yup, of course. Her incision is bleeding.

"Fuck," I say. "We need to end this. Where's the bride?"

"Over there." Cherry points to the spin pole. Sure enough, the bride is laughing and spinning like a child on a merry go round.

"Go sit down in the back. I'll figure this out."

I tell the bride we need to call the limos back, that her friends are sick outside and we're so sorry, we have to shut down the party a little bit early. I take her to the locker where we put all the cell phones so she can locate hers, and I promise her we'll give her a 50% discount on the party because of this mishap. I don't need word getting out that a party at Cosmo was such a disaster on my account.

Fucking Jell-O shots.

She calls one of the limo drivers for me and hands me the phone. I explain what's happened and he says the fleet will be back in ten minutes.

I cut the music to a chorus of very loud groans and announce that the party has to end early. "Your cars are on their way. Please come get your personal belongings and you can wait outside."

By the grace of God, somehow the women listen, even though they're pissed. Indigo and Saffron help me get them outside. I settle up the money with the maid of honor, and, true to my word, give her 50% off, which – since the strippers already took their share, leaves me and the girls with $400 for the night. $100 each.

I'd make more on a Wednesday at the Diamond Excelsior pub.

Finally, they leave. Cherry covers her incision with Band-Aids, since that's all we have, and she leaves too, at my insistence. She can't be mopping or picking up heavy trash bags, anyway, and she'll need to see a doctor ASAP. Saffron, Indigo and I are left to clean up the extremely foul mess.

"I'm sorry, you guys," I say. "It was my fault. If we had stuck to the plan and had Jell-O shots ready, this never would have happened."

"Well, now we know," Saffron says.

"Yeah. I'll never break the protocol again, that's for sure."

"You think Cherry will tell Arrow?" Indigo asks.

"Shit. I hope not," I reply.

My stomach turns.

And this time, it's not because of the persistent aroma of vomit in the air.

CHAPTER TWENTY-ONE

BRADY

When I get the call from the Skeeve, I'm actually kind of glad, because I'm starting to run low on cash.

Over the past few weeks, I've taken Gretchen on quite a few nice dates, I got her tire fixed, and kept a good amount of fresh food in the house at all times. I also bought a new pair of shoes for my interview along with a new suit, got the suit tailored, and filled up my gas tank twice. The call comes when my bank account is just under $500.

"Brady," Steve says when I pick up the phone. Not *hi*, or *what's up*, or even a simple *hey*. Nope. Just my name.

"Yeah, hi, man. What's going on?"

"Listen, I got a request for you this weekend."

"A request? What do you mean?"

"Apparently, some chick saw you dance and specifically requested that you perform at her party. It's on Saturday night. You free?"

"Sure. What's the costume?" I ask. The thing is, his words don't really register; the idea that someone *specifically* requested me. I'm still new; there's no reason for this to happen. But I'm so head over heels for Gretchen that my brain's been acting funny lately. Like, normal things I might question just totally go unnoticed on my radar.

They say being in love will fuck up your head. I don't know if I'm willing to admit it to myself yet, much less out loud, but if this isn't love, I don't know what is.

"Bride wants you to be a cop," the Skeeve says.

I nod to myself. "'Kay. Is it a solo gig?"

"Nope. Five of you – but she wants you front and center. The specific request is that you are not to dance with anyone besides her."

Weird. "Can people request that?"

"For enough money, these girls can request anything," he says.

I don't like it. I should say no. But I think of Gretchen, and how, depending on how much I'll make for this gig, I'll be able to float through the rest of the summer and take her out on a few more really special dates. "Is there any kind of bonus? Or incentive?"

"Funny you should ask. Bridal party's paying extra for their demands. So, if you say yes, you get your normal rate plus a $500 bonus. Plus tips, of course."

In other words, it's a thousand dollars no matter what. For an hour of my life. "Okay. I'm in."

"Great. I'll throw in the thong again since you're doing me a solid. I need you to meet with the guys – it's Max, Tommy, Dex, and Billy – before the end of the week. Touch base with Max. He's got the info. I'll make sure he picks up the costume for you, too."

"Sounds good. Will do. Thanks, Steve. Appreciate the hook up."

I explain the situation to Gretchen, who thinks it's odd and immediately wonders if the girl in question is Miranda.

I hadn't considered it, but once she mentions it, I figure she's probably right. She did mention being engaged, after all. Still, it's just an hour, and for that kind of money, I can fake it. Gretchen says she understands, but I can feel the strain in her voice.

"Babe," I tell her that night in my apartment. "What do you have to be worried about? Do you have any idea how crazy I am about you?"

She sighs. "I know. I'm crazy about you too. I just – I feel *jealous.* I know it's petty, and that you were with her like forever ago, but I still don't like the idea of you dancing with her."

"I don't like it either. How about this. If you want me to call it off, I will. It's not worth it to me to make you upset."

She ponders this, taking a bite of the loaded nachos I made us for movie night. "Thank you, Brady. I guess it'll be fine."

"It's all for the money. You know I have zero interest in seeing her."

"I know. It's just, I feel like the last week's been a lot, between Cherry going back out on bedrest and the three of us running these parties alone. Too many mishaps. And now, to have to worry about you on top of it..." Her voice trails off.

The mishaps she's referring to include one night of vomiting clientele, another night where the maid of honor didn't bring enough cash to cover the balance on the party (a fact which Gretchen didn't find out until after the party ended), a third night where the bridal party surprised the bride with the trip to Cosmo and brought the bride's mother and grandmother, who were both appalled and took down the entire vibe, and a fourth night where two members of the bridal party got in a fist fight, and Indigo took a shot to the lip trying to break it up. So, yes. Her concerns are fair. I reposition myself on the couch so that I'm facing her, and take her free hand in mine. "I know. It's been a shit storm lately," I say. "Summer will be over soon, and then we can all go back to our regularly scheduled programming."

"What will that even look like for us?"

"I'm not sure, exactly," I admit. "But it starts with the two of us, happily together, you in your last year of grad school, me working at a good job. We'll be able to put this whole business of working at Cosmo behind us and move on to bigger and better things."

At this, she smiles. "I like that picture."

I lean in and kiss her. "I do, too."

We table the Miranda issue as kissing turns into a whole lot more on Luis' couch. We move to the bed and spend the next several hours enjoying each other, showering together, and then returning to the bed for a second round.

We do not watch the rest of the movie.

By Saturday, we've discussed it a few more times, but it's basically been decided that the show must go on, regardless of who's in the audience. I practice with the guys on Friday – Max teaches me some steamy choreo to a mixed number that begins with *Sound of Da Police* by KRS-One and includes a very sexy remake of *Every Breath You Take* by the Police, *Wait (the Whisper Song)* by the Ying Yang Twins, and ends with *Chains* by Nick Jonas. It's an insane compilation of songs that actually all work together surprisingly well. The dance takes about eight minutes total. Also, the props are kind of cool, and include long handled flashlights, handcuffs, and a bulletproof vest.

By the time Saturday comes, I'm almost looking forward to it. Gretchen's going to think it's crazy hot.

Me, the boys, and Big Mike pull up to Cosmo in two cars: Mike's F-350 and Max's Jeep Wrangler. I'm pumped for the night, looking forward to making some serious cash and hopefully not having to do this anymore. Gretchen's over it; I think at this point she's just eagerly awaiting Arrow's reappearance and the start of the school year. It's become too stressful for her, but, ever the trooper, my girl soldiers on. And same for me. I just want to be a grown up already. I've gotten a taste of what it could be like to have my own place, a serious girlfriend, and almost even a decent, steady job that I didn't get simply by being a blood relative of Chef Braxton Hawthorne. It's nice behaving like an adult. I'm ready to retire these shenanigans and do it for real.

But, for tonight, I'm an officer of the law.

We do our thing, knocking loudly on the door. Surprisingly, Gretchen opens it.

"Oh, no," she says, in a voice of fake surprise. "Officers, what can we do for you?"

"There's been a violation here," I reply, in an exaggerated, deep voice. "I'm afraid we have a search warrant. Let us in, little lady." She smirks. I definitely sound like I'm channeling my inner wild west, which is ridiculous. I wink at her as she steps to the side. Indigo kicks on the music as soon as the door shuts behind Big Mike.

And there she is, just as Gretchen expected.

Miranda.

The girl who, in another lifetime, actually mattered enough to hurt me and who, in this current lifetime, has become something of a nuisance.

We walk up onto the stage as the KRS-One song fills the air. The lights cut to blackness and the girls all scream as we kick on the flashlights, waving them around as we get into a V-formation. It's reminiscent of the lights on a cop car, which is kind of cool – Max and Tommy, who are on either side of me, each have a red tinted light and a blue tinted light and the rest of us have regular, white lights. Wave, wave, wave until the beat drops, the purple lights come back on, and we begin to dance. Our moves are smooth, we weave in and out through one another into a variety of formations, then begin to strip off our outer layers as singles, fives, tens and even twenties begin to fly at us from the dance floor.

Miranda, I notice, is wearing a barely there, white mini skirt with an extremely tight white tank top that reads "Bride" in neon pink. Several of her friends are wearing a pink version of this same outfit with white writing, each touting their position in the lineup: Maid-of-honor, Brides-maid #1, #2, and so on. It's been done. They've each got a dick-shaped pacifier hanging from a string around their necks, which I find hilarious. The maid-of-honor tries to tongue it down while she watches us dance, and it looks like she's trying to suck a micro-penis. I try not to gag and instead keep my eyes on Gretchen, who's setting the next round of Jell-O shots out on a table in the back. She looks beautiful, as always. Her hair has faded to a pinkish blonde, and she's wearing a rhinestone covered bikini top with fringe across the bottom, paired with black pleather hot shorts that leave most of her booty on display. I'm upset that I'm not allowed to dance with her tonight, and I swear if any of the other guys go near her, I'll sic Big Mike on them.

My plan with Miranda is as follows: I'll finish my dance on stage with the guys and then the clock will start ticking. I only have to stick around for 45 minutes more after the number ends. I'll do a basic rock move side to side with my ass sticking out so she can't grind herself up on my junk. I'll hold her hands if I have to so that I create natural space between us – and I'm wearing gloves, so it won't even be skin to skin contact. I'll two step and dance some of the other routines in the space in front of her when the music picks up and is a little faster, essentially dancing with *myself* instead of her, but facing her. And I will limit the conversation to an absolute minimum.

I don't know why she even wants me here. She's getting *married*, for Christ's sake.

The group number ends, and I take a deep breath, give Gretchen a wink, and begin to keep up my end of the bargain for this paycheck. I approach Miranda, reach out to take her hand, and begin to two step with her. Admittedly, this comes off a bit like an eighth grade boy-girl dance move. But she doesn't really have much of a choice. She asked to dance with me, and here I am.

She leans in and puts her face next to my ear. "I want to talk to you, Brady."

"Sorry, no can do," I reply. "You're paying me to dance, not to talk."

"I just want to clear the air. Can you *please* just step outside with me and give me two minutes to explain?"

I sigh and look at the clock. 44 minutes to go. "I'm not leaving," I say. "You want to talk, go ahead."

She shakes her head, frustrated. "Fine," she says, then takes a heavy breath as I continue to two-step. "Can you hold still for a sec?"

I do. She looks at me and nods. "I never slept with him."

"Who? Stacks Phillips?"

"Yeah."

I fold my arms across my chest. "Then explain the pictures."

She shakes her head. "They were Boudoir Shots. You know those pictures you can take for, like, your soon to be husband?"

I shrug. "Not really."

"Well, Stacks was representing a client who was trying to sue the photographer for a personal injury claim. The client said the place was unsafe. I wanted to secure a spot in the firm beyond my internship, and I figured if I went in and checked it out for myself, I could testify as a witness in the case and then maybe he'd promote me."

My obvious confusion must be evident in my expression, because she continues to explain.

"So, I did the boudoir shots and I sent them to Stacks in an email with the subject line *info for your case*. But then his wife saw them and, well, you know the rest."

"And that was all?" I ask.

"Yes – but it all escalated so quickly that I could never really explain it to you. My parents took away my phone when they sent me to California. They didn't want me to be in touch with anyone."

"So, what brought you back?"

"The holidays. We always celebrate at our Cape house, and after missing a few years of Christmases, I wanted to come back home. My sister set me up on a blind date with a cop here – figured, if I was home, I should at least have a little extra protection – anyway, now we're getting married."

"Why are you telling me all this?"

"Because, Brady. I always felt bad about how we ended things. Plus, I don't think I ever really got over you. And now, seeing you like this, I felt like it was the universe giving me a second chance to make it right with you." She bites her lip coyly. "Or maybe, it's just the universe giving me one last hurrah before I go off and get married." Miranda places a finger on my abdomen. "I mean, you don't think this is all just a coincidence, do you?"

I remove her digit from my stomach. "I do, actually. And I have a girlfriend."

"So? I have a fiancé. I'm not suggesting we *do* anything. I just wanted to clear the air. You know. Move on from all that."

"Fine. Consider the air cleared."

She nods, and a smirk plays on her lips. "Okay. So, then, dance with me, Brady."

I literally am squished between a rock and a hard place. The boys around me are killing it. They're grinding up on the ladies, playing it up hard. Then the boys surround the two of us, yielding a surprising reaction from her. Instead of looking around, Miranda hones in on me with laser focus, as if she's determined to get me to do the kinds of moves those guys are doing. While I begin to shuffle innocuously from side to side, Miranda frowns. She places her arm around my waist and says, "Come on. For old time's sake." I take a step back, creating distance, letting her story sink in. I don't know if I believe it's true, but at this point, what does it matter, anyway? We've been done for so long, and I am head over heels for Gretchen. I just need to get through the next – I check the clock – 39 minutes.

But Miranda's not having it.

She begins dancing as if *she* is the stripper. She licks her finger and traces it down the front of her body. She drops to the floor and pops back up again.

"What are you doing?" I ask.

"I said, dance with me," she whines.

"I *am*," I insist.

She pouts. "You can't tell me you don't miss me, even just the tiniest bit?" She pushes her breasts up and begins to play with her nipples through her shirt. No shame, this girl.

"Miranda, stop," I say. "That's enough. I'll dance with you, but as I said, I have a girlfriend. You're getting married. And most importantly, I'm not interested."

Evidently deaf to my words, she goes too far.

Miranda turns around, facing her back side to me, bends over to put her hands squarely on the floor, and reveals to me that she is wearing nothing underneath that skirt.

My eyes frantically dart around the room, looking for Gretchen, making sure she didn't see what I just saw. She's dancing with Max now, but he's keeping a respectful distance. I'm sure he's just pacing himself. Sometimes the girls are so thirsty that dancing with Cosmo employees becomes a welcome reprieve. Her back is to me, though, so my wild gaze goes unnoticed by her.

Miranda turns back around to face me, and, pleased with herself for shocking me, flashes me again, this time from the front, She lifts up her skirt and reveals a clean-shaven ham wallet that I want exactly zero part of. I lean in towards her and say, "If you do that again, we're done here."

"I'm sorry, Brady," she sulks, and then, her expression turns diabolical. "But I'm a paying customer, so I call the shots tonight. You don't have to touch me. You just have to dance with me." She gives me the bitchiest grin. "Assuming you want to get paid, that is."

I shake my head, willing myself to keep it together. The whole reason I'm here is for the paycheck. So I can make ends meet and do nice things with and for my girlfriend.

I take a deep breath and pretend to smile.

Miranda, still facing me, takes a step closer. "Absolutely no touching," I remind her. "You touch me, we're done here."

Instead, she continues to touch herself. Over the skirt, over the tank top. Her hands snake up and down her body and she writhes into the touch as if she is genuinely arousing herself.

"Enough," I say, and she laughs. "I'm serious."

"So, when did you become a fuckboy anyway, Brady?" She's trying to get a rise out of me. *That's fine,* I decide. *Two can play that game.*

I ignore her question, plaster on a fake smile and – not sure where this comes from – start doing the running man, just to piss her off. Out of the corner of my eye, I see Big Mike laughing. It's about the least sexy move someone can do in a thong. And there's not a damn thing she can do to stop me.

The running man becomes the sprinkler. Then, I begin to floss. Next, I dab. I do the gritty back and forth in front of her as she grows increasingly agitated with me, folds her arms over her chest and huffs. Finally, I get sturdy, and Big Mike is in fucking stitches. I look like a fool, but hey, *I'm* not the one who rolled up with no goddamn drawers on like a ratchet piece of street trash.

Miranda stops dancing, and puts her hands on her hips in aggravation. "Will you please stop?" she yells at me. I see Gretchen turn around, and she starts laughing, too.

"Nah, Miranda. I can do this all day," I announce. "It's a killer workout for my glutes."

A few seconds later, most of the people in our immediate vicinity are laughing along with Gretchen and Big Mike. Miranda's face twists up like she might cry. Finally, she screams, "You know what, Brady? Fuck you," and storms past Big Mike out into the parking lot.

Once I get my fit of giggles in check (yes, I am wiping tears from my eyes), I resume dancing for real. I work the room like I normally would, noticing that the maid-of-honor has chosen to evacuate the dance floor and locate the blushing bride outside in the gravel lot. *Good for them*, I think. *Like I give a shit.*

Later, Big Mike is put in the position of having to collect our money. He explains to the bridal party that I did exactly what I promised to do and that Miranda was wrong to flash me multiple times. Big Mike is *big*. His voice *booms*. And he's there to protect us – whether that means keeping unwanted hands (or mouths) off of us, keeping us from getting in fights with ladies who drink too much, or, in this case, collecting our payments.

Miranda screams at Mike in the parking lot that she did *not* order my brand of foolishness and did *not* want to become the butt of the joke at her own bachelorette party, but Big Mike responds that she should have been respectful about the limitations and stopped flashing me the first time I asked her to. Eventually, the bridal party pays us what they owe us, and the rest of the party is cut short. Miranda's furious. She orders herself an Uber, leaving the rest of her party to pay the remainder of the Cosmo bill. When the Uber pulls up to the parking lot, she yells one final thing at Big Mike.

"You're all going to fucking pay for this! Mark my words."

Then, she's gone.

CHAPTER TWENTY-TWO
GRETCHEN

After our recent debacle with Miranda, which Brady handled *brilliantly* (if I do say so myself), Brady informs me that he's done stripping. "I've made enough money to finish out the summer," he explains. "This will give me the freedom and time I need in order to buckle down and find a real job."

"I'm not against it," I reply. "Save your stripping for my eyes only."

"Exactly," he says. "I like it better that way, anyway."

I love that we both want to be done with the grind (no pun intended) of the adult entertainment industry, and that we're also both diligently planning for our next steps once the summer ends.

I'm lying in bed with Brady on the last Monday morning of July. We slept naked, as we often do, and waking up, we're just a tangle of limbs marked by his profound morning wood. I can't help myself. I roll on top of him and kiss him, and he welcomes me into his mouth. My nipples pinch at the touch of his tongue against mine, and the sensation hits me right between my legs. It's amazing how hot this man makes me. I bite his lower lip, then move down to his neck, and try to head lower when he stops me.

"Uh uh," he says. "Don't you dare."

"Don't I dare what?" I ask, my face against his chest.

"Don't you try to go down on me just because I'm hard."

"Why not?" I ask.

"Because you'll break my cardinal rule."

"Which is?" I ask, raising an eyebrow.

"Ladies first."

Seriously, I could try to dream up a fictional man and would never even come close to the real one I've got.

He flips me onto my back, kisses down my body and places his palms on my inner thighs, holding me open. He looks at me, first between my legs, and then up at my face. "You are so beautiful, Gretchen. I could stare at every inch of you and it would never get old."

"Well, don't just sit there staring. That's weird."

He removes one of his hands and rests his face on my inner thigh, getting a better look. "No, it's not. I'm appreciating you. Besides, I'm getting to it. Don't worry, I won't make you wait very long."

"Are you –" I stop myself, craning my neck to the side. Goddamn it. He *is*. He's touching himself while he looks at me. "No fair, Brady," I squirm. "You can't do that."

"Does it bother you?" he asks.

"No," I say. "I just – do it to me instead," I beg.

"I think you like being teased," he says, and he's right. It dawns on me that I've never been so open in bed with anyone before. He doesn't stop stroking himself, but he does lean in and give me a long lick, ending with a tender kiss that I grind my hips up to meet, searching for pressure from his tongue. "Tell me what you want, Gretchen. I'll do anything."

The old me – that is, me before Brady – would never, *ever* ask for anything in regards to sex. But this version of me enjoys the freedom that being in a healthy, stable relationship with the world's hottest former stripper can bring.

"Fuck me," I say.

"Already?" he asks.

"With your mouth," I clarify.

"Damn," he whispers, and kisses me again. "Gladly."

I can feel him working himself faster as he buries his face into me. I'm so wet, and he knows exactly how to move his mouth to get me to come for him. He uses his free hand to play around at my entrance, then finally slides a finger inside me, and I can feel him stop moving his other hand – the one that's wrapped around himself. "You okay?" I whisper.

"Yeah. Just got pretty close, so I had to stop before I ruined it."

"Mmm," I reply, as Brady plants his lips back on me. With his newly free hand, he reaches up and grazes my left nipple. My body arches into the touch. His finger moves faster inside me and his other hand takes turns hopping from one peak to the other, pinching lightly and flicking each nipple until they're both solid little marbles. Each touch sends me closer to the precipice. I moan, and Brady knows that means to go the tiniest bit faster, so he does. My orgasm comes hard at first, and I can feel myself constrict around his finger, hooked perfectly as it is, bringing me so much unfiltered pleasure. The next waves follow, and I jerk into the sensation until all that's left are delicious aftershocks.

"Now, your turn," I say. I reposition myself so that I can take all of him into my mouth, eliciting guttural groans that provide instant gratification. Carefully, I move up and down, sometimes slowly, sometimes faster. He gets worked up into a frenzy pretty quickly, so I offer him a change in positions, and he gratefully accepts. On all fours, I welcome Brady to take me from the back, which I know is his favorite, especially when he's carnal like he is first thing in the morning. He grunts and thrusts, grabbing my hips for support, and I can feel his entire length fill me each time. My eyes roll into the back of my head as he comes inside me. Then, we collapse onto the bed. Brady cleans us up with yesterday's boxers, which were left on the nightstand specifically for the possibility of a morning like this.

He hugs me afterwards, and the lust is now replaced with an overwhelming tenderness. He pulls back to look me in the eye. "I love you," he whispers.

I can't control it. I grin like a fool. "Say it again," I murmur.

"I love you, Gretchen."

"Mmm. I love you too, Brady. So much."

And this beautiful Monday morning is what sets the scene for what I imagine will be a glorious week.

The next day is August 1st. There's a shift in the air once August hits; at least, this has always been true for me. When you grow up in a summer town, it's hard not to see August as the beginning of the end. School usually starts either right before or right after Labor Day, and so there's one more month – or, sometimes more accurately – four more weeks to soak up whatever gifts the season has left to give.

It's ironic that August 1st is when I hear from Cherry that Arrow has convinced Jenny it is time to move on. Which means she'll be coming back to the Cape with her family in tow. I wonder what that will mean for Cosmo, but I don't ask. It will be interesting to see if maybe they'll finally open up that dental office they spoke about all those years ago. Or maybe just something a little more – kid friendly? Wholesome? I don't know. Of course, the news does not come without its downside: because Jenny's coming back with her, they have to pack up her whole apartment and move it here. Which means they'll be renting a U-Haul and driving it all the way from Arizona to the Cape. According to Cherry, their hope is to arrive by Monday the 7th.

Maybe then I can quit my job.

I've enjoyed it, don't get me wrong. But I have enough money. I've got big plans to get an after-school job while I student teach so that I can finally start my life as a certified teacher next year. I've got an amazing boyfriend *who loves me* who is also looking at real jobs in economics that I don't entirely understand.

I would really like to see where this new path takes me. And, just like how Brady's done with stripping, I'm getting tired of Cosmo. I love the *dancing*, I've discovered. I just don't enjoy the business side of things. Also, there's no life for it beyond the summer.

Anyway, Arrow knew I was only temporary when she hired me. And I'm sure we can both agree that I did way more than either one of us ever expected me to.

August air smells like anticipation. Impending change. And I can feel it more this year than ever.

Brady's big interview is this Friday in New York. I'm excited and nervous for him. He says he'll leave on Thursday afternoon and stay overnight in a hotel in the city, since the interview is at 9:00 a.m. He's invited me to join him, but with Arrow still out and Cherry back to shot-girling for me (carefully, as her doctor was pissed when she reopened her incision), I can't in good conscience abandon the club this weekend.

Plus, just knowing there's an end in sight makes it easier to forgo the idea of road-tripping to New York with Brady. I remind him that when (not if) he gets this job, I'm sure he'll have to go in for meetings every now and again. So we'll be able to go down and visit whenever we want. Who knows? Maybe his company will even pay for it.

That's how finance and marketing and all those industries work, right?

Everyone's excited for Brady's interview. Big Mike makes him a Spotify playlist to get him pumped. Brady's mom sends him a handmade dreamcatcher that she bought at an open-air market made by a Meskwaki native. With it, she sends a card that says something about chasing your dreams. It's very sweet. "She's a little out there sometimes," Brady explains, "but I think you'd like her." He calls her to thank her, and she reminds him that she'll be in Connecticut for a writing conference that overlaps with his time in New York, and would he like to see her? Of course he would. Brady's good like that.

Even my parents are excited for him. My dad tries to look up what a Market Research Analyst does, but can't quite figure it out. My mom bakes him cookies for the long car ride to New York, which she gives to me on Wednesday morning when I swing by the house to pick up some mail that came for me over there.

Things are finally coming together, I decide, listening to Sheryl Crow's *Soak Up the Sun* in my fresh-tire Fiesta on the way back from Eastport. *It feels so good to be in such a healthy place.*

Wednesday night, though, I'm finishing up a (thankfully uneventful) shift at Cosmo when I see that I missed a call from my dad.

I check the voicemail. "Gretchen, it's me. Listen, I wanted to let you know that me and your mother decided to surprise your friend Brady at the Diamond Excelsior tonight. Wanted to wish him luck on his interview, and figured we'd never been there, so might as well go while we actually know someone who works there. Except, honey, that's the thing. I don't know how to tell you this except to just come out with it. I think Brady's been lying to you. He wasn't at the Diamond Excelsior. At all. We even asked for him by name, and the server we spoke to said he hadn't worked there in months. I wanted to come down to the pub and talk to you about it, but your Mom said not to upset you at work. I don't like the sound of this, though, Gretchie. Call me in the morning, honey. I think we should talk about this. Love you."

Fuck.

I hate to wake him, but as soon as I get home, I knock on Brady's door.

"Hi, babe. How was work?" he says, opening it, rubbing his eyes.

"It was fine. I'm sorry that I woke you," I say, kissing his cheek.

"No worries. I wasn't totally asleep. Just dozed off watching Netflix."

"Brady, we've got a problem."

He furrows his brow. "What's wrong?"

"Apparently, my parents went to the Diamond tonight to wish you luck. They sat in the main restaurant and asked for you by name – only, someone said you haven't worked there in months."

"Oh. Shit."

"Yeah. My dad's pissed."

"Hm. That was nice of them to go over there. I feel bad." He rubs his forehead.

"Yeah, kind of out of character. They must like you. They don't eat at expensive places like that for no reason."

"Hang on, just let me think."

I lean against the kitchen counter.

"Okay. What if..." His voice trails off.

"I'm listening," I say.

"What if we say that I got moved to the golf side?"

"Go on."

"Like, you know how by the pro shop there's that restaurant where the golfers eat?"

"Mulligan's?"

"Yeah. What if we say I moved over there? It's still part of the Diamond."

"I guess we could say that. But wouldn't it be a downgrade?"

"Not if I was the restaurant manager."

"That could work. Unless..."

"Unless what?" he asks.

"Unless they go there to try and visit you."

Brady takes a step towards me and reaches his hands around my waist. "Well, they won't go this week, since I'm out of town anyway. Hopefully, that will give everyone a chance to settle down. By next week, maybe it won't be on their radar anymore. Especially," he goes on, kissing me on the forehead, "if I get the job in New York."

"Okay. That's fair."

"You just need to be convincing when you tell them. Like there's nothing to be concerned about at all. Like it was just a misunderstanding or an oversight."

I nod. "Got it."

I put it out of my mind for the rest of the night, curl up in Brady's bed, and help him get over his pre-interview jitters.

Twice.

CHAPTER TWENTY-THREE

BRADY

Driving *to* New York is no problem at all, but driving *in* New York? Holy hell. That's another story altogether. People are crazy. That's really all I can say.

I don't know what I thought New York City would be like. I remember going on a class trip there when I was in the fifth grade. We went to see the Broadway rendition of *Grease* and it was really cool. But we drove in on a coach bus, and all I remember is playing with my PSP for the hours-long trip down. I do not remember every turn being a near-death experience. I do not remember pedestrians playing Russian Roulette with their lives, jaywalking without even so much as a "look both ways" mentality. I remember eating pizza and thinking the slices were so big. I don't remember the atmosphere absolutely *reeking* of weed, or seeing quite so many panhandlers on the street. I also don't remember parking costing $80, but of course, I was not responsible for parking a vehicle overnight when I went there the last time.

It's a *vibe*, that much is certain. The fact that I make it to my hotel is nothing short of a miracle. And thankfully, the hotel is close to the office where my interview is being held, so I can walk there the following morning. There are five different food choices on my block alone, and I opt for pizza, because it brings back happy memories. It is handed to me on a thin, white paper plate tucked into a brown paper bag, and within moments of holding it in my hand, the bag is translucent with grease. It tastes good, though. Like good enough that I wish I could save some for Gretchen.

The hotel is fine. The room is small but clean, and the view of city lights and the people down below me on the streets who are tiny dots, like ants scurrying this way and that, is insane. The sound of sirens is never ending, and I can hear it even through the floor-to-ceiling windows of my room. I try to drown it out by watching SportsCenter, which I leave on all night, because I'd rather sleep with the sound of people analyzing baseball than the melody of mayhem that exists outside my door.

Fun to visit, for sure. Maybe not alone, and maybe not under such nerve-wracking circumstances, but still. I just don't know how anyone would ever be able to *live* here.

I sleep. Well, sort of. I drift in and out. At 6:00 a.m., I give up, head down to the gym and run a few miles on the treadmill just to burn off the nervous energy. I grab breakfast from the complimentary selection in the lobby (a packaged muffin and a cup of coffee that is extremely strong). I go back to my room, get showered, packed, and dressed in my new suit. I stick my hands in the pants pockets to flatten out the fabric against my legs. That's when I discover the little piece of paper in my right pocket. *A receipt?* I wonder.

I pull out the paper, unfolding it. It's a note.

You're going to kill it, babe, it reads. *I believe in you. Love you so much! Xoxo, G.*

I steel myself. *She's right,* I decide. I *am* going to kill it.

For her.

For *us.*

I check out, drop my bag in my car in the hotel's parking garage, and head to the building that houses Gildersleeve Marketing Group. It's in Suite 1626, which, according to the map in the lobby, is on the 16th floor of the building. I go up in the elevator at 8:40, with about ten other people, all of whom ignore one another and either look straight ahead or down at their phones.

Once I locate the correct suite, I find a receptionist at a large glass front desk. She's changing out of sneakers and putting on a pair of high heels.

"Morning," she says. "How can I help you?"

"I have a 9:00 appointment with John Stellaris?" I ask, even though I realize it's not a question.

She clicks around on her desktop computer. "Brady Hawthorne?" she asks.

I nod.

"Have a seat. His team will be with you shortly."

I sit in a leather chair next to a glass table with a small stack of magazines on top of it. *Forbes. Time. The New Yorker.*

I opt to flip through my portfolio, which houses five copies of my resume (printed on fancy paper), a pad of lined paper, and a silver Diamond Excelsior pen. I focus on my breathing. Close the portfolio. Scroll through my phone. Put the phone away. Want to seem adult. Secure. Capable of eye contact, not always glued to a screen.

I pick up a copy of *The Wall Street Journal* that sits on the mahogany coffee table in front of me. I'm not reading the words. I'm just pretending to. It feels like forever, but finally a tall, broad man with white hair and a grey pinstripe business suit enters the waiting area.

"Brady Hawthorne?" he asks.

I stand up, smooth out my jacket. "Yes, sir. Mr. Stellaris?"

He shakes my hand. "Please. Call me John."

"Nice to meet you, John. Thanks for having me."

"Thanks for coming. Follow me," he says.

We head down a hallway into a room with a long, executive-looking conference table in the center. It's surrounded by easily a dozen black leather office chairs on wheels. All but four of them are filled.

I scan the room quickly, positive that there must be a mistake. There are eight people in here.

"Have a seat, Brady," John Stellaris says. *Fuck. I only have five copies of my resume.*

"We'll start with introductions," John goes on, and while each high-level adult member of this team introduces him or herself, I try – really, really try – to remember their names. I pretend we're playing that old game, *We're going on a picnic, and I'm bringing...* but by the fifth person I've forgotten the names of the first two people, and I'm starting to sweat.

Breathe.

John takes the lead on questions, at least at the beginning. He asks me about my previous work in the industry and why I left. (Easy softball. COVID. No one can argue with that.) He asks me what I enjoy about market research. I go on for a bit. I describe growing up in an area fueled by tourism and learning the role market research can play in creating a viable economy. I discuss the impact of the pandemic and how market research elevated the health and pharmaceutical industries during that time. I explain that in such a volatile business environment, market research analysis remains more important than ever, as we need to forecast trends in order to keep companies sustainable and relevant.

They like my answers.

A lady with her hair up in a bun and glasses asks me the next set of questions, beginning with where I see myself in five years.

Married, I say, surprising myself, but warming inside at the fact that it might be true. *Working my way up a ladder in a job I can be passionate about.*

She asks about my greatest strength, followed by my greatest weakness. I say that my two biggest strengths are being a hard worker and being extremely loyal, and my biggest weakness is that I sometimes invest too much of myself into my work.

She asks for an example of that.

I tell her that right after the pandemic, I worked for my father, because he needed good help and no one wanted to return to the service industry. I put in 110% of myself, only to learn that working with family is complicated. I struggled to delineate between personal and professional there, which is why I ultimately left, I say.

She thanks me for my honesty, scrolls down the resume she's got up on an iPad in front of her, and asks me when that was.

End of May, I confirm.

She asks what I've been doing since then. Side hustle jobs, I tell her. Anything to keep afloat while looking for the next big thing, which, I speculate, might be this interview right now.

She smiles.

A different man takes over. He asks about how I heard about the position (found it online), why I want to work at Gildersleeve (seems like a fast-paced environment with top-notch professionals looking to make a real difference for the clients they serve), and what my timeline for moving to the city will be if I get the job.

Record scratch.

"I'm sorry?" I ask.

"I asked you what your relocation plans look like," he clarifies. "Because the position comes with an allocation for that."

I clear my throat. "I was under the impression that the position was remote," I say calmly.

"Hybrid," he clarifies. "Three days in, two days from home. We believe in balance here at Gildersleeve."

"Does it matter which days, from a scheduling standpoint?"

"Not unless we have meetings like this. Otherwise, most of us opt for Mondays and Fridays from home."

My mind races. The Acela train brings commuters to and from Boston, New York City, DC, etc. regularly. People do this. They make this type of thing work all the time. I nod at the table. "That sounds good."

"Were you not expecting to move closer to the city?"

I think on my feet. "I'm open to anything. I've been interviewing in Boston and DC, too. So, I haven't made any concrete plans, because that would be putting the cart before the horse." They chuckle.

The rest of the interview goes well, but my chest feels like there's something lodged in it. My phone vibrates in my pocket on two separate occasions, and I'm sure that at least one of those calls belongs to Gretchen.

We wrap it up, and I thank the interview team for taking the time to meet with me. Stellaris says they'll be in touch very soon. Sounds like potentially good news. He walks me out, shakes my hand, and tells me I did great in there.

In the elevator on the way back down to the lobby, I check my phone. First up is a text from Gretchen. *I got called for an interview by Eastport, babe! It's for an after-school counselor position, working with grades 1-3. I'm so excited! Hope your day is going great! Xoxo!*

There's also a text from my mom. *Still on for dinner tonight? I got a room with two queen beds in case you want to stay the night.*

I reply to my mother first: *Yes, can't wait to see you! I'll let you know about an overnight. Let me see how traffic is. I'll keep you posted on my travels.*

Then to Gretchen: *So exciting! Can't wait to hear all about it. Call you in a bit.*

But I can't shake the feeling in the pit of my stomach.

Before I head back to the car, I stop into a kitschy souvenir shop and buy Gretchen an *I ♥ NY* t-shirt. I grab myself a bagel with cream cheese for lunch and eat it on a stool overlooking fast-paced Lexington Avenue. Even at lunchtime, the city is fueled by an energy I'm not sure if I could ever match. It's thrilling, but I feel like my blood pressure has been through the roof ever since my arrival.

I muster up the courage to drive my car out of there, and by the time I've left the Bronx and am driving up I-95 into Connecticut, I can finally feel my shoulders begin to drop. I talk to Gretchen on the phone, and she shares all the exciting details of the interview she's got lined up next week. She asks me how my interview went, and I keep it vague, but let her know I have a good feeling, and that I'm just nervous about it. I ask about her dad; how did it go when she told him about my "switch" over to Mulligan's? It went fine, she assures me. All is good again. She asks if I'm coming home tonight or planning to hang with my mom. I tell her I'm not sure.

"You should stay, Brady. She probably really misses you. I'm sure she'd love to see you."

She's right, I know, but I tell her I'll play it by ear.

It takes just over three hours to get to the Marriott hotel in Mystic where I'm meeting my mom. She's left a hotel key for me at the front desk. Once in the room, I marvel at the quiet. No sirens. No noise. Just the hum of the air conditioning unit. I change out of my suit and into a pair of jeans and a polo shirt. Then, I lie down on the spare bed and close my eyes.

Next thing I know, I'm waking up to the sound of my phone vibrating. I check the time. It's 4:45. The call is from a 212 number.

I clear my throat and answer it.

"Hello?"

"Brady, hi. John Stellaris here."

"Hi, John."

"I'm just calling to let you know that the team and I were very impressed by you. We'd like to offer you the job," he says. "Starting salary would be $70,000, along with full health and dental, a 401k, and a $10,000 relocation package."

I'm stunned. I never imagined this could happen so quickly. "Wow," I say. "Thank you."

"Of course, take your time and think about it. We don't need to know until Monday," he continues.

Monday? "Sure thing, John. I just need to discuss it with my girlfriend."

"Roger that," he says. "Give me a call by COB Monday. Meantime, enjoy the weekend. And congratulations, Brady. We really think you'll be a valuable asset to the firm."

"Thanks, John. I really appreciate the opportunity. Very exciting."

"Great. Talk soon."

"Bye," I say, hanging up and rubbing my eyes.

Oof, I think. I look at the other bed and notice a stack of my mother's notebooks sitting there.

Suddenly, I'm really grateful to have some time with her.

I think you're right, babe, I type. *I think I'll stay the night here with my mom.*

Aw, Gretchen writes back. *That's great. Hope you have fun.*

Thanks. Love you. Have a safe night.

Love you too. Enjoy!

I set the phone down on the nightstand and work on intentional breathing to calm my heart rate.

For someone who's supposed to be so excited about adulting, I'm suddenly realizing that it might not be all roses and sunshine.

Nope.

Something tells me a storm is definitely brewing.

CHAPTER TWENTY-FOUR
GRETCHEN

The 24-hour period from waking up on Friday to waking up on Saturday is seriously reminiscent of a fever dream.

Brady's interview is Friday. While I'm waiting to hear from him, my phone rings. I don't recognize the number, but it's a local 508 area code, so I pick it up.

"Hello?"

"Hi. May I speak to Gretchen Andrews please?"

"This is she."

"Gretchen, hello. My name is Charlotte Fiore. I'm the director of after-school programming at Eastport Elementary."

"Oh," I say, clearing my throat. "Hi!"

"I'm calling in response to your application for a position with us," she says. "We'd like to set up an interview with you."

I shoot a fist up into the air but don't emit the screeching sound that my body wants to send up with it. "That would be lovely," I say, sounding like composure personified.

"How is next Tuesday? Say around 2:00?"

"Sure. I can be free then."

"Great. You'll be meeting with me and possibly the school principal, Mrs. Trout."

"Sounds perfect. Can't wait."

"I'm looking forward to it. We'll see you then," she says.

We hang up the phone and I immediately text Brady with my good news. When he calls to tell me about his interview, we're like the human version of a ping pong game at lightning speed, shooting information back and forth at each other. I'm excited about my new developments, and it sounds like his interview went really well. I'm a little bummed that he'll be staying with his mom for the night, but also, I think it's good. He never gets to see her and again, it seems like fate that she should be right in the middle of his trek home at some random writing conference on the East Coast.

Life is so good sometimes.

Tonight's party should be pretty run-of-the-mill. 25 girls. The bride is from Watch Hill, Rhode Island and is filthy rich. Like, Taylor-Swift-is-her-neighbor rich. Her name is Sweden McFarlowe. The maid of honor is her sister, Vienna. Evidently, the McFarlowe family tree is comprised of airline industry titans. They name their family members after some of their favorite travel spots.

I cannot make this shit up.

Oh, to be of means like that. I felt like I was approaching baller status when I opened up a CD last week so I could put $2,000 in as an official "rainy day fund." So, yeah. That's not exactly the same level as the wealth we're talking about here.

Anyway, this party that we're throwing for Sweden is not even her *real* bachelorette. It's just the first stop on a two-week bachelorette *trip*. First stop, Cosmo, then the next morning a private jet will be flying the girls to Nantucket for the weekend, then on to Milan (ironically, that's the name of Sweden's brother), and then to Zaknythos, an island in Greece.

This party is literally the pre-game to the pre-game.

Anyway, no pressure. I feel like we'll show them a good time and they'll be on their way to bigger and better a few hours later. I just hope they tip us well. Sometimes, the wealthiest people are the ones who tip the worst. So, fingers crossed.

Me and the girls meet at Cosmo at 4:00 to make Jell-O shots and practice a new routine that we'll be using tonight. We get the sense that this particular crowd has poled before, so we can't slide by with dip turns and back knee hook spins. We need to teach at least a few advanced moves, so we opt for the Cradle, the Superman and the Stargazer for those of them who know how to climb, along with more basic moves for those who don't. It should be fun, actually, since I've never taught these moves before. I *know* them, but they're hard to master, so teaching them will be a different story.

The other piece about this party that's different is that each girl gets a pair of pole heels to keep as a souvenir. We've got a good amount of stock in the back room, and we normally charge $80 per pair, but the maid of honor was happy to throw down $100 per pair when she offered me an extra $2,500 plus the cost of the bill, so who was I to argue?

Arrow would be proud, I decide.

We arrange the heels by size – they're all the same: black, patent leather booties with a zipper up the inside and rainbow flashing lights in the clear platform heel. They're the industry standard, eight inches tall.

They've ordered firefighters for the striptease, so Max, Billy, and Tommy are performing. Max is as good as they come, so it'll be fun for the ladies. It's not as much fun for *me*, since it's not Brady, but these guys are really nice and very talented, so it should be smooth sailing.

8:00 p.m. rolls around and the ladies arrive in a caravan of pink Escalade limousines. Very subtle. Sweden is surprisingly sweet and funny – way more down to earth than I was expecting. She thinks the "shoe shopping" portion of our party is cute, although, she shares, she often has a tough time walking in heels, especially ones this high.

"Baby steps," I advise her. "And if you keep a hand on the pole, you'll be fine."

Several of the girls have *definitely* poled before. Once the music gets going and the shots are distributed, they start doing tricks, some of which are even better than I can do. Sweden has fun watching from the sidelines, cheering on her sister and her friends as they spin and flip.

The format of the night is the same as always: once the party settles in, we teach the moves and the choreo and then the small groups dance for each other until the strippers arrive. This group is a bit more wild, though. They decide to *strip* for each other, which I'm guessing is maybe a touch more European than what we're used to. But I try to remain calm. We're all ladies here; it's nothing we haven't seen. I will say that I'm a bit shocked to see not only dresses and shirts go flying around, but also the occasional bra. The girls are *not* wasted, though, which is really all that I care about after the last major disaster. My big goal is a vomit-free night. If these girls are comfortable dancing up on each other with no clothes on, who am I to judge?

Sweden is perhaps more conservative than some of her friends, so her dress is still on when it's her group's turn to perform. By contrast, Vienna might as well be naked, her thong is so tiny. Sweden should definitely be in a group with other beginners, but her sister has decided they must remain together, and as the beat drops to Cardi B's classic, *WAP*, Vienna is ad-libbing all over the place, hands on her knees, twerking on the ground, doing pole splits and inversions galore while the rest of her foursome tries their best to do the moves we went over together.

Vienna is something of a show-stealer, I realize. It makes me feel almost sort of bad for Sweden, who clings to the pole for dear life in her new bioluminescent footwear. Their dance ends, and the crowd cheers, even though poor Sweden was definitely sitting up front on the struggle bus to Strip Town, USA.

To be clear, a snapshot of the party at this moment is as follows: Me, Saffron, and Indigo, all in typical work fashion: push up bras, pleather hot shorts, rhinestone belts, 8-inch glow heels, now each hopping on a pole and preparing to dance back-up for the impending strippers. Cherry is wearing a similar getup only instead of working the floor, she's doling out shots. 25 girls – seven with their breasts fully exposed, dancing all up on each other to *Milkshake* by Kelis. It's definitely the wildest party hosted at Cosmo this summer.

Then, there's a knock on the door.

Cherry goes to open it – Max comes in with a giant fire-hose in his hands and as I look over at Big Mike, who takes up the rear of the stripper conga line, I try not to laugh at how staged this all is. They come in, and Big Mike gives me a nod as he heads to the back of the club where the bathroom is. He must need to go bad, because he beelines past all the half-dressed Eurogirls, a man on a mission. Max is so cut, though, that he sucks up all the attention in the room anyway. It doesn't even matter if the bit looks contrived – the girls are eating it up. His eyebrows go up when he sees how many girls have opted to set their chichongas free tonight, like it's just as much a show for him as it is for the hot-and-bothered ladies on the dance floor. Billy and Tommy are also pleasantly surprised by this turn of events. After his whole, "We got a call that something in this building was *smoking*," announcement, Max and the boys start fucking the air to *Hot in Here* by Nelly. The girls scream, the dollars come flying, and the vibe is excellent.

Until there's a second knock on the door.

"Ooh, is that your backup company?" Vienna cries. She takes off for the door, clutching her naked breasts with one arm as I look over at Cherry, who raises her eyebrows at me and shrugs.

"Yum!" Vienna screams. "We've been a naughty bunch of girls, Officers! Please, come punish us!"

"Officers?" Cherry mouths at me.

And these are the last words I hear.

Before.

My.

Father.

Walks.

In.

CHAPTER TWENTY-FIVE

BRADY

"Sweetheart!" my mom exclaims when she enters the hotel room. "Honey, let me look at you!"

I stand up, setting the TV remote down on the bed. "Hey, Ma."

"Give me a hug! You look great, Brady!" She squeezes me tightly. "And, wow. So firm," she comments, squeezing my left bicep. "Been working out, huh?"

"Jeez, way to embarrass a guy." I laugh.

"Sorry! Sorry. You just look so grown up is all."

"Well, thank you. You look nice, too. You changed your hair," I say, because one cannot help but notice that yes, my mother has dyed her hair the colors of a rainbow. Red bangs, orange crown, then blonde, green, blue, and purple down her back.

"You love it, don't you? It's called *rainbowmbre.*"

She looks a little like a *My Little Pony*, to be honest. But it's fine. Somehow, my mom can pull off some wacky shit. "Really nice."

"So, dish! I want to hear everything."

"Actually, I'm starving. Can we go eat?"

"Of course, of course," she says. "Let me just freshen up. There's a cute little spot called Olde Mistick Village that I want to go see."

"As long as they have food there, that sounds great."

They do. We go to a place called The Jealous Monk, where we share something called a Pretzel Charcuterie Board and I order a Monk Burger. Mom orders a salmon BLT. I get a beer and she gets a hard cider, and only once the drinks and apps have arrived do I start to settle in and feel ready to talk.

Not that we haven't been talking this whole time, mind you. Mom goes on about her writing. She's working on a new novel (her "WIP," she calls it) about a ghost that lives in a cornfield. It's supposed to be a metaphor, and I don't 100% understand it, but that's fine. She's happy, and I'm happy for her. After all those years of misery with my father, she deserves it.

Speaking of his royal dickface, Mom informs me that he tried to contact her after our falling out, but she very clearly sided with me and told him the bare minimum. He wanted to know where I moved to, what I'm doing for work – and none of that is any of his business, Mom says.

Then she tells me she's seeing someone. His name is Rank. No, not *Frank*. Rank. As in *The King* ranks *higher than the nine in cards. Or, your breath smells* rank.

Poor guy.

She met him at yoga. He sells fancy mailboxes for a living. She's happy.

That's all that matters.

She asks me again. "How are *you* doing, sweetheart? Tell me everything." She sips her cider. "I want to know about the girlfriend, the – oh, wait. Is it okay that I call her that?"

I chuckle. "Yes, Ma. Gretchen's my girlfriend."

She claps. "I love it!" she exclaims. "Okay, so I need to know about her, about the job interview, about your living situation. Wherever you want to start. The floor is yours." My mother beams at me.

"I guess I'll start with Gretchen. She's amazing. I'm really into her."

"Yeah?"

I nod. "She's funny, smart, beautiful. Total package," I say. "She's studying to be a teacher."

"And what does she do now?"

"She's in school. She's in the process of trying to get an after-school job for the year. But I met her at the Diamond Excelsior. She was a waitress at the pub."

"Nice," Mom says. "Good, honest work."

The irony of this is not lost on me, but I ignore it and go on. "The only issue is, she's definitely a Cape Cod lifer."

"I knew there was a *but*."

"Well, it's *not* a but, though. It's just, I got a job offer today."

"Brady! That's amazing!"

"In New York," I add.

"Wait – you mean, the job you just interviewed for? They offered you the position on the spot?"

"Not exactly. I had the interview this morning, and they called me later in the day. But I have to give them an answer by Monday. And I don't know what to do."

"I thought you said that job was remote," she says.

"I thought it *was* remote. But apparently, they wrote 'hybrid' instead of 'remote' in their listing and I confused the two. They said it's two days from home, three days in the office."

"I see." Mom chews on a cheese-dipped pretzel thoughtfully.

"I think the job is such a great fit in every other way, Ma. It's in market research, which I love, the pay is excellent, good benefits. There's even a 401k."

"But..."

"But, what about Gretchen? I love her."

She swallows back a grin. I'm sure she'd classify this in the *Aw, look how cute* category. "And there's no way she would move to New York?" she asks.

"She can't. She's in the process of being placed in her student teaching for the year. She *owns* her condo. Like, what 26 year-old do you know of who actually owns real estate?"

"Sounds pretty put together."

"She's amazing," I admit. I sip my beer.

"So, what is it? You don't think you can do the long distance thing?"

"No, it's not that – although, quite honestly, I *do* think that would be challenging. I just..." My voice trails off. "I just feel like she has it all figured out. She has a plan, and it's a solid one. I, on the other hand, have basically been unemployed all summer, squatting in someone else's apartment. I feel like she deserves *more*. And so, here's my chance to *be* something. To be, I don't know. *Worthy* of her. But the only way to do it is to compromise how comfortable we are right now by making things difficult for us."

My mom nods, processing my verbal diarrhea over her BLT. "What if –" she begins, "and, now, just hear me out – what if a challenge is exactly what you guys need?"

"How do you figure?"

"Well, it's been easy so far, right?"

"I guess," I say, thinking back on how we met, how we both lost our jobs, how we stumbled into the same living situation and the same line of work. "Yeah, maybe not *easy*, exactly. But definitely *convenient*."

"Right. That's what I mean. It's been convenient. But, Brady, *life* is not always convenient. If you guys are going to work for the long haul, you're going to have to face challenges at *some* point, you know?"

I take a bite of my burger, considering her point as I chew. "I just don't want to mess up a good thing." I leave out the fact that up until today, being with Gretchen has been the *only* good thing I've had in a really long time.

"Of course, honey. I understand that," she replies. "Just remember, sometimes overcoming obstacles makes a relationship stronger."

"Yeah, and sometimes it makes a relationship fall apart."

"But wouldn't you rather discover that now? As opposed to finding out that you don't have what it takes to weather a storm together *after* you're married and have a child?" I hear the undertones. I know she's referring to the life she had with my dad.

Gretchen and I are *nothing* like my parents.

"I think we *do* have what it takes, Ma. I really, really like this girl."

"So then, you should talk to her about it. See if you guys can come up with a solution together."

I nod. "You're right." I sigh. I feel a little lighter. *We can figure it out. As long as we have each other, we'll be fine.*

"Sometimes that happens," she says with a smirk.

"Thank you. Really. I feel a lot better."

"My pleasure, sweetie."

"Now, can I ask you an important question?"

"Sure."

"Have you ever driven in Manhattan?"

"God, no!" she exclaims.

I laugh, and we cheers our drinks to that.

The rest of the evening goes really smoothly. I miss my mother, I realize, and I wish Gretchen was here so she could meet her. They would hit it off instantly, I'm sure.

After dinner, we walk around the cute little shops in Olde Mistick Village and I stand off to the side as she tastes a variety of fancy infused honey, pores over a high-end store featuring kitchen gadgets, and peruses a purveyor of lotions and soaps. When she's finished with her shopping, we drive back to the hotel. I check the time. It's after 8:00. I want to call Gretchen but I know she's working tonight, so I figure I'll shoot her a text to say goodnight and save my phone call for the morning.

Needless to say, I am more than a little bit alarmed when my phone wakes me up at 2:30 in the morning. It's set to vibrate, but it's dancing all over the nightstand like nobody's business. And it's a 508 number, but not one that I recognize.

I pick up. "Hello?" I whisper.

"Yo, Brady, it's Mike."

"What's up, man? You okay?"

"Not really. I'm sorry to wake you, but bro, we need your help."

"We? Huh?"

My mom rolls over in her bed. "Everything okay, honey?" she asks.

"Yeah, Ma. I'm sorry. Go back to sleep," I say, hopping out of bed. I go into the bathroom and squint at the light, closing the door behind me. "What happened? What do you need?"

"There was a bust at Cosmo. Cops raided the place."

"Oh, shit."

"We're all being held at the Wellingham Police Station."

"Held?" I ask, rubbing my eyes.

"Like, in jail. We were arrested."

"Who was?"

"All of us, dude. Me, Gretchen and the girls, Max, Billy, Tommy, and even two of the chicks from this party. Shit got out of hand tonight."

My heart drops when he says Gretchen's name. "Okay, so what do you need? What can I do?"

"We each need to post bail of $500. Also, I need you to call Gina."

"Okay. I'll figure out the money. How do I do that? Can I use a credit card?" I start to sweat. My trip to New York was expensive, but I still have $1,200 in my bank account, so at least I can cover Big Mike and Gretchen. "Also, why didn't you call Gina?"

"It has to be cash, Brady. And I called you first because –"
He lowers his voice and says something else.

"Wait. What? I can't hear you."

"Gretchen's not allowed to leave," he repeats, only a fraction of a decibel louder.

"Why not?"

"Her dad won't let her."

"What? Why not?" *I don't understand. What the fuck is happening right now?*

"Gretchen's dad led the raid, Bray."

CHAPTER TWENTY-SIX

GRETCHEN

Little known fact: the jail cells at the Wellingham police station are in the basement.

From the outside, the precinct looks pretty similar to a house. But they renovated it a few years back and turned the basement into a space with three jail cells. They even hosted an open house to show the renovated space to the community.

Because the Wellingham chief is his friend, my dad went to that open house. I remember him telling me and Mom that it was pretty exciting to see what they did over there.

I can assure you my father never anticipated that his child would be taking up residence in one of those cells.

But by Saturday morning, not only am I locked up in a cell, I'm the *only* one left.

Last night was *mayhem.*

I can only remember pieces of it. Everything happened all at once. The cops came in, a tornado of activity went down, an ambulance arrived, more squad cars came, and ten of us were carted off to jail for processing.

I can only share the highlights that I actually saw.

After Vienna opened the door essentially naked and *invited* the police to enter, my father walked in with four other officers: the Wellingham chief and two of his guys, and – to add insult to injury – my ex-boyfriend, Keith.

Cherry cut the music, and the party girls actually *booed*. I got down from the pole and walked over to the officers, yes, in platform glow heels and not much more than underwear.

"Gretchen?!" my father cried.

Cried.

He could not believe his eyes.

Keith – *Keith, of all fucking people!* – started questioning Vienna. "Do you have ID?" he asked.

Vienna is not very bright, I learned. She wasn't 100% sure that this wasn't still part of some stripper act. She replied, "Do *you* have ID, Officer?"

"I'm asking you a question, ma'am," he clarified, eye-balling me.

Then Vienna ran both hands down his chest and said, "Ooh, yeah. Call me ma'am," as her palms landed *on his penis.* I could not believe my eyes.

"Nope," Keith said. "This is not happening." He turned her around and cuffed her, and Vienna, the *fucking moron,* smiled like she was into it!

Meanwhile, Sweden tried to come for her. "Vie, *stop it!*" she screamed. "I think these are actual –"

Her sentence was cut short by her ass tumbling to the ground like a house of cards. She clutched her ankle. "Oh my God, oh my God, oh my God," she howled. Tears sprung to her eyes. "I definitely just broke my foot," she seethed. Three of her friends crouched down around her. One of the officers radioed an ambulance.

Big Mike, Max, and the two other strippers made moves to leave, but, no, that wasn't happening. The Wellingham cops began questioning them. Pretty soon, Max was being handcuffed and led outside. Big Mike tried to stop the cop, resulting in his arrest.

Cherry brought the Wellingham chief over to the locker bank and tried to answer his questions. He asked for a building permit, proof of inspection from the health department, a whole litany of things we did not know where to find, if they even existed. He pointed out that the lockers were blocking the fire exit. Eventually, he cuffed Cherry, too, explaining that he needed to bring her in for more questioning. Many of the girls attending the party were released to leave. One, who was drunk and topless, yelled at Keith for 'putting his hands on Vienna' and ended up in cuffs as well.

It all happened around us, as if me and my father were stuck in a standoff in the eye of a hurricane. He couldn't say anything, couldn't do the job he had been sent in there to do. He could only look at me with disgust and shame, and worse, disappointment.

An ambulance that ironically came from the fire department was on the scene moments later, and that was when my father turned around, walked over to Keith, who was questioning someone else, whispered something in his ear, put two sets of cuffs in his hand, and left.

Then, Keith approached me and, shaking his head, began to recite my Miranda rights.

I pushed him. "Don't *touch* me," I said.

But he did. He spun me around, handcuffed me, and added *resisting arrest* to my list of violations.

Other stuff happened, but it was all too much to register. Here is what I know:

The girls were split between two cells. The guys were in the third cell.

I did not get to make a phone call. Everyone else did.

There was a warrant out for Joyce Cooke's arrest. I almost didn't realize they meant Arrow when I overheard this piece of information.

Bail was set at $500 per person. The arraignments would take place on Monday.

We were fingerprinted. Our pictures were snapped. Our phones, keys, and money were taken away from us, and we were each given a receipt for our things. The list of charges was endless: no liquor license, potential exploitation of sex workers/no adult-entertainment license, violations of building codes/zoning laws, Board of Health violations, fire code violations, tax regulations, reckless endangerment, disorderly conduct, noise and nuisance violations, and for me and one other girl, resisting arrest was also on the list.

People were brought in for questioning in a different room, one at a time. Not me, though. No one asked me anything.

I think it's possible I had a panic attack, because after I got in the police car, I went mute. I could not speak to anyone. The shock was more real than anything I've ever felt, but at the same time, I was disconnected from it all, as if I was having an out-of-body experience.

At some point, I fell asleep on the blue bench in the jail cell.

But this morning, I woke up to find I was the only one left.

My voice came back, but I've been sitting here for the past ten minutes, listening to the silence.

I hear a door open upstairs.

"Hello?" I call out.

An officer who I do not recognize comes to my cell. "What do you need?"

"Is my dad here? Chief Andrews, from Eastport?"

"Don't think so. Let me check." He uses a phone to call someone and ask.

"He said he'll be in at nine."

"What time is it?"

"Just after seven."

"Okay," I say.

I wait. There's very little else you can do in jail. I replay the events over in my mind – the ones I can remember – and little details emerge, like the look on Keith's face when he saw me, which was an odd combination of sad, smug, and surprised. I think about my interview for Eastport Elementary, the fact that I got fingerprinted last night, but not in the way I would have preferred, and I wonder if I just threw my entire life plan out the window by ending up here. I think about Arrow, about Kit and Jenny, and about what will happen to all of them given this new series of unfortunate events. And of course, I think about Brady, wondering if he'll be disgusted with me.

Wondering why he hasn't come for me yet.

I breathe with intention, trying desperately not to panic. The officer has taken up residence at a desk on the other side of the bars I'm locked behind, and I ask him to turn around so that I can use the toilet. When I'm done, I wash my hands in the small, metal sink, lie flat on my back on the bench seat, and stare at a speck on the ceiling.

Until my dad arrives.

I hear his footsteps. He greets the guard and then dismisses him. "I need to speak to my daughter alone," he says. The guard heads up the stairs and shuts the door behind him.

My father pulls up a chair outside my cell. He sits down, rests his elbows on his knees, laces his fingers together, rests his forehead on his hands.

And begins to cry.

I have never seen my father cry before.

It is the most gut-wrenching experience of my life. Without words, I can see that I have broken him. Hurt him beyond measure. Gravely disappointed him. His shoulders heave as the tears fall from his eyes and onto the tile floor.

My own eyes fill with release, an understanding that yes, this is horrible, but it happened, and my dad showed up. He came back for me. He wouldn't be crying if he didn't still love me.

I fucked everything up, and I'm sorry.

I try to say the words aloud, but it comes out as a gasp, because my tears have become sobs. He looks up. He wipes his eyes. He stands up, grabs a few tissues from a box on the small, steel desk nearby, and silently offers one to me.

I stand, approach him at the bars, and gratefully accept his offering.

Our eyes meet.

He shakes his head and sits down in the chair again.

I return to the bench.

"Brady came to bail you out," he says.

"He did?" I hiccup.

"He asked for me specifically," he continues.

"I didn't call him, though," I say, confused.

"His friend did. Mike."

I nod.

"He told me everything."

My insides clench. "What do you mean?"

My father sighs and remains quiet for a moment. Finally, he speaks again. "Gretchen, you have been lying to your mother and I all summer."

I look down at the floor, wiping the fresh tears from my eyes.

"Mommy is beside herself."

His words stab me.

"She doesn't understand any of this."

I say nothing.

"I'll wait, Gretchen. It's Saturday, and I have nowhere to go. But neither do you. Not until you tell me your side of the story."

I inhale. Blow my nose. Wipe my tears.

And tell him everything.

I start with David Krumholtz. Then, Brady moving in next door. Jenna helping me get the job at Cosmo. I tell him about Arrow, about Brady working for the Skeeve, about the parties getting more and more wild once Arrow was gone. I tell him I did not know that Cosmo was an illegal establishment. I thought maybe the stripping side of it might have been shady, but the pole side seemed legit to me. He asks me when I've ever had a legit job that paid all in cash, and I shrug and tell him he has a point. I explain that I was going to quit, I was just waiting for Arrow to get back. I tell him me and Brady just want to move forward and start the next chapter of our lives together.

I tell him that I'm sorry.

"Why didn't you ask us for help? After you lost your job at the Diamond Excelsior?"

"I already owed you guys money."

"So?"

"I was embarrassed. I didn't want you thinking I couldn't handle my own life."

He gestures at my current living situation. "*This* is you handling your life?"

"I'm just doing my best, Dad." I sigh. "And I'm sorry, but you've always set the standards pretty high. I didn't want to disappoint you."

"I can be a little overprotective, I'll give you that. But you just told me that your boyfriend is a stripper."

"*Was* a stripper. And you said *Brady* told you everything!"

"He must have left that part out."

"Whatever. He only did it a few times. And it didn't bother *me*, which should be all that matters anyway."

"As your father, I think I'm entitled to have an opinion on that."

"I don't know. Are you? This is *my* life."

"It's my responsibility to raise a good person, to turn a *good human* out into the world."

"Am I not a good human, Dad? Have I really turned out *that bad*? Do you mean to tell me that you've never lied, or done something slightly out of character, in an act of desperation?"

"Not like this," he says.

Something dawns on me. "You're doing it right now! Didn't you just tell me that Brady bailed me out of jail *hours ago*?"

"Yes."

"So why am I still here?" I ask.

"Because I wanted to talk to you."

I fold my arms across my chest. "So you kept me in *jail* for longer than necessary so that you could talk to me? Does that not seem like an act of desperation?"

"Don't, Gretchen. Do *not* use that tone with me."

I stand down, realizing that I am, in fact, still locked up in a jail cell at his hand. "Fine," I mumble. "Can I ask you a question, though? Because this is the one part that doesn't make sense to me."

"Go ahead."

"How did this all happen?"

"What do you mean?"

"All of it, Dad. How did you find out about Cosmo?"

"It wasn't me, Gretchen."

"Huh?"

"It was Keith."

I shake my head. "I don't understand."

"Apparently, Keith's fiancée had her bachelorette party at your establishment, and she said she could tell something was amiss. So he started digging around. Staked out the place a few times."

"Keith is engaged?"

"Yeah. He's getting married in a few weeks."

"So the bachelorette party was recently?"

He nods. "Not long ago, yes. But anyway, he said that one night he was watching and several young girls came outside the warehouse throwing up. And he saw a big group of guys go inside. He assumed they were adult entertainment, and looked for licensed adult entertainment providers locally and came up empty handed. So he knew something illegal was going on. He tipped me off, and I got in touch with Wellingham. We planned the bust together."

"That's so weird," I say, thinking. "I've never had an unhappy bride, except -"

Oh my God.

Miranda.

"Dad, what's the bride's name?"

"What?"

"Keith's wife? Fiancée? Is her name Miranda?"

"In fact it is. I could never forget that name, you know. Because of Miranda rights."

That fucking bitch.

CHAPTER TWENTY-SEVEN

BRADY

When I finally wake up, it's after 1:00 in the afternoon. My head pounds, like worse than if I was badly hungover.

Then it all comes back to me and hits me like a tidal wave.

He tried to end my relationship with Gretchen. He specifically said the words, "You will give her some space."

Then, he just walked away. And I let him.

To be fair, he was carrying a gun.

Let me back up.

I got the call from Big Mike. I had to wake my mom up and explain what was going on, but I didn't have a lot of time to waste, since I was a three hour drive from Wellingham, so I gave her a kiss goodbye and told her I would call her from the car to explain, which I did. My poor mom was so confused at first. But I walked her through the whole story step by step, and (in true Mom fashion) while she was disturbed to hear that I had been stripping, she was happy to hear that I had "reclaimed my love of dance."

Go figure.

I think she was able to let it go pretty easily because I told her I was done with it. Also, we'd just spent a whole evening together discussing my plans for the future.

I stopped at the ATM and basically drained my bank account between the $1,000 I needed for bail plus the $40 non-refundable fee per person I'd have to pay to the bail clerk. By the time I arrived at the police station, it was almost 6:00 in the morning. I informed the officer at the desk that I had come to post bail for Gretchen Andrews and Michael Evans. The bail clerk had already been sent there for several others from the party, so I didn't have to wait, which was good. I paid the money and was issued a receipt for each of them. Then, Gretchen's father came out into the waiting room.

"Brady," he said.

"Hi, Mr. Andrews."

"You bailed her out?"

I nodded. "Yes, sir."

"You knew about this?"

"About what, exactly?"

"Her employment situation?" he asked.

"Yes, sir," I said.

He bobbed his head up and down, stuck in his thoughts.

"Brady, I need to ask you something. And I need you to be honest with me."

"Okay."

"Is my daughter a stripper?"

"God, no!" I replied. "No, sir. Not even close. She was hired to be a shot girl. She sometimes pole dances, but never without her clothes," I explained. "Honestly, sir. Never."

"Okay." He exhaled. "One other thing."

"Sure."

"The other girls are saying she was left in charge. Is this true?"

"Unfortunately, yes. Arrow thinks highly of Gretchen."

"I wasn't sure if they were just trying to throw her under the bus, you know?"

"No. They seem to all have a good rapport."

"Thank you, Brady, for telling me this."

"Of course, sir."

"How was your interview?"

Eager to give him any sort of good news, I said, "It went really well. I got the job."

He gave me a pat on the back. "Congratulations, son. That's nice for you."

"Please don't tell Gretchen. She doesn't know yet."

"I won't. I'll leave the news to you. But I need to tell you one more thing."

"What's that, sir?"

"Annie and I think Gretchen is going to need to move back home for a little while. We are concerned about her decisions, and we think she might need a little reset."

"But she's got lots going on, sir. She has an interview coming up, and her student teaching. Some digital something-or-other class, too. Summer's almost over."

"I don't think you understand the gravity of what just happened here, Brady."

I shook my head, exhausted and confused. "What's that?"

"Gretchen will never be a teacher on Cape Cod."

"What? Why not?"

"Because she just got arrested, for one thing. And there are three reasons that *employed* teachers are ever dismissed here: insubordination, incompetence, or immorality. My daughter was just arrested for operating an illegal strip club. Bad news travels fast in Cape Cod, and whether or not the judge only slaps her with a fine, no self-respecting local school is going to look the other way and hire a pole dancer to teach their kindergarten babies how to read."

"I mean, I wouldn't put it like *that*, exactly."

"Brady, maybe you wouldn't – but a school administrator certainly would. Also, please keep in mind that this is happening right now. It's not like she did this ten years ago and is looking for work. This is *fresh*."

I nodded my head, realizing that he was probably right. Dread filled my throat.

"So Gretchen is going to need to take some time, you understand. To figure her life out."

"And you don't think she can do that in her own apartment?" I asked.

"I don't know, Brady. This is the first time I've ever had to navigate my only child doing something so ridiculously stupid. Not to mention illegal."

He was getting worked up. I could see that. "I think that if you were to look at it from her perspective, it might make a little more sense to you." Even *I* could tell there would be no rationalizing at this point, though.

Then, bad turned to worse.

"Tell me something, Brady," he said. "You bailed out another person tonight. Michael Evans, right?"

"Yeah."

"How do you know him?"

"We're friends. We go way back."

"So you knew he was in this line of work?"

"Oh, sir. Mike's a security guard. He's not a stripper."

"He's a security guard at an underground adult entertainment venue where my daughter has been working all summer long," he attempted to clarify.

"Yes. That's correct," I said. Because, really, what do you say in this kind of situation?

"Listen, Brady," he went on. "I can see that you're trying to make something of yourself, and I applaud you for that. But I've got to level with you, son. I think you might be hanging out with maybe not the best crowd of people, and while Gretchen's trying to get her life back in order, I think it would be best if the two of you took a little hiatus from this relationship. I think that might be the healthiest thing for her."

To be fair, it was late, and I was exhausted. And, not for nothing, Big Mike's *such* a good dude. So, this man was coming at my best friend and my girlfriend all at once, and I couldn't keep my tone in check. "What?" I said, in a voice louder than perhaps I should have used.

"You heard what I said. It doesn't have to be forever, but for now, Gretchen is going to need a fresh start, and I advise you not to get in the way of that."

"Sir, with all due respect, I am not going to stop dating your daughter. She's a grown woman. And we're in love."

"Brady. I appreciate your willingness to fight for her. But this is not up for discussion."

"It's not your choice to make," I said.

"Watch yourself, kid," he warned me.

"Mr. Andrews, I appreciate how much you love Gretchen," I said.

"Then you will give her some space," he demanded.

I wasn't done with the conversation, but he turned and walked away from me, put some kind of magnetic card up against the door, and buzzed himself back inside.

It only took about a half hour for the door to buzz again. This time, Big Mike walked through it.

He gave me a handshake, followed by a hug. "Yo, man. Thank you."

"Of course, dude. No worries. Thank *you* for calling me."

"Listen, I'll get the bail money back after the arraignment on Monday. They basically just keep it as collateral to make sure you show up."

"It's fine. I know you're good for it. How are you? You okay?"

"Bro, that shit was *wild*." He lowers his voice. "I really can't talk about it here, but it was the craziest night I've ever seen in this line of work."

"Yeah. Definitely sounds like it. Hey, do you think you're going to lose your teaching job over this?"

"For what? I didn't do anything illegal. I was just in the wrong place at the wrong time."

"Yeah, I guess." I sighed. "Gretchen's dad just came at me, telling me to leave her alone, that she needs a reset or some shit. He said she won't be able to get a teaching job because of this. You think he's right?"

"I'm not sure, Bray. To be honest, I think she's on the hook for more charges than I am."

"He made it sound like nobody will ever hire her."

"I don't know. It *is* a small town mentality out here, that's for sure. But yo, one step at a time, right?"

I shrugged. "I guess."

"Let's get going. You've got to get some sleep. I say this with love, bro – you look like shit."

"Thanks," I say. "You're one to talk."

He patted me on the back. "C'mon."

"I'm not leaving until she comes out."

"Oh, Gretchen's not being released."

"Why not? I paid her bail."

"I heard her dad tell the guard to hold her until morning. Think he's trying to flex."

Fuck. "You sure?" I asked.

"Yeah, man. I heard it myself."

So, I left with him. Reluctantly. Drove myself home. I texted Gretchen to let me know when she got out, and I also left a note on her door. Then, I came inside and immediately passed out.

Until just now.

I check my phone first, of course. Nothing but a text from my mom, just checking in on me. I take Advil and make myself some toast.

I don't know what to do.

My head starts to clear, and I realize that if Gretchen's not home, she can only be in one of two places: a) jail (but I can't imagine her not getting out by *now*, especially since I drained my bank account to ensure her freedom), or b) her parents' house. I need to talk to her, but I keep hearing her father's voice booming in my head, and I want to approach this situation with care.

So, instead of being a hot head and driving up to Eastport, I stay at home.

And wait.

CHAPTER TWENTY-EIGHT
GRETCHEN

I am not okay.

I'm wearing an oversized Wellingham PD t-shirt and pleather hot shorts, and I'm barefoot, because my choice of footwear last night was not appropriate for my brief incarceration.

By the time my father releases me from jail and drives me back to my parents' house, I am rapidly deteriorating.

I need to talk to Brady.

But first, I need to talk to my mom.

We pull up into the driveway and I feel the tiniest bit of relief at the familiarity of the seashell gravel crunching beneath the tires. *Home,* I am reminded by the sign on the porch, *is where our story begins.* I suppose that's true. It really all began with my parents falling in love and settling down in this house, in this town. They had me, and placed all their hopes and dreams and wishes upon me, and I did everything I could to make them proud.

Until I didn't.

I walk up the driveway straight to the back deck, where I open the slider to the kitchen. My mom rushes at me and wraps me in a warm hug. "Sweetheart," he says, burying her face into my hair.

She begins to cry.

The weight of all my decisions, everything I've done this whole summer, all comes crashing down on me and I can feel myself crumble. "Mom," I whisper. My shoulders sag. I begin to sob in her arms, and she holds me up as the catharsis of letting go washes over me. We stand there like that as my father enters the kitchen, and no words are exchanged as he wraps us both in a family embrace.

"It's going to be okay, Gretchen," my mom whispers into the group hug.

It takes a few minutes and several tissues for me to catch my breath, but I finally do. My father is quiet. He excuses himself to go lie down. Mom offers to make me breakfast, and I politely decline, but she starts cooking anyway. It calms her nerves. She makes me a plate of bacon and eggs along with a fresh cup of coffee, and my body surprises me by gratefully accepting all of it. Turns out I'm actually very hungry.

"Baby, are you okay?" she asks me.

I sigh. "I thought I was."

She nods, patiently waiting for me to go on.

"I made a mistake."

Sitting across the table from me, she crosses her legs and sips her coffee. Then, she asks, "Honey, which part of it was a mistake?" The cadence of her voice calms me, reminding me that this is a safe space.

I inhale, appreciating the cacophony of scents that make up the airspace around me. Bacon, salt air, mom's lavender essential oils. "Taking the job, I guess?"

"Everything happens for a reason," she says. "Do you believe that?"

I nod, swallowing a bite of scrambled eggs. "I do."

"What did that job give you, besides money?"

A headache? Jail time? Possibly an ulcer? "Brady," I say. "And self-confidence," I admit.

"Tell me more about that," she says.

"I know you probably think I must be some kind of slut for pole dancing –"

"Don't assume, Gretchie."

"I'm kind of *good* at it."

"You sound surprised."

I shrug. "I *was* surprised. It takes a lot of strength. Like, in your core."

"Maybe you're stronger than you give yourself credit for."

"Maybe."

"No," she corrects us both. "Definitely." She places her hand on mine.

"I messed everything up."

"How?"

"Daddy says I'll never be able to get a job as a teacher."

"It won't be easy. Especially not in this area."

"What am I going to do, then? I have my interview this week."

"Talk to your advisor. Be truthful, and see what she says."

At this, I nod. "I'm embarrassed, though."

"Don't be. We were all young once. She'll understand. I promise."

"Dad also said that he thinks I should move back home."

"Do you want that?"

I shake my head. "No. I felt like I was finally getting somewhere. Summer changed me, you know? I went from being some pub waitress who was basically just coasting through life to becoming someone with a serious boyfriend and actual career prospects on the horizon. It's bad enough that *this* happened. I don't want to move back in like some baby who can't handle her own life."

"Then don't," Mom says.

I smile, and it feels good. "I need to talk to Brady," I tell her, squeezing her hand. "Thank you."

"I love you, sweetie."

I kiss her on top of her head and head for my old bedroom. Sitting down on my bed, I pull my phone out of my back pocket.

He picks up right away. "Finally!" he exclaims. "Are you okay?" Poor guy sounds like an unraveling fidget spinner of apprehension.

"Hi," I reply.

"Where are you?"

"My parents' house."

"How's your dad? How are *you*?"

I exhale. "It's been a long night. I've been better."

"What can I do?"

"I'm not really sure." Then, I remember that he bailed me out. "Thank you for posting bail, though. I'll pay you back."

"Don't even think twice about it. I just need you to be okay."

"I'm okay, Brady. But I found something out. You won't believe this."

"What is it?"

"Miranda was the one behind the bust."

"What? How?"

"Remember I told you about my ex-boyfriend, Keith?"

"The cop?"

"Uh huh. Well, apparently he's engaged to Miranda."

"Wow, really?"

"Yeah – and she was the one who told him that Cosmo was a shady establishment. So he launched an investigation. But I don't think she cared so much about that –"

"Definitely not. That was a revenge move."

"That's what I was thinking, too."

"I can't believe her!" he says, agitation rising in his voice.

"It's okay, Brady. Not worth getting upset over."

"She got you *arrested*, Gretch. She put your whole *career* in jeopardy!"

"Yeah. I know. But I don't think it was me she was after."

"She was trying to get back at me for – for *what*, exactly? For not accepting her ridiculous advances?"

"For not dancing with her the way she wanted you to, I guess. For not making her feel like the only woman in the room." Despite myself, my lips curl into the tiniest smile. "You really do have a way about you, babe. I imagine you'd be very difficult to get over."

"I doubt that." He shrugs.

"You said that she tried to apologize to you, right?"

"It was the most twisted attempt at an apology I ever saw, Gretch."

"Well, I don't know, then. Anyway, I just wanted to share that with you – that Miranda was the reason this whole thing happened. Thought you'd like to know."

"Babe, I'm so sorry. It's my fault." He sighs. "Jesus Christ."

"No. I don't believe that. Don't do that."

"Goddamn it. This is such a mess." He pauses. "Are you coming home?"

"Yeah."

"When?" he asks. "Do you need me to come get you?"

"Actually," I realize, "I need to get my car."

"Let me bring you."

"Okay."

"One thing, though."

"What's up?"

"Your dad – he kind of told me that I should give you some space. So, I'll come get you, but I need you to just come outside. I don't want to see him right now."

"He did what?" I ask.

"I'll tell you all about it when I see you. I just wanted to let you know."

"Thanks. Yeah, come get me, please. I'll handle him."

CHAPTER TWENTY-NINE

BRADY

A few hours later, we're sitting on Gretchen's couch. She looks exhausted and I know I should probably give her the chance to take a shower before I lay this on her, but I can't hold it in anymore.

"I don't know how to say this, so I'm going to just say it," I begin. "I got the job."

Her eyes go wide. "Seriously? That's amazing!" She hugs me tight. "I'm so happy for you! Finally, a piece of good news!"

I squeeze her hard, then release. "There's a catch."

Her eyebrows knit together. "What is it?"

"It's in New York. Well, three days a week, anyway."

"I thought it was remote?" she asks.

"I did, too. Apparently not."

"Oh." She looks down at her hands and begins to pick at the edge of a throw pillow.

"They need to know by Monday," I continue.

"So what are you thinking?" she asks, her voice hollow.

I shake my head. "I don't know. I wanted to talk to you about it. I'm sorry for dropping it on you like this when you've got so much on your plate –"

"No," she replies. "It's fine, Brady. This is a good thing. I mean, right?"

"Hey," I say. I place my hands on her upper arms. "Look at me." She looks up, her lashes covering about half of her gaze. "Your father said –"

"I don't care what he said," she shoots back. "He doesn't get to decide my future."

"I know. I just think this might be for the best."

"How do you figure *that*?" she asks.

"He wants us to have some space. This would give me a chance to establish myself somewhere. It doesn't have to be forever."

"Hang on. Are you saying you want to *move* to New York?"

"God, no. But I could commute."

"From where, Brady?"

"I don't know. Boston, maybe?"

"So you want to move to Boston?" she replies.

"No – I'm not saying that. I don't know," I mumble. "I just wanted to discuss it with you. I need to find a new place to live at the end of summer anyway."

"Okay. Slow down. I'm hearing you say that you're tossing around a bunch of ideas in your head that would all move you away from me, and that this would be a good thing because it's what my *dad* wants. Correct me – am I wrong? Is that *not* what you're saying right now?"

"Jeez, Gretch. I'm just trying to figure this out. I'm sorry. They gave me a deadline of Monday."

"I have my arraignment on Monday."

"I know, babe. I'm sorry. Bad timing."

"No, it's fine. I just – I need to think."

"Should I –"

"Go? Maybe. Just let me shower. I'll come by in a bit."

I don't want to leave, but if she needs some space, I guess I should. I stand up and head for the door. "Hey," I say, turning to face her. "I love you. You know that, right?"

She nods. "I love you, too."

"Okay." I offer her a weak smile.

After I close the door behind me, I stand there for a second, wondering if I'm doing everything wrong. I begin to walk back to my place, which is when I hear it.

The sound of her bawling pierces through the otherwise quiet hallway.

I let myself into Luis' condo, sink my head into my hands and take a deep breath.

Somehow, I will fix this, I decide.

I open my laptop, power it on, and get started.

CHAPTER THIRTY

GRETCHEN

The next two days are a whirlwind.

My dad and I get into it, but thankfully, my mom is on my side. She convinces my father that I don't need to move back home, that it's clear I've learned a lesson, and that if I'm going to learn how to be an adult, I have to do it on my terms. He pushes back, asks who's going to come and bail me out when I can't figure out how I'm going to pay my mortgage or my bills, and Mom tells him that I have to be given the chance to at least try to handle my life in my own way.

He is not happy, but he relents.

My mom has always had a way with him. I guess when you love someone like my dad loves her, you can learn how to bend without breaking.

On Monday, I appear in court. My mother wants to come with me; I tell her no. The way I see it, this is the first step of my next chapter, and my father has already informed me that he doesn't believe I will end up being sentenced. Brady wants to come as well. I also tell him no. I'm not sure why, but I need to do this on my own. It's surprisingly not as awful as I expect it to be, since it appears that I am only at the beginning of what will be a longer process. I meet with a probation officer first, who runs a check for a criminal record and determines that I qualify for a court-appointed lawyer. The session clerk reads me my charges, and it is decided that because I have no record and I am not a flight risk, I can be released on personal recognizance. A trial date is set for Monday, September 25th.

Jenna meets me for lunch after it's over, regaling me with the story about her role in Friday night's disastrophe. Evidently, she was working the ER when a girl came in with a triple fracture and complete dislocation of her right ankle. She was wearing one pole heel, and Jenna knew right away that I was *not* having a good night. Sweden needed two surgeries, and Jenna was there to assist with the first one before her shift ended. She tried to get in touch with me, but of course I had no phone at the time. As soon as she learned that I had served jail time, she insisted that we schedule a catch-up lunch as soon as humanly possible.

In the afternoon on Monday, I have an emergency Zoom meeting with Jane Bishop. I'm grateful to her for making the time given her busy schedule, and I tell her this. Then, I break the news to her about the recent developments in my personal and professional life. I ask her point blank if I have just destroyed my chances of becoming a teacher. She says that I will not be able to be hired in the midst of criminal proceedings, so I should inform Eastport that I am unable to accept their interview for after-school at this time. She says she will contact the principal and defer my placement at the school to a later date, citing a personal emergency as the reason. She says she will keep it vague, which will likely give the district the impression that it is health-related.

Of course, bad news travels fast in a small town, so there's no telling what the impact of that might turn out to be, Jane warns me.

"Should I take my digital literacy class?" I ask.

"No," she says. "I advise you to defer the entire semester. Give the trial a chance to play out. Then, pick it all back up next semester."

"Okay," I say, and while I'm not happy about losing four more months to uncertainty, I *am* happy to at least have the beginning of a plan for my imminent next steps. I do what she says to do; I call the director of the after-school program, Charlotte Fiore, and let her know how sorry I am to have to step back from the interview process at this time.

On Monday evening, Arrow returns to Cape Cod with her family, according to a group text sent out by Cherry. She turns herself in to the authorities, intending to make the process as smooth as possible for everyone. She's hired a lawyer, has money for bail, and is in good spirits, Cherry says. She got her family back, and even though she has to face a trial and possibly even jail time, she knows she has a support system here that will help her take care of Kit and Jenny, which is really all that ever mattered to her anyway.

I tell Cherry that if Arrow needs help with Kit, I'm available.

There's a knock on my door around 6:00 in the evening. Brady's car has been gone all day, so I imagine it must be him.

And I'm right, only it's not *just* him.

He's with my parents.

"Um," I say, upon seeing the three of them on my doorstep. "This is… weird."

Brady smiles, and I notice he's holding a bouquet of flowers. "Can we come in?"

"Depends," I say, putting my hands on my hips. "Are you all here to stage some kind of intervention?"

He gives me a kiss. "No."

"Okay, then." I step aside, and am greeted by each of them. My mother has a pan in her hands, and my father is holding a big bag. Brady hands me the flowers. "We brought you dinner," he explains.

"And I baked brownies," Mom says. "Though I'm not sure they'll be as good as yours."

"Thank you?" I ask, still very confused by this turn of events.

"Come," my Mom says. "Let's eat. Your father grilled some skirt steak, and I made potato salad and a roasted corn salad. Brady got us a beautiful rosemary focaccia from ACK Gioia."

"Is this some kind of celebration?" I ask.

"Sort of," Dad says. "It's been a good day. There's been lots of progress."

I raise an eyebrow at this, but let it go while I set the impromptu table. Mom sets out the food they've brought, Brady puts the flowers in a vase, and within minutes, we are seated in front of plates filled with food.

"Well? What's this all about?" I say.

"I accepted the job," Brady begins.

"You did." I know this is supposed to be good news, but the last real conversation we had about this ended with me feeling all kinds of uncertainty over this particular opportunity. I swallow my corn salad and try to smile.

"I came up with a plan," he continues. "And then, I cleared it with your parents to get their blessing."

"Why do you need my parents' blessing to accept a job?" I wonder aloud.

"Just listen," he says. "First of all, I needed to find a place to live, right?"

"Yeah."

"So, I spoke to Big Mike about it. He lives in Bourne with Gina, and they have a spare room." He takes a sip of water. "They're going to rent it out to me for the next year, which will buy me some time to figure out a more permanent solution. It also gives me time at my new job to prove myself."

"Okay."

"So, hang on, because I've got it all written down." He takes out his phone, opens his notes app and sets it on the table. "Bourne is a half hour away from Kingston in normal traffic. Now, I only have to be in the office on Tuesdays, Wednesdays, and Thursdays, so I just had to figure out a way to get in once a week and a way to get out once a week."

"And a place to stay," I add.

"I'm getting to that," he says. His face is all flushed. *Hear him out,* I tell myself. *He looks excited.* "So, the first train out of Kingston is at 5:30 a.m. If I take that to South Station in Boston, I'll get in at 6:30. I'll have enough time to grab some food and then get on the Acela train to Penn Station, and it'll get me in at 10:50. I can be at my desk by 11:00."

"Isn't that late?" I ask. "Aren't they a 9 to 5 operation?"

"I asked when I called them today. They said they could make accommodations for that. And since I won't be using my relocation package for actual moving, they said I could use it to supplement my transportation."

"Wow," I say. "That's pretty cool."

"Yeah, so on Tuesdays, I'll time shift and work from 11:00 to 7:00. Then Wednesdays I'll do extra hours from 9:00 a.m. to 7:00 p.m., and Thursdays I'll do 8:30 to 2:30, get on the Acela at 3:00, and that'll get me into Boston at 6:45. I can pick up dinner in Boston and take the 8:45 back to Kingston, which will get me home at 9:45. I'll be in the house by 10:15."

"That's so much travel," I say.

"But it's only once a week. The way I figure, I have to do it for a year so that I can prove myself. After that, I'll either be used to it, or they'll get more flexible with me, or I'll start looking for a job closer to Boston. And with a year of experience working at a high-end New York City firm, I'm sure I'll have a way easier time of it as far as the job search is concerned."

"I mean, probably. Where are you going to sleep when you're in New York, though, Bray?"

He grins at me. "My mom has a connection at the West Side YMCA. They're one of the pre-eminent YMCAs in the country when it comes to arts stuff, so she knows people there. Evidently, they have guest rooms. Kind of like a cross between a hotel and a hostel type of situation. For two nights, it's only $232 if you book it in advance. It's right in midtown on Central Park West."

"And what is all the train fare going to cost you?"

He looks at his phone. "I've got that, too. It comes out to $662 for 10 trips on the Acela train and $110 for 10 trips on the T. That means each week, I'll be spending $154 on travel. So, if you add up the travel and the lodging, it comes to $386 a week. Over the course of the entire year, it's a little over $20,000 – and considering the fact that I have a $10,000 untaxed relocation stipend, this is, like, a huge benefit."

"I am just now understanding what a nerd for numbers you are," I say.

"Gretch, do you understand what this means, though?"

"It means you're happy?"

"It means I'm not leaving!"

My mom smiles at him. My father nods, and I can tell there's more to this than meets the eye.

"That's great, Brady. I'm happy for you."

"I know Bourne feels kind of far, but it's not New York."

"Oh my gosh, definitely not."

"And it's also going to save me from having to pay for New York real estate. But that's a whole different economic picture that I won't go into right now." He's *beaming,* and I can't help but smile.

"You can save more money. I get it," I say.

"As a nest egg," he clarifies.

"Sure."

"You're not understanding me," he says. "I spent some time with your parents today, Gretch."

"I can see that, given that you've all conspired to bring me dinner."

"I wanted them to get to know me. To know how serious I am about you. About us. And also, to know that I'm not just some random stripper. I have a plan – and now, a *good job* – and I love you."

The words make my heartbeat speed up. "I love you too, babe."

"No, but I mean like I *really* love you. Like, forever love."

"Me too," I say, looking him in his eyes.

"Gretch. Your parents are right that you need some time to figure out what your next move is going to be. But I want them – and you, obviously – to know that whatever it is, I'm here for it. I'm here for the long haul. I understand the idea of a parent wanting to make sure that their child lands on their feet. But, that's the thing your parents *didn't* know."

"What?"

"That you already did. With me."

"What do you mean?" I ask.

"I'm going to work like crazy this year to launch a career for myself. Start saving, and all that good stuff." He inhales deeply. "And then, I'm going to ask you to marry me."

My mouth goes dry, and my eyes sting with tears. "Wait. What?"

Brady's grin is like pure sunshine. "Not yet, silly. And not like this. Don't worry."

"Are you serious?"

"Yes, I am. I just needed to figure out the logistics. And I had to talk to your mom and dad."

I look at my mom. "Is this real?"

She nods.

"Brady's a good man," my father says. "He really cares about you, Gretchie."

"He reminds me of the way your father was with me all those years ago," Mom adds. "We couldn't wait to figure out our happily-ever-after. But Daddy was willing to put in the work for it. Just like Brady."

"Marriage isn't easy," my dad says. "It's full of challenges. I wasn't about to let my daughter get swept away by some guy who wasn't ready to take her seriously. It took your mom reminding me about how we started out to realize that sometimes, being scrappy and opportunistic just shows how much heart you've got."

"Which is why, when Brady called me and asked if he could share his plan with us, I had to say yes." Mom is glowing.

Brady leans over and gives me a kiss on the cheek. "Everything will fall into place, Gretchen." He takes my hand in his. "You'll see."

Even though I still feel like an overwhelmed train wreck thanks to my job situation and my grad school plans being put on the back burner, compounded by the fact that I spent the morning in court, I look around and see the three people I love most in the world looking at me with hopeful expressions. And, I don't know.

Somehow, I believe him.

Maybe it *will* turn out okay.

EPILOGUE

BRADY

TEN MONTHS LATER

The dance recital begins at 7:00 p.m., and I can tell Gretchen is nervous.

It's only five numbers. The Twinkle Toes are up first with their dance to *Shake it Off,* by Taylor Swift. The Crazy Eights (so named because there are eight of them and they're all eight years old) are up next, dancing to Pharrell Williams' *Happy.* Then, we've got The Tweenyboppers, which is our largest group – 16 kids in all – and they're doing a six minute hip-hop/step combo to a mix of recent songs. We round out with a group that calls themselves High School Musical, and they'll be doing eight minutes of choreo to a Bruno Mars medley of songs. After all of that, the recital will end with a surprise performance.

Miss Joy (formerly known to some of us as Arrow) is our choreographer and costume designer, and as Gretchen leads the Twinkle Toes out onto the stage behind the curtain, Joy's niece, Kit, stands front and center, proudly donning her red and black fluffy tutu skirt over a black leotard. I give Gretchen the thumbs up from the side of the stage where the curtain ropes are. Gretchen breathes deeply and then exhales hard. "Okay," she says, her eyes sparkling. "Here goes nothing."

She slips out between the ginormous curtain panels and stands on the stage in front of the red sheaths of fabric. "Good evening, parents, families, and friends," she says into the microphone. "Thank you so much for being here with us tonight to celebrate All-In Dance Studio's first annual student recital!"

The crowd of about a hundred spectators cheers. In the front row, Gretchen's parents gaze up at her. A huge bouquet of flowers sits across Annie's lap. Jenna's sitting a few seats away, clapping wildly. Next to her, Cherry, Indigo, and Saffron are all in a row. Of course, they go by Cheryl, Kim and Maria now. Big Mike is in the back row seated between Gina and my mom. And backstage are Arrow and her sister, Jenny. Notably missing is my dad, but that's okay. He's been notably missing since my first dance recital, if we're being honest, and it just doesn't bother me anymore. I'll be a better father one day just by learning from his mistakes.

I got the idea for the studio from Gretchen when she started her gig as a nanny for Kit last September. They had just moved here from Arizona, and Arrow turned herself into the Wellingham police. She was arraigned and went to trial, and her attorney offered a plea bargain to the judge. In exchange for a reduced sentence of three months at Barnstable County Jail, Arrow would commit to 200 hours of community service in the town of Wellingham, along with payment of a $30,000 fine. It would wipe out about half of what remained of her savings, she later told Gretchen, but she didn't need the money as much anymore now that she had her family with her. Besides, she wanted to work closer to her home in Plymouth, so that she could be actively involved in Kit's life.

Gretchen's deferral of her final year of graduate school became permanent after her trial. She pleaded not guilty to the charges brought against her, and even though she won the case, the local schools were all aware of what had happened and the fact that one of the people responsible for operating the club was the daughter of the Eastport Police Chief. So she gracefully decided not to drag her father's name through the mud or bring any further speculation to her family or the town, and instead figured she would begin to think outside the box about other potential career paths she might be interested in exploring. She wanted to give back meaningfully to the community that raised her, she said. She told her mom she really loved the self-esteem she felt from dancing, and I took it upon myself to do a little market research analysis during my extremely lengthy commute.

Turns out, the market for youth dance programs on Cape is fairly saturated, in that there are a good amount of studios. But most of them focus on competitive dance, and all of them are very expensive. A few have scholarship opportunities, but nothing is low cost or donation-based, except for the one-off programs offered at the Boys & Girls Club or the YMCA. Which meant there was plenty of room for local arts grants to help support a new not-for-profit venture to bring dance to all local children in an equitable way, without cost to families who couldn't afford to otherwise sign their kids up.

The first thing I had to do was find a space. I wanted an affordable location for a start-up, where the investment wouldn't be too overwhelming. I looked into storefront rentals, but the real estate market in the Cape is wild, as I've mentioned before.

It was actually Max who reminded me about the Harwich Cultural Center. It used to be a school, so it's filled with classrooms and there's even an auditorium there. You can rent a classroom for $15 per three-hour session, because the Cultural Center is supported by local grants as well – in turn, making the arts available to the community via low cost rentals.

I had to file for non-profit 501(c)(3) incorporation, along with a business license. The most expensive investment was insurance, which was needed in order to rent the space. And, of course, my background check, which was crystal clear. I put everything in my name and rented the space with the sprung studio floor that me and the guys had used for practice. I even had the ability to rent out their auditorium in the event that we were planning to have a recital.

I saved up $2,500 from my first several paychecks and spoke with my company about donating a match for a start-up non-profit. They said yes, so I had $5,000 in capital to get All-In Dance Studio off the ground.

I did it all on the train, and all without Gretchen's knowledge.

On Christmas Eve, Gretchen and I slept (in separate rooms, obviously) at her parents' house. We wanted to be together on Christmas morning, and since she's never had a Christmas without her parents, that was the only choice. But it worked out, because her mom and I had become rather adept at cooking up surprises for Gretchen, and this one would be one of those stories she'd be telling to our grandkids someday.

I woke up on the couch in the living room at the Andrews' house. The Christmas tree had been left on all night, and the rainbow colored lights, along with the (mostly handmade) ornaments reflected the love that lived within the little Eastport cottage. Some people like their Christmas trees flashy and showy, or worse, stoic, with simple white lights and not much decoration, in an effort to appear elegant. This tree was a testament to a lifetime of family memories, starting with baby footprints pressed into clay and including beaded garlands made over the years by a much younger Gretchen and her mom. There were tons of pictures that had been turned into ornaments documenting happy times, vacations, summer days. There were even craft stick, tree-shaped picture frames surrounding some of Gretchen's old school photos. A tree like that is more than just decorative. It's a living tribute to the power of family.

And under that tree, amidst the wrapped packages and shiny bows, sat a modest box. I didn't want it to look like anything jewelry-related, because the last thing I wanted was for Gretchen to be disappointed by what was inside.

Later that morning, with warm mugs of coffee in our hands, the four of us took turns opening gifts, and I handed Gretchen the box. It was about the size of a ream of paper.

She opened it slowly. Once she pushed back the tissue paper, she found a business plan and incorporation papers for All-In Dance Studio, along with a key to room 127 at the Harwich Cultural Center.

"What is this?" she asked. Amusement played on her face.

"It's a fresh start," I said.

Now, just six months later, on the last Friday in June, here we are, hosting a dance recital for the community.

Business is going well. The plan is to stay at the Harwich Cultural Center while we diversify and develop our funding sources, and eventually to run a capital campaign for a brick and mortar space with multiple rooms inside.

I'm still doing my thing in the city, and it's not perfect, but it's definitely a career path and a fantastic learning experience. I don't mind the grind for now with all the travel, especially since I use that time wisely, planning surprises for my girlfriend, planning for our future, you know. Typical commuter-type stuff.

Gretchen handles the day-to-day operation of the dance business, and she still helps out with Kit in the mornings. There are 12 classes a week – three for each age group – and they all happen after-school and on the weekends, so Gretchen has some time available during the day. Arrow works for us, now, in addition to filling her time with a variety of community service projects on the outer Cape. She puts together the dance routines, teaches them to Gretchen, and Gretchen teaches them to the kids. I help out with the older kids, especially the boys. It's empowering for children to see that dancers come in all shapes, sizes, and genders.

She's beaming, watching the littlest dancers in our studio perform a routine they've practiced for months onstage in front of their proud families. The little girls have on bright red lipstick, and their excitement is palpable as they hop, pose, create lines and very simple formations in groups and work through their moves. When they are finished, no one cheers harder than my girl.

She looks absolutely gorgeous in her costume. I'm simple; I'm in black pants and a form fitting black v-neck t-shirt. But Gretchen's my star, so when I came up with my most recent big idea, I had to get her something incredible to wear.

The dress is black with silver ombre, covered from the neckline to mid-torso in sequins. It hits at her mid-thigh, so it's sexy without being too revealing. The shoes are proper closed toe, t-strap ballroom shoes, appropriate for Latin dance. The heel is low and they're comfortable, which is the most important thing.

The groups of kids go out in succession, like we rehearsed, and I can tell Gretchen's getting more and more anxious. When the teen group goes up, Gretchen rejoins me by the side of the stage at the curtain. She rubs her hands together. "I can't believe we're actually going to do this," she whispers.

"Nah," I say. "It'll be fun. Plus, I feel like this is one dance that *you* actually owe *me*."

"Depends on how you look at it, I guess," she replies, smiling at me. "I mean, you're the one who broke my toes."

"Pretty sure I've repaid that debt."

I slide my arm around her, hoping she can't feel the bulge in my pocket.

After what feels like an eternity, our High School Musical group is done. "Come on," I say, holding her hand. "Let's do this."

Arrow steps out on the microphone and says, "We have a very special final production for you this evening. Our owners, Brady and Gretchen, have put together a number for you. This is a rumba, but they've added some hip hop and their own little flair to it. We hope you enjoy."

The audience applauds, and the lights turn red.

Then, the curtain opens, and we are standing, her facing away from me, poised and positioned center stage, as the music starts.

Of course, it's our Christina Milian song. The one we really never got to finish.

There are some fluid steps before the beat drops, and when the lyrics begin, I spin her around, and, facing each other, we begin the steps. I count in my head, the way I always did when I was little. *Slow, quick, quick, spin, quick, quick, lift, dip, slide, quick, quick.*

We're dancing. And it's beautiful. My heart soars. My love for Gretchen is simply unmatched by any emotion I have ever felt.

During the bridge of the song, there is a moment where I slide across the floor on my knees. The prep for this is a spin out from her and a two-step away, just to create space. During this time, I slip my hand into my pocket and grab the box.

She doesn't see it coming. But her parents know, and my mom knows, and Arrow knows because she worked the move into the choreo for me.

I slide up to Gretchen on both knees, then, instead of popping up from the floor, I open the box and show her the ring.

She freezes.

The music keeps playing.

The audience screeches and whoops, applauding for us. It's so loud that I wonder if she can even hear me when I ask her, "Will you marry me?"

But she nods, and smiles that perfect smile of hers, and tears streak through her stage makeup. I stand, place the ring on her finger, pick her up and spin her around.

My fiancée.

When I finally put her down, we embrace, and she squeezes me with all her might. "Damn it, Brady," she says in my ear. "You interrupted our dance!" Her laughter lights my soul on fire.

"I guess I'll have to owe you one," I say.

The curtains close, and the show is over.

But everything else is just beginning.

Acknowledgements

Every novel is its own journey, but this one was particularly special since it took place during a challenging time in my life and featured an unlikely cast of characters.

When I turned 40, I felt a myriad of things. Most notably, I found myself fitting neatly into the mid-life paradox of busy but discontent. With the major boxes in my life checked off (marriage, house, kids, career), I was grateful but still felt like something was missing.

Something big.

It was twofold: on the one hand, I suddenly felt very old. And not in a "wow, she's so wise" kind of way. More in the run-of-the-mill, invisible kind of way. After having had two children, I felt like my body wasn't what it once was. Compounding that, there was the issue of my occupation. I love my day job, but I've always had a passion for writing. I dreamed of becoming a novelist when I was a little girl, and when the clock struck 40, I could feel that dream slipping further and further out of my reach.

So in the same year, I took two huge steps: one into an MFA program, and the other into a pole studio. And both of those decisions changed my life in the very best way possible.

The women at Dream Dance Fitness taught me that age is just a number, and I learned that at 40, I could be sexier and stronger than I ever was at 25. So to Misha, Tash, and the powerhouse team at DDF, a million thanks. Hopefully this book will give a little something back to the pole community by promoting the strength, glory, and inner beauty of women at every age that can be unearthed through the sport and art of pole dancing. I reclaimed myself and became unapologetically authentic as a result of my time at Dream Dance.

Between dancing and going back to school, I learned how to turn my experiences into stories, and I'm now part of the romance community in publishing, thanks to the dedication of my agent, Elizabeth Copps. E, thank you for being the world's best everything! There are no words to express how much you mean to me; there's no one I'd rather be partners with on this publishing journey.

The other major partner in my life is my beautiful husband, Chris. Thank you for loving every version of me. I look forward to having morning coffee with you on a porch in Cape Cod when we're *really* old... but I also look forward to all the days between now and then. You are the human equivalent of challah bread with Temptee cream cheese, and I love you forever (and ever).

To my girls, who are growing up so fast, thank you for turning me into a wild robot. One day you'll understand why I cry all the time now. I love you both plus one anything you say, and it doesn't matter how big your feet are because my cubit will always be bigger.

To David Krumholtz, thank you for being so cool when I reached out about using your name in this book. Congratulations on your incredible success – it couldn't have happened to a nicer person. I can't wait to see what you'll do next!

To Kristan Higgins and Al Davis, for your endless wisdom, advice, and support, thank you.

To the real Big Mike, who is one of the best people I've ever been privileged to know, thanks for letting me base one of my characters on you. I hope you feel like I did him justice!

To my friends and family near and far, thanks for all the support you've given me along the way. I'm grateful for every single one of you.

Last but really first and foremost, thank you to YOU: the person reading this right now. Time is the most precious commodity we have, and I'm honored that you've chosen to spend some of yours with me. This time around, I built a street team to help promote this book, and I've gotten to know many of my readers on a much deeper level thanks to that. I'm endlessly grateful to my readers: I read the Goodreads reviews, the Amazon reviews, I love the posts on social media, and I get giddy when one of you e-mails me! Without you, I'm just writing into the void. So my deepest thanks goes out to you! I hope we can spend more time together again soon!

About the Author

KJ Micciche is a novelist who hails from Queens, New York. A self-proclaimed workaholic, KJ runs a non-profit organization that teaches kids with dyslexia how to read. In her limited free time, she writes novels with humor and heart. Proud mom of two beautiful girls, KJ and her family live on Long Island and summer in Cape Cod.